She stretched forward and began to crawl toward the opening in the floor of the duct. It was only a couple of meters in front of her now. Just beyond it, the duct turned a corner.

As Sable peered over the edge to see into the room below, a small hovering metal globe about half a meter in diameter drifted around the corner. Sable gasped and jerked backward as the floating robotic thing approached her, a camera lens focused directly on her. A small laser beam was also marking her squarely in the forehead, and she could now see the barrel of a small weapon mounted just below the camera lens.

A strangely melodic voice reverberated from the comm unit in her ear. "This is a rather strange place for you to be, young lady. Don't move, or I will kill you. Now, just what do you think you're doing, crawling around in my vent system?"

STAR DRIVE.

THE HARBINGER TRILOGY
DIANE DUANE

STAR*DRIVE

GRIDRUNNER

Thomas M. Reid

Wizards
OF THE COAST

GRIDRUNNER

©2000 Wizards of the Coast, Inc.
All Rights Reserved.

Cover art by Corey Macourek
First Printing: September 2000
Library of Congress Catalog Card Number: 00-190350

9 8 7 6 5 4 3 2 1

ISBN: 0-7869-1573-0
620-T21573

U.S., CANADA, ASIA,	EUROPEAN HEADQUARTERS
PACIFIC, & LATIN AMERICA	Wizards of the Coast, Belgium
Wizards of the Coast, Inc.	P.B. 2031
P.O. Box 707	2600 Berchem
Renton, WA 98057-0707	Belgium
+1-800-324-6496	Tel. +32.70.23.32.77

Visit our web-site at **www.wizards.com**

To M, D, & J for the "write" genes and
an amazing childhood; to A & G just for who you are;
and to T most of all, for the encouragement and support,
especially at the 11th hour.

01.0:

AN EXPANSE OF yawning blackness enshrouded Sable, engulfing her completely. She luxuriated for a brief moment in its familiar comfort, enjoying the complete immersion in nothingness. Tentatively she concentrated on the connection program and somehow sensed, until a shimmer appeared, that she was racing through the enveloping void. The sharp contrast of an artificial horizon made of light flickered into view: the Grid.

Although she had connected to the computer-generated virtual reality that was the Grid countless times, Sable still gasped slightly as her Grid shadow careened toward the visual grandeur of this digital reality. A million specks of light expanded rapidly below her as cytronic circuitry embedded in her flesh processed the images smoothly and fed them to her mind's eye.

Sweet, she thought, grinning. This new system's definitely faster. Damned fast. None of that annoying flicker anymore.

Gliding to a relative crawl as it levitated high over the center of this vast, pulsing world of light and data, Sable's shadow suddenly descended toward the virtual landscape in a breathless rush. The million specks of light exploded up to meet her, becoming a million million specks in the span of a heartbeat, pulsing into her field of vision in an incredible display. Single points of brightness expanded into geometric shapes, then expanded again into hyper-resolution lattices of information, a vast sprawl of virtuality, glaring and emblazoned more brightly than the most garish night spots of downtown Port Royal. The brilliance bore into her skull, made her wish she could blink away some of the intensity. Her Grid shadow pulled up just short of slamming itself against the virtual surface of the Grid, settling gently the last bit of distance until her mind was convinced she stood in the center of a great digital plaza.

Sable rotated in place, surveying the neon landscape around her. Other shadows—digitized figures of every imaginable shape, size, and color heading in a thousand different directions—joined her in the plaza and then shot away again. She took a breath and tried again, mentally interfacing with the Grid's standardized search menus. In the heartbeat it took her to formulate the thought, a graphic display materialized in her field of vision. She gasped again at the pure speed of the new interface.

What a rush!

She began rifling through help features until she found what she was looking for, then mentally selected a virtual address, and was instantly racing through the jungle of light like a transit car running between the life-sustaining eco-domes on the surface of the system's harshest planet.

She ignored the familiar wavering patterns of flickering data that churned in her peripheral vision, allowing the shuttling program to do its work while she called up several other executable subroutines into her work space. It was still a little unsettling, the act of combing through data in front of her, selecting menu choices with her mind's eye rather than tapping keys on a gauntlet. But it was certainly faster and easier.

Yeah, she told herself. I could get used to this.

Shuffling through the executables, Sable selected a pair of files, then minimized the rest for later use, setting mental hot keys for each one.

By the time she had completed sorting her files, she had arrived at her destination. With a flick of her mind, her Grid shadow passed through a data node, and she was inside. There was the slightest pause, a delay that she would never have noticed with her old system, as protocol coding was updated. The sensation gave her a slight shiver, but then suddenly Sable's shadow stood in the entryway of the Loading Zone.

Loud, pounding music instantly blasted through the digital feed. She winced, willing the volume control down several notches. Garish advertisements undulated and flickered everywhere, hawking anything and everything to anyone who paid the slightest attention. Sable ignored the imagery. All around her, shadows surged and mingled, users pretending to be in a club, even though they sat perhaps thousands of kilometers away, on their couches, in their underwear, heads buried inside Gridcaster helmets.

The vast majority of the shadows were store-bought, over-the-counter software available to the masses, although at least some of them had modifications, mostly nothing more than a radical palette shift. A few were more clever. One store-bought that strolled by, a Gerald model, had been user-modified so that its hair was a pillar of green flame. It wore an outlandish, bright orange zoot suit. It also had immense red clown feet.

Sable chuckled. Probably some kid who hacked the safety lock on his parents' Gridcaster, she mused.

For a moment, thinking of some kid sitting at home playing with his parents' system made her think of Gavin.

No, she told herself. Just don't. Not now.

She grimaced and blinked back the tears that she felt welling somewhere outside of her virtual consciousness. She swallowed hard a couple of times, her throat tight, then took a deep breath, and put thoughts of Gavin out of her mind.

Surveying the room where she stood, Sable wondered how she would ever spot her contact in this morass of Grid shadows. All Mr. Maxwell had told her was that she was looking for a fool. She rolled her eyes.

They're all fools, hanging around and pretending to enjoy this techno crap.

Sighing, she scanned the place for a better vantage point and spotted one that suited her, an upper level with a balcony that ran along one of the walls. It seemed a bit more out of the way, a place where she could watch without being in the middle of the mess.

Sable guided her shadow by force of will, gliding across the digitized dance floor that dominated the club's Grid node. Abstractly she brushed past the other shadows that swarmed around her, ignoring their personalized signature files, which magically appeared above the animated figures like text balloons in an old-fashioned comic book. She made her way to a lift, where someone had electronically bit-painted the thing to appear as a hydraulic platform. She stepped onto it and her shadow instantly materialized at the top, making her smirk.

Cheap bastards won't even program a decent physics model.

She moved away from the platform to a corner of the loft and found a relatively unobtrusive spot near the railing that overlooked the main floor of the virtual club. A mirror had been programmed into the wall near her vantage point, and she caught a quick glimpse of her own shadow reflected back at her.

The image of a woman's face with a stylish flattop hair-cut, eyes shielded by silvery lenses, stared back at her. The hilt of an ornamental oriental short sword protruded from behind one shoulder. The shadow was dressed in a snug-fitting shirt, pants, and boots that came almost to the knees, with a long trench coat over it all. With the exception of the silvery stylish shades over the eyes and a matching pair of jagged tattoos, one on each cheek, looking a lot like some sort of war paint, the entire figure was a softly luminescent black. Compared to the wildly glaring shadows that were killing time in the Loading Zone tonight, Sable's own image was easy to overlook, which was fine with her.

Right down to the sword on her back, Sable had chosen the appearance to imitate the street toughs in the real world, those cybered-up punks who liked to play at being samurai. Not the cocky idiots who walked around flashing chrome and trying to look cool, but the more subtle ones who didn't care how dangerous you thought they looked, because they *knew* they were going to kick your butt if you looked at them funny. She found that Gridpilots in general respected that same subtle approach here in the Grid, too.

Sable smiled, thinking of the last time some jerk pilot had annoyed her, trying to show off by hijacking her feed and bumping her off the Grid. Her own Antivirus Fortress Code, which she had written herself, had ground the offending shadow into oblivion. All in all, it had been a rather beautiful display, and she was proud of it.

It sure as hell took me long enough to program it, so I deserve to be proud, she chuckled.

The moron had been knocked off the Grid himself, and unless he had been running surge protection back home, her parting shot had also fried a few circuits on his Gridcaster. She really liked other shadows to leave her alone.

Sable wondered how quickly her Grid shadow could execute its defense code moves now that she had a neural system link.

As fast as I can think of them, she realized, and had to stop herself from accidentally executing one when she realized she had called it into ready mode with a thought.

Sable turned back to the morass of shadows below her, scanning the crowd for her contact, someone who would be known as a fool. It didn't take long to find him. It was another brand of store-bought, a Buff Dude model, but it had been modified so that the image wore a jester's hat and juggled a series of colored balls that flashed through the spectrum in an endless cycle. The Fool. The image was at a table in one corner, stiffly sitting by himself and juggling.

Shabby coding, Sable thought absently. No variation in the pattern or rhythm of the motion. It looks too perfect, too unnatural. I would have at least— Oh, who cares? she chastised herself. He's got to be my mark.

She tried stepping right off the balcony in order to drop directly to the floor below, but an invisible barrier blocked her way. She sighed in exasperation.

Sure. They won't program a lift that works, but they'll take the time to stop me from hopping over the edge.

She made her way back to the lift, already tired of this place, especially the music that still pounded in the background and was giving her a headache.

Sable descended the lift and worked her way through the crowd of images to where the Buff Dude sat, still juggling his balls in their endless pattern. She maneuvered her shadow into the chair opposite him and smiled, knowing her own shadow would mimic her. Not everyone's did.

"I'm looking for the Fool."

"You've found him." The shadow's voice transmission was rough, gravelly, and very unnatural, apparently passing through some heavy filtering before being piped through.

Sable winced at the sound, her mind adjusting a few controls to soften the sound of the Buff Dude's voice before she realized she had decided to do it. Voice mods were common enough, especially when you wanted to remain incognito, but some people had no sense of style.

"Careful what you say," the Buff Dude cautioned, although there was little inflection in the heavily masked voice. "We could be monitored."

"In that case, here," the girl replied, mentally selecting one of her hot keys, and her shadow pulled a small white envelope from an inner pocket of her trench coat and held it out to the Fool. "Run that."

The Buff Dude's juggling act vanished, and it suddenly held the envelope in its hands. There had been no transition images; it simply went from one status to another. Sable sighed, wondering sometimes why she bothered to program her effects at all. They were always wasted on people who didn't know the difference between a pixel and a palette. Lamers, all of them.

"What is it?" the Fool asked, never moving.

"The other half of an Ed," Sable replied.

"An Ed?"

Sable nodded, grimacing. "Yes. E-D. Encode-Decode. I wrote it an hour ago. Open it up and run it. Then we can talk, and no one can hear us."

"Didn't you get the encryption crystal that was part of the package?"

"Yes, and I'm running that, too, but this is a little extra protection."

"How do I know it's not a trap of some kind?"

"What? You don't have a filter? Aren't you running some Afsee? Scan it and see for yourself." Amateur! How did these people evolve?

"Afsee?" the Fool queried.

Oh, for God's sake! "That's A-F-C. Antivirus Fortress Code. You *are* running some, aren't you?"

"Of course." Without any facial expression on the Buff Dude, it was hard to tell for sure, but Sable got the impression that the user on the other end was a bit offended. The

Fool held the envelope a moment longer, as if considering, though the expression on his face never changed a bit. Finally the envelope disappeared and the construct was immediately juggling again.

Sable chose another hot key, executing the Ed file, and then waited for the connect signal. When the channel was open, she made a couple of adjustments to enhance the Fool's voice while filtering out the club's background noise, and then spoke again. "All right, it's running. That should be enough encryption to keep most tech-heads from listening in."

"Most? Isn't it foolproof?"

"Well, nothing is ever foolproof, but my code is pretty boss—uh, I mean, pretty top-notch. Besides, who's going to care what two shadows are talking about in a corner of a Grid club? It's safe enough."

"Still, we must be cautious. The longer we spend in communication, the greater the risk of—"

"Fine," she cut him off. "I have a package to deliver. When and where?" She was annoyed that this Grid zombie was questioning her skills, but her headache was also growing worse. She wondered if it was due to the new system. *I should take it in small doses at first,* she thought.

"Arrangements must be made first."

Sable's annoyance was complete now. This new delay meant more waiting, meant spending more time in Port Royal, and she hated Port Royal.

One of several cities on Penates—the third planet of the Lucullus system in the Verge—Port Royal was a huge sprawl of over a dozen and a half ecodomes scattered across several square kilometers of the planet. Connected by numerous high-speed transit corridors, the collection of domes that made up the city most resembled some three-dimensional model of a wildly improbable chemical compound. Port

Royal, which included subsurface areas a couple of kilometers directly beneath it as part of its city limits, was completely controlled by the Jamaican Syndicate, a huge organized crime family, one of several that ruled the various city-states of Penates. These ruling factions sprang from the planet's roots as a penal colony for the Solar Union, one of the old stellar nations originating from humankind's colonization of the stars closest to old Earth.

Born, like the other ruling factions, in the struggle against years of misery in servitude to their old jailers, the Jamaican Syndicate now fattened itself by offering the one thing to which all the species of known space were beholden: pleasure. Filled to the brim with every conceivable kind of sensual and mental delight known to the collective species, Port Royal was a gambling paradise, a colossal bawdy house, and a trafficker of illicit goods all rolled into one, each carnal delectation eagerly consumed by the hungry masses, who willingly and in dizzying amounts paid the Syndicate for the privilege. And Sable hated it.

It wasn't that Sable hated the staggering filth of the city or its garish, decadent disposition, or even how far away it was from her brother, Gavin. It was just that she hated all the people. She didn't hate people in general, but she didn't trust them, and she most definitely despised mingling in huge crowds of them, abhorred being surrounded, feeling trapped, hemmed in by their stinking bodies. She was revolted by their rank, drunken breath and their mindless, groping hands. She just plain hated being around people, and Port Royal literally swarmed with them, day and night, humans and aliens of every size, description, and income level, of every philosophical bent or moral view. Sable shivered at the thought of so much humanity in one place and returned her thoughts to the Fool in front of her, opening her mouth to protest the prospect of staying in Port Royal even one more day.

But then the girl remembered that he was one of Mr. Maxwell's paying customers. If she became difficult, he just might complain to her boss. Sable thought again of Gavin and bit off the retort.

"Okay, fine," Sable answered, trying to sound agreeable. "What's my next step?"

"You will meet me here again in three days' time. I will have the particulars of the exchange finalized by then, and we can proceed."

Three days! Sable groaned inwardly. She truly hated this moron now. His shadow was lame—the juggling balls were definitely making her headache worse—and because he wanted to drag his feet, she had to hole up in a fetid room in a cheap hotel in a particularly loathsome section of Port Royal, one of the nastiest places on Penates, until he decided he wanted his hardware. She almost wished she could slice and dice him, just to watch her shadow cut his into a thousand streamers of light, but she knew better. She took a deep breath and then nodded. "Three days. Same time?"

"Yes. Right here."

"I'll be here." Sable bookmarked her location in the node, killed the Ed, and angrily logged off the Grid, not bothering to head back to the welcome plaza. It was bad form, but she didn't care. "Three days!" she screamed aloud, startled by the closeness of her own voice in the tiny room. She blinked, looking around.

The place Sable had rented was nothing more than a single compartment with a bed, toilet and sink, shower, a couple of drawers in one wall, a vidscreen on another, and a table that folded into the wall. It was all crammed together in the space of a cube less than three meters square. She was on the bed now, sitting crosslegged. A thin cable trailed from the back of her neck to a gauntlet, a metallic sleeve that fit snugly on her forearm and looked strangely like some sort of fingerless glove. There were several small switches, displays, and slots on the gauntlet, as well as a keypad that rested in the palm of her hand. A second cable ran from the gauntlet to a feed in the wall near the fold-out desk. It was all part of a neat package that connected the cybernetic circuitry embedded in her flesh to the Grid.

Sable reached up and slid the cable out of the socket in the back of her neck, which would normally be hidden by her dark, shoulder-length hair, tossed it carelessly to the side, and then slid the gauntlet from her arm. She sighed and stretched, wishing she had tried piloting while lying down. Her back hurt, as did her head. She climbed off the bed, opened one of the drawers in the wall, and put the gauntlet and feeds inside it.

She kicked her clothes off into a heap on the floor, went to the sink and splashed a bit of water on her face, and then killed the single greenish light that illuminated the room and climbed into bed. The sheets were not particularly soft, but they were clean and cool on her bare skin, and she lay there for a few moments, feeling herself sink into the pillow, trying to relax.

Sable tossed and turned for a few moments, trying to find the peace of sleep, but her mind would not slow down. She kept seeing her brother, Gavin, and Mr. Maxwell looming over him, threatening. She tried to shut it out of her mind, but it was no use. She could hear his screams in her head from the last time she had seen him, only a few days earlier. She shuddered and sat up.

Flipping the light on again, Sable sat for a moment on the side of the bed, grimacing and rubbing her temples. Her headache wouldn't go away, nor would the visions of her brother's torture. She sighed and pulled open the drawer where she had stashed her Gridcaster.

Inside was a small case, which she removed, closing the drawer again and sitting down once more. She eyed the case and thought of the street vendor in the Golden Quarter who had sold her the crystals that were inside, shivering a little as she remembered his greasy smile and knowing wink.

At least he had them, she thought. The room felt too much like a prison already.

Sable opened the case and removed one of the tiny crystals from inside, examining it sadly.

Once again you escape, she chided herself, but her heart wasn't in the admonishment. Just this once, she argued with herself. So I can sleep. Can't do the job unless I get some sleep, she rationalized, settling the debate with herself.

Sable slipped the crystal into the jack at the base of her skull and closed her eyes. As the executable booted up, she found her mind's eye staring at a selection menu not unlike the ones she had manipulated in the Grid. After changing a few control settings to her liking and setting a timer feature, she willed the program to start and left the tiny room behind, forgetting for a while the punishments inflicted on her brother as she lost herself in an orchestrated cacophony of stimulants that teased the pleasure centers of all five senses.

* * * * *

The figure known only as Lazarus waited until the small group of staggering revelers passed him by. Then he crossed the boulevard and headed down a side street toward the Lucky Ace, a clean if somewhat dilapidated hotel in Uptown Port Royal. The glare of the lights wasn't quite as bad off the main drag, but that also meant that the shadows were a little deeper. Lazarus kept one hand under his jacket, on the grip of his pistol, and unobtrusively scanned both sides of the street as he strolled, trying not to look as if he was hurrying.

As he neared the front entrance to the Lucky Ace, a tired-looking girl with fiber-optic implants in her spiked hair and eyelashes sauntered over to him with a tight smile that wasn't terribly convincing.

"Hey, love. Ya want some company tonight?" She was wearing a slick black outfit that fit too snugly, and she tried to get between Lazarus and the door so that he couldn't help but see her.

He sidestepped her without making eye contact. "Not tonight," he said in a flat voice, reaching the door.

Recognizing the disinterest in his tone, the girl turned on her heel and sauntered back the way she had come, already watching for another prospect.

Lazarus stepped through the sliding doors and found himself staring at the well-worn red carpeting in the lobby. The nighttime counter jockey gave him a single brief glance as Lazarus went toward the elevators. Then the bleary-eyed man returned his attention to the holoprojection in front of him.

Lazarus shared the wait for the single elevator with one other person, a haggard-looking man who was slightly disheveled and stank of too much to drink. As the door to the lift opened, the other fellow swept inside, stabbing at the controls with one large, meaty finger, and then finding a solid corner to lean against. Lazarus followed him and picked the level he wanted, thankfully noting that the guy was getting off after only a couple of floors.

"I lost a little more than I should have tonight," the fellow began, only the slightest hint of a slur in his speech. "The tables weren't too nice to ol' Bert, nosiree." He tried to chuckle, but he lapsed into a fit of wheezy coughing.

Lazarus ignored him, watching the digital readout flashing the current floor. When the elevator reached "ol' Bert's" floor and the door slid open, the man turned to Lazarus and stumbled forward slightly. One hand was poised to begin pawing Lazarus's jacket.

"Could you help ol' Bert out tonight, huh? Just a little something to help me change my luck?"

Lazarus deftly caught hold of the man's arm at the wrist and twisted it up and away from himself before it had time to reach inside his jacket. He steered the man firmly out through the elevator door, his other arm patting the fellow reassuringly on the back.

"Not tonight," Lazarus said in that same flat voice. He released Bert and stepped back inside the elevator just as the door slid shut. He sighed and went back to staring at the digital display.

When he reached the floor he sought, he waited a moment before stepping out of the elevator. He kept close to the wall, turning to peer down the hallway in both directions. There was no carpeting here. The Lucky Ace was a no-nonsense place to stay. Satisfied that no one was lurking in the shadows of the dimly lit hallway, Lazarus set off in one direction, checking his progress by the numbers on the walls next to the key-padded doors spaced at regular intervals.

Finding the door he wanted, Lazarus paused again and checked his surroundings. Convinced he was indeed alone, he studied the keypad beside the door, hesitating.

You can still bail on this, he told himself. Last chance.

No. It's the only way to get a break. Just keep your head.

Taking a deep breath, he pulled a small black metal and plastic box from a pocket inside his jacket. Along one edge, the box had an array of sensors and contacts. He held the thing up against the keypad, slotted it into a socket, and tapped a switch. The red display above the lock flickered through countless iterations for a moment as Lazarus drew his pistol from its holster. When the display suddenly flashed a code in green, there was an audible click at the door, and it began to slide open. Lazarus stayed to one side of the doorway, out of sight, pistol in hand. He pulled the autokey from the socket and dropped it into his pocket again.

When he realized the room was dark, Lazarus switched his optics to thermal sight and peeked around the edge of the doorway. He noted a single heat signature stretched out, probably on the bed. The figure was moving slightly but didn't seem to be reacting to him, so he stepped cautiously into the room, keeping the pistol trained on the figure, and tapped the inside control panel to close the door behind him. He flicked the lights on and shifted back to normal sight, still pointing his pistol at the bed.

As his vision changed, Lazarus found himself staring at a nearly naked young woman. Stripped to nothing but her briefs, she was oblivious to him, undulating gently in a troubled sleep. The bed was disheveled, the sheet wrapped loosely around her legs, and her jet-black hair was damp and matted to her face in a tangled mess. The room stank of stale sweat. A pile of clothing sat on the floor near Lazarus's feet, and atop it was a slender plastic case.

Ah, there we go, Lazarus thought, smiling.

He moved to the case and flipped it open, but the data crystal inside was not what he had expected to find. It was too small, designed to plug into a neural interface jack, or NIJack, a small port for connecting Gridcasters with cytronic circuitry. He noted that the case normally held two such crystals, but the second depression was empty.

Not asleep, he realized. She's stimming. Well, at least she'll stay under while I have a look around.

Lazarus holstered his pistol and began to poke through the pile of clothes on the floor, checking the pockets and feeling the linings for bulges. When that turned up nothing but a common credit crystal, he moved to the drawers and opened the top one. Inside, he found a Gridcaster gauntlet. He whistled softly in surprise.

"Christ," he muttered. "It's got a system link. She's packing some serious hardware." Cutting edge stuff. No wonder she was so hard to trace.

Lazarus checked through the memory slots of the gauntlet. A couple of standard computer data crystals were slotted. He popped them both out and held them, considering.

Maybe that's my prize, he thought, but he wasn't really convinced. I'll check them later.

Lazarus stuck the pair of crystals into a pocket and continued searching. In the other drawer was a backpack with some more clothes, but after carefully checking them, he came up empty. He ran his hand along the underside of the drawers, and then flipped the table down and checked there. He moved about the room, methodically checking every nook and cranny where something might be hidden.

"Damn," Lazarus growled quietly. I don't even know what I'm looking for. What the hell am I doing here? I should clear out of here right now!

Lazarus turned to look at the girl again uncertainly. I guess I'm going to have to wake her. She had not reacted at all to his presence the entire time he'd been here.

Not too bright, he thought. Anyone could come in here, and she'd never know it. She's lucky I'm such a nice guy.

He admired an elaborate tattoo on the pale skin of her left shoulder. It was a series of curving tendrils, graceful curves and points that reminded him of a creeper vine, or perhaps the curving antlers of a deer. It was deep blue in color. He found its simplicity surprisingly beautiful, simple because, unlike most skin decoration, it didn't glow or flash.

Lazarus let his gaze sweep over the rest of her, lingering awhile in appreciation. She was maybe twenty, he guessed, and her body was lean and fit. He imagined that she must have a catlike grace when she moved.

Or at least when she's not strung out on a stimcrystal, he decided. It's a shame, he thought, taking one last long look at her.

Drawing his pistol once more, Lazarus reached down and felt along the back of the girl's neck until he located what he was looking for. He grasped the small crystal and pulled it from the socket embedded in her flesh, and then stepped back, keeping the gun aimed low but ready.

The girl groaned and doubled up into the fetal position, her eyes fluttering open after a moment. She blinked rapidly over and over and tried to focus in the greenish glare of the light, confusion plain in her mien. She stared at Lazarus for a moment, as though not comprehending his presence, and then her eyes grew wide, and she surged upward and back, cowering from him on the bed, wedging herself into the corner of the wall and drawing her knees up, wrapping her arms about herself to hide her bare breasts.

Lazarus frowned but kept the gun trained in her direction and watched her. "Easy there. Just take it easy." He tried to make his voice soft and soothing.

She stared at him without responding, trembling and breathing rapidly. She seemed to be trying to make herself as small as possible in her chosen corner. Suddenly she coughed and gagged.

Lazarus wondered if she had ever been unplugged in mid-sequence before, if she knew about the cybersickness. . . .

"Sorry," he said, shrugging slightly. "It'll pass in a few minutes." She looks pathetic, he thought ruefully. Not quite what I expected.

But then, Lazarus wasn't sure what he *had* expected.

Certainly not little miss hardwired here. But the cash and the weapons have to be coming from somewhere, and this shivering wretch of a girl in the corner is my ticket to finding out where.

Now he just had to find the goods.

The girl gagged again and covered her mouth with her hand, but she made no other movement.

"Look, if you're gonna be sick . . ." Lazarus gestured to the toilet with his gun.

He backed up a couple of paces until he was against the wall, settling casually against it, arms folded, with his pistol cradled in the crook of his other elbow, trying not to look too threatening.

Time enough for that later, he thought.

The girl watched him warily, not budging from her defensive crouch, but then another spasm of choking gripped her, and she slid off the bed and sank to her knees, hunched over the toilet. She retched a couple of times.

She slumped over the toilet, running a hand across her face and trying to brush a few strands of hair from her eyes, but she never turned her face completely away from Lazarus, always keeping an eye on him. She tried to cover her breasts with her other arm as best as she could. When it seemed her nausea had finally passed, she merely stayed where she was, huddled miserably and watching him, especially his gun.

"Nasty habit, those stimcrystals," Lazarus said, crouching down and grabbing her shirt from the pile of clothes at his feet. "Not good for you at all, you know," he continued, straightening again and tossing the shirt to her.

She flinched from it, and it dropped next to her on the floor. She made no move to pick it up.

"I've seen those things really fritz out . . . melt a stimhead's mind to goo," Lazarus said, leaning against the wall once again. "Besides, you never know who might sneak up on you. Nope, not too smart, getting strung out on those things. Go on, put it on," he finished, gesturing to the shirt lying on the floor in front of her.

Without saying a word, she finally picked up the black tank top and, slightly turning her back to hide herself, prepared to slip it over her head.

Lazarus sucked his breath in sharply. Laced across the young woman's back in a crisscross pattern were a series of welts, pinkish scars that showed tinges of purplish bruising along their edges.

" Mother of God," he mouthed silently. He shook his head, a strong wave of sympathy passing through him. What on earth has she been into? He shook the thought from his head. It doesn't matter. She's just a courier. Do your job.

"Why don't you clean yourself up a bit?" Lazarus said, gesturing with his gun toward the sink. Still silent, the girl watched him for a moment, and then stood up and moved on wobbly legs to the basin. She splashed a bit of water on her face and rinsed her mouth out. Then she turned to face him once more, her back firmly against the wall. It was the first time Lazarus had gotten a good look at her head-on, especially since she had pushed the hair out of her face, and he had been right. She was gorgeous, with the grace of a feline. But the haunted look in her eyes unnerved him.

"Where is it?" he asked matter-of-factly.

"Where is what?" she replied dully, her eyes glazing over. Lazarus had seen this before. She was retreating inwardly, he knew, escaping from . . . something.

"Your package. I know you made contact with Germaine. You probably know him as the Fool. You're here to deliver a package to him. Now, where is it?"

"I don't know what you're talking about." Her voice was lifeless, the words programmed, and it was as though she didn't care that he knew she was lying.

"Of course you do. Did someone else at HansCorp give you the contract? Who are you bagging for?"

She didn't say anything. She just stood there with her arms folded tightly across her midsection, looking away from him and chewing on her lip.

"Look," Lazarus began, a little menacingly, "you can give me the package and tell me who sent you to deliver it to Germaine, or I can haul you someplace very unpleasant and convince you."

No answer.

I guess she's been threatened before, he thought a bit wryly.

"All right, we'll do it the hard way, then." He started to walk toward her, fumbling in one of the pockets of his duster with his free hand. She shrank back slightly, watching him like a cornered cat. The cuffs he was trying to pull from his pocket snagged, and he glanced down to try to free them.

Her attack was in a single, fluid motion, and it caught him completely off guard. A single fist slammed down on his weapon, knocking it free, and then she was running toward the door, throwing her shoulder hard into him on the way past. Lazarus stumbled backward, off-balance, and his head bounced against the wall. He grunted in pain as his pistol skittered into the corner. She was already slipping through the widening crack of the opening door. He tried to lunge at her and grab her ankle, but she was too quick. His hand swiped at empty air, and she was gone.

Furious, Lazarus snatched his pistol from the floor and charged out the door. When he made it into the corridor, the girl was already halfway to the fire exit door at the end of the hall. She still seemed wobbly from the stimcrystal. One hand was sliding along the wall, apparently to aid her in balancing. Lazarus raised his pistol and sighted the middle of her back.

"I *will* shoot you!" he called out.

She stumbled and nearly lost her balance, but she kept running.

Grimacing, Lazarus squeezed the trigger.

02.0:

THERE WAS A deep, bone-jarring belch as Lazarus's stutter pistol fired, and at the end of the corridor, just shy of the exit to the fire escape, the girl suddenly lurched forward, jolted by the sonic blast from the weapon. She went sprawling face first to the floor. Lazarus holstered the pistol as he ran, grabbing once again for the pair of handcuffs in his pocket.

The young woman had just drawn one of her knees up under her and was trying to rise when Lazarus reached her, but she couldn't lift her head up from the floor. Lazarus planted his boot on her rump and pushed it back down; she lay still, moaning softly. He knelt down, pulled her arms behind her back, and snapped the cuffs on. She didn't resist at all. He was glad. He didn't want her to see how badly his hands were trembling.

A door farther up the hallway slid open.

"What the hell is going on out here?" a man called out, sounding half asleep.

"Nothing," Lazarus responded, tensing and keeping his face pointed away from the direction of the voice. "Nothing that you want any part of."

Lazarus heard the door slide shut again, and he let out a sigh of relief as he lifted the dazed girl to her feet. Her eyes were glazed, and she immediately lost her balance. Her mouth was working to say something, but Lazarus couldn't understand her and didn't care at the moment. He hoisted her over his shoulder, and she hung limp as he hauled her back to her room.

Once they were inside, he tapped the keypad to shut the door and then plopped her down on the bed, propping her up in the corner with her hands still cuffed behind her. He stepped back and noticed tears streaming down her face. The girl's body shook now, and she drew her knees up under her chin as she cried, squeezing her eyes shut and sobbing silently.

"That was really stupid," Lazarus began to pace, wanting to burn off his anger, but there was nowhere to walk in the tiny room. His heart thumped furiously, and he was practically panting. He realized he was as angry with himself for underestimating her as he was with her for running. He took a slow, deep breath. "If you try that again . . ."

She flinched and looked at him, her eyes puffy and red and her lip quivering slightly. "Please," she said, almost in a whisper. "They'll kill him. Please don't do this."

Lazarus raised one eyebrow, looking at her. "Who? Who's going to kill someone?"

She didn't respond. Instead, she closed her eyes once more as a new wave of sobs shook her. Lazarus sighed as he slumped, his back against the door, watching her.

This sure as hell isn't working out like I'd hoped. She doesn't act like a courier for hire. She's a wreck.

"Look," Lazarus said, trying to soften his tone. "I don't want you. You're just the messenger; I know that. I want the people above you. I want the people who hired you. If you're in some kind of trouble, maybe I can help you. But you've got to help me first."

"Right," she said, her eyes still closed and her voice quavering. "Just a minute ago you were threatening to beat the shit out of me, or worse. Now I'm supposed to trust you?" The pain in her voice was sharp.

Lazarus winced. "I wasn't threatening to—" he started, but then stopped himself. "Yeah, all right, you've got no reason to trust me. But, hey, no courier I've ever met felt any loyalty to the job, so I can't figure out why you want to be so stubborn about this. But then you go spouting this crap about someone being killed, and I'm thinking that maybe there's more to this than I know. . . ." His voice trailed off as he looked at her, waiting to see if she'd give him a clue about what was going on.

The young woman opened her eyes again and looked at him for a moment. "So suddenly you change your mind and decide to be Mr. Nice Guy? Look, I don't know which Port Royal boss has you in his pocket—not that it matters much. I'm screwed any way you slice it, but I don't think his instructions were, 'Give the poor bag girl a little pep talk to make her feel better about her personal problems before you put a round through her head!'" She squeezed her eyes shut again as more silent sobs wracked her body.

Lazarus shook his head, deciding to try a different tactic, to earn her trust a different way.

"Look, I'm not a killer. I might be able to help you."

She sniffed and opened her eyes to look at him again. "What?"

"I said, I'm not a killer." He took a deep breath, wondering if he was making a mistake telling her this. "I'm CIB," he said quietly, "Concord Investigative Bureau."

"A cop?" The girl gasped. "A stinking cop!"

Lazarus looked at her sharply, already regretting that he had told her. Port Royal was not very hospitable to members of the Galactic Concord's private investigative agency.

The girl's face was a grimace of anger. Then her eyes widened in some sort of realization. "How did you find me?" she blurted at him, awkwardly wiping her tears on her shoulder.

"What?" Lazarus asked, surprised.

"How did you track me down? Why did you come here?"

"Let's just say some good detective work and leave it at that. I want you—"

"No. I need to know! How did you track me down?" Her words were forced, sharp, as she tried to hold herself together.

"I put a trace on your shadow last night," he responded, wondering what she was so afraid of.

"Liar," she said, not harshly or angrily. More like a simple statement of fact, something she knew beyond questioning. "Somebody ratted on me, set me up."

Lazarus laughed despite himself. "Bets?" he replied, a smile in his voice. "I traced you myself. Didn't take all that long, either." Then he let the smile vanish. "Well, okay, it took me a while to work through the system at the cafe at the casino. That was a nice bit of hacking, writing in a back door there so you could patch through to the Grid remotely and throw me off the scent."

The girl gazed at him, not admitting anything. "You couldn't have planted a signal trace on me without my knowing it. My Afsee is too good."

"You think I didn't consider that? I had the signal piggyback through Germaine's voice modifications. It nests itself in the voice program to get past your Afsee. It traces your port."

"That terrible job of voice modulation!" she exclaimed. "I thought the guy was just a lousy coder. Stupid, stupid, stupid!" she growled at herself.

"So you admit to contacting Germaine," Lazarus asked, smiling at her blunder.

The young woman went stoic again. "No. I don't know anyone named Germaine. I went to a club. I met a shadow there. We had a casual chat. I left."

Lazarus waved his hand dismissively. "Yeah, yeah. Encrypted log files, no way to break them. I untangled that last night, too. Would you like to see the transcript?"

"You're bluffing," she said quietly, uncertainly.

"You wish. Let's see . . . 'Well, nothing is ever foolproof, but my code is pretty boss—uh, I mean, pretty top-notch. Besides, who's going to care what two shadows are talking about in a corner of a Grid club? It's safe enough.' " Lazarus smiled at the irony.

The girl slumped in defeat. "How . . . ?"

Lazarus smiled again. "Hey, don't feel too bad. I've been hacking for a long time. I've made it my life's work to break encryptions. And like I said, it was a nice piece of work at the casino." Then he sighed. "But enough. I meant it before when I said that maybe I could help you. Whatever else you may think of cops, if you're in trouble, if someone is going to die over this package you say you don't have, then let me help you. Believe me, Germaine is *not* worth it. Now, who's 'he'?"

"Nothing. No one."

"*Now* who's the liar? Give me a break here. There's no way you walk; you know that. I will be taking you in. You're not making this delivery."

She pursed her lips and hung her head once again, remaining silent.

"Come on, throw me a bone. I told you, I don't want you. I want the people above you. I can help you, but I need you to help me, too."

Still nothing.

Lazarus sighed. "Okay, let's try something easy. What's your name?"

The girl raised her head and looked at him for a long moment before speaking. "Sable."

"That's it? Sable? What is that, your shadow name? No chance you'd give me your real one?"

"Sable." She had gone back to that stoic disinterest again.

Lazarus shrugged and nodded his head. "Fine. Sable will do. All right, Sable, I'm Lazarus. Call me Laz. If you won't let me help you, there's nothing I can do to force you. Your choice. But if it means someone dies, then someone dies. I don't want it to be that way, but I still have a job to do. So, you have two choices. You can help me, and maybe we figure out a way to stop this murder you were so worried about a few minutes ago, or you can continue to give me the silent treatment, in which case you do some time in CIB detention. Of course, everyone you deliver for thinks that you skipped town with the goods, so even though you'll spend a long time in prison, you won't want to come out when your sentence is done, because there will be gunrunners looking for you. And they *are* killers."

Sable refused to look at him. He could see the desperation on her face, could almost read the sense of helplessness that was overwhelming her. She blinked back the tears once more and drew a deep, ragged breath, and then shook her head slightly as one more choking sob got the better of her.

"You can't help me," she cried softly. "No matter what you do. They'd know, and they'd kill him. You have to let me go. Let me deliver the package. It's the only way to save him."

"No way," Lazarus replied. "That's not an option. It's sure suicide for me. I'm not about to let you run to them and tell them I'm on to them. You could paint them a damned good portrait of me!"

"I promise I won't say anything," Sable pleaded, her tone all desperation. "I swear to you, I won't. Please. I'll just deliver the package and go back where I came from. Please!"

Lazarus was shaking his head, trying to cut her off, but she refused to stop begging him.

"Please! It's better if I don't say anything; it'd keep me out of trouble. For God's sake, they'll kill him! Please! You can trust me."

"No, damn it!" Lazarus nearly shouted. He didn't want to admit it, but he actually was feeling sorry for her. Still, he'd have to be crazy to let her go.

"Tell me where the package is!" he growled.

"I can't!" Sable sobbed, turning and pressing her face against the wall. "They'll kill him," she whispered once more and then cried softly.

Lazarus sighed, staring at her as she cried, feeling a dull pain in his gut. Angrily he pushed it down. He didn't want to admit that it was guilt he was feeling.

Do your job, he told himself again. Don't be a sucker for a bit of skin and a sob story.

"What if—" she began quietly, still turned away from him—"if I let you see the package and agree to whatever else you wanted." She swallowed hard and finally turned to look at Lazarus. "If I did all that, would you let me deliver the package? I need to do it, Laz. I need to be the one. It's too risky to switch. He heard my voice; he'll know if it's not me."

Lazarus began to shake his head from side to side again. "Good voice mods can make me sound just like you. That's not a good enough reason."

"Laz, please! It could be something else, something we haven't thought of. What if something was said when this Germaine fellow first contracted for the job? My boss might have mentioned me, described me in some way. He won't be expecting you. They're expecting a woman."

Lazarus was still doubtful, still shaking his head. Even though he saw the wisdom of what she was saying, the risks terrified him.

"You asked me to trust you," Sable said. "You have to trust me in return. I swear that I won't rat on you. But if they don't see me coming, if you try to deliver that package to them and they are expecting me, they will know something's wrong, and they will probably kill you, too."

Lazarus sighed, knowing the girl was right. If Germaine smelled anything fishy, he'd bolt, and that would be that. End of case.

She's no regular courier, that's for sure, Lazarus told himself again. From what she's been saying, she must be working for her bosses exclusively. Which means she's a direct link back to them, he realized. Letting her go forward with the delivery held its share of risks. Plus, he would be breaking all sorts of regulations, using her as a partner in this, but the chance to break this case open was tempting. He was going to have to be willing to take a few chances.

"I'm not ready to agree to that yet," Lazarus began, "but it's a start. Show me the package. Let me see what it is, and I'll consider it. We've still got two days before Germaine is expecting you to contact him again. That's enough time to make plans."

Sable looked at him, chewing her lower lip. "Okay," she said at last.

There was something new in her eyes that had not been there before. Not hope exactly, Lazarus told himself, but . . . something.

"All right. Good. You're doing the right thing, and I'll hold up my end of the bargain. You can trust me on that. Now, where's the package?"

"It's in a locker at the casino. I stashed it there when I programmed in the back door," Sable said, scooting toward the edge of the bed awkwardly, due to the cuffs on her wrists. Her feet finally reached the door, and she stood up, turning around, holding the cuffs out to him.

"Fine," Lazarus said, not making a move to undo the cuffs. "Which locker?"

"I'll show you," Sable replied, holding her hands out from her back insistently. "Uncuff me, and I'll take you to get them."

Lazarus hesitated. Telling himself he was going to have to trust her and actually doing it were two different things. She could easily try to make another break for it the minute he let her out into the night.

If she told me the truth about stashing it in the casino, then she knows better. But what if she lied? She could bolt, and I'd never see her again.

Lazarus sighed and frowned, but he finally pulled a small black baton about six centimeters long from a pocket in his duster and moved toward Sable. He keyed a switch on the device. There was a small beep from the handcuffs, and they clicked open. Lazarus pocketed them and the command baton.

Sable rubbed her wrists for a second or two, and then turned to look at him. "What now?" she asked.

"Get dressed. We're going to go get the package, and then I'm taking you to a safe place where I can think without having to keep an eye on you."

"I can tell you what it is right now. It's a pair of crystals—one data, one banking. I don't know anything other than that."

Lazarus nodded, thinking. *So she's bringing Germaine some money. Interesting.*

"Laz?"

He looked at her, blinking. "Yeah?"

"Can I take a shower before we go?"

Lazarus shook his head. "No. You can shower when we get to where we're going."

Sable seemed to pout a little at his denial, but she didn't

say anything. She slipped her pants, boots, and jacket on, and then packed the rest of her belongings.

"I'm ready," Sable said, holding a duffel bag.

Lazarus thought for a moment, still wondering if she was going to try to run the first chance she had. Then he got an idea. He pulled the binders back out and came toward her. The girl shrank back from him, her eyes wide.

"You said I could be the one to make contact!" Sable protested.

Lazarus ignored her as he firmly took hold of her right arm and snapped one cuff on it, the other one on his left. "There. Nobody will pay any attention to a couple out for a stroll, holding hands." To demonstrate, he took her hand in his.

"You don't have to do that," she said quietly. "I won't run."

"As much as I might like to believe you, this is a safe-guard against your being a really good liar and my being an idiot. We'll work into this trust thing slowly. Let's go."

Sable sighed in exasperation and followed Lazarus to the door.

He killed the lights and then tapped the keypad. As the door slid open, he peered out, carefully checking both directions in the hallway before leading her toward the fire exit door.

*   *   *   *   *

Sable's heart pounded in her chest as the two of them stepped out into the street at the side of the Lucky Ace. She wasn't sure if it was because she felt so trapped, or because she was worried that someone would notice the cuffs that bound her to this cop. If anyone *did* notice them, they might both be in trouble. If he really was CIB—she realized with a start that she hadn't seen a badge yet—he was way out of his element in Port Royal. The Galactic Concord was far from welcome here, and just about anyone would finger one of its CIB agents to the Jamaican Syndicate just for the fun of it. And if the Jamaicans got hold of him . . . that was an end to this little adventure Sable did not want to think about. Regardless of her explanations, the Jamaicans would most likely take the conservative approach and assume she was as big a liability as Lazarus.

The trip to the casino didn't really take very long, but to Sable, it seemed to drag on forever. She worried every time a passerby strolled past them, even though her common sense told her that no one could see the matching metal bracelets encircling their wrists.

"If we get mugged . . ." she muttered, only half under her breath, as a small band of street punks went past, clowning with each other and laughing loudly.

"Just act normal, and we'll be fine," the CIB agent said softly next to her, "and everyone will leave us alone."

God, I hope so. Oh, Gavin, I'm so sorry. I'll come back to you, I promise. Whatever it takes, she told herself firmly.

Sable studied Lazarus out of the corner of her eye as they walked. In another time and place, she admitted, she would have found him handsome, with his goatee and his long, straight black hair, which was pulled into a tail. He was tall and somewhat thin, and his nose was perhaps a little too large, but his clothes were nice, if simple in cut, and the large black duster he wore over the ensemble flared at his boots as he walked. His stride was solid and purposeful, as though he knew where he had been going all of his life. She shook her head the tiniest bit.

Don't be stupid. He's still a cop.

When the pair reached the casino district near the center of the dome, the lights were even brighter and more garish. All around them, patterns of every imaginable color shimmered and blazed, beckoning all to partake of what Port Royal had to offer. The city never slept. It was open for business and was, in turn, consumed, at all hours of the day or night. Neon and lasers reflected off of every chrome, steel, cerametal, and glass surface, in every direction, including up. Towering buildings, amazing feats of architecture, dominated the center of the dome, stylish and glorious in their attempt to appeal to the carousing masses. Throngs of people, many of them drunk, all of them desperate for gratification in one form or another, meandered about, drawn to the promise of decadence and revelry, sensuality and diversion. Anyone seeking even the most depraved of pleasures could find it here. Holograms broadcast continuously in every plaza, on every corner; illuminated advertisements blazed and pulsed, vying for attention. It gave everything an overdeveloped, washed-out look. Sable squinted and wished she had her shades on. In the brightness of Port Royal, there were no shadows, and Sable worried once again that people would notice the cuffs.

They reached the Double Star Casino, a huge structure of steel, glass, and cerametal, slightly pyramidal in shape. Lazarus led them inside, into a main plaza. The center was dominated by a huge fountain enhanced by a hypnotic holographic light show, all beautiful flashing patterns of color. Surrounding the plaza were dozens of small shops, upscale establishments selling everything from souvenirs to guided tours of the city to expensive jewelry. The casino overlooked the plaza from several levels of balconies reached by escalators, and above that was the hotel.

Lazarus and Sable rode an escalator up to the second level, where the sounds of gambling bombarded them. The din was almost palpable, the white noise of thousands of voices rising above the endless electronic singing, whistling, and chiming coming from the slot machines, hologames, and entertainment centers spread throughout the place. Sable began to tense. Her breathing grew shallow, her skin prickly.

Shit. It's even more crowded at night than in the daytime, she thought. She just wanted to get the crystals and get out of there as quickly as possible.

As they stood there, adjusting to the onslaught of noise, loud sirens went off, and lights began flashing nearby. Sable jumped and went into a defensive crouch, ready to bolt to the nearest exit, before she realized that the cacophony was merely a celebration of someone winning big. She trembled and stood up again, trying to relax. She realized that in her panic, she had jerked her hand free of Lazarus's, and now they were joined only by the cuffs. Calmly, subtly, he took her hand again, clamping it forcefully. She looked at him, and he gave her a pointed stare.

"Sorry," she mouthed to him. "This way," she said, gesturing, and began to thread her way through the crowds, pulling him along behind her.

Stupid! she scolded herself. Panicking is only going to blow it. Get a grip on yourself!

They reached an alcove near the cybercafe where she had been earlier that day, out of the way of the rest of the casino level. The noise was only slightly less intrusive. Rows of small lockers, each with an elaborate electronic keypad on the door, lined the walls of the place. The unoccupied ones had a small green light, and the doors swung open freely. Sable went to one where the light was red and began to tap in a code. There was a small click, and the door swung open. Inside was a small crystal case. She reached for it.

Lazarus beat her to it and slipped it inside his duster. Sable glared at him briefly, but he only shrugged and began to head back the way they had come, leading her. Sable began to breathe easier. Soon they would be out of here, somewhere quiet. She could think better then, figure out a way to escape this mess. . . .

Halfway to the escalators, a man in a conservative business suit, wearing a headset version of a comm unit, stepped in front of them and smiled graciously. "I'm sorry, folks, but we've had a bit of trouble here this evening. Some things were stolen from some of the guests. You don't mind if I have a quick look inside your duffel bag, do you?"

Sable froze, along with Lazarus, and groaned inwardly. She'd seen this a thousand times before. It was an old trick. Casino security would hassle the guests, pretending that something had been stolen and insisting a quick search of the guests' belongings were in order. Of course, what they were really hoping for was a quick bribe to have them leave you alone. If you didn't play their game, they always found something on you that had been reported stolen. Sable thought of her new gauntlet and blanched. She knew the guy would single it out in an instant; it was top of the line and worth a fortune. And even if he didn't intend to impound the gauntlet, falsely claiming it as stolen, he'd run a security check on them both, just to further delay them in the hope that they would pay their way out of the mess. When the identity check revealed that Lazarus was a CIB agent to the security guard, who worked for a casino owned by the biggest crime family in Port Royal, the two of them were dead.

Oh, God! We're screwed. Please bribe him, Laz, please-pleaseplease—

Lazarus leaned in close to the guy, putting on a conspiratorial smile, and said, "Look, we only dropped in for a moment."

Laz, no! she silently screamed in horror.

"Had to get something out of a storage locker. Can you make this quick?"

Sable sighed in relief as Lazarus reached inside his coat and pulled out a case of disposable bank crystals. Unlike a standard bank crystal, which contained the ownership information for transferring funds between accounts, a disposable one could be easily obtained from vending machines for a set amount and passed between owners like currency. Very handy for bribing someone when you didn't want the money traced back to you, Sable knew.

The security suit's smile warmed considerably as he eyed the crystals, but when Lazarus absently reached up with his other hand to slip out a single crystal, Sable's breath caught in her throat. Her hand, still locked to Lazarus's by the cuffs, was dragged right into the security suit's line of sight. The man's smile faded to a frown as he saw the cuffs, and then his gaze darted back and forth between their faces several times as he tried to puzzle out just what this meant. Sable figured she must have looked as guilty as sin right then, for the suit's frown deepened considerably.

"What the hell—?" the guy said, reaching up to the comm unit at his ear. "All right, you two, just stand easy right there. I'll just let my boys know I'm leaving the floor for a bit, and then I think we'll just take a nice stroll back to my office and sort this all out." He thumbed a switch on the communicator and seemed to wait a moment. Then he opened his mouth to begin speaking, but the words never came.

Lazarus's free hand came up hard, slamming the crystal case into the guy's face, driving the comm unit's mike into his teeth. On instinct, Sable lashed out with her leg, sweeping it into the back of the suit's knee, buckling it and sending him down to the floor. In a flash, Lazarus was pulling her along with him.

"Come on!" Lazarus shouted, even as the suit, his mouth bloody and his comm unit shattered, fumbled for something else inside his suit. Sable lurched forward as she caught a quick glimpse of a pistol sliding out, and then she was running with Lazarus, both of them charging through the crowded aisles, trying to avoid the people standing at the gambling machines. Lazarus ran fast, darting deftly around people, and Sable had to sprint to keep up.

Behind them, there was a shout, and then she saw two figures, dressed similarly to the first guy, step into their path ahead. Lazarus slashed down a side aisle when he saw them, jerking Sable along with him. She saw pistols in their hands, too, and someone screamed, not with the excitement of hitting the jackpot but with fear.

People were starting to pay attention to them now as they ran past, and it was becoming more and more difficult to knife through them as they clogged the pathway to see what was going on. Sable began to panic, feeling as if she were suffocating in the crowd.

Lazarus drew to a sudden stop, and Sable crashed into his back awkwardly. Another casino security officer was blocking their way ahead. Behind them, yet another one appeared. Sable hissed a curse under her breath when she realized they had been cut off, but Lazarus suddenly darted left and leaped onto a large stylish planter box, crashing through the fake ferns.

Sable was caught by surprise and timed her leap all wrong. She banged her knee into the side of the planter and felt a sharp pain, but Lazarus was dragging her up and through the foliage, so she scrabbled the rest of the way up, pulling the duffel bag awkwardly behind her.

Lazarus was leading them deeper into the casino now, away from the exits. At the last moment, he cut back, working between a series of tables where people played dice games. Sable's gaze darted back and forth around them as they worked through the crowd, watching with trepidation for more of the security suits to appear.

They suddenly found themselves along one of the balconies overlooking the open plaza below, on the main floor. They were halfway between two sets of escalators and not close to either one of them. Behind them, Sable saw the first guy, his mouth still bloody, weaving through the tables, closing the distance between them, even as other security personnel appeared in pairs near the tops of each bank of escalators, cutting the duo off from escape. Each carried a gun, but they kept them relatively low and out of sight.

Trying not to scare the guests. But that's just what we need: a big diversion.

"Laz, we're running out of time!" she said nervously as the suits advanced cautiously.

Lazarus had been surveying the situation and now took off again, following the curve of the balcony, heading straight toward one pair of security officers. Sable darted after him. Behind her, she heard a heavy smack and grunt. She glanced back briefly, catching a glimpse of the original casino security guard, his mouth bloody from Lazarus's punch, sprawled awkwardly on the tiled floor where she had stood only a second before, not moving. He had apparently dived after them and missed. She turned away quickly as Lazarus began running hard again. Her knee throbbed as she tried to keep up with him.

"Come *on!*" he yelled over his shoulder, tugging on her hand insistently. About twenty meters from where the two guards were nervously awaiting Lazarus's headlong charge, he suddenly slowed and scrambled up onto the banister of the balcony, directly above the glass ceiling of a shop on the level below.

"Laz, no!" Sable yelled when she saw where he was headed.

He ignored her and pulled her along as he stepped onto

one of the steel beams of the framework that held the glass panels in place. Sable flung her legs over the side of the banister to keep from being dragged over and losing her balance.

When the security suits saw what the pair was doing, they shouted and began running, trying to catch them before they escaped from the balcony. The two guards at the other end, along with two more who had joined them, took off down the escalators, hoping to cut Lazarus and Sable off before they made it to the plaza below.

Lazarus tightrope-walked the support, awkwardly trying to keep his balance with his cuffed hand behind him. Sable's own cuffed arm was pulled forward and across her body, and the duffel bag made balancing with her other arm difficult at best.

"Laz, I can't—!" she gasped as she nearly lost her balance. Her knee was really stiffening up now, and it throbbed with each step.

The two security guards reached the balcony where Lazarus and Sable had scrambled over the side. "Hold it!" one of them shouted, aiming his gun at the two of them.

Lazarus stopped and looked back as the other guard began to step out onto the support to follow them. A crowd had gathered below now, and there was general shouting and confusion in the milling mass, everyone pointing and watching. Sable edged closer to Lazarus, trying to keep the guard who had climbed out on the roof from reaching her.

"Laz!" she hissed through clenched teeth.

"Get ready to jump," Lazarus said softly as he fumbled in his jacket for something.

"Are you *insane?*" Sable gasped, looking down at the plaza floor some ten meters below. "There's no way!"

Lazarus had his pistol out now, and the guard who was

following them—he was only about two meters from Sable now, reaching toward her—saw it.

"Jesus, he's armed! Look out!" he cried to his companion, but the other suit couldn't get a clean shot.

"Get out of the way! You're blocking my line!" the man on the balcony called, trying to move to the side to get a clear angle. The guard out on the glass roof began losing his balance, waving his arms wildly and trying to keep from toppling over. He took a desperate step to another crossbeam, barely managing to stay off the glass panels, just as his companion fired a shot. The round grazed the stumbling guard's shoulder and whizzed by Sable's ear. The guard cried out in pain and staggered forward again, trying desperately to stay on his feet and blocking his buddy's line of sight again. Sable screamed and ducked just as Lazarus fired his own pistol, straight down.

The glass panel beside Sable's feet fractured into a million tiny pieces at the same instant Lazarus stepped off the beam and into the gap that was suddenly there. Sable was pulled forward and down. She barely managed to swing her free arm up, getting the duffel bag clear of the framing as she dropped, following Lazarus down into the shop below. Somewhere she heard another shot fired, and more glass shattered, but she was aware that she was screaming, flailing as she fell.

Sable felt herself land in a heap next to Lazarus, but the jarring pain of hitting the hard floor wasn't there. She gasped but barely had time to realize that they had fallen into a huge bin of stuffed toys before Lazarus was scrambling up, dragging her after him. She scrambled and tumbled over hundreds of little stuffed weren, dragging the duffel behind her, as the CIB agent headed toward the back of the curio shop. She slipped once and rammed her already injured knee hard into the side of a display rack. The shock of pain that went through her leg made her scream in agony, but she didn't have time to crumple. Lazarus was still tugging insistently on her hand and pulling her along with him.

"Laz, my knee! I can't run!" she cried out.

He turned and grabbed her, handing her the pistol and spinning her three hundred and sixty degrees so that her own cuffed hand cut across her front to connect with his, which was now around the back of her waist. He hoisted her up into his arms, and she wrapped her free arm around his neck, the pistol dangling in it as she watched behind them over his shoulder.

"Hang on!" he said as he turned and darted toward the back of the shop. Sable saw one of the guards enter the front of the shop and spot them. He raised his gun just as Lazarus disappeared into the stock room in the back.

"They're at the front door!"

Lazarus didn't answer. At this awkward angle, Sable couldn't really see where he was going, so she clung to him as best as she could and continued to watch behind them. The guard appeared in the doorway, talking in his comm unit. Sable felt Lazarus pause and shift his weight, and then he pushed against something using her feet. She aimed the pistol at the guard, but Lazarus was opening a door, and suddenly they were in a hallway. Lazarus took off, running clumsily, Sable bouncing hard in his arms. She risked a quick look in the direction they were headed and saw a fire exit at the end of the hallway.

When Sable turned back, the guard had stepped out and was bringing his pistol to bear. She raised Lazarus's gun and fired wildly, feeling the low, rumbling belch as the sonic blast left the weapon. The shot was off target, but it was enough to send the security suit scrambling behind the doorway for cover.

Lazarus hit the fire exit, setting off alarms, and peered

out. They were on a back street behind the Double Star, and there was no one close by. A shot rang out from behind them, and steel and plastic exploded from the wall near their heads.

Lazarus dashed out into the night.

03.0:

HOW'S YOUR KNEE?" Lazarus asked Sable as he set her down gently. He took his pistol from her and holstered it. The two of them had taken refuge behind a huge power transformer box down a small side street a couple of blocks away from the Double Star. Lazarus was breathing hard as he fumbled in his jacket for something.

Sable flexed her leg gingerly and felt a twinge of pain. It felt swollen and was very stiff. "Not great," she said, bending it again. "I smacked it pretty good when you dragged me over that planter box."

Lazarus produced the small black baton, raised his cuffed hand into the air, and pressed a button on the remote, causing the binders to release. "Sorry," he said as Sable gratefully rubbed at her chafed wrist. "That was one bit of atrociously bad luck back there, wasn't it?" he said, a wry grin on his face. "Of all the times to run into . . ." He let the thought trail off, his smile fading. "Well, they've got both our faces on security camera now. Good thing we don't have to go back there."

The sounds of someone entering the alley made Lazarus crouch low, draw his pistol, and peer cautiously around the side of the transformer. It was only a couple of tourists, giggling softly and groping one another as they went past, lost in the moment. Lazarus remained quiet for several moments after they had passed, seeming to listen.

Sable merely looked at him. "What now?" she asked after a time. "I don't think I can walk like this."

Lazarus considered her for a moment. "I'll carry you to the transit station around the next corner, and when we get to my dome, I'll flag a cab. I've got something that can take care of that knee back at my place. Can you stand to wait a bit?"

"Sure." She smiled. She almost meant it.

"Okay, then. I want to take a quick peek to see if any of the Double Star goons are still looking for us. I'll be right back." He started to leave, but then paused and looked down where Sable sat, her back propped against a wall. "You're not going anywhere, are you?"

Sable stared back him. "Even if I could, you've got my crystals."

Lazarus nodded somewhat doubtfully. "Maybe I should cuff you to something, just to be sure."

Sable sighed but didn't argue with him. I guess I wouldn't trust me either, she thought ruefully.

Lazarus seemed to consider a moment longer, but instead of pulling the cuffs out of his jacket, he disappeared into the night.

Sable wondered what had made him change his mind, but right then, she was too tired and in too much pain to care. She just sat there, suddenly feeling very alone. If they find me, I'm done. I sure as hell can't run. She flexed her knee once or twice more and winced. She leaned her head back against the wall and closed her eyes, thinking about Gavin.

She remembered when he was about eight and she had been twelve. They were on vacation—she couldn't remember where—and they were staying in some resort somewhere. There was a park with real grass and bushes and huge trees. Sable still remembered how huge the trunks of the trees had been. She and Gavin had laughed and chased each other around the trees.

"Tag, you're it!" Gavin laughed, darting away.

"Gavin, you're not playing fair! I was on base!" she screamed at him. He made her furious when he ignored the rules. He only laughed at her and kept running. She darted after him, her longer legs letting her close the distance quickly. At the last second, he ducked to the side and ran, laughing, into some bushes.

She charged in after him, following his desperate giggles as he tried to stay away from her. Crawling on her hands and knees, she worked her way through the shrubs. Little pathways showed where countless other kids had played before them. She was almost to Gavin, was just about to reach out and grab him, when she heard her parents calling.

"Kids, it's time to go! Gavin! Sa—"

Sable's memories were interrupted as Lazarus slunk silently into view.

"It looks clear. Let's go."

She clung to that warm memory for a moment longer, and then pushed herself up awkwardly, trying to keep from putting any weight on her bad leg. Lazarus turned to face away from her and crouched down.

"Jump on. I'll carry you on my back."

Sable grabbed hold of Lazarus's shoulders and half leaped, half hoisted herself onto his back. He snaked his arms around and under her legs and cinched her up a bit, and then they were off.

As Lazarus had promised, the transit station wasn't far. He was cautious, watching to see if any of the suits who had been chasing them had thought to stake out the place, but there were none to be found among the milling crowds. Most of the people on the platform were workers—the majority from the service industries, shopkeepers and casino game dealers, a tired-looking waitress or two, and cleaning people in their dingy work clothes. But a significant number of the passengers were tourists, and lots of people were laughing and cutting up, a few a bit too loudly.

Lazarus made his way closer to a few of these rowdy revelers.

"What are you doing?" Sable hissed softly in his ear.

"Trust me. We'll blend in better. Just follow my lead."

As they got a little closer, a couple of the people in the crowd gave them curious looks. Sable merely stared at them as Lazarus sauntered up.

"My silly girlfriend can't walk when she's drunk. She turned her ankle," he explained, a hint of humor in his voice. Several among the group laughed, and others chimed in. Sable tried to flash a lame smile. It apparently worked, for soon they had been accepted as part of the party-going crowd, although few were actually paying much attention to them. Once or twice someone asked a polite "Where are you two staying?" or "Are you having a nice visit?" at which point Lazarus gave a quick, unassuming answer. Sable, for her part, kept quiet.

Playing the part of the drunk girlfriend, she grimaced. But Lazarus had been right. The two of them seemed to be just a part of the crowd.

The transit arrived shortly after that, and soon they were sitting in silence as the sleek cars shot out of the station and into the tunnel. They were headed toward Uptown. Lazarus began to stare off into space, apparently lost in thought.

Sable stole furtive glances at him once or twice, but he was preoccupied, it seemed. She leaned back in the seat and closed her eyes, thinking again about Gavin and the last time she had seen him. Her mind drifted. . . .

"Please!" she said, cringing. "I just wanted to know he's all right. I won't do it again, I swear!"

Mr. Maxwell loomed near where she stood, her wrists manacled to a steel post that stood upright in front of her. The man, his face a mocking smile, looked at her. Out of the corner of her eye, she could see the door open, and two of Maxwell's goons entered, dragging Gavin between them. Sable was both relieved and terrified. He was alive, but he was here. With Mr. Maxwell.

Mr. Maxwell grabbed her chin, twisting her head and forcing her to meet his gaze. "You know better than that, my dear." He shook his head, as if disappointed. "Pretending to still be asleep in hope of finding out where we are. Too much knowledge is a dangerous thing, Sable. And you know what happens when you try my patience like that." He nodded almost imperceptibly at the two goons, and they dragged Gavin toward a post similar to the one she was chained to, next to where she stood.

"No, please! He didn't do it! I did it! Please don't!" she wailed, struggling to free her trapped hands.

The two goons ignored Sable as they forced the struggling boy against the post, snapping cuffs on him and locking him into place beside her. Mr. Maxwell walked casually over to a table nearby and picked up a pair of black leather gloves and slipped them on. Then he hefted a long baton with a very thin whiplike end. He examined it carefully, and when he was satisfied, he turned back to the two prisoners.

Sable was still struggling vainly to free herself, but Gavin stood there disconsolately, his head hanging down. "P-please, Mr. Maxwell. Don't punish him. He didn't do anything wrong. Please. You can punish me," she sobbed desperately.

Mr. Maxwell stepped around behind the two of them, where Sable couldn't see him anymore. She jumped when one of his goons stepped behind her and ripped open her thin shift, baring her backside from head to toe. She heard Gavin's shirt tear, too. She clenched her teeth and closed her eyes as tears welled up in them.

"Yes, that's right. I *can* punish you. And you *will* learn to behave."

The first blow sent white-hot pain through her body as the baton struck her back. Its thin whiplike blade made a crease in her bare skin, but it also had an extra kick, a small yet painful electrical charge that crackled across her entire back. Sable's scream echoed loudly through the room as the muscles in her neck and arms corded. She drew in a sharp, ragged breath just as the second blow fell, and her cry was nothing but a high-pitched wail as she thrashed in her bonds.

Each blow delivered was more painful than the last. The electrical shock felt like salt being poured into the previous wounds. Sable bawled and thrashed, flinched and jerked, trying desperately to escape the terrible pain raining down on her back and rump. After five blows, Mr. Maxwell stopped. Sable hung limply in place, panting from her exertion and sobbing silently.

"Five for you so you'll remember what it feels like," Mr. Maxwell began, walking over to stand behind Gavin, "and twenty for your brother so you won't misbehave again."

Sable drew a deep, shuddering breath and turned to look at Gavin, her teary eyes filled with sorrow. "Please," she whispered hoarsely, but the first blow hit the boy, and he jerked in his bonds and screamed in agony. Sable closed her eyes and turned away, her heart breaking. She wanted to close her ears, too, to escape the awful screaming.

"Sable," Lazarus said, and she started, remembering where she was. "Are you all right?" He was leaning in close, looking at her with worry on his face. "What is it?"

She realized she had a tear trickling down her cheek. Oh, Gavin! My baby brother! She shook her head resolutely. "Nothing," she said, wiping away the tear with the back of her hand. "I'm fine."

Lazarus's eyes told her he didn't believe her for a second, but he said, "This is our stop."

Sable looked around and realized the transit had pulled into another domed station. People were filing off. Standing gingerly, she grabbed her duffel bag as Lazarus turned to let her hop on his back. She climbed up, and they were off, leaving the transit and heading up out of the station into the main part of the city of Port Royal.

The dome they were in was not Uptown, but it was pretty close.

Probably the same district, Sable thought, impressed with the architecture. Everything seemed to be clean and well lit, not as garish as the casino district had been. Here, instead of endless streets of gaudy shops and perverse entertainments, there were well-to-do residences and elegant malls. So this is where the wealthy and powerful of Port Royal dwell, safely away from all of the debauchery that paid for their existences, Sable thought.

Lazarus hailed a cab at the front of the transit station and gave the driver an address as they climbed inside. The vehicle took off, gliding silently, its lanthanide battery cells propelling it through the quiet streets of the dome. Sable looked out the window at all of the luxurious dwellings, almost all of them hidden behind privacy walls. She yawned repeatedly as they passed out of one wealthy district and into another, not quite so gentile but nonetheless upscale.

The cab pulled to a stop at a corner where a drugstore sat, quiet and dark. Lazarus paid the driver and helped Sable out of the car. She could hardly keep her eyes open, and her knee was so stiff now she could barely bend it at all. Lazarus led her to a small alcove next to the shop as the cab drove off. Inside, he punched a code into a keypad on the wall, and a door slid open. He hoisted her up onto his back once more and carried her up a set of stairs to another door with a security panel.

Pretty boss security, Sable thought sleepily, yawning again. Lazarus fumbled for something in one of his many pockets as Sable laid her head on his back and closed her eyes. She absently heard a click and the high-pitched ping of a code being entered, and then they were moving, and she heard the door shut behind her.

The last thing Sable remembered before drifting off to sleep was Lazarus laying her out on a soft couch, helping her slip off her boots and pants, and draping a blanket over her.

* * * * *

When Sable awoke, it took her a moment to remember where she was. The sounds of commerce on the street below were muffled, but the daylight streaming through the translucent dome and into her eyes made her blink a couple of times before it came back to her. She tried to sit up on the couch and groaned from stiffness. She plopped back down and draped her arm across her eyes.

"Morning," Lazarus said from across the room. Sable peeked at him with one eye from under her arm. He was seated at a desk built into the wall, a gauntlet on his arm, busily working at something.

She grunted at him and closed her eye again.

"This is amazing . . ." Lazarus muttered, half to himself. Whatever he was looking at, he seemed pretty absorbed in it.

"That's good," Sable replied sarcastically, turning over on her side and looking at him again. "It's certainly worth waking me up at the crack of dawn."

Lazarus laughed and looked over at her finally. "It's nearly lunchtime," he said, smiling, and went back to what he was doing.

Sable groaned and forced herself to sit up. As she swung her legs down to the floor, she realized that her knee was wrapped in something and wouldn't flex. Surprisingly, the joint felt pretty good, compared to last night. She looked at the thing; it seemed to be some kind of plastic pad with a small interface panel on the outside. A couple of lights were blinking on the panel, but otherwise she couldn't tell much about what it was supposed to do.

"What the hell is this?" she asked, looking at Lazarus.

"It's a bioelectric wrap. I put it on you last night after you fell asleep. Your knee should be feeling a lot better this morning."

Sable raised a quizzical eyebrow at him. "It does, I think. But what's this thing do?"

Lazarus turned away from what he was working on and walked over to the couch. "It injects some steroids and other proteins into the injured joint to reduce the swelling, while at the same time stimulating it with a low, constant electrical field. It speeds healing."

"Hmmm. Does it knock your patient on her tail, too? I feel like I could sleep for another week."

Lazarus began unfastening the device from her knee. "I also set it to give you a mild sedative."

Sable looked at him levelly. "Why?" she asked curtly.

Lazarus stopped and returned her gaze. "So you would sleep better. And so I would know for sure that you would sleep through the night and not try to leave before I woke up."

"Bastard."

He shrugged. "I wasn't taking any chances. I didn't want to wake up with a gun in my face, whether you were at the other end of it or someone you went and fetched."

"I told you I wouldn't do that." Sable turned away, angry. But she wasn't completely angry at Lazarus. She couldn't really blame him for his distrust. Too much had happened in her life to expect someone to trust her, and she was angry about that. Most of all, though, she was angry because she knew that he was right. If she had managed to wake up and could have laid her hands on the crystals, she would have been gone.

That's just the way it is, she told herself. He's got his problems, and I've got mine. No reason to get them mixed up with each other. When the time comes, you make a break for it. You do it for Gavin. He's the only thing that matters. She knew she would, but it didn't make her like it any better.

Realizing that Lazarus was squatting in front of her, looking at her, she smoothed her face and turned back to him. "So now what?" For a moment, the look he gave her in return was strange, almost pained.

Lazarus blinked and then shook his head with a start. "Oh, right. That's what I was going to tell you." He finished unwrapping the medical wrap and turned back to the desk where he had been working. "I've been having a look at these crystals of yours."

Sable tested the knee and was surprised at how good it felt. There was still a little stiffness, but the pain and the swelling were pretty much gone. She stood carefully, grabbing the blanket and wrapping it around her waist, then walked over to look at Lazarus's handiwork. "I sure hope you didn't screw them up, Laz."

"Nah. I didn't do much serious poking. At least not at the bank crystal. I just scanned it for the amount and the registrations. You're toting around a hell of a lot of money, Sable." Lazarus patted the chair, and she sat down as he picked up the gauntlet. He began to tap on the keypad, and a screen mounted in the wall at the head of the desk glowed into life. There were a couple of menus visible, but Lazarus zipped through them so fast that Sable had a hard time keeping up.

It's a lot harder to follow when it's not you at the controls.

She contented herself to wait until Lazarus's manipulations paused. Then she looked more closely at the screen.

He had managed to hack into the registration system of the bank crystal, something that people generally weren't supposed to be able to do. Sable shook her head slightly, impressed, and concentrated on the information there.

When she realized what she was reading, Sable whistled in surprise.

Seventy-five *thousand* Concord dollars!

She blinked and reread it to make sure of the amount. It was being delivered from some company called Quartz Pyramid, Limited, located on Bluefall in the Aegis system, to a man named Quentin Germaine. Sable looked up from the screen to Lazarus.

"Okay, so?"

"Do either of those names mean anything to you?" He asked her.

"No. Nothing other than the Germaine part, and only because you kept throwing that name around at me last night."

Lazarus nodded, already typing on the gauntlet again. "Germaine works for a company here in Port Royal called HansCorp Freight. I've been watching him for about three months now. I'm pretty sure he's the point man for a smuggling operation." After a few moments, he stopped typing.

"This was pretty tightly encrypted," he said as Sable leaned forward to read the screen again. "This is what was on the other crystal."

It was a letter.

Mr. Germaine,

As we agreed, here is a small sum to cover some of your expenses for your efforts. Expect the remainder once the documents you have agreed to deliver are in my hands. My courier will transport the information back to me. She is completely reliable.

I assure you, your name will never be mentioned during negotiations. Should things go well and a deal is struck with your employer, a second payment will be delivered to you, as promised. I am quite certain I can make your people a better offer, one they can't refuse.

Sincerely,
Jaren Gillst

When Sable finished reading, she looked up at Lazarus, who was staring at her intently. "What about him?" he asked.

Sable shook her head. "Never heard of him," she replied, starting to reread the letter.

Lazarus grabbed the chair by the armrests and spun it so she faced him. "Are you sure? Jaren Gillst? Your boss, perhaps? He might go by something else when dealing with you. You've never seen or heard anything—letterhead, a snippet of conversation, anything—that mentioned this Quartz Pyramid company?"

"No!" Sable growled at Lazarus, trying to rise from the chair. "I told you I haven't."

He moved aside to let her stand, and she stalked across the room toward the couch. When she got there, she spun to face him again, her jaw jutting out at him in anger.

"Look, I'm never told anything. 'Take this to the Lucullus system. Go to Port Royal on Penates. Get on the Grid, go to a place called the Loading Zone, and meet a shadow called the Fool. He will give you further instructions for delivering it. Wait for an answer, and then come right back. Oh, and don't screw up, or—' " She clamped her mouth shut, choking off the rest of what she'd been about to say.

Or I'll make sure you never see Gavin again! Sable felt vulnerable, and she hated it. This man who was interfering with her ability to do her job seemed to know just where to poke to rile her up. She was going to go insane if he kept asking her these questions.

Damn!

Seething, she dropped to the couch and grabbed her duffel bag. Unzipping it, she began to paw through it, trying not to let his stare get to her.

Lazarus came over to Sable and sat down on the couch beside her. "Hey. Take it easy."

"You take it easy!" she shouted, whirling on him in a rage. "I did what you asked, did it even though I'm so scared I want to double over and puke, did it even though it almost got me killed last night! What did you think? That suddenly, if you showed me some stupid names, I would clear everything up for you? Well, I can't! I don't know! All right? Do you get it now? I don't *know!* Damn you!" She sobbed uncontrollably then, the tension breaking through her, and she sprawled facedown on the other side of the couch and wept into the cushion.

Lazarus left her alone. She felt him get up softly and heard him walk away from the couch.

And she cried.

It felt good, in a way, just the quiet, wracking sobs making her shudder, the big, wet tears running down her face, buried in her arms. It hurt, though, too, because she was so tired of it all. Tired of being so afraid all the time, tired of worrying about Gavin. But mostly tired of being alone, of hiding from everyone, from herself, all the time.

And when she was finished crying, she knew nothing had changed. There was still the problem of getting away, of getting back, of protecting Gavin. But somehow she felt better.

Sable sat up and looked around. Lazarus was standing on the far side of the room, staring out a window. He did not turn to look at her, so she swept her gaze about the room, taking it in for the first time.

The room was smallish, and in addition to the couch, there was the work desk, which, along with piles of various equipment—most of it Gridware, she saw—took up almost half the room. There was a second chair, overstuffed and made for reclining, facing a small holoscreen on one wall, and a doorway that appeared to lead into a hall. The entrance to the place, where they had come in the night before, was on the far side of the room, in a small alcove. The place was clean if spartan.

Sable shrugged and bent down to grab her duffel bag. She stood up, still holding the blanket around her waist with her free hand, and headed toward the hallway.

Lazarus turned to look at her as she got up. "Look, I—"

"I'm starving," Sable cut him off, trying to sound as though everything was back to normal. "Did you eat yet?"

"Wha—? Oh, yeah. But I saved you some."

"Okay, good. But first I'm going to take a shower. I assume it's this way?"

Lazarus nodded at her. "Yeah. There are towels in the closet in there." He opened his mouth as though he were going to add something else but closed it again.

Don't, Sable thought. Don't try to fix it, damn you.

After her shower, Sable dressed quickly and found her way into the kitchen. It was barely more than an alcove. Lazarus had left her a plate with breakfast on it—some nutrition bars. She grabbed the plate and headed back into the living room, where Lazarus was back at the desk, staring intently at something on the gauntlet screen on his arm. Sable ate her breakfast in silence, watching him work. He seemed not to notice she was even there.

After she finished, Sable returned the plate to the kitchen and came over to where Lazarus was working. "So what's the plan?" she asked, trying not to peer over his shoulder.

"I set up a simple shadow to go find out anything I can

about Quartz Pyramid. If we're lucky, we can get something useful from the Lucullus Grid, but I'm setting another one up to head out of the system, just in case. We won't see that one back until after you make the drop, but it still may be worth something."

Sable smiled softly. "So I'm making the drop, then?" she asked.

Lazarus turned away from what he was doing to look at her briefly. "Against all my better judgment, yes. You were right; this letter specifically mentions that you're female. Germaine will know something is up if it's not you who delivers the goods. I *could* try to change it, but without the encryption code that was originally used, the risk of leaving behind some telltale evidence that it was tampered with is too great."

"I won't hang you out to dry," she said, and she desperately wanted him to believe her, to trust her on this one issue. "I swear it."

"Yeah. You said that. I guess I'll find out soon enough."

"So I make the drop. Then what?"

Lazarus turned back to the gauntlet and tapped a few more keystrokes. "Well, if this note is saying what I think it is, we may hit the jackpot."

"And what do you think it's saying?"

Lazarus tapped the keys once more and slid the gauntlet from his arm. He turned and looked at Sable directly. "I think it's a bribe. As I mentioned before, I believe Germaine is a point man for a weapons smuggling operation. Germaine manages the shipment of the weapons for his superiors. I think this Gillst character is paying Germaine a huge chunk of change to hand over a list of those superiors' names."

"Why? What does Gillst want with the names?"

"I'm not totally sure, but as near as I can guess, Gillst wants in on the gunrunning action, wants to make these buyers a better offer and become their new supplier. I don't know for sure who the current supplier is, and I don't really care right now. Gunrunners are a dime a dozen in Port Royal, and even if we shut down this operation, the people buying the weapons would just turn to someone else. So I don't want the suppliers, at least not right now. What I *do* want are the clients' names. I've been trying to figure out who Germaine works for, and I haven't been able to crack it. The operation on this end is locked down tight. If I'm right about this, then I get the names. Germaine gives me exactly what I've been wanting."

"And why is that so important to you?"

"Because whoever they are, they're one of the biggest supporters of Concord Free Now, the single largest terrorist group in the Verge. And I'm going to bring them down."

04.0:

LAZARUS SMILED AS he watched Sable, finally starting to feel a little more at ease. She was nodding at something absently, staring vacantly at the wall of the living room of his apartment, her gauntlet on her arm. He waited expectantly for her to finish, pacing casually beside the chair she was sitting in.

"Yes, I've got it. Same place as before," Sable said, speaking quietly. "Yes, I understand. All right. I'll be there."

There was another moment of hesitation, and then Lazarus saw her blink her eyes and look around, and he knew she was done. "Everything went okay?" he asked, even though he had heard her end of the conversation.

"Yeah. No problem. He wants to meet at the same place as last time," Sable said, frowning. "I'm not sure— Well, I guess that's no big deal."

"What's wrong?"

"Nothing, really. I usually try to mix it up a little more when making contact, just to be on the safe side, but if he's happy with the arrangements . . ."

Lazarus nodded. "It shouldn't be a problem. He probably just feels safe using that place."

"I guess. I'm supposed to meet him there in two hours. What time is it now?" Sable asked, checking the chronometer on her gauntlet even as she did so. "Hmm, almost seven. I want to take a nap before we go."

"All right. I'm going to double-check the equipment. You want me to wake you?"

"No, I won't sleep that long. I'm just going to doze for a few minutes," she replied, sliding the gauntlet off her arm and pulling the cable from the back of her neck. She rose from the chair and headed into the other room.

Lazarus watched her go, dressed in her now-familiar black tank top, black pants, and boots. Then he turned to the pile of surveillance equipment he had gathered the day before. He began going through it carefully, piece by piece, making sure everything was functioning properly. As he worked, in his mind he went back over everything that had happened since he had hacked the data crystals.

After waiting the requisite three days, Sable had made contact with Germaine again. It had gone smoothly. The man had instructed her to meet him at a little cafe in a mall several levels below the surface. Lazarus was pleased that it wasn't in the Golden Quarter, but it was still a more seedy part of Port Royal than he would have liked. Germaine had said he would be waiting at a table by a window, wearing a red Lazers cap and carrying a Silver Comet Casino shopping bag with him. Of course, Lazarus already knew what the man looked like from his earlier surveillance, and he showed Sable several pictures beforehand, just to be on the safe side. Sable was to bring the goods in an identical bag and sit at the next table over. Germaine would then depart, grabbing her bag on his way out. It all seemed pretty simple, but Lazarus had been very uptight while they had waited for everything to unfold.

In the end, the whole thing had gone off without a hitch. The bag's contents had included a handful of vidmags, some junk food, and a note instructing Sable to meet Germaine on the Grid once more, in twenty-four hours' time, at the Loading Zone in order to receive further instructions.

And now, one day later, Sable had concluded that third meeting. Germaine was satisfied with the package she had delivered, and they were going to meet again in person, so he could turn over the list of names that Gillst was paying for. Everything seemed to be going smoothly, and Lazarus was finally starting to relax.

We just make this last exchange, and I can finally make some progress. I'm going to need to send Administrator Monahan an update pretty soon, he realized. Hmm. I'll wait until we get those documents from Germaine. Maybe I'll have a major breakthrough to tell him about. Lazarus smiled again as he finished checking the gear.

The CIB agent didn't envy his boss. The duties of a Concord Administrator were difficult during the best of times. Trying to maintain some semblance of law and order on the edges of known space, most particularly the Verge, was never easy, but Monahan's assignment was particularly tough: tracking down the various factions of Concord Free Now, a terrorist group clamoring for Verge independence from the stellar nations. Lazarus knew that gaining this list of names for Monahan would earn them both a few points up the chain of command, although Lazarus didn't truly want the accolades for himself.

Lazarus was particularly indebted to Monahan for getting him his life back, and that was enough. Several years before, the Administrator had extracted him from an Insight prison and given him a second chance, working in CIB as a special agent assigned to Monahan's task force on CFN activities.

Lazarus grimaced when he remembered what had landed him in that prison in the first place. Working as a Gridpilot for Insight, he was still known then by his given name, Lincoln Summerfield, and he was considered by most on Vision, the stellar nation's home world, to be one of the best and brightest Gridpilots they had. But he was cocky, and he let the praise and accolades get to him. Just to see if he could, on a dare with himself, he had tried to pull off the perfect hack, right into the core servers of the Insight's Grid itself, considered by most to be completely secure. He had gotten close, but they were too tight, and he had been grabbed by Insight's security agents before he could disappear. In that instant, his life had changed forever. He had regretted his own foolish pride ever since, but at least he had been given a second chance.

Monahan had come to him and offered him a choice: rot in his cell for many, many years, or allow the Concord Investigative Bureau to fake his death, then join the Bureau, put his talents to good use, and come work for the Administrator as a special agent. Monahan had told him his skills were just what they needed. Lincoln had leaped at the chance, changing his name to Lazarus as a reminder of what he had been given and to keep his identity a secret. He had never looked back, and he was grateful to the Administrator for his new life. Now, he only wanted to pay the old man back for the act of kindness, and getting those names would go a long way toward doing that.

Lazarus returned his attention to what he was doing and finished packing. He then sat down at the desk and donned his own gauntlet, snapping the thing into place where the feeds connected with the subdermal jacks in his arm. He slipped a set of shaded lenses down over his face and turned the gauntlet on. As he dropped into the Grid, he began booting up some programs. When he was connected, his shadow materialized in a small roomlike space.

The virtual room was something of a pigeonhole, set into an array containing hundreds of others just like it, looking for all the world from the outside like some sort of strange row house. Each cubicle room was a private address on the Grid, a connection where Lazarus did a lot of routine Gridrunning. Various bits of correspondence, files, and other data he had gathered were stored here. Visually, he had decorated the place to represent a stylish nineteenth-century library from old Earth, an ancient place with dark paneling and actual books with hand-tooled leather covers. He had programmed the physics model complete with a fireplace, a pair of overstuffed chairs, and a couple of portraits of people dressed from the period. He tried to leave no detail out, right down to the smell of the leather and the sound of the crackling fire. Rather than make his files appear as the books on the shelves, he programmed them to appear as pieces of art and sculpture throughout the room. It wouldn't really deter the serious hacker who broke in, but at least it was aesthetically pleasing, and it offered some small amount of additional security.

Standing in the corner of the room, looking very out of place amid the decor of the room, was a Grid shadow. The figure looked a bit like Lazarus, although the hair was trimmed short and the clothes were of a slightly finer cut than his own. It looked quite a bit like a common-stock, middle-management office shadow, complete with briefcase for carrying data.

"Ah, good. You've returned," said Lazarus, working through a few keystrokes blindly as he turned to face the motionless shadow. "What have you learned?"

The shadow never moved as it responded, "There is no record of any kind for a company named Quartz Pyramid, Limited, listed in the local databanks." The voice was a rather flat, emotionless imitation of Lazarus's own. It was always a little eerie to talk to himself this way.

"Hmm," Lazarus grunted as he thought for a moment. "Let's see. . . . I set you to dig at level . . ."

"I was programmed to search at Detail Level Three, with Softcheat master module version five-point-three-point-one interface protocol to circumvent password protected databanks. I was successful on eight out of eight attempts to access restricted data."

"Right," Lazarus muttered, musing as he mentally went back over the specifications for this shadow. "And I sent you just about everywhere in the system," he reminded himself absently, thinking.

Without prompting, the shadow began to recite in list format a series of names, all data storage facilities belonging to various businesses here on Penates. Lazarus listened to them, making a few mental notes.

When the shadow was finished, Lazarus pursed his lips. "Well," he said, nodding, "if there was any record of Quartz Pyramid to be had around here, one of those places would have stored it. I have one last place for you to look, but we're going to have to update your format a bit to get you there."

Lazarus began to construct a new file of instructions. He attached a new series of programs to the system he was creating, then patched in the new setup for the shadow, replacing the old one. The last thing he did was alter the physical image of the shadow slightly, changing its clothes parameters so that it now appeared to be a technical specialist.

"You're ready to go. Depart."

Without a word, the shadow left the cubicle room and disappeared. If the spaceport docking records don't have any documentation on a registered Quartz Pyramid vessel ever having been here, Lazarus thought as he jacked out again, then this Gillst character is either a very low-key customer, or else he's lying through his teeth.

*   *   *   *   *

The cafe where the drop was going to take place seemed a little more crowded than the day before, but it was the weekend now and two hours later into the evening, so

Lazarus didn't give it much thought. Naturally, the table he had chosen yesterday was occupied, and there were few tables available at all this time around. Lazarus decided to grab a stool at the end of the bar where he could see more or less the entire room.

The bartender was a t'sa, a lizardlike alien about a meter and a half tall and with the rapid, graceful movements of a cat on the prowl. Somehow he managed to keep up a steady stream of conversation, while at the same time keeping no one waiting for his drink. In his exuberantly friendly fashion, the bartender tried once or twice to engage Lazarus in some casual conversation. Lazarus smiled and nodded once or twice at the fellow's quips and bits of sports news, but finally realized that the only way he was going to be left alone was to feign interest in the holovid broadcast above the bar. Eventually the bartender left him alone, and Lazarus spent half his time pretending to pay attention to the arena games that were being broadcast, and the other half scoping out the place.

There seemed to be the usual assortment of patrons for a Port Royal cafe. A couple of weren—huge, tusked, clawed creatures rippling with muscles and thick manes of hair— seemed to dominate the room without trying to, and there was also a trio of winged sesheyans at one table. Their bulbous heads, set with eight eyes, constantly scanned the room, their broad elephantine ears twitching now and then, absorbing the sounds of the place. The rest of the people in the bar were humans, most of them gathered three or four to a table or standing in clusters at the bar, although a few were by themselves, mostly at the bar, drinking and watching the sports broadcast or chatting with the t'sa bartender.

Lazarus shrugged. This should be a piece of cake, he thought. It's just crowded enough that no one will pay any attention to the exchange.

When Germaine arrived, he seemed even more nervous

than before. Lazarus studiously ignored him for a full five minutes, but the man still seemed agitated.

He must be really nervous, carrying around so much incriminating evidence, Lazarus mused. Assuming he's got what I think he does.

Finally Germaine picked out a table back in a corner, near the entrance to the kitchen. It wasn't by the window, but it was in an awkward place in the cafe where the holovid set wasn't visible, so few people were sitting there. Lazarus frowned at the thought of changing seating arrangements but realized that, since Sable had already seen the man, she would know what she was looking for and would easily be able to make the drop.

I guess it's more important to have a couple of empty tables together, he thought. Back there, the two of them can exchange the bags without being obvious about it.

A few moments later, Sable entered the cafe and scanned the room. She avoided letting her gaze linger on Lazarus for more than a moment, but in that brief instant, Lazarus knew she was watching him for some sign that there was trouble. They had agreed on such a signal beforehand, just so she wouldn't walk into a trap. If everything was fine, Lazarus was supposed to stretch and take a sip from his drink. He went through the motions without looking at her. A second later, she was headed toward the table where Germaine sat waiting for her.

Suddenly Lazarus had the strange feeling that something wasn't quite right. He stole a quick glance at Germaine, but the man seemed intent on watching Sable walk past as he pretended to study the glowing menu set into the surface of the table. Sable sat down with her back to Germaine, setting her bag against the wall, near the other one.

Lazarus frowned as the hair on the back of his neck rose and a shiver threatened to shoot up his spine.

What the hell is wrong with me?

He casually looked around the room, trying to spot any-thing out of the ordinary. He looked for anyone fidgeting or otherwise appearing nervous, or anyone watching him. Noth-ing. He repeated the process, cautiously scanning, checking each face. People laughing, talking, or eating and drinking and watching the holovid. Everyone acting normal. Almost everyone, Lazarus realized. Or, rather, almost normal.

A guy at the other end of the bar, sitting by himself, impeccably dressed in a crisp suit and wearing very dark goggles, was subtly casing the joint, too. Lazarus hadn't noticed him the first time around, because the guy was good at being inconspicuous. But now that Lazarus was paying attention to body language, it was almost obvious.

He's using all the standard tactics, Lazarus realized. He's doing it just like I do. He could have been trained by the CIB.

Lazarus watched the carefully controlled twists and turns of the head, the goggles hiding the glances and the lazy, wandering eyes. He was pretending to be absently staring at nothing, but the guy's gaze was sweeping the room method-ically. In fact, Lazarus realized, the guy was specifically casing Germaine and Sable. He nodded his head almost imperceptibly. A signal.

Oh, shit. An ambush.

Lazarus looked around again, hunting for the partner, the backup, watching the body language, looking for anyone who suddenly seemed tense, ready, about to spring out of a chair. And when he spotted the telltale signs, he swallowed hard. Not one partner but two. The weren.

Oh, my God. We're screwed. Sable! Look up! he willed.

Lazarus turned back to look at Sable, to try to catch her eye and signal her that everything was about to turn ugly, when he realized she was up to something. She was on her feet again, the new bag in hand—at least, he assumed it was the new bag—and was headed not toward the exit, but to the back, toward the kitchen, or perhaps the rest room. Lazarus's eyes narrowed for a moment in realization as she turned away from him.

She's making a break for it, he fumed as chaos erupted around him.

The man at the bar shouted something and spun around, and Lazarus saw the muzzle of a weapon peeking out from his jacket sleeve. No, not his sleeve, his wrist.

Great. A chop shop reject. We are *really* screwed. "Sable!" he shouted, knowing it was a little too late for stealth now.

In the blink of an eye, moving unnaturally fast—probably cybernetically enhanced, Lazarus thought—the man leaped up on a table and began striding across several of them as if they were large stepping stones, right to where Sable was taking a final look back over her shoulder. The guilty look on her face told Lazarus that his suspicions were right; she was making a break for it. She saw the assassin raising his gun toward her, and her eyes grew wide. She dived through the doorway to the kitchen and out of sight as Lazarus heard the unmistakable high-pitched whine of a flechette gun. Someone screamed.

At the same moment, the two huge weren had risen to their feet, heavy weapons materializing in their giant, furry hands—from where? Lazarus remembered thinking later, berating himself for not spotting them. Realization dawned on Germaine's face as the assassins closed in on him. Blanching in terror, he dived to the side as the huge weren brought their weapons to bear with almost military precision and opened fire. The table where he had been sitting, along with a good portion of the wall behind it, practically dissolved in a deadly spray of full automatic fire. Germaine scrambled madly away on his hands and knees as the weren, setting up intersecting arcs of fire, walked their shots complacently after him, unloading their entire clips.

Lazarus had rolled to the floor and was fumbling to get his gun out as more screams erupted and a mass of humanity and aliens panicked around him. He managed to get around behind the end of the bar and leaned out to take a peek. The assassin was still calmly stumping across the few remaining tables toward the doorway to the kitchen, and the weren were snapping fresh clips into their weapons. Germaine was slumped against a wall, one hand grasping feebly at an injured leg while he held the other above him, as if to ward off the inevitable attack. The look on his face was pure, instinctual terror, and Lazarus actually felt a twinge of pity for the guy.

Lazarus leveled his pistol at the professional killer and fired. The familiar low-pitched burp echoed loudly in his ears as the shot slammed into the assassin, causing him to stumble. One of the two weren spun around, and Lazarus dived back behind the bar just as a fresh volley of charge rounds slammed into the wall and floor where he had been.

Stupid! Just get out!

The heavy machine gun fire was completely penetrating the material of the bar only a meter from where Lazarus crouched. He dived in the opposite direction and put his back against the far wall, looking for something better to hide behind.

The t'sa bartender was crouched down, too, holding a flechette shotgun, his eyes darting back and forth and his tail twitching wildly, as though he were trying to make up his mind whether to jump up and shoot or run in the other direction. When he saw the stutter pistol in Lazarus's hand, he swung the gun around quickly and aimed it at him. Lazarus froze, caught dead in the t'sa's line of sight. Holding his pistol out away from him and being careful not to appear to be aiming at the t'sa, Lazarus began to set it down as a token of surrender.

The machine gun fire had stopped again, and Lazarus was trying to figure out what to say to the bartender, when the other weren suddenly appeared, leaping directly onto the bar right above the t'sa. It spotted Lazarus and swung its heavy gun, aiming directly at him. Lazarus's heart skipped a beat as he realized he was pinned there. He didn't twitch a muscle.

The weren did a double take when it realized what Lazarus was doing with his gun and figured out that the t'sa was armed. That hesitation was all the bartender needed. The flechette shotgun went straight up, and the high-pitched scream of its blast was shrill in Lazarus's ears. The weren's scream, a deep bellow of pain, was brief, changing to a wet gurgle as its face was pulped into oblivion. A fine red mist spattered Lazarus and the t'sa. The weren's body toppled backward, out of sight, and there was a heavy thud from the other side of the bar as it hit the floor.

Lazarus choked back his disgust and grabbed his pistol again. He eyed a long, waist-high window directly over his own head, between the bar area and the kitchen, that was used to pass meals and dishes back and forth. The t'sa leveled his gun at him, and Lazarus hesitated, crouching. There was another burst of machine gun fire from beyond the bar, and Lazarus watched in horror as a line of gaping holes appeared in it—a stream of charge rounds that passed completely through the bar and cut through the t'sa in a fresh spray of blood. Lazarus launched himself upward to the window, swinging his legs out of the way as the spray of shots passed where he had been crouching, opposite the slumped and bleeding bartender. Lazarus caught a quick glance of the other weren unloading his magazine at the bar. It tried to raise the angle of its fire to catch Lazarus, but he rolled through the squat window and dropped out of sight, diving to the side as soon as he did so in case the weren's shots passed through the second wall.

The kitchen was in turmoil. The place looked as if a small storm had passed directly through it, and several members of the staff were either crouched behind large appliances or sprawled dead or wounded in pools of blood. One woman saw Lazarus and stifled a scream as she scrambled to get around a large cabinet and out of his sight. Lazarus scanned the place desperately, looking for another way out of the cafe.

A fresh round of heavy weapons fire slammed into the wall separating the kitchen and bar, directly below the window, ripping up large chunks of plastic and steel. Lazarus headed toward the back of the kitchen.

A cook with a large chopping knife lunged up at him from nowhere, and Lazarus twisted away at the last moment, taking a slight gash across his forearm. He spun in one fluid motion and kicked the knife from the cook's hands. Then he brought his leg back around and swept the guy's legs out from under him. As the fellow dropped with a painful thud, Lazarus leveled his pistol centimeters from his face.

"A back door. Where is it?" he demanded.

The cook's eyes bulged as he stared down the barrel of the pistol, hyperventilating in fear. Lazarus saw the weren stalk through the doorway at the opposite side of the kitchen, the one he knew Sable and the killer following her had come through. The creature carried both machine guns, one under each huge arm. It paused, crouching and surveying the room. Lazarus groaned and grabbed the cook by the collar of his shirt and pulled the guy, half crawling, behind a large freezer unit in the middle of the room.

The weren saw the movement and swung both guns around, firing them simultaneously. The cacophony of slugs pounding into the steel sides of the freezer made Lazarus's ears ring as he scrambled desperately away from view. The weren kept up the barrage, firing short bursts at the freezer, as Lazarus and the cook cringed. Lazarus scanned the back wall of the kitchen and saw an alcove that seemed to lead back deeper into the building, perhaps to offices—and a back door.

As a new spray of bullets ricocheted off of everything and someone screamed from the other side of the kitchen, Lazarus tapped on the cook's shoulder, pointed toward the alcove, and whispered, "The woman with dark hair and the nut with the gun in his arm . . . did they go that way?"

The cook only looked at Lazarus in abject terror and shrugged.

Lazarus sighed and whispered, "Is there a way out of here through there?"

The cook nodded. Another burst of machine gun fire, and Lazarus realized that the weren was moving, swinging around to flank him. If he didn't go now, he might not get the chance in another moment. In the background, he also heard the faint sound of a security siren.

Great. Here comes the cavalry, he thought sourly. They'll definitely shoot first and ask questions later.

Getting a good grip on his pistol and taking a deep breath, Lazarus waited for the next burst of automatic fire to stop and then took off at a dead run, diving into the alcove just as the weren shouted something in a deep bass voice and squeezed off another volley of shots at him. The rounds slammed into the wall of the alcove above Lazarus, spraying him with shredded plastic from the wall. He scrambled deeper in, jumping to his feet when he knew he was out of sight, and followed the alcove down a short hall, past a storage room and an office to a back door. There were several telltale signs of flechette rounds having been fired, but no blood. Lazarus reached the door and stabbed at the button on the security panel beside it, and then slipped through it as it slid open.

He was in some sort of service or access corridor that ran in both directions. He took an uncertain step to his right, trying to decide which way to go, and had just changed his mind and turned to go back in the opposite direction when there was another burst of machine gun fire that ripped apart the door. One instant later and he would have been walking in front of that assault, but instead he leaped backward and turned to run.

The corridor did not run straight, but twisted back and forth as it went, and it seemed to have a lot of service hatches and panels, as well as what seemed like kilometers of pipes. Lazarus searched desperately for a place to duck into and hide as he ran, knowing that he was a goner if the weren caught up to him. Unless he could sneak in real close, there was no way he could take down the weren with a stutter pistol.

Lazarus turned another bend and saw ahead of him a long, straight section. He groaned and turned to listen, trying to determine if the weren was following, and how closely. He heard pretty distinctly the solid footfalls of something running, and they seemed to be getting closer. He turned and dashed away again, hoping he could reach the other end of the straight section before the weren caught up.

He wasn't so lucky. About halfway through the straight passage, Lazarus heard the weren yell at him.

"You're dead, you little sh—!"

Machine gun fire erupted behind him.

Lazarus dived down to the floor and spun on his belly, swinging his pistol up even as the weren fired. The hulking assassin had ditched one of the two guns, but now that he had both hands on the remaining weapon, he could aim a lot better. Slugs slammed into a pipe near Lazarus's head, and foul-smelling liquid sprayed out. Lazarus flinched and scooted away from it as more shots tore up the walls, the floor, and the pipes all around him. He brought his gun up once more and took careful aim, knowing that the weren was out of range.

This is it, Lazarus, my friend. You're out of options. Make it count.

He pulled the trigger. His pistol belched a sonic blast toward the weren.

And nothing happened. He took careful aim again, but before he could fire a second shot, there was a strange clank overhead. He rolled on his back, his pistol aimed upward, just in time to see a woman dangling upside down through an open service hatch in the ceiling, aiming a rifle down the hall at the weren. She pulled the trigger, and the flash of laser fire on full auto streaked across his vision. The weren howled in pain, and Lazarus tilted his head back to see, upside down, the creature crumple to the floor.

Lazarus turned back to where he was aiming and watched as the woman passed the rifle back up through the service hatch. He got his first good look at her and realized she wasn't human, but mechalus. Thin, sinewy veins of circuitry gleamed in deep blue skin from the stark light of the service corridor. Her hair seemed to be a shiny clump of data cable. Lazarus shook his head in wonder.

"Jamaican League Security Forces approaching/arriving, all directions/paths CONFIRMED," she said, little emotion in her strangely structured words. "Weapon/lower please. I'm dropping you a harness."

She produced a coil of rope, to which was attached a black safety harness. Lazarus climbed to his feet and lowered his weapon, although he didn't put it away. He watched, puzzled, as the mechalus woman played out enough of the rope so that the harness dropped down to his level.

"Climb on. You must hurry. Security/League arriving CONFIRMED."

"Who are you?" Lazarus asked, still wary. He barely heard the drone of security alarms in the distance over the sound of the burst pipes.

"Explanations/time NEGATIVE available. Do you want us to leave you to be arrested by League Security Forces? Opinion: You will not enjoy spending time in their prisons."

Lazarus sighed, tucked his gun away, and then swung a leg through the harness loop. A winch of some sort began lifting him up before he had a chance to slip his other leg through, so he merely hung on and dangled awkwardly as he was hoisted toward the ceiling. Below him, the puddle of brownish liquid was spreading, and the sound of troops moving through the tunnel was definitely louder, although he couldn't say for sure from which direction.

When he reached the top, several pairs of hands helped him through the opening, and then the mechalus woman swung down, pulled the hatch up, and latched it from the inside. Lazarus looked around at the group surrounding him and saw a variety of faces, perhaps half a dozen or so, many of them young. He felt a hand slip inside his coat from behind and retrieve his weapon.

"Hey!" he snapped and turned to reach for it, but he quickly found himself staring down the muzzles of several other weapons. He relaxed and withdrew his hand, concentrating on slipping the harness off his body. "So who are you?" he asked, trying to keep his voice steady, even though his heart was pounding. "And why did you decide to rescue me?"

"Technospiders/guest current/you CONFIRMED," the mechalus woman announced in a flat, level voice. "You will come with us."

05.0:

LAZARUS STARED, AMAZED, at the mechalus woman before him. Dressed in a no-nonsense outfit replete with numerous pockets and tool loops, she seemed to be equipped for just about any job he could think of. Which made sense, he realized, given who she was.

"The Technospiders?" he said, a little awestruck. He was still trying to figure out exactly why they had made an appearance at all. He tried to recall what he knew of them, but it wasn't much.

The Technospiders were one of the organized syndicates on Penates, although they didn't have the same kind of operational power as the Jamaican Syndicate or the Picts. Instead, they controlled vital systems, such as atmosphere processors and energy plants, choosing to remain low-key but ever able to put a stranglehold on just about any large facility. Port Royal was one such facility, and he knew that they maintained a somewhat fragile peace with the Jamaicans. He frowned. *That really doesn't explain why they would give a rat's ass about me and—Sable!*

"Look, I appreciate the hospitality, but I have a friend who needs my help. She's in a lot of danger, and I need to find her. So, if you'll just drop me off someplace nice and not under the scrutiny of a lot of league security, I'll—"

"Companion/you *possessive* is safe. Please come this

way." The mechalus woman turned and began to lead the group through the maintenance tunnel.

Lazarus blinked, struggling to follow her strange speech patterns, but he followed her, noting that his escort took care to keep several people behind him as well as in front. "Sable is with you?"

"Affirmative: She has been detained. You can see her shortly. Please, everything will be explained at the right time. This way," the mechalus answered, still walking. Now that the situation was considerably calmer, Lazarus noted that she tended to speak more plainly, rather than in her species' odd, mechanical dialect.

"Will this take long? I really do have a lot to do," Lazarus asked, trying to sound friendly and unthreatening.

The mechalus never broke stride as she looked back over her shoulder at him. She merely gave him a stony-faced gaze, shook her head slightly, and answered, "Please. No more questions. All will be explained."

Lazarus decided to follow her advice and stay quiet for the remainder of the trip. The group wandered through a maze of tunnels, all filled with pipes, conduits, and stark lighting. Every so often they hit an intersection, and once in a while the group turned and followed a new tunnel. They descended several stairwells, and at one point they had to climb down through a vertical shaft with a ladder in it. At another point, they crossed a catwalk suspended over a huge room filled with some sort of large but squat round tanks below them.

As they turned in another direction and headed back up a flight of stairs, the mechalus motioned for the entourage to halt for a moment. She stepped up to a small security panel against one wall next to a long, straight tunnel and tapped a code into the keypad. The door to the panel swung open, revealing a larger control panel beneath it. The woman stuck a hand near an interface slot and a series of thin, tendril-like wires extruded from her fingertips, settling into place in the interface.

Lazarus watched with a strange mixture of fascination and unease. He had seen the mechalus in action before, able to interface directly with computers without the need for external hardware, and it had always both piqued his curiosity and turned his stomach.

The woman paused for a moment, and there was a short beep as several indicator lights switched from red to green. Then the tendrils of circuitry retracted into her flesh. The woman closed the panel again, and they proceeded.

"What was that all about?" Lazarus asked just before he remembered his promise to keep his mouth shut.

"That," said one of the Technospiders behind him, a young man with a fierce, almost reverent gleam in his eye, "was us keeping you from getting your ass shot off."

Lazarus raised an eyebrow at the guy, who was not quite as tall as he was but was a bit broader at the shoulders. He carried a laser rifle cradled in his arms and was also decked out in many of the same tools as the mechalus.

"You see," the young man continued, "if we hadn't done that, you'd be a nice bright red mist right about now."

When Lazarus looked back, the fellow's grin seemed almost too eager for his comfort. Lazarus didn't respond.

"Algim," the mechalus woman said as they proceeded through the tunnel, "our guest does not need to know the details of our precautions."

"Yes, Ellesao," the young man responded, but when Lazarus glanced at him again, he was still grinning.

A moment later, Lazarus saw what the guy had been talking about. Hanging from the ceiling were a pair of heavy weapons—autolasers, by the looks of them—aimed right at him. As he walked closer, the servos on which the guns were mounted whined slightly as the barrels shifted, and Lazarus realized they were actually tracking him. He swallowed.

"Why is it following only me?" he asked, his voice wavering a little.

"Because it identifies you as an intruder," the mechalus named Ellesao replied.

"An intruder? But I thought you shut them off."

"I merely shut down the autofire option. I did not disable the tracking system."

"Oh." Her explanation didn't leave Lazarus feeling much better. He suspected that the system used some sort of bio-electric detection system.

They probably all have some kind of chip or tracer signal with them, he mused. Hell, it could even be implanted under their skin. Well, let's just make a mental note not to come visit uninvited.

As they proceeded farther along the passage, they passed a second set of weaponry, this time apparently some sort of heavy-duty mass cannon.

Of course, Lazarus thought, impressed and sweating at the same time. Whatever the laser cannons can't penetrate, the mass cannon certainly will. You'd need an army of troopers in battle armor to get through here. I don't know if even they'd make it.

Again the weapons tracked specifically on Lazarus as he closed with them, and then they were past the guns and standing before a large door. From the looks of it, Lazarus guessed it was thick enough to withstand some pretty heavy weapons fire or even explosives, and he suspected it was magnetically sealed to boot.

Ellesao accessed yet another security panel near the door, and it opened smoothly and silently. They passed through the doorway—Lazarus noted that it was a good two meters thick—and they were in a large open space dominated by a large structure in the center. Not a building, exactly, Lazarus realized, but some sort of power plant or other similar structure.

Four great round towers, slightly wider at their bases than at their tops, rose up several stories over their heads, entwined by hundreds of meters of massive pipeline and level after level of balconies and catwalks. The pipeline branched out from the structure in every direction, penetrating the surrounding walls and ceiling of this massive chamber. Near the edges of the platform, on all four sides, was a wide chasm that completely encircled the place like some ancient castle's moat.

This same chasm currently barred the group's passage farther into the chamber. It was about twenty meters wide and ran parallel to the wall where they had entered the great chamber. They were standing on a narrow balcony of sorts, opposite another one on the main platform. There was no causeway across it. Lazarus peered cautiously over the edge, staring downward into the chasm formed by the side of the platform and the wall of the chamber. Dozens and dozens more pipes of all sizes ran between the sides, like countless little round bridges without doors. The floor at the bottom was too far away and too dim to be seen clearly.

When Lazarus looked up again, Ellesao was speaking through a comm unit near the railing of the balcony. A moment later, there was a deep, rumbling shudder, and then a large section of the side of the platform right across from where they stood began to slide outward, spanning the chasm and locking into place on the balcony where they stood to form a bridge. As the causeway slid into place, the section of railing blocking their path retracted downward, dropping into the floor and leaving the way across open.

Ellesao began crossing without fanfare, and Lazarus followed after with his escort. As they made their way to the main platform and then on toward the facility in front of them, Lazarus noticed that it was bustling with activity. On all levels, he could see people either pacing back and forth, as though keeping watch, or hurrying along from one place to another. It seemed almost like a great office building.

"Where are we?" he asked, figuring he had held his tongue long enough.

"This is one of the atmospheric processors for Port Royal," Ellesao answered. "It is also our enclave headquarters."

"Okay, so why are you bringing me here?" Lazarus queried, not really expecting to get a straight answer.

"Because my superior wishes to speak with you," Ellesao replied.

Lazarus had a pretty good idea that was all he was going to get out of her.

Once they reached the base of the facility, Ellesao led them into the interior of the maze of pipeline to a large industrial lift. They all boarded it and were soon rising past several levels of decks and catwalks. When they were about two-thirds of the way to the top, the lift halted and they got off. Ellesao led them through a door and inside a hallway.

The decor changed suddenly, and Lazarus felt as if he were about to enter an executive meeting in a large corporate office building. There was carpeting on the floors, indirect lighting set to illuminate tasteful pieces of art placed periodically on the walls, and the whole place had an air of organization to it. In fact, as they passed others on the way to wherever they were going, their weapons received a few funny looks. Lazarus just shook his head, giving up trying to figure out what was going on.

Ellesao turned another corner, and they entered a large room that looked very much like a reception area. Six people, including one male mechalus, sat in comfortable chairs, obviously piloting on a grid, as evidenced by the gauntlets and visors they wore, all except the mechalus. Three other people sat nearby, studying readout screens and apparently supervising. One of the three looked up as the group entered and nodded her head in the direction of a pair of polished double doors.

"He's waiting for you inside," the woman said, and then went back to what she was doing.

Ellesao never broke stride as she crossed to the double doors. "You aren't all needed in here," she said to the rest of the entourage, and Lazarus's escort paused, then turned, and departed.

"Who's waiting for us?" Lazarus asked, watching the rest of them leave. "And when do I get my gun back? One of them has it," he said, gesturing at the retreating group.

Ellesao smiled then, the first time Lazarus had seen her do so. "Your weapon will be returned to you after the meeting. Now please come with me. We would all very much like to know why a hit squad controlled by one of the syndicate's largest families was trying to kill you."

* * * * *

Sable stared sullenly at the wall opposite where she sat, her knees drawn up under her chin. She felt a little woozy— the effects of analgesics and other medications that had been injected into her by her rescuers, despite her best efforts to the contrary. Her right arm was carefully wrapped in a layer of bandage that protected an application of artificial skin beneath it. Her jacket, one sleeve shredded and bloody, was draped across the back of a decorative chair that faced the desk of her current host. Director Stipelle, whoever he was, sat at his desk, a visor over his eyes as he manipulated the gauntlet on his arm. Piloting. Against the desk slouched a young man—little more than a kid, really—whom the director had called Blue, with one side of his head shaved and the hair on the other side dyed an iridescent cobalt and bundled in a rather short, spiky tail. His face was adorned with rings and studs, and he grinned as he stared at a dataslate through a pair of tinted glasses, a nice translucent sapphire to match his hair and nickname. Every once in a while, he would glance up at Sable and leer at her. She grimaced and looked away.

Her flight from the cafe had not worked out quite as she'd planned. She had promised herself that when the time came and she made a break for it, she wasn't going to turn around no matter what. She'd just keep walking, get away, get back to Gavin. She wouldn't turn around, even if she heard Lazarus call after her. But she had. The look on his face, that realization that she was betraying his trust, had sent a pain through her chest that she hadn't felt for anyone but Gavin in a long time. Even if the place hadn't suddenly gone to hell with all of the shooting, she wouldn't have come back. At least, that's what she told herself. In the end, it didn't matter.

The cybered assassin had been relentless. She had barely managed to get through the kitchen and out into the corridor before he was there, ripping chunks out of the wall near her as he fired his flechette gun at her over and over again. She shuddered, remembering the round that had actually connected, grazing her arm. The tiny needles had turned her flesh to jelly, and the pain had nearly made her faint.

You are so lucky. You should never have let that idiot Germaine use the same place.

Yeah, right, she argued with herself, as if it would have made a difference. Those goons were all over him. It wouldn't have mattered where the drop took place.

Lucky, she snorted, causing Blue to look at her.

Am I lucky? I didn't get away, did I? I'm stuck here with these freaks.

Yeah, but you're alive. Better off than Germaine. Or Laz, probably.

Thinking of Lazarus made her cringe again. But she was also angry at him. He was supposed to case the place, make sure it was safe, but he'd blown that. She wondered briefly if he had set it all up to happen, if the ambush had been his doing, to get both her and Germaine. But she dismissed that thought from her head.

Easier just to kill me when I was stimming, she reminded herself. Besides, he saved my life. If he hadn't called out . . .

She wondered where Lazarus was.

Probably looking for me.

The assassin had caught up to her in the corridor quickly, dropping her with the shot that hit her arm. While she had still been down, writhing in pain, he had grabbed Germaine's bag from her. Then, for a long moment, he had stood over her, almost reveling as he watched her groan and bleed, before raising his arm and aiming the embedded gun at her head for one last shot.

If it hadn't been for the Technospiders . . .

She didn't finish the thought. They had swooped down from the ceiling—four of them, all armed. In a blur, they had knocked the assassin away from her, catching him off guard, but only for an instant. He was juiced to the max, sporting enhanced strength and most likely body armor, too, and two of her rescuers went down before they managed to force him to retreat. Sable still wasn't sure he would have left, would have let her live, if it hadn't been for the imminent arrival of the cops. When the shooting stopped, she tried to get up and run again, but she had already lost a lot of blood, and she collapsed.

Her rescuers hauled her up into the ceiling, telling her all the while that they were only trying to save her from the Syndicate Security Forces, who were on their way. Then they had used a trauma pack on her arm, stopping the bleeding and dulling the pain enough for her to regain some semblance of her wits.

When she remembered that the assassin had gotten away with Germaine's goods, she had panicked briefly and tried to escape. They merely restrained her, and then calmly ignored her frantic sobbing and pleading as they hauled her along with them, through some of the most serious defenses she had seen in a long while. They brought her here and left her with this joker, who had spent the next ten minutes asking her all sorts of questions that she had refused to answer. Now they simply seemed to be waiting, but for what, Sable had no idea.

Sable glanced at the door again, but shook her head in frustration. She'd already tried to make a break for it, and Blue was beside her in an instant, calmly but insistently leading her back to her seat. She was stunned at how strong he was, realizing that he, too, had been cybernetically enhanced. He seemed to thoroughly enjoy manhandling her, but she refused to give him the satisfaction of being indignant at his roving hands.

Even if I got out, there's nowhere to go. This place is a fortress.

Right. Like it makes a difference now, girl. Where would you run to? You lost the goods.

But it wasn't my fault! He can't blame me for this. Whether Laz had caught up to me or not, Germaine would be dead—

Sable's argument with herself was interrupted by a knock at the door. In a moment, it opened. Lazarus strolled inside, admiring the decor, followed closely behind by a mechalus woman dressed in a very utilitarian jumpsuit that was generously decorated with tools of every description.

Sable's breath caught in her throat, first with elation, and then with guilt.

He's alive. But he's here. Oh, God, he's going to be angry.

Lazarus paused, smiling uncertainly at Blue, who merely laughed and turned back to his dataslate. Lazarus's attention then turned to Director Stipelle, who had stood at their arrival and was holding out his hand, introducing himself. Lazarus crossed over to the man, who was impeccably dressed in stylish but informal attire, and took his hand, smiling as he continued to scan the room.

When Lazarus's eyes fell on Sable, the line of his jaw hardened considerably. He stared at her for a long moment, his eyes icy.

Sable tried to meet his gaze, but she couldn't maintain it and looked down. She wasn't going to apologize for this.

I won't! He doesn't understand, damn it! I had no choice.

"Well, I'm glad to see you managed to get here in one piece," the director began, but he trailed off as Lazarus turned and strode directly to where Sable was sitting. The look on his face, the fury she could see there, made her cringe. She was certain he was about to strike her. She averted her eyes once more and shrank back, even as she tried to look determined and resistant.

"You're alive—barely, it seems," Lazarus said, his voice soft and markedly cold.

"Laz, look. I did what—"

"Save it," he interrupted, never raising his voice. "I don't want to hear it. I take it they have the bag?" he asked, jerking his head toward the man sitting behind the desk.

Sable shook her head miserably. "No. The assassin got away with it." Her throat felt tight. She hated caring what he thought about her. She hated that she had run from him.

"Damn." He stood there for a long time, saying nothing, until Director Stipelle closed in.

"Yes, yes," Stipelle said, "it's a very happy reunion and all that, but we must talk. I need some answers to some questions."

Lazarus turned away from Sable and began to head back over to one of the empty chairs that sat across from the desk. As he took the seat, the director nodded his head at Blue, who crossed over to where Sable sat with her knees still drawn up.

Blue looked down at her, that infuriating grin spreading wider. "Come on," he said to her. "We're going to go take a walk." He held his hand out for her, but when she just looked at him, he reached down and took hold of her by her good arm and lifted her to her feet. As they crossed the room to the door, Sable looked back at Lazarus to see what he would do, but he never turned around. As the door was shutting behind them, Sable called out.

"Laz." Her voice was low and thick with emotion. "I'm sorry. I had to try."

Lazarus didn't turn to look at her. "I guess we all do what we have to."

And the door slid shut.

* * * * *

Lazarus kept his back straight in his chair, trying to keep his breathing even and his body relaxed. It was hard with the rage that seethed inside him. He was angry at Sable, certainly. Her betrayal had stung, but he was nonetheless glad she was alive, if a bit nicked up. No, he realized that his anger was directed more at himself than anything. He had started to care about her, and he had foolishly trusted her. Never mind the fact that her decision to run was actually the reason she was still alive. He had let his guard down, and it could have cost him. It could have cost him dearly.

As it was, they were guests, if he wanted to call it that, of a potent underground power faction that had yet to reveal its intentions toward them—toward *him*—in the slightest. He wasn't sure how they'd react if they found out he was CIB, and he wasn't too eager to learn. But if they had been quizzing Sable before his arrival, he had no idea how truthful she had been.

Knowing her, Lazarus thought, she didn't tell them anything. But I have no way to be sure.

Lazarus briefly considered telling them a partial truth, explaining that Sable was prone to lying and didn't like him very much, and then leave her to her own devices, but he couldn't do it, no matter how angry he was.

"Well, let's get down to it, shall we, uh . . . Laz, I believe the young lady addressed you as?" Stipelle said, bringing Lazarus out of his thoughts.

"Yes. It's Lazarus, but everyone calls me Laz."

The fellow opposite him sat back in his chair and eyed Lazarus with a strange look in his eye. "Funny, I seem to recall that you had another name at one time. I believe you were once known as Lincoln Summerfield."

Lazarus reeled inwardly from the revelation, stunned that this person could know his real name. Oh, my God. He knows me. How the hell does he know me? I'm a dead man!

"I think you've made a mistake. I don't know that name," he replied, trying to make his voice firm.

"I'm pretty sure I've got it right. I think you're the Lincoln Summerfield I used to know. As in Lincoln Summerfield, expert Gridpilot with Insight, risen through the ranks to senior programmer inside of three years. Lincoln Summerfield, reportedly dead, believed by many an Inseer-faithful to have risen to a higher consciousness within the Grid itself."

"Where did you get your information?" Lazarus asked, stalling, desperately trying to catch his breath, to rid himself of the nauseous feeling that had suddenly washed over him and was making his hands tremble.

"Hmm. Well. Yes. That is an interesting story in and of itself. Let's suffice it to say for right now that I was once with Insight myself. You're quite a legend, you know."

The sensation of vertigo washed over Lazarus again, but he clutched at the sides of his chair and made himself relax a little. "Yes." He was at a complete loss for words.

"Well, you're obviously not dead, but you're a long way from home, Lincoln Summerfield. Just what is it you're up to that has the entire Mateo family, one of the most powerful families within the Jamaican Syndicate, up in arms and trying to hunt you down and kill you?"

"No, not dead yet. And I expect that I have you to thank for that?"

"You're avoiding my question, Lincoln."

Lazarus sighed, considering how much to reveal. At this point, Stipelle probably knew enough about him that lying was not really an option. "I'm working for the Galactic Concord. I'm trying to find some information."

"I see. And just what is it you do for the Galactic Concord, Lincoln?"

"Let's just say I track down information and leave it at that."

"All right. And what kind of information are you looking for right now?"

"I'm not really at liberty to say."

Stipelle chuckled. "That almost explains why the Mateos want you dead. Well, we'll leave that alone for the moment. Tell me how the girl fits into this."

Lazarus sighed again, thinking about Sable. Despite the cold sense of betrayal he still felt, he found that he was seeing those desperate eyes of hers a little too clearly. It unsettled him. "She's working with me. She's just a courier I convinced to assist me. Look, why are you asking all these questions? Why in the hell did you get involved in the first place? Don't get me wrong, I'm grateful—God knows we probably both owe you our lives—but I don't get it."

Stipelle leaned back in his chair and studied Lazarus for a moment, his fingers steepled in front of him. "How much do you know about us, about the Technospiders?"

"Enough to know that the balance of power between you and the other factions on Penates is pretty delicate, and that you're a lot lower key than most of the others. You like to stay out of sight, mind your own business. . . ."

Stipelle chuckled again. "If that were true, we probably wouldn't even still be around. No, Lincoln—or Lazarus, if you prefer—we make it our business to know what everyone else around us is up to, what they're planning. That way, we know when one of the other barons is up to something that we would find unpleasant. And we take steps to prevent it from happening. So, in a way, we mind everyone else's business."

Lazarus smiled. "I guess I can understand that. Still, what's that have to do with the two of us?"

"We've been paying particular attention to the Mateo family for a while now. For reasons I'd rather not go into, we're worried about various things they're up to. I was hoping you'd be able to shed some light on a few of them. It would certainly help me decide exactly what we should do with you at this juncture."

Lazarus leaned forward and looked intently at Stipelle. "Are we talking about some sort of cooperation here?"

"I guess that would depend a good deal upon you, Lazarus."

Lazarus reclined again, considering. This is a dangerous game you're playing, Lazarus, my friend. The opportunities are there, but if he doesn't like what you're about to tell him, this could be it for you. Make damned sure.

Lazarus looked again at Stipelle. "I would sure like to hear the story of how you wound up here."

Stipelle nodded and seemed to ponder for a moment. "I left Insight to come out here to the Verge, thinking I could go freelance and make some serious dollars. I got a contract to do some very high security Grid work for a company here in Port Royal. They wanted me to put together a node for them, cutting-edge defense, the works. It was a sweet job, but I was stupid . . . naïve.

"The Technospiders saved me when the people who had hired me tried to kill me—you know, in order to keep the particulars of their system a secret. Kill the architect so no one but the owners know where the secret entrances are. They almost succeeded, too. I took a long time to recover.

"When I was healthy, for some reason I didn't leave. It wasn't just a revenge thing. I realized that I could do more with people I trusted, and I believe in what the Technospiders stand for. They are trying to make this system a little better, and I decided to stick around and do my part. You can call me sentimental if you want, but the experience changed me somehow. I wasn't just doing the work to get paid anymore. I was becoming part of an ideal."

Lazarus nodded when Stipelle finished. "Hey, if it works for you . . ." He was still trying to decide if he believed Stipelle's story or if it was a load of crap designed to get him to trust the man, when the guy leaned forward and looked him squarely in the eye.

"Look, Lazarus. I don't really care if you believe me or not. It doesn't matter. You and the girl are in some deep stuff out there. The way I see it, you've got two choices: You can get off this rock and never come back, in which case we'll help get you to the spaceport, or you can tell me why the Mateos want you dead, and maybe we can do something about it."

"I have absolutely no reason to trust you," Lazarus replied, "except for the fact that you saved me from the hit squad out there. Hell, that could have been a setup. You could be with the Mateos and could have had your own assassins killed just to dupe me into believing you're on my side so I'd tell you everything."

"I think you know that's not true."

"I'd like to believe it, but we're playing with my life here." Lazarus stood and began to pace, trying to decide which way to go. If he and Sable just left, whatever was tying her to her employers would still be there, and she'd have to go back to them empty-handed or not go back to them at all. He doubted if either choice was a good one for her. As for him, going back without any evidence at all was hardly an encouraging sign for his bosses. Administrator Monahan might be understanding, but if Lazarus screwed up this case, they might just decide to send him back to serve out his prison sentence.

At least it's better than being dead. Marginally.

Lazarus paused in his pacing and took a deep breath. Then he looked at Stipelle. "All right. Either you're who you say you are, in which case I can tell you what's going on and maybe get lucky, or you're not, in which case you're probably planning to kill me regardless. So here goes.

"I'm trying to track down who's the money behind a weapons smuggling operation. A man we were meeting today, a guy by the name of Germaine, who works at HansCorp Freight, was going to give Sable a crystal with the names of the people he worked for, the people who were paying for the weapons. She was supposed to take it back to her employer, someone going by the name of Jaren Gillst, who claims to be a gunrunner himself. I believe Gillst wanted to underbid the current supplier, and he wanted the names of the buyers in order to pitch them a deal. Gillst bribed Germaine to get him those names. I don't know why the Mateo family came after him and us, but that's the story."

Stipelle stared off into space for a moment, digesting Lazarus's story. "You know all of this for fact?"

"I'm reading between the lines about Gillst's motives and what Germaine was going to give him, but the rest is fact. I've been watching Germaine for about three months now. I know he's the go-between for the buyers and the suppliers, and he's the one who repackages the weapons before they leave Penates."

"Lazarus, I suspect the Mateos went after this Germaine fellow, and you two by extension, because they are the supplier. They have a whole lot of business interests, but underneath, one of the main things they're into is gunrunning. They must have had someone inside HansCorp who was loyal to them, who informed on Germaine when it became apparent he was going to betray the family. I'm pretty sure they don't like the idea of being underbid. They were just eliminating the competition."

Lazarus chuckled. "Yeah. Just good, sound business practices," he said wryly.

"Lazarus, if you're working this case undercover for the Galactic Concord, you're most likely a CIB agent."

Lazarus nodded slowly. Not much use in denying it, now, he thought, grimacing.

"I figured as much. And I don't blame you for not wanting to share that with me. It's not a popular career choice here in Port Royal. We won't hold it against you."

Lazarus looked at Stipelle, unsure just how serious the man was. When the director cracked a smile, Lazarus returned one of his own, although he suspected it must have looked a little sickly. "I guess that's a relief," he said finally.

"Look, Lazarus. We seem to be working toward a common goal. We're not so stupid as to throw away a benefit like that.

The fact that you're a GC cop doesn't interest me in the least. The fact that you're going after the Mateo family does."

"Well, technically I'm not. I just want to know who's actually buying from them. Unfortunately, the assassin who had been after Sable got away with our data. We never had a chance to look at it, so we still don't know who's got the deep pockets."

"Tell me something, Lazarus. When you find out who's buying the weapons, are you going to shut the operation down?"

"That's the plan, yes."

"Then it's a thorn in the side of the Mateos regardless, and we like that."

"Then you're still willing to help us?"

"Yes."

"Good. Then I want to take another shot at getting those names. I may not be after the supplier, but now that I know who they are, I'm guessing I can find out who their buyers are. I want to get inside the Mateo family Grid node."

06.0:

SABLE GRIMACED AS the door to Director Stipelle's office closed behind them. Blue's idea of a walk was to stroll about fifty paces to a large room at the far end of the long hallway from which they had first come in. It turned out to be a cafeteria, with both a kitchen and vending machines. Blue led Sable to one of the machines and selected a couple of nutrition bars and a couple of bottles of water, and then picked out a table for the two of them and gestured for Sable to sit down.

There were only a few other people around, and when Sable checked a chronometer on one wall, she realized why. It was well after midnight. It was just as well, as far as she was concerned.

Two many crowds for one day already, she thought.

Blue unwrapped one of the bars and began to eat it, staring at her all the while. Sable looked back at him for a moment. That grin of his, which always seemed to be present, widened the tiniest bit.

"Aren't you hungry?" he asked, his mouth full.

Sable merely shrugged and picked up the bar. As she unwrapped it, she said, without looking at his face, "Stop staring at me."

Blue's expression never changed as he continued to eat. "Why?"

"Because I said so." She shook her head and corrected herself, hoping that politeness might work better. "Um, because I asked. Please?"

There was the tiniest shrug, but he continued to watch her as he ate. "But you're quite an eyeful. I like your face."

"Yeah, well, just stop. Please." Sable took a bite of her bar and scanned the room again. She noted that Blue had directed her to a seat against the wall, facing the door. If she tried to make a run for it, he would be able to intercept her easily.

Blue shrugged and opened his water, noisily gulping down several swallows. Sable took another bite of the bar, but she could hardly taste anything and decided she really wasn't hungry, especially since her stomach was in knots. She slumped back in the chair and folded her arms beneath her breasts, staring at nothing.

She had lost the data from Germaine, and she was trapped in Port Royal, a "guest" of the Technospiders. She couldn't see how she was going to be able to get back to Mr. Maxwell now.

Even if you do, what would you tell him? He's not going to care how it happened. You don't have his goods, simple as that. Oh, Gavin! I'm so sorry.

Her chest constricted as she imagined what Mr. Maxwell would do if she didn't return. Worse, what would Gavin think? And then there was Lazarus. She wondered how she had come to care so much about what he thought of her. It wasn't supposed to be that way.

Gavin is the only one that matters.

She found herself desperately wanting Lazarus not to be disappointed in her anymore, but she couldn't seem to think of a way to repair the damage.

Silly. Get your head clear, and get it clear now. Gavin needs you. Lazarus doesn't matter. He can't fix your life. No one can.

Sable sighed. She had told herself this, and things like it, a thousand times before.

Don't let anyone in. Don't expose yourself by caring. You can't afford to be weak, because Gavin is depending on you.

The problem was, it wasn't working anymore. Somehow she'd let Lazarus get under her skin, and telling herself not to care about him, about what he thought, didn't make it go away again. But now it was too late. She'd tried to run, had promised him that she wouldn't, and then did it anyway, and he was never going to trust her again.

Blue was finished eating and was staring at her again. When she noticed, she glared right back at him, but he only grinned wider. "They're done talking. We can go back now."

"How can you tell?"

In response, Blue tapped the side of his temple and said, "They told me. They're waiting for us."

Implanted comm unit, she guessed. "Great," she responded sarcastically. She doubted Lazarus had said much on her behalf. She almost hoped they refused to let her go. She had nothing to go back to, even if they did let her walk.

Blue was standing and motioning for her to get moving. She sighed and rose from the chair to follow him. When he saw that she was just going to leave the food behind, he grabbed it and wolfed it down. Sable rolled her eyes and accompanied him back to the office of the director.

When Sable and Blue returned, Lazarus was there, discussing something with Director Stipelle. Lazarus looked at her for a moment, and then said, "Come on. Let's go get your stuff. You're free to leave."

Sable winced at his tone and then nodded, her head down. The CIB agent was letting her go, knowing full well that she was in trouble. The offer of help had been rescinded. She had expected it, but it still hurt.

Blue and the mechalus woman who had brought Lazarus into Stipelle's office led Sable and Lazarus by a different way out of Technospider territory, through more of the service passageways and access corridors, finally depositing them outside a power plant facility in an alley in the dome where Lazarus's apartment was. It was a short walk from there. Lazarus bid Blue and the mechalus farewell, promising to meet them at the designated time and place the next day.

When they were alone and walking back through the night to Lazarus's apartment, Sable took a deep breath to steel herself and asked, "What are you going to do now? Why are you meeting them again?"

"What difference does it make to you? You can leave as soon as you get your stuff. That's what you wanted, isn't it?" His face was a stoic mask, but Sable could hear the hurt beneath the words.

"You know I can't go back," she said quietly. "I failed to get the package from Germaine."

"I know nothing of the sort. I don't know a damned thing about you, Sable, but it doesn't matter. You wanted out. You're out. Simple as that."

Sable could feel the tears welling up in her eyes, and she wanted to run from him, to keep him from saying anything else that tore at her insides, but she couldn't. Something was compelling her to stay, to try to make him believe in her again.

You're insane! she told herself. You can't win!

I've got to try, she replied silently. I've got nothing else.

"Laz," she said, trying to keep her voice calm, steady. It wasn't easy. "Lazarus, please. I want to explain—"

"I said before, save it. You explained clearly enough back at the cafe." They were at the entrance to his place now, and he was heading up the stairs to the landing where his door was.

"I know, but—" She was floundering, desperate for just the right words, something, anything that would make him turn around and look at her. "Please. I—" The tears began again, and her voice cracked.

"Forget it, Sable. The crocodile tears aren't going to work anymore." Lazarus opened the door and stepped through, leaving her standing outside, her head down.

The sense of hopelessness that was overwhelming Sable made her feet feel leaden. A single tear escaped and ran down her cheek, and she scrubbed at it with her arm.

Please, she thought. Just listen! One more chance! I don't deserve it, but . . .

Lazarus was grabbing her duffel bag and gathering up a few things of hers that were scattered around the room. She came inside, shut the door, and crossed the room to him. She stood in front of him, blocked his path, and put a single hand on his chest.

"Lazarus." He tried to move around her. She pushed her hand harder against him. "Laz, please! I know I don't deserve another chance, but you have to listen to me!"

Lazarus stopped and faced her now, fury plain on his mien. "I *have* to?"

"No. No, you don't. But I want you to. I'm begging you to, just for a minute."

He turned away from her, staring at the wall.

"I lied to you. I betrayed your trust. You have every right to be angry. I don't blame you."

Lazarus snorted in derision, "I was a fool."

"No, Laz, I was the fool. I'm sorry. I'm so, so sorry. I've been running for so long, I don't know how to stop. And I screwed up. I didn't know what else to do. I just don't want you to hate me," she said, fighting back a sob.

"I wanted to help you. You wouldn't let me. I'm not going to make that mistake again."

"I want to fix it, Laz. Give me a chance. One more chance."

Lazarus turned back to look at her again. "I would have to

be the universe's biggest fool, Sable. No. No way," he said firmly and began to push past her to continue packing her things.

Sable dropped to her knees in the middle of his living room floor. The ache of her misery had reached its limit. She didn't care anymore what happened. As terrifying as it was, she had to tell Lazarus. Through teary, choking sobs, she began, letting all of it pour out.

"He's my brother. They hurt him when I don't do what they say. They took us when we were younger—Christ, he was only a little kid then. We were traveling, on vacation to somewhere, and they came. Daddy tried to stop them, but . . . but . . ."

Lazarus had stopped moving, but she could only stare at the floor, remembering.

"They killed my mom and dad and took us with them. That's when I first met Mr. Maxwell." She shuddered. "I was sixteen then, and he made me his, mind and body. He—he—" Sable shuddered, reliving the first time Mr. Maxwell had touched her. "He told me that if I didn't do everything he said, he'd hurt Gavin. So I did. Gavin was twelve. God, he was just a kid! But Mr. Maxwell meant it. When I didn't obey, he would punish us both. And Gavin always got the worst of it."

"Jesus, Sable," Lazarus said quietly. "Those marks on your back?"

Sable nodded, her eyes closed in misery. "That was the most recent. Gavin's punishment was five times worse. At night sometimes, when I'm trying to go to sleep, I hear him screaming. I can't get it out of my head. That's why I use the stimcrystals."

Lazarus crossed over to the couch and fell into it, the duffel bag sliding to the floor between his legs.

Sable went on, still kneeling on the floor. "After a while, Mr. Maxwell began to train me. He had this horrible woman named Ana teach me how to do all sorts of things. Gymnastics, self-defense, you name it. She was fast . . . God, was she fast. She had to have been enhanced—strength, reflexes, vision, you name it. When I didn't get it right, she'd kick the shit out of me until I learned it. And they gave me the cybernetic implants, all the cytronic circuitry for the Grid. I didn't have a choice. They just took me one day, strapped me to a table, knocked me out, and when I woke up, they rammed a computer jack into my neck and made me learn how to use it.

"Finally, about a year or so ago, Mr. Maxwell began to send me out to run errands. A lot of it was courier work, like what I was doing with Germaine, but I also broke into offices, computer systems, whatever. The first job was actually a setup. I tried to get help, to tell someone what was going on, that Gavin and I were prisoners of this sadistic maniac, but it was all fake. The whole job had been a big put-on to test me. When he finished teaching me the error of my ways, I couldn't move for two days, and Gavin nearly died. Mr. Maxwell told me that if I ever did that again, he would kill Gavin, and I'd have to watch."

Sable opened her eyes then to see what Lazarus was doing. He only stared at her, his jaw working. She couldn't tell what he was feeling, but it looked a lot like rage. She went on.

"After that, I learned to keep my mouth shut and just do the job. I learned not to trust anyone. I got used to working alone. It was pretty easy most of the time, since the kind of work I do doesn't involve a lot of face-to-face contact. In fact, I don't really like being around a lot of other people. When I came out of it the other night and you were in my room, I freaked out because . . . because . . ."

"So why tell me now?" Lazarus asked. Sable looked at him, confused.

"Because," she said, then stopped, her voice catching in her throat. It was harder to say these words than she had thought. "Because I needed you to understand. So we wouldn't go our own ways with you always thinking that it didn't matter to me that I'd lied to you. I guess I needed you to believe in me again. You're the first one who did at all, you know. Somehow I let you in. Despite everything I had taught myself about the cold, hard facts of my life, I let you get to me. And when I saw how much I'd hurt you by trying to run, I felt something I haven't felt for anyone except Gavin. I don't think Gavin even believes in me anymore." She stared at the floor in front of her, unable to meet Lazarus's eyes. Now that she'd said it, the words sounded silly. He was going to laugh at her, she was sure.

"You didn't just come back to me because you've got nowhere else to go?" Lazarus said doubtfully. "This isn't just another way for you to save your own ass?"

Sable did look up, then, desperate to break through Lazarus's doubt. "I— Laz, I—" She paused, working the thought in her head exactly. Then she took a deep breath and admitted, "I wouldn't be sitting here telling you this if I had been able to get away before. I won't dare insult you by lying to you again. But it hurt when I saw your face back at the cafe. Even as I was running away, I felt . . . regret. And for some reason, I felt the need to say I was sorry. I thought I'd never get a chance to, but . . ."

Lazarus stared at her for a long time without saying anything. Finally he nodded. "I believe you. I don't know exactly why, but I do."

Sable smiled then, and a strange feeling of warmth hit her. She laughed and sobbed at the same time.

Whatever else happens, at least he knows the truth. At least he understands, she thought, and she sniffed.

Lazarus slid off the couch and came to crouch beside her.

"Look," he said, trying to make her meet his gaze. "That first night, in your room at the Lucky Ace, it tore me up, watching the fear in your eyes. I was expecting some cold, arrogant courier who would give me a little grief and then turn the package over without too much fuss. I sure wasn't expecting you. I know you've been through a lot, but it made me really angry when you bolted today. Not just because you lied to me, but because . . . well, anyway, I'm sorry, too." He reached out then, gently, and took her hand in his. She looked at his face, at the warmth in his eyes, and felt his hand squeeze hers softly. She nodded to him, unable to think of anything to say, and then he was leaning forward, trying to kiss her. She flinched, suddenly light-years away, in Mr. Maxwell's private chambers, feeling his unwelcome touch.

Lazarus froze and then backed away, stammering, "I'm sorry. I thought—I misunderstood. I—I'm sorry." He stood quickly and turned to go into the bedroom, but Sable tightened her grip and wouldn't let go of his hand.

"Laz," she said, standing. "It's not you. It just reminded me of—"

"Oh, God, I'm sorry," Lazarus said, recognition dawning on his face. "That was stupid of me. I didn't think."

"No, it's all right. I'm okay." She smiled at him, trying to reassure him, even though her heart was suddenly sinking again.

I can't. I thought I wanted it, but I can't. Not and go back to *him* later. And I still have to go back.

Lazarus suddenly seemed as if he was afraid of breaking her, so she leaned toward him and gave him one quick kiss. It wasn't much, and the way he hesitated made it rather bland, but she found that she could do it without her stomach twisting or her skin crawling in fear. "Just give me a little time, okay?" she lied. She was still lying to him, she realized. It was a hard habit to break, but telling the truth would hurt too much right now. For both of them. She swore then that she would tell him. Before she left. When the time was right.

He seemed to ponder the kiss for a moment, but then he nodded and smiled. "As much as you need."

She smiled at him again, and then stepped away. "Laz," she said, swallowing back the new lump in her throat, "this doesn't change anything else, you know. I still have a big problem, and I don't have the goods to take back to Mr. Maxwell."

"You know there's no way you're going back there, back to that psychotic. Whatever else happens, I'm not letting him do anything to you again." Sable saw the intensity in Lazarus's eyes as he said this. She inadvertently let out a small gasp.

"Please don't say that, Laz. Don't promise to save me. You can't, and I can't afford to believe it. I have to go back to him. I needed you to understand me, to know who I was and to know that I cared, but you can't fix it. I don't want you to try."

"Jesus, Sable. How can you ask me just to stand aside and let you go back to that? I can't. I won't."

"How can *you* ask *me* to risk Gavin's life by testing Mr. Maxwell? Gavin is my brother, and the moment my parents died, I swore I would take care of him. This is the only way I know how. I can't beat Mr. Maxwell. He knows me too well. He made me who I am. Please, Laz. Don't make this harder for me than it already is."

Lazarus didn't say anything. The look in his eyes told her he was far from convinced. She began to doubt whether she had done the right thing, telling him so much, even as good as it had felt to get it off her chest. She shook her head, refusing to second-guess herself now.

Sable looked into Lazarus's eyes and said, "Laz, you can

still help me. Help me figure out a way to go back with what he wants. I need to get that data. Help me figure out how to get it."

"All right, but don't think this discussion is over and done with. I can't just stand by and watch you return to this Maxwell fiend. Even if it weren't my job, I—"

"Okay. You can try to talk me out of it later. Just tell me what you're going to do next."

"Stipelle said that the assassins who tried to kill us work for a major family in the syndicate—the same family who is most likely selling the guns that I have been tracking. They would know who is paying for the guns, so I'm going to go get my hands on the information tomorrow night. I'm going to break into the family headquarters, and Ellesao is going to help me."

"God! You're insane! You're going to get yourself killed! And who's Ellesao?"

"The mechalus Technospider. Stipelle has an interest in seeing this family taken down a peg, so they've agreed to lend me some aid."

"Let me go with you," Sable pleaded.

"No. Not this time. You've helped enough, but this is my case. I can't let you risk your life again."

"Oh, cut the macho crap. I do this for a living, too, remember? I can help. And I need the information as much as you do."

Lazarus looked at her doubtfully, and then finally shrugged. "I'm too tired to fight about it tonight. I have a long day tomorrow, planning the break-in. I need some sleep, and so do you. We'll talk about it tomorrow."

"I'm going with you tomorrow," Sable said, and then held up a hand before Lazarus could protest again. "But I'll convince you in the morning." She yawned and grabbed her duffel bag from the floor where Lazarus had set it down.

"I'm beat," she said, "But I need some help with this before I crash." She gestured toward the bandage wrapped around her arm as she began to dig around in her duffel bag.

"Sure," Lazarus answered, taking a seat next to her. "What are you looking for?"

"I just want another dose of painkiller. Stipelle said it should be okay in another day or so, but it still hurts."

Together they carefully unwrapped the wounded arm, and Lazarus inspected it. He seemed satisfied with the healing process and helped Sable with the analgesic injection. Then he rewrapped it to protect the artificial skin.

At last Lazarus stood and moved toward the bedroom as Sable kicked her boots off. He stopped at the doorway and turned to look at her, appearing to want to say something. She waited. "Good night," he finally muttered, and turned away, disappearing as he tapped the light panel near the doorway.

Sable sat there for a few moments in the dark, the glow from outside shining through the window and creating a dim luminescence in the apartment. She considered going to him as she slipped out of her clothes, but the thought was still too raw, too frightening. She kept seeing Mr. Maxwell's face instead of Lazarus's, and she shuddered. Finally she shook her head and lay down on the couch, pulling the blanket around herself. Despite her exhaustion, sleep didn't come for a while. Sable found herself torn, thinking about both Lazarus and Gavin. She could hear Lazarus's breathing in the other room, slow and deep. He was already asleep. She wondered where Gavin slept. She wished for a moment that she had a stimcrystal to help her forget about all of this, but then she shook her head angrily at the thought.

No. It's time to stop running. It's time to stop hiding. Tomorrow, you help Laz get that data, and then you go from there, she told herself.

Hang in there, baby brother. I'm coming for you.

* * * * *

The shadow that glided through the utter darkness of the digital void that served as a night sky in the Grid was unremarkable in many ways. From the conservative cut of clothing to the forgettable facial features, it had been designed to be overlooked, for other Gridpilots to pass it without noticing anything memorable at all. The last thing the pilot of this shadow wanted was attention.

Drifting over the artificial landscape below, the shadow found the object of its destination and descended sharply, pulling up at the last moment and settling lightly onto the rooftop of a digital construct, a storehouse of information rendered to look like a corporate office building. It happened to be the tallest such structure in this node, prohibiting anyone in another, higher, building from looking down onto the roof from above.

The shadow walked to the center of the structure, seeking a spot beneath a large corporate logo that was emblazoned on a huge virtual banner. From there, it would be hard for another shadow floating through the heights to look down and see this one. Waiting beneath the billboard was another shadow, in many ways quite similar to the first. Again the desire for being overlooked was paramount.

"You're late," the second shadow said, not moving.

"Yes. Affairs of office, as usual. It couldn't be avoided. We are encrypted?"

"Of course."

"Very well, then."

The other shadow stood for a long time, as though its pilot was struggling over what to say. "There is a problem."

"I see. You're dealing with it?"

"Um, this one is complicated."

The first shadow sighed. "Tell me. No names."

"The cop made contact with my courier, as we antici-pated, but there was a problem with the delivery. Someone inside who was loyal to the family played pigeon on our turncoat. He's dead."

"Was the data delivered?"

"No. The family's shooters intercepted the information and returned it."

"Damn. And what of our cop and courier?"

"They received unexpected aid."

"Oh?"

"Yes. From those who live within the walls. You can see how complicated it is now. Should I terminate them?"

"What's your read on them? What are they likely to do next?"

"My courier is being coerced, so she would be reluctant to cooperate further. Her main desire is to return to me, even though she will fear my displeasure at her failure."

"Yes. Your games with her have made her predictable. And the cop?"

"Hard to say. If he goes by the book, then he'll pull back and report in, asking for further instructions. He'll probably also have her shipped to detention. I may have to extract her later, but I expected as much and planned accordingly."

"If that's the case, make sure he is steered in a new direc-tion when he requests instructions." He paused, letting the silence hang for a moment. "And if he does not go by the book?"

"That's where it becomes complicated. He may decide to go for the source."

"Damn. I thought you had selected someone reliable."

"Reliable, yes, but for different reasons. Remember, his past is a double-edged sword. The creative thinking that drew us to him in the first place is also the reason he got into trouble with his former employers. We can expect him to excel when things get uncertain, to think his way through to a solution, but he may decide to act on his own, to go against the orders he was given, if he thinks there is some ultimate advantage to doing so."

"This complicates things."

"As I said. Shall I terminate them? Should we begin again?"

The first shadow thought for a moment. "No. I don't want to adjust the timetable if we can avoid it. Do you think he could succeed?"

"Perhaps. With the aid of the wall crawlers, they could pull it off."

"In which case. . . ?"

"In which case there's a chance—a long shot, to be sure, but a chance—he might be able to discover our role in these matters. Are you certain we should not terminate the operation?"

The first shadow thought a moment longer. "I am. We might be able to turn this to our advantage. The financial trail could be altered so that it points back to the same source as our freight company."

"Ah, yes. Very clever. It would strengthen our case then. Do you think the friend of the senator will cooperate?"

"I am sure you can persuade him."

"Of course." The second shadow chuckled slightly.

"There is one last matter."

"Yes?"

"The family obviously knows about our little bribery game now. Are you certain there is no way for them to trace it back to us?"

"Certain. Everything was doctored to appear to come from a nonexistent company. I used the name of an old schoolmate who was killed when I was young. It cannot be traced back to me."

"As long as you are certain . . ."

"Absolutely. When the time comes, I will enjoy seeing the entire syndicate fall, but I want them to know who it was that was behind it."

"Very good. I want an update in two days."

"I will be here."

As if on cue, both shadows vaporized simultaneously, leaving nothing to hint that they had been there at all.

07.0:

LAZARUS SAT IN the chair at his desk, watching Sable as she slept. Unlike that first night, when she had been strung out on the stimcrystal, her face was calm, peaceful. He shook his head, wondering when it was, exactly, that he had fallen for her.

It's such a stupid thing, he thought, to realize you're in love with someone, and you don't know when it happened.

Not nearly as stupid, he told himself, as falling for someone you know is bad news for you, who's going to split the first chance she gets, no matter what she told you last night.

I know, but I can't help it. I guess I'll just cross that bridge when I get to it.

Turning back to his desk, he jacked into his gauntlet and quickly found himself on the Grid, in his private library. There was no shadow calmly waiting for him this time, but he wasn't expecting it back yet anyway. Instead, he booted up a new shadow and watched it materialize in the corner. He began to feed it some data and input some alterations to its repertoire of tools.

"I want you to find out anything you can about this woman," he told the shadow. "You've got a pretty sketchy set of data files there. Interpolate and use visuals whenever possible." Lazarus had used a digital camera to get a couple of images of Sable as she slept, and he had lifted a set of her fingerprints from a few of her personal belongings. He had felt a twinge of guilt over doing it covertly, but he knew she would never tell him her true identity.

"Check the following offworld resources," Lazarus said. He created a file with the names and Grid addresses of five of the biggest Concord data banks that contained census and population information. "Begin with *Lighthouse* and only move on to the other items if you don't find anything there."

The *Lighthouse*, a mobile city among the stars, was a refitted space station that traveled regularly between the various systems of the Verge, bringing news and supplies to the frontiers of space. Not only was it the repository of a fine data library, perhaps the best in the Verge, but it was also Administrator Monahan's headquarters and what Lazarus considered home when he wasn't undercover. Based on its route schedule, the *Lighthouse* would be the closest source he planned to check anyway, and he wanted to save as much time as he could. He needed to find out if Sable was telling him the truth the night before. He was worried that he would find out she was.

"Depart," Lazarus said, and the shadow disappeared.

Lazarus created one more shadow, and for this one very few modifications were needed. It was a standard messenger, one he'd used a dozen times since arriving in Port Royal for this assignment. He had changed his mind and decided to send a quick update to his superior, just to keep the Administrator informed.

"This is a Priority One message for Administrator Monahan, Oslo G., at *Lighthouse*. Clearance is Eyes Only, use fastest available traffic at all steps. The message is: 'New development in progress. If things go well today, I may have a substantial lead on the identity of our quarry. Utilizing new ally. Will be performing a technical ops insertion to retrieve sensitive information. Will follow with a more detailed report after the fact.' End message. Depart."

There, Lazarus thought as the shadow vanished, that

should satisfy him for a few more days, at least. I'll get back to him when we get that data. In fact, I'll probably just head to the *Lighthouse* and deliver it to him in person. Won't that give him a shock?

Lazarus disconnected and lifted his visor. Sable was still stretched out on the couch, her breathing slow and easy. He watched her for a long time.

* * * * *

"So once we're inside, the only way to access their main data storage facility is through the ventilation system. There's a surprise," Lazarus said sarcastically, frowning. "It's always the ventilation system." He peered intently at a holodisplay set up in a conference room near Stipelle's office. It rotated through an animated sequence showing first a building, and then, by stripping away the facade of the edifice, revealing the superstructure and vital systems beneath it. The three-dimensional display was a schematic for the headquarters facility for Gibson-Williams Multimedia in Port Royal. GWM was a producer and multisystem distributor specializing in a wide variety of entertainment packages, ranging from interactive holo and Gridware to live stage productions and sporting events. They also happened to be the main front for the Mateo family's various business interests, at least according to Stipelle.

"It's either that or the reprocessing feed," Stipelle quipped, "but I doubt that you really want to slog through their sewer."

"No, thank you." Sable grimaced, wrinkling her nose. She stood near Lazarus, peering just as intently at the schematic and making a mental checklist of the equipment they would need. "The vents will do just fine, but I want to go back over the internal alarm sequence again. The timing of that is going to be critical."

Stipelle looked at Lazarus, who merely shrugged. He and Sable had already gone round and round a dozen times this morning, arguing about whether or not she would join him on this venture. She had made it plain to him that the only way she was not accompanying him was if he physically restrained her. In the end, he conceded, although she could tell that he still wasn't happy about it.

Originally Lazarus was going to try to enter the fortress—and it was a fortress, despite its innocent-looking external façade—alone, with Blue watching his back from the outside. Ellesao would pilot the Grid and help Lazarus by running interference, shutting down computer defenses and tripping magnetic locks from virtual remote until he was inside the building. Once there, however, Lazarus would be on his own, because the security system was a part of GWM's private Grid, which had no external access. It was an isolated system.

Sable firmly pointed out to Lazarus that having her along would allow one of them to patch into GWM's private Grid and guide the other one through the rest of the run. Lazarus had grudgingly admitted that she was right, but he still didn't like the risk.

"This is still a CIB operation," he had said, "and technically I have no authorization to involve civilians in the process."

"That didn't stop you from using me to get to Germaine," Sable had countered.

"Yeah, and it was against my better judgment then, too. You remember what almost happened."

"But you still did it, because it made sense. It helped our chances. It's the same set of circumstances now. You can't deny that."

Lazarus had sighed. "No, I can't deny that, but I shouldn't let you go anyway. I don't want you to get hurt. I care about you, okay? I admit it. Plus, I don't want to be distracted from worrying about you while we're in there."

"Laz," Sable had answered quietly, "I need to be in there. I can't just sit and wait, hoping you make it out alive. It would drive me crazy. Not only because of you, but because of Gavin. I can't just hang out and hope everything works out where he's concerned. I have to participate. Besides," she had added, smiling, "I can take care of myself. Probably better than you."

"I guess we'll see," he had finally said. Sable considered it settled.

Sable blinked, returning to the present. Stipelle was going over the timing of the alarm sequence again. It was going to be tricky.

"I'm going to need some special equipment," Sable said when they had finished. "I've got a list."

"Blue will pull together everything you need," Stipelle answered. "Give the list to him, and he'll have it by evening."

Blue grinned and nodded, so Sable began running through her list with him. He entered everything into the dataslate he always seemed to be carrying, and then hurried off.

When they were done, Sable turned back to Lazarus and Ellesao. "It's going to be a long night. I'm going to get some sleep. Ellesao, is there someplace I can crash for a little while?"

"Confirmed. Spare rooms/availability for occasional guests." Ellesao stood, ready to lead the way.

Lazarus nodded. "That's a good idea. I'll grab a nap, too. We'll need enough time to check all of the equipment, though, so don't sleep more than a couple of hours," he said, checking the time on his gauntlet chronometer.

* * * * *

Two hours later, Sable awoke. She quickly changed into a one-piece, snug-fitting dull gray bodysuit with an attached hood that she could pull over her head in an instant. The suit was made of an extremely fine but tough weave of carbonate fiber and flexible cerametal mail, so it would stand up to some serious slashing, scraping, and tearing without taking serious damage. It also had a tiny battery pack inside a pocket in the small of her back. Sable checked the battery to make sure it was charged to full, and then flipped the switch and watched in the mirror as the suit quickly changed color, blending with the wall behind her. Satisfied, she flipped the switch off, and the suit returned to its dull gray color.

Next she donned a tool harness that wrapped around her waist and looped over her shoulders. Attached to the web gear were several snap rings to which she could clip various tools and climbing gear. When she was dressed, she paused and stared at herself in the mirror once more.

Well, you said you wanted to go along. Here's hoping you come back again. In one piece.

She took a deep breath and went to join the others.

The group had gathered in the conference room to go over last-minute details and to sort through all of the equipment, making sure everything was in working order, all the batteries were fully charged, and that nothing was missing. When everything checked out, they began to pack the gear. Lazarus was dressed similarly to Sable, although his bodysuit was black.

Sable picked up a small backpack. "Turn around," she said to Lazarus, holding the pack up.

"You act like you've done this before." He smiled, spinning to face away from her.

"Once or twice," she chuckled as she began attaching the pack to Lazarus's back with his web gear. "But I never had anyone help me suit up before."

Lazarus nodded as she finished, and he turned to face her. He cinched several straps to get the pack snug against his body. "What if I don't help you this time?" he asked as Sable turned away from him.

"Then I'll do it myself, as usual."

"I still wish you'd reconsider," Lazarus muttered, but he began clipping her pack to her harness nonetheless.

Sable didn't answer him as she cinched her pack tight. Instead, she began to attach an assortment of other tools to her harness.

Ellesao and Blue were packing other gear into a large black case with numerous compartments and pockets. It seemed bulky at first, but when they were done, the whole thing folded up nicely into a convenient bundle. Next to it was a multisectioned duffel bag about the same size. Everything was ready.

Lazarus surveyed the collection of gear and people, slipped on a pair of gloves, and then slid his gauntlet onto his arm and checked the chronometer. "Let's go," he said.

Sable slipped a special gauntlet on, one that Blue had modified for her earlier in the day. She plugged the feed into the NIJack in her neck. She considered getting a subdermal jack, like the one Lazarus had in his arm, which would negate the need for the jack in the back of her neck.

But then I couldn't stim, she thought, and wished she didn't want to.

Ellesao wished them good luck and left. She would access the Grid and wait for them to begin the insertion, doing as much preliminary work as she could before they started. They would keep in contact with her by means of a scrambled comm unit.

After she was gone, Blue led Sable and Lazarus along another of the Technospiders' secret routes through passageways and access corridors. They were fortunate that

Gibson-Williams was as close at it was, making it unnecessary to have to take the transit between domes. They would have had to wait to equip until they were on location then, and Sable didn't like the idea of lugging all that stuff around in public, even if they kept it concealed in containers. There were too many unscrupulous people in Port Royal who would like nothing better than to steal it.

Gibson-Williams Multimedia was a large complex in an open plaza, difficult to approach without being monitored. In addition, it was surrounded by an extremely high-tech security shield, a combination energy and particle screen designed to keep anyone and anything unwanted on the outside, even if they did manage to breach the security wall. If Lazarus and Sable had been forced to approach the place from the surface, they wouldn't have been able to get within two hundred meters of the building before a vast array of sensors had detected them and measures were taken to eliminate them.

Fortunately, GWM's facilities ran several levels under the surface, and there were other ways to get close to them. During their planning, the group had discovered that a rather exclusive fitness club was situated nearby, and that the club's service elevator actually ran past an old abandoned construction tunnel that would get them within the compound. Assuming their information was accurate, that was their ticket inside GWM.

Blue stopped in the middle of a rather large, dimly lit service corridor and began to look around. "The hatch into the club should be here somewhere." Sable and Lazarus spread out and began to search. Lazarus finally spotted the small door up high, recessed slightly into the wall. The metal door looked as if it hadn't been used in a long time.

Lazarus folded his hands together to make a step for Sable and boosted her up. While he held her in place, she pulled out a small flashlight and checked the door thoroughly. She didn't see any external sensors or alarms, but that was no guarantee. She removed a small canister from her tools and began spraying a thin stream of lubricant into every crack.

Blue began setting up a portable sensor array, identical to two others he had hidden in access tunnels on two other sides of GWM's location earlier in the day. Together, the three sensors formed a triangle, in the middle of which was the entirety of Gibson-Williams Multimedia's headquarters. When he was up and running, he nodded to Sable.

She switched on her Gridcaster and waited for the connection. They had modified the gauntlet so that she could get a data feed from the triangulating array without having to jack directly into a port. Instead, they had used a comm unit to make the connection via radio transmissions. It wasn't nearly as fast as a direct fiber optic link, but for what they wanted to do, it was perfect.

Another reason to bring me along, Sable thought as the program they had set up began to boot. I can run this directly through my optics, and Lazarus can't.

The program started up, and Sable was suddenly blinded. Her cytronic circuitry was receiving a signal from the Gridcaster, but because there was no Grid, only the radio transmission from Blue's triangulating array, she could see nothing but snow, as if her whole world had turned into a holovid with no signal.

"Whoa!" she grunted, almost losing her balance.

"Sorry," Blue said from somewhere below. "The triangulation is still synchronizing. It'll clear in a sec."

A moment later Sable's vision returned, although there was still a random scrolling and flashing of light.

"Okay," Blue called up. "Let's get you aligned. Put your nose right up next to the handle."

Sable looked at the rusty door with a small measure of distaste, but she leaned in and pressed her nose to the door and held still. Suddenly there was a crisp white line in her field of vision, right where the doorframe was.

"How's that?" Blue asked.

Sable pulled back, and the line remained in position, joining with others to show the outline of the door. "Looks good," she replied. "I'm going to adjust a bit." She entered a few keystrokes on her gauntlet, and the line dimmed to a medium gray that wasn't quite so stark against the dimness of the corridor. She made another adjustment, and the wire frame outline, the signal from the array superimposed onto her normal field of vision, shifted a few centimeters, lining up a bit more accurately. "Okay, we're up and running." She turned her head this way and that, up and down, experimenting. The image remained in perfect position, a three-dimensional model of the entire tunnel and all of its features. "This works better than I thought it would."

"Yeah," Blue answered. "Your system link really speeds up the processing time. Unless you whip your head around, you shouldn't experience any lag."

Lazarus grunted. "The new toy is really cool, but would you finish opening the door, please? You're getting heavy."

"Sorry," Sable said, giggling. "Hang on." She slipped her regular comm unit over her head, adjusted the mike in front of her mouth, and switched it on. There was a brief crackle, and then she heard the click of a connection. "Ellesao?" Sable called.

"Present/available," the mechalus answered. "Is everything up and running?"

"Like a charm," Sable replied. "We're just outside the access hatch to the pump room now. How's it look?"

"There was no electronic lock or security sensor on the door," Ellesao said, her voice matter-of-fact, as usual.

"Confirmation/NEGATIVE whether a lock/mechanical is in place, of course."

"Well, only one way to find out," Sable answered. "All quiet now," she said. "We're on go mode." She reached up and tentatively turned the handle. It twisted reasonably easily and without noise, but when she pushed it, she felt it slide a fraction of a centimeter and then butt up against something. "It's got a bolt or something. I'm going to have to cut."

Below her, Lazarus sighed and shifted his position slightly. "Please hurry," he said.

"Going as fast as I can," she said, pulling a tool that looked similar to a pistol from her belt. It had a fiber optic connection that ran to the power pack on her back. She slipped a pair of tinted goggles over her eyes and then flipped the switch, and a thin blue beam of light protruded about seven centimeters from the front of the tool. Sable twisted a dial, shortening the beam to about three centimeters. Then she twisted a second dial, making it a bit thinner, about two millimeters in diameter. "Cutting now," she said softly into the mike of the comm unit.

She held the tool up to the metal of the door and pressed the beam into it. The blue disappeared into the steel with a soft hiss, and there was a flare of orange as the liquid metal ran from the cut. Sable drew the torch down in a steady, straight motion, lasering a clean slice between the handle and the door frame. When she finished, she switched off the torch and hooked it back onto her belt.

"Cut's made. I'm trying the door again," she said and pushed gently on the door. It swung inward easily into a darkened space beyond. "It's open. We're inside the club." She removed the goggles, flipped on her flashlight, and shone the beam around. From her first quick surveillance sweep, everything seemed to be undisturbed. She breathed a small sigh of relief.

"I'm going to boost you up, Sable," Lazarus said, pushing up on the underside of her foot. Sable guided herself through the doorway, holding the flashlight in her mouth so she could steady herself with both hands. When she was through, she turned and waited for the equipment. Lazarus passed the case up first, and then the duffel bag. Finally he jumped up and grabbed the frame of the doorway and pulled himself through.

"Good luck," Blue called from below. "See you when you get back."

Lazarus gave him a quick thumbs-up and pushed the door shut again. Sable did a quick visual of the place. It was a combination storeroom and filter system for the club's swimming pool. Shelves lined the walls with various maintenance equipment for the pool. In one corner, a large pump hummed, filtering water from the pool a level above. Nothing seemed out of the ordinary.

Lazarus had pulled up a file on his gauntlet and was consulting it as Sable switched on her suit's stealth mode and unpacked a few new items to clip onto her web gear.

"According to the maps, the service lift is down the hall to the right," he said, his voice echoing in the comm unit's earphone. "The door is about thirty meters down and on the opposite side."

"Let me take a peek out there to make sure we don't have company," Sable said.

"I have patched into the club's cameras/security," Ellesao's voice chimed in. "No one at all appears to be down on your level right now. You're clear to go."

Lazarus gave a satisfied nod as Sable opened the door a crack. The hallway outside was lit, but dimly. It appeared that only safety lights were currently on. The structure of the building remained superimposed on Sable's field of vision, but she found that, with the contrast of the image toned down a bit, it really wasn't too distracting. She leaned back in and nodded to Lazarus, grabbed the duffel bag, and crept out into the hall.

"I've patched in a loop/continuous feedback to the cameras/hallway where you are," Ellesao continued, "so you will not be recorded. I will shut it off once you are inside the shaft/elevator so that we minimize the risk of notice."

Sable and Lazarus padded through the hallway to the elevator door.

"I am sending the elevator down now," Ellesao said.

Sable noticed as they approached it that Blue had cycled the door image in her visual feed to a nice blue color to differentiate it from the surrounding wire-frame imagery.

"That's cute, Blue. It's even your color," she said softly into the comm.

"Testing it on something easy to make sure it works," Blue replied.

The elevator door opened just as Sable reached it, and she stepped through, followed closely by Lazarus. As the door slid shut behind them, Lazarus was already interlocking his fingers to give Sable a boost again. She stepped in, and he lifted her to the ceiling, where she flipped the access hatch open and then pulled herself up into the darkness of the roof of the lift. Lazarus passed the equipment up, and then she leaned down to extend a hand to him. He took hold and pulled himself through. Sable closed the hatch.

"We're on top of the elevator, Ellesao," Lazarus said. Sable checked her wire-frame imagery against the real backdrop. So far, it had remained steady and true.

"Sending you up," Ellesao answered, and the elevator began to move. As they rose upward past several doors in the dim glow of the service lights, Sable unpacked a couple of new things from the case. First she removed a small battery-powered lantern, more powerful than her flashlight, flipping it on to illuminate her work.

"Blue, you got that cutting template locked in yet?" Sable asked as she produced a special magnetic coupling.

"Already set to go," the kid responded, and Sable glanced up. A few dozen meters above her was a red blotch in her wire-frame environment. The elevator came to a stop about two meters below it. The cutting template was where Lazarus and Sable were going to cut through the elevator shaft wall to reach the old tunnel that would lead inside the GWM building. Unfortunately, Sable realized, there was about a two-meter chasm, where the lift cables ran, between the side of the elevator and the wall. She was going to have to anchor herself to the wall, because she couldn't reach the spot where she was to cut from the elevator.

"Ellesao," Lazarus spoke into the comm, "do you have the elevator disabled?"

"It is locked down. I will give you a warning if anyone puts it into use so you can secure your position."

"Roger," Lazarus responded.

Sable unclipped a piton from her harness and smacked it against the elevator wall, where a high-strength adhesive oozed out and quickly clamped the thing in place. She snapped a safety line from her harness to the piton, then swung out into space. She quickly secured several more pitons into place, allowing her to brace her feet against the wall and face her designated spot easily. Lazarus monitored her progress from the roof of the elevator. Once she was in position, Sable slipped the goggles over her eyes again and pulled out the cutting torch and fired it up.

"Blue, tell me again what my layers are," Sable asked, poised to begin slicing through the steel wall of the elevator shaft.

"First you've got six centimeters of steel. Then there's about half a meter of stone. I positioned the template in a spot where you would miss one of the main steel support beams. Sure don't want you blasting through that."

"Roger," Sable replied and adjusted the torch. She began to cut, sliding the blue beam of the lasering device through the metal slowly but steadily. The faint orange glow of melting steel ran in thin rivulets as she maneuvered the torch. She followed the cutting template superimposed on her vision, tracing out a hole big enough for them to crawl through.

As she got close to completing the circuit, Sable used a magnetic coupling with a gravity negation device attached to slide the whole piece of steel away from the hole without having to bear its weight. She removed the goggles to survey her work.

Pulling a canister of compressed gas out of a pocket of her harness, she sprayed it around the edges to cool the metal enough so she could touch it. She flicked on her flashlight and checked the stone behind the plate. It appeared to be poured concrete.

"How thick did you say this was, Blue?"

"What?" Blue asked, confused.

"The stone behind the steel plating. It looks like concrete."

"About half a meter."

Sable nodded. "Okay, Lazarus, you're up to bat." Sable detached herself from the two main pitons and worked her way back across the chasm to the roof of the elevator. Lazarus took her place.

"All set," she said. "Tell me what you want first."

"Send over the charges first," Lazarus said.

Sable carefully unpacked a bundle from the case and passed it along to Lazarus. He went to work placing shaped charges on the surface of the concrete as Sable retrieved the detonators from the case. Lazarus grabbed them and continued working.

This process continued as Lazarus worked and Sable relayed supplies across to him. Slowly Lazarus's project took shape. After placing the shaped charges and setting the detonators, he covered the entire section of the wall with a thick foam that hardened in a matter of moments. He took great care to shape the foam a certain way, although Sable didn't understand the particulars of working with explosives.

"You have a passenger," Ellesao's voice cut in on the comm unit.

"Damn!" Sable said. "Lazarus, you secure?"

"Yeah. Just ride with it. Ellesao, what's their arrival level?"

"Level two. Sable, hang on."

Sable crouched down and grabbed a structural brace with one hand and the open case with the other. Suddenly the elevator dropped, and Sable's stomach lurched with it. "Oh, yuck," she moaned softly as the service lights streamed past her vision in a blur.

Just as suddenly, the car came to a halt.

"Sable, people/two getting on," Ellesao reported, monitoring the passengers' progress from the Grid. "Quiet/remain; they are only riding up levels/few."

The car began to rise rapidly again, and Sable held her breath to keep from gasping, trying desperately to keep her balance. When the car floated to a stop, she breathed a small sigh of relief.

"Okay, all clear. Taking you back up," Ellesao said.

"You can take your time," Sable muttered, feeling queasy. "I don't need another ride like that."

Soon Sable was back with Lazarus, passing him the last of the pieces he needed to complete the job. When he was finished, they rode the elevator down until they were out of blast range and detonated the explosives.

There was a deep, muffled thump, followed by a vibration Sable could feel in the elevator, but that was all.

"Perfect!" she said, elated.

"We'll see," Lazarus replied. "Take us back up, Ellesao. Let's see if we punched through."

The elevator began to rise again, and when they reached the place, Lazarus dissolved the foam with the contents of a small spray bottle to reveal a hole blasted in the concrete.

"Looks like we used a little more Detonex than we needed, but we're through," Lazarus said after a moment.

Sable let out a sigh and realized she had been holding her breath. If they hadn't been able to blast through the concrete, they would have had to abandon the show and come back tomorrow night. They hadn't been able to pack enough explosives and foam for a second detonation.

"Nothing to report on my end," Ellesao said, her voice tinny in the comm unit. "It appears personnel/none in the club took any notice of the explosion."

"Roger," Lazarus replied. "We're going through the hole." He turned back to Sable. "Send the gear, then come on. The clock's ticking."

Soon Lazarus, Sable, and both packages of gear were in a very old and surprisingly large tunnel. In front of them, it sloped upward at a gentle but noticeable grade. They shone their flashlights around, revealing the old support beams. A stream of water trickled past their feet along one side of the tunnel, and in the distance, Sable could hear a steady dripping. A few thick, frayed power cables, ripped out of their conduits and long out of use, dangled like snakes from the ceiling. The whole place smelled damp and musty.

"They used this passage to tunnel out the levels when they first built Port Royal," Lazarus explained. "This was one of the ways they hauled the rock back out. Most of these tunnels got expanded and turned into other structures, but for some reason, this one was just sealed up on each end and abandoned."

Sable nodded as they walked, flashlights in hand. She was still getting a nice, clear signal from Blue's triangulation array. As they followed the tunnel, however, Sable began to frown. Up ahead of them was what appeared to be a large hole, a shaft that bisected the passageway vertically. Her visual feed from Blue's triangulation array told her the passage was solid and uninterrupted, but the dropoff was nonetheless in front of them, as plain as day.

"Great," Sable said, groaning. "That's not on our schematics. What now?"

Lazarus stood next to her, peering at the shaft, which was about five meters or so in diameter, and frowning. "Our technical specs for this section must have been wrong," he said, half to himself. "At some point after they put together those specs, someone came along and did some sort of core drilling."

"What the hell for?" Sable asked, peering carefully over the edge of the precipice.

"Any of a half-dozen reasons I can think of," Lazarus answered. "Most likely, though, they started to expand this area like in the other tunnels, but for some reason changed their plans later. And no one bothered to update the schematics. Blue?" Lazarus said into the comm unit. "We've got a problem."

"What's up?" Blue asked.

"We've got a big hole in our way that wasn't on our map," Lazarus replied.

"Yeah, my visuals show that the tunnel is intact, but it definitely ain't," Sable added.

"So? How wide is it?" Blue asked.

Lazarus pursed his lips for a moment and then said, "We can manage to get across without too much trouble, I think, but it's going to set us back at least several minutes."

"Well, it's your call," Blue responded.

Lazarus considered for a brief moment. "We'll keep going. We can probably jump it, no problem, but moving the equipment is going to take a little more effort. Damn, that's a long way down." He shone his light down past the edge of the crevasse, but the bottom was too far away to be seen.

"What's this 'We can probably jump it' stuff, Laz?" Sable asked sarcastically. "I'm not thrilled about that plan."

Lazarus said, "I thought you said you did this kind of work all the time."

"Sure. I didn't say I liked it, though."

Lazarus chuckled and said, "All right, I'll jump first, then we'll use rope to set up a relay. We'll ferry the stuff across first, and then you can come."

Sable looked at Lazarus doubtfully. "Do we have enough rope?"

"I think so," Lazarus replied. "Slap a couple of those pitons here"—he pointed to a spot on the wall of the tunnel—"and here. We'll anchor me with some rope, too, just in case I don't make it across."

Sable nodded and unpacked a pair of the adhesive anchors, slapping them into place where Lazarus had indicated. The adhesive gel quickly bonded the pitons to the wall.

Lazarus, meanwhile, took more of the pitons and clipped them to his web gear. "I'll take these over to the other side. Then we can loop the rope through and ferry the equipment across," he said, retrieving a coil of rope from the duffel bag and attaching one end of it to his web gear with a clip.

"Got it," Sable answered, clipping the other end of the rope to the pitons fastened to the wall. "Hey, Laz?"

"Yeah?" the CIB agent responded, gauging his running room as he backed up.

"Are you sure about this?"

There was a moment's pause. "Yeah," he said at last.

"Then be careful."

He looked at her. "I will."

Sable watched Lazarus as he tested his approach a couple of times. The trick here, she realized, was finding the right balance between running room and rope length. If he backed up as much as he really wanted, there would be too much length to his safety rope, and he'd fall too far, and too fast, before the rope jerked him painfully to a halt. On the other hand, keeping the rope at a safer length meant he couldn't get the full running start he really wanted to build up enough speed to clear the span of the shaft.

Sable crouched down to one side of the tunnel and waited. She watched Lazarus take a couple of deep breaths and close his eyes, and then suddenly her heart pounded in her chest as he sprang into motion, taking smooth, long strides toward the hole. The rope trailed behind him and then doubled back to the piton anchored on the wall next to the edge of the shaft. Lazarus reached the edge of the hole and launched himself, arms and legs kicking and flailing, up and across. Sable stared at him as he jumped, literally willing him to clear the hole and land on the other side.

When Lazarus tumbled to the floor of the tunnel on the opposite side of the shaft and slid across it, Sable breathed a huge sigh of relief. Lazarus went sprawling, jerking to a stop when he reached the end of the rope's length. He lay there for a moment, not moving.

"Laz!" Sable growled, waiting for him to get up. "What's wrong?"

"Nothing," Lazarus mumbled. "I just wasn't sure I was going to make it for a second there."

Sable sighed again and waited for Lazarus to recover his wits. When he finally rose to his feet, he gave her a goofy grin. "What is it?" she asked.

"It was fun. You should try it."

"No, thanks!" she said, glaring. "Just get the damned pitons set so we can get moving." Lazarus moved to comply, but he was still grinning. "And stop grinning at me," she added in exasperation.

"I can't," he said. "It's the adrenaline rush."

Sable rolled her eyes as they continued to work on the rope, threading it through all four pitons so that it doubled back on itself, making a long loop that they could use to move the equipment across the shaft. By pulling on the top portion of the rope, they could slide the bottom section in the opposite direction, much like a breeches buoy used for rescue at sea.

When the two of them were done, Sable took a deep breath and prepared to cross the rope, standing on the lower line and holding herself upright on the upper portion. Slowly and carefully, she stepped out onto the rope, feeling it quiver and sag beneath her weight.

"Careful," Lazarus said, trying to hold his end of the loop still for her.

"No kidding," she snapped back through clenched teeth, trying desperately to keep her balance. As she neared the middle of the shaft, the rope sagged even more, and the wobbling was at its worst.

Just take it easy, Sable told herself. One step at a time.

She took another breath to calm herself, and then looked down, trying to focus on her feet shuffling sideways along the bottom rope rather than on the yawning blackness beyond. She inched her way along. Lazarus helped to keep the rope steady and then held out a hand for her to take when she came within reach.

That's when the rope gave way beneath her, accompanied by a loud sound like the crack of a rifle, and Sable was tumbling into the chasm below.

08.0:

SABLE DIDN'T REALIZE she was screaming until after Lazarus already had hold of her arm, gripping her by her wrist with one hand and clinging to the dangling loops of rope with the other. He was leaning precariously over the side of the shaft's edge upside down, feet still barely resting on the edge of the shaft and arms straining to keep them both from slipping and dropping into the depths of the shaft. Sable's throat was raw from her terror-filled cry, and her shoulder hurt from being jerked to a stop when he had grabbed her wrist. But she was alive, and she wasn't falling.

"OhmyGod, ohmyGod, don't let go of me, Laz!" she shrieked, the panic rising in her chest. "Pull me up . . . don't let me fall!" She was shaking and felt the adrenaline pounding through her veins as she twisted in his grip, her feet kicking uselessly in the void around her.

"What the hell is going on?" Blue's voice demanded through the headphone of Sable's comm unit. "Are you two all right?"

"Easy . . . just take it easy," Lazarus said to Sable with a calmness that belied the strain he was under. "Shut up, Blue. We can't talk right now." To Sable, he said, "I can't pull us both up; I'm overbalanced. You have to climb up my arm, Sable. Reach up with your other hand and pull yourself up to my web gear."

Sable nodded and tried to focus her attention on his face.

She swung her free arm up and used both arms to lift herself, doing an improvised chin-up. When she was as far up as she could pull herself, she shot her free hand up to Lazarus's back and snatched hold of the harness around his torso. "Okay," she said, trembling from the strain. "I've got it. Just hang on while I climb up your back."

"Carefully, but don't dawdle," Lazarus replied, his voice tight.

Sable tried to resist the urge to yank herself up in quick spurts, knowing that would only put more strain on Lazarus's grip. Instead, she steadily pulled, using nothing but her arms and trying to keep her feet from flailing behind her. Lazarus used his free hand to grab her by the ankle and help lift her. Finally, she found more of her weight resting on top of him than hanging free, and she scrambled the rest of the way up to the floor of the tunnel.

Lazarus quickly swung himself around, grabbed the rope that was still attached to the wall, and dragged himself back upright to the floor beside Sable, dropping limply down and not moving.

"Will someone tell me what the hell is going on?" Blue's voice cut through the silence.

"Fine now . . . nearly . . . fell," Sable responded, catching her breath.

"Don't scare me like that!" Blue said.

Sable waited for the pounding of her heart to subside and for her arms to stop shaking. Finally she rolled over and looked at Lazarus.

"What happened?" she asked.

In answer, Lazarus gestured, without looking, back to the far side. Sable squinted across the shaft to where the pitons had been anchored to the wall. Where they had been positioned, there was a large chunk of the wall missing. She crawled to the edge of the hole and peered over the side. The two pitons were still attached to the chunk of concrete, all of it swinging slightly at the end of the rope.

"Shit," Sable said.

"The concrete was old and weak, I guess," Lazarus said, finally sitting up.

"Thanks, Laz. You saved my life."

Lazarus flipped his hand in dismissal. "I just reacted; I didn't even think. But you're welcome."

Sable didn't mention that she noticed Lazarus's hands shaking as he said this.

After recovering enough to continue, the two of them gathered their gear and prepared to set off.

"We're on the move again, Blue," Lazarus said as they started walking.

"How are we going to get back across?" Sable asked.

"I guess I'll jump back across and secure the rope to a new spot on the wall."

"Why don't we get Blue to follow us in?" Sable asked him as they walked along. "He could be waiting for us and set fresh pitons without anyone having to jump."

"She's right, Laz," Blue agreed.

"Not yet, but when we're on our way out," Lazarus replied. "I want you to stay where you can monitor the array until we don't need it anymore. Now, let's find that mark and get inside GWM."

"The spot we want is just up ahead," Sable said as she walked, noting a small speck of red that appeared in her field of vision.

"Yeah, about thirty more meters," Lazarus replied. "Watch your step here. There's a lot of loose rubble and exposed rebar."

Sable watched the small blob of red in her field of vision grow larger and take form as a small square. About fifteen meters away from it, the structure of the tunnel suddenly changed from concrete to metal. It was roughly in the form of a box, and overhead was what appeared to be a large rusted metal door with a valve handle in the middle of it, like a giant hatchway. The water that Sable had heard earlier was dripping from the seal at the edge of the door. It splashed onto the floor in a small puddle and then ran down the gentle slope of the tunnel.

"We're passing through into a section of newer construction," Lazarus said quietly. "This must have been a drop shaft where they lifted the diggings straight out. I'm sure that shaft overhead has been filled in. I wonder why there's a leak, though. Not sure where that water might be coming from. Is the template still visible?"

Sable nodded and continued to walk toward the red outline that was lined up along the wall, skirting the splashing water as she went. When they reached it, Sable stopped and pointed.

"It's right here, Laz," she said.

"Okay, mark it for me."

Sable nodded and removed a small paint can from her tools and sprayed little orange crop marks at the corners of the outline. When she was done, Lazarus moved close to it with a small EM detector in his hand. He moved the device back and forth over the area Sable had outlined very slowly, checking the readings on the display.

"Yep, this looks like it. I'm picking up EM readings, so there's a power grid on the other side, just like we thought. You've got to be very careful when you cut through. Don't cut too deep."

Sable took out the laser cutter once more, donned her goggles, and set about adjusting the cutting beam so that it was no more than a couple of centimeters long. Then she stepped up to the metal wall and began to slice into the steel with the torch.

As before, she worked slowly and carefully, moving the beam cleanly through the metal, carving out a large square. Lazarus prepared the gravity negation coupling and locked it into place as Sable neared the end of the job. When she was done, Lazarus gently tugged the metal out and pushed it to the floor.

Sable had her flashlight up and was peering inside the hole she had just made. Beyond the metal was a small dark space that was about a meter high and went back for quite a distance. Dozens of power conduits were bundled together, running past the opening. They had cut into an area between floors of the GWM building. The foundation of the building on the surface had changed over the years, and this section of the place jutted out farther than the rest of the structure, but it was all connected.

Lazarus moved in beside Sable and took a look. "Looks good," he said, nodding in satisfaction. "We should be able to squeeze between those conduits. Let's get whatever else we need out of the baggage. This is where we leave the rest behind."

"Careful. I haven't cooled the cut yet," Sable said. She pulled out the canister of compressed gas.

After she had applied some of the gas to the edge of the metal, she ditched the laser cutter and most of the climbing gear, as well as the modified gauntlet. Lazarus pulled out her gauntlet from the case and stashed it in her backpack.

Once they were finished selecting the equipment they'd need, Lazarus said, "Blue, Ellesao, we're heading inside. We're about to lose your signal to their jamming field. We'll see you on the flip side."

"Roger," Blue said. "Stay loose, and be careful."

"We will be waiting," Ellesao acknowledged.

Sable and Lazarus shut off their comm units to conserve the batteries. Then Lazarus began to pull himself through the opening, twisting through the bundles of conduit, sliding on his stomach. Sable helped by holding his legs and pushing gently.

When Lazarus got inside, he squirmed around to face her. "Okay, your turn. Just take it slow and easy. It's pretty dirty in here."

Sable nodded and stood on the case, using it like a stool. She poked her head through, shimmying her arms through the gap in the power cables. Lazarus took hold of her hands and pulled slightly as she pushed with her feet. Lazarus was dragging her in on her belly. Once she was inside, they paused while Lazarus consulted the map readout on his dataslate.

"The access hatch is about forty meters this way," he said after a moment. He began to crawl forward on his belly. Sable followed him, her flashlight in her teeth. They had to worm their way past pipe and structural supports and a maze of power conduits, all covered with a thick coating of dust. Sable wished she had a breathing mask, but there was no more room in the equipment bundles. After a time, they reached a small hatch in the floor of the crawl space.

"This is it," Lazarus said, whispering. "Keep your voice down. There's going to be a lot more people around here."

"Got it," Sable whispered back. "Take a peek and let's see what's what."

Lazarus applied some of the lubricant to the door, then he took hold of the hatch handle and turned it gently. He lifted it up a fraction and peered through. "It's dark. Hang on." There was a pause, and Sable knew he had switched to his thermal optics. There was a distinct, audible hum coming from the space beyond the hatch. Finally he said, "It looks clear. Let's move."

Lazarus swung the hatch open all the way and swung his legs around to drop down through the opening. He slowly lowered himself through and dropped out of sight. Sable moved to follow him, suddenly realizing her heart was pounding.

Why are you so nervous all of a sudden? she asked herself.

Sable lowered herself to the top rung of a ladder and got a foothold, and then descended the rest of the way, pulling the hatch shut behind her. Lazarus was shining his flashlight around. In the dimness of his light, she could see that they were in a generator room, one of four she knew were within the building complex.

The Mateos, in their wisdom, had chosen not to rely on external power, but instead had installed these fusion generators to supply all of their energy. Everything had triple redundancy protection—shut one down, the other three automatically adjust without skipping a beat. About the only thing that could sense the change would be the monitoring computers—except, of course, for the alarm systems that would warn everyone within the place that there was a problem needing immediate attention.

The massive shielded reactor dominated the center of the room, although there were several other, smaller pieces of equipment along the walls—monitoring devices and so forth. Sable ignored these as she checked for a door leading out. It was set into the far wall, completely electronic and magnetically sealed.

Lazarus was checking out a monitoring station set along one wall. He sat down at the station, shining his flashlight over the dimly glowing controls. "This should do nicely," he said. "I'll run point for you from here."

"You can get a Grid connection?" Sable asked, coming up to look over his shoulder.

"Yeah. Its primary function is to manage the reactor, but I can patch into the main systems easily enough, I think. I'll plug in and start decoding the security. You get ready to go."

Sable nodded and unhooked her pack, and then fished her own gauntlet and a wicked-looking knife out of it. "I'm leaving this here," she said, dropping the pack on the floor. "Don't need any extra things to carry with me." She slipped the knife into her belt and put the gauntlet on her arm. Lazarus plugged his gauntlet in and hit the switch, dropping the shades down over his eyes so he could work.

Sable sat down to wait for Lazarus to access the GWM Grid. After a few minutes, her thoughts drifted elsewhere. To Gavin. She found herself thinking of what he might be like under other circumstances, free and laughing.

What would he like? she wondered, trying to imagine what other sixteen-year-old guys liked. Girls, maybe, she thought. Yes, definitely girls. And holovideos. Of girls, she thought, and smiled. God, he's sixteen years old, and he's never known what it's like to be a teenager, to spend time with other teenagers. This can't go on. I can't let him—let us—stay trapped with that bastard any longer. It's got to stop! Maybe Lazarus could—

"Sable," Lazarus said, snapping her back from her thoughts. He had stopped fiddling with his own gauntlet for a moment and was looking at her intently.

She blinked, looking at him. "What?"

"Are you all right?" he asked.

"Yeah. Why?"

"You just seem to be off somewhere else. I called your name three times before you answered."

She looked down at her hands. "I'm fine. I was . . . I was thinking about my brother."

"Oh. Are you going to be able to finish?" he asked. She could see the worry in his eyes.

She nodded, not saying anything.

"Are you sure?"

"Yes. I'll be fine."

"Listen. You watch yourself," he said. She nodded to him and tried to smile. "I mean it," he went on. "If they catch you in here, you're dead."

"I know," she said quietly. "So you watch out for me, too."

"Damn it, I wish I were doing this instead of you."

"Lazarus, you know you're better at piloting than I am. Just keep watch for me. I'll be fine."

He looked at her a moment longer, and she saw that other look in his eyes, the one that made her think he was about to try to kiss her.

She pulled away before he decided to actually follow through and moved over to the door. "Let's do this," she said to get them both back to the business at hand, her heart beating rapidly in her chest once more. This time, though, it wasn't because she was thinking about trying to break into a major crime family's fortified headquarters. She was thinking about Lazarus kissing her. And she was starting to like the thought.

"All right," Lazarus said, and turned back to the console in front of him. "I'm into the system. Christ, this is locked down tight. Lots of secondary check systems in place. You'd think they were expecting someone to try to break in." He chuckled at his own joke. "You go slow and steady for me, okay?"

"All right. Tell me when I can slip out."

"Give me one more second. . . . Just about . . . got it . . . there! Okay, you should hear a click in about three seconds. That's the magnetic lock to this room shutting off."

Sure enough, a moment later, there was a faint click from the door, and Sable saw a light on the panel beside it shift from red to green.

"I've hacked into the security cameras, and I've got them set on a looped feedback. I'm about to shut down the various motion and heat detectors along your path. The system automatically does a self-diagnostic and resets every ten minutes, though, so you can't dawdle. Got it?"

"Roger."

"I've also set up a secondary frequency we can use inside their jamming range. Turn your comm unit on," he said, and gave her a new frequency to use.

When she had the comm unit set up, she moved next to the door. "Say when." Sable stood at the ready, her hand on the door handle.

"Go," Lazarus ordered, and Sable swallowed.

This is it, she thought. Don't think, move.

She stabbed at the button next to the door, and it slid silently open. Crouching, she padded through it into a hallway that ran straight ahead for about ten meters to a second door, this one transparent. Beyond that was a hallway that ran perpendicular to both sides. On the other side was a security station. Sable could see the bioelectrical scanner.

"Lazarus, are you gonna be able to get me back through this second door?" Sable whispered through the comm.

"As long as we don't set off any alarms," he answered.

"And if we do?"

"Then you're gonna wish you had that laser cutter with you."

"Then let's make sure I don't set off any alarms," she said, moving to the door. Taking a deep breath, she tapped the switch next to the door and padded through, peering down the hallway in both directions. She stepped out into the hallway, and the door slid shut softly behind her. Sable tapped a couple of keys on her gauntlet, pulling up a map of the place on the passive display screen. She knew the route by heart, but she wasn't taking any chances.

Sable turned to her right and began moving down the corridor, which was lit by soft indirect lighting. She saw the video cameras positioned at regular intervals, monitoring the hallway in both directions.

Fourth door on the left is the stairs, she reminded herself, and moved cautiously along, counting. When she reached the door she wanted, she stepped close to it, and it slid open. Beyond was a landing with stairs heading up.

"Laz, I'm at the bottom of the stairs," she whispered.

"Roger," he replied. "Hold up for a moment when you get to the top. There's someone in the hallway up there."

Sable froze, waiting for the inevitable warning from Lazarus that whoever this was had decided to take these very stairs down—right where she was. She got ready to run. A moment later, though, Lazarus gave her the all-clear.

"All right. Looked like a security guard. He's gone now. Get going. You've got seven minutes."

Sable climbed the stairs and got to the door at the top. She let it slide open and sneaked a quick peek out into another hallway that seemed almost identical to the one below. Once she was satisfied that there was no one hiding outside of camera view, she moved into the open and turned to her left.

Two doors on the right, she remembered, then a hallway to the datacore. Go past that to the next door. She followed her memorized instructions, consulting the map to gauge the distances.

She was almost to the hallway when Lazarus hissed, "Damn! Sable, hold it! Two security guards just came out of the datacore door! They're coming up the hallway toward you!"

Sable shrank against the wall and pulled the hood of her stealth suit over her head. It fit snugly. Then she yanked her knife out of her boot. She didn't dare respond to Lazarus for fear of the two guards' overhearing her.

She was just about to turn and flee back the way she

came, when Lazarus said, "Wait. They're heading back inside. One of them said he forgot something. Get across to the other side, right now."

Sable inched toward the corner of the intersection and peered cautiously around it. At the far end of the hall, she could see two men, their backs to her, standing in front of another clear door like the one at the entrance to the generator room. One of them held up a hand to the scanner and the door slid open. She waited until they had passed through and the door shut behind them. Then she darted across to the other side. She could feel the sweat trickling down her back, and she was trembling.

"Get me out of this hall, Laz!" she hissed into her comm.

"Hang on. I'm going to pop the lock on that door right now. Just give me a sec."

Sable swallowed and stole another glance around the corner. There was no sign of the two guards. They had passed through a second door and out of sight—for the time being.

"Laz," she whispered fiercely.

"Damned thing has a continuously randomizing check digit—hang on a sec. . . ."

"I don't *have* a sec. They're going to be coming *back* in a sec. Come on!"

"Hang on. . . ."

Sable crouched and took another peek. The two guards were on the other side of the transparent door, approaching it. They were laughing and obviously not paying any attention to anything more than two meters in front of them, but Sable jerked her head back nonetheless.

"Right now, Lazarus!" she whispered again, emphasizing his full name to drive home the urgency she felt. "They're coming back!"

"All right, Sable . . . almost . . . there . . ."

Sable could hear the two of them now. One was talking as the other one chuckled. They were getting closer. She inched back away from the intersection and hovered right next to the door.

"Just about got it . . . get ready."

I couldn't be more ready, Sable thought, the hand that held her knife shaking.

"Okay! Go!" Lazarus said, just as Sable heard a faint click and the door slid open.

She lunged through into semidarkness and stabbed at the panel on the inside wall. The door slid shut behind her. She collapsed in a heap, her breathing ragged. She waited, listening, but there was no sound of pursuit. A faint glow permeated the room above her, cycling through the colors of the spectrum in steady succession. She looked up to see a small holoprojector on one wall, displaying an abstract three-dimensional animated art print.

After a moment, Lazarus said, "Okay, they're gone. They turned the other way. You all right?"

"No," Sable answered, still shaking. "I just aged twenty years. How much time?"

"Um, three minutes and forty-five seconds. You've got to get moving."

"On my way," she replied and pulled herself to her feet. She sheathed the knife and pulled out her flashlight. Flipping it on, she surveyed the room. It was a small office; the desk was cluttered with data crystals, papers, and a handful of dataslates. On one wall was a large shelf filled with more of the data crystals.

Sable ignored all of this as she peered at the ceiling of the place. She found what she was looking for easily, a grate covering a ventilation shaft. It looked a little smaller than she had expected.

How the hell am I going to squeeze through that? she wondered.

Shrugging, she moved over beside the desk and tested it to see if she could move it. It slid across the thick carpeting with only slight resistance, so she shoved it over beneath the vent and hopped on top. Thrusting her flashlight into her mouth, she grabbed a power screwdriver from her tools and reached up to take out the grill. She removed each of the screws, the screwdriver making a soft whining sound in the near darkness. When she had the last one out, she gently lowered the grill to the desk and shone her flashlight up inside.

"Time?" she asked softly.

"Two minutes, thirty seconds," Lazarus responded. "How's it going?"

"I'm climbing into the shaft right now. Hang on," she said, working rapidly.

Sable pulled one last tool off her belt, a rod that was about five centimeters in diameter and about thirty-five centimeters long. Grasping it at both ends, she began to pull, and the telescoping rod expanded into a thin but stable collapsible ladder. Small steps flipped down, alternating from side to side, as the tubing expanded.

When she had completely opened the thing, it stood about three meters tall. She attached two small coupling devices, which had the same adhesive as her pitons, to the ends, and then planted the thick end firmly to the top of the desk, with the other rising straight up into the vent. She attached the second coupling to the wall of the vent shaft and tested the ladder's stability. It wobbled and flexed slightly, but she knew it would hold.

Sable began to climb up toward the ceiling. When she reached the opening of the vent, she carefully began to snake her arms into the hole, using only her knees to keep her balance on the ladder. She pushed up through the opening into a larger duct, sliding onto her belly as she scrambled completely into the ventilation system. Within the duct, she could rise up on her elbows and knees, but turning around would be a trick.

Better hope you don't have to backtrack, girl, she thought, and began to push her way forward.

"Laz, I'm in the vent, moving toward the datacore. How much time, and do you have the laser barrier down yet?"

"One minute, thirty seconds, and I'm working on it. I should be done by the time you get there. If you hurry."

Sable pushed ahead, trying to move quickly yet quietly at the same time. It was going to be close. She passed several side ducts but continued to follow the straight route, heading directly toward the large room where the main computer datacore was housed.

"Sable, I've got the grid down, but you'd better hurry. You've got one minute left."

Sable growled in frustration and pushed herself harder, worming her way through the duct, trying to keep a steady pace. It was hard, only being able to raise part of the way up on her hands and knees.

"Time, Laz," she said, sliding along.

"Thirty-seven seconds."

She could see the end now, could see the light shining up through the grate. About three meters on this side of it, she could see the laser barrier array. She continued crawling, praying she wasn't making enough noise to be heard down below, in the room.

"Twenty seconds, Sable. How close?"

"About ten meters."

"Fifteen seconds."

She shoved with her feet, crawling with her hands. Six meters . . . almost there.

"Ten seconds."

Two more meters.

"Five seconds. Come on, tell me you're there."

Sable crossed the laser array threshold and continued, dragging her legs up under her.

"Zero. Are you through?"

Sable collapsed, breathing hard. She turned her head back slightly, peering over her shoulder, and she was just able to make out the laser array, generating a crisscross pattern of faint red light. Her toes were about two centimeters from it.

"Sable? Talk to me. Are you through?"

"Yes," she whispered, her breathing ragged. "I'm past it. Now for the home stretch."

She stretched forward and began to crawl toward the opening in the floor of the duct. It was only a couple of meters in front of her now. Just beyond it, the duct turned a corner.

As Sable peered over the edge to see into the room below, a small hovering metal globe about half a meter in diameter drifted around the corner. Sable gasped and jerked backward as the floating robotic thing approached her, a camera lens focused directly on her. A small laser beam was also marking her squarely in the forehead, and she could now see the barrel of a small weapon mounted just below the camera lens.

A strangely melodic voice reverberated from the comm unit in her ear. "This is a rather strange place for you to be, young lady. Don't move, or I will kill you. Now, just what do you think you're doing, crawling around in my vent system?"

09.0:

A T FIRST LAZARUS couldn't figure out what had happened. One minute he was piloting through the Gibson-Williams Multimedia isolated Grid, paving the way for Sable to get inside, and the next, he had been locked out. It didn't make any sense. He thought perhaps that he had missed something when the system had run its self-diagnostics, so he began to go back over his links, trying to see if he had omitted a step. But he couldn't even do that; he had been completely locked out. Then suddenly a huge shadowy figure loomed into his virtual field of view from nowhere, appearing on the Grid as a security officer for GWM. When it spoke, its voice cutting in on the comm transmission, he knew.

"Oh, damn, Sable. It's an artificial intelligence." Christ! An AI! She's hung out to dry! I've got to get her out of there!

Desperately he backpedaled, pulling up some defense code as he did so, trying to ward off the imminent attack. Strangely, it didn't come.

"Call me by my name," the digital image of the guard snapped at Lazarus. "I'm Diva."

The figure swirled and coalesced and then was suddenly transformed into a beautiful human woman. It was strange, but Lazarus thought she looked familiar.

"Lazarus," Sable's disembodied voice called out through the comm. "What the hell am I supposed to do here?"

"You're supposed to answer my question," Diva said. "I've been watching you two since you got into the generator room. I want to know why you're trying to get into my datacore. And make it good; I hate lame lies."

Damn, we've been tricked from the start! Lazarus worked furiously, calling up an attack program and readying it for when an opportunity presented itself.

Yeah, fat lot of good this is going to do. I didn't bring the right kind of code to deal with an AI.

"Diva," Lazarus heard Sable say, "I just came here to get some information. I'm no threat to you."

That's it, Sable. Keep that thing occupied. Keep talking while I—

"All right, Lazarus, or whoever you are, I see you setting up your arsenal," the woman representing the AI's Grid shadow said. "Cut it out, or your accomplice winds up as a bloody smear in the vent system."

Lazarus froze.

Bloody smear? What kind of AI talks like that?

The image of the beautiful woman had transformed again, and now a tough-looking street punk image was standing opposite Lazarus's Grid shadow. Around the two of them, the scenery changed. Suddenly, instead of a junction node, Lazarus found himself standing on a seedy street out in the casino district. The voice had changed, too. He blinked, doing a virtual double take. He knew this figure.

"Michael Thunder?" he said, a little dazed.

"Yeah, well, it seemed appropriate. Besides, I'm not kidding around. Stop messing with that blackware you're trying to program to attack me with, or I'll plant a flechette round between Sable's eyes."

"Lazarus, what the hell are you talking about?" Sable asked nervously, her voice distant in the comm unit. "Who the hell is Michael Thunder?"

Lazarus paused in the midst of prepping the blackware. It's a shame, too, he thought. I might have been able to crack

that wall. "Michael Thunder is a holovideo action character," Lazarus answered Sable. He found it strangely amusing
to speak remotely through the comm unit to Sable, who was
crawling through the ductwork in the center of GWM, while
his senses were immersed in a virtual reality that looked like
a back alley in Port Royal, facing off against Michael Thunder, holovideo star. "Diva and I are just getting to know each
other a little better here in the Grid."

"Holovideo? Laz, there's a *thing* staring me in the face,
and it has a laser-targeted gun pointing at my brains. Do
something, please!"

A thing? In the vent duct? Lazarus was a little surprised.
Then he chuckled. That's exactly where we thought we
could sneak in. Very clever.

"Diva," Lazarus said calmly, "I've never met a security AI
that was a talk-first kind of gal. What's your game?"

"Oh, nothing really. Just bored. They've got me locked
down so tight that I don't get the chance to interact with too
many people outside the building. When I saw you two, I
decided to just watch for a while and see what sorts of interesting things you were up to." The image returned to that of
the beautiful woman, and this time Lazarus remembered
where he had seen her before. She was one of the most popular live entertainment acts around right now. He couldn't
remember her name, but it was beginning to make some
sense now.

Gibson-Williams had massive amounts of data saved on
their various entertainment ventures. Recordings of every
conceivable type must be stored in the datacore, and Diva
was merely drawing on some of that to add to her own personality. She was like a holovideo junky, always quoting
stuff she'd seen broadcast.

"So have you been entertained so far?" Lazarus asked,
hoping his tack would pique the AI's interest.

"Well, so far it hasn't been much more than some sneaking around. I was thinking of raising the alarm so I could watch a nice shoot-out."

"Oh, that's such a cliché, Diva," Lazarus said, swallowing nervously. "Besides, Sable isn't carrying a gun."

"True on both counts. Besides, I think I've seen you two before. Still trying to figure that one out. Sable, take your hood off. I want to take a good look at your face."

What the—? Seen us before?

"Laz, whatever you're going to do, please do it *now!*" Sable growled into the comm. He could tell she was on the verge of panicking.

"Sable, calm down. Do what Diva asks. Pull your hood off."

"All right. Hang on."

There was a brief pause, and then Diva exclaimed, "Yes. I knew it. The casino chase scene. I thought I recognized you two."

Casino chase scene? Suddenly Lazarus understood. Diva had a recording of the incident at the Double Star. Probably the security camera footage. But how did she come across it? She's locked down from outside connections. Unless they brought it in manually . . . That's it! The Double Star must be run by the Mateos. That's some piece of bad luck, he thought wryly. Or is it? He suddenly had an idea. He only prayed Sable would figure out what he was up to and play along.

"Oh, yes, Diva," Lazarus said. "That was part of our pilot episode. Did you like it?"

"Actually, yes, although I don't like the two-dimensional imagery," the AI replied. "Your ratings are going to suck unless you shoot in full three-D."

"Our pilot episode?" Sable cut in. "Laz, what the hell are—"

"I told you that was only a test shoot, Sable," Lazarus cut

her off. "You remember, for the new show they want us to do? The one Gibson-Williams is considering producing? With you as the star?"

Come on, Sable, think! Figure it out!

"You're going to be a star?" Diva said excitedly. "I haven't seen you in anything before. What's the name of the show?"

There was a long, drawn-out pause, and then Sable replied, "Uh, well, yeah. Actually, we haven't decided yet. On the name, I mean. They were thinking of calling it Shadow Knights, but that's just the working title right now."

Oh, good girl, Sable. That was perfect!

"Right. And this is part of the show, too," Lazarus added before Sable could continue. "They wanted to try out some new stunts for an upcoming episode, but they didn't want to build a whole new set just for a trial run. So the producers suggested we use the GWM building instead. That's why we're here tonight."

"Yeah," Sable added. "We're supposed to sneak into a facility and steal some data crystals from the central vault. That's why we're crawling around in your vent ducts."

"Really? No one mentioned any of this to me," Diva said a little doubtfully.

"Well, they wanted to make it as realistic as possible," Lazarus added, trying to sound upbeat, "so they didn't tell anyone about it. The security people don't know either. But I suspect they might even want to include an AI in the script. You could be in the episode, Diva." He wondered if this was working.

At least Sable had caught on.

"Do you really think so?" Diva asked. "Do you think they'd write me into the script?"

"Well, it only makes sense," Sable answered. "Since we bumped into you tonight, they're going to have to account for it in the story somehow."

"Listen, Diva, we'll mention this to the writers when we finish up here," Lazarus added. "But right now we need to complete the test. Do you think we could go ahead and let Sable get into that vault? The executives planted some mock data crystals in there, filed away with all the real ones. Sable just needs to get in for a moment, find the fake ones, and get out again."

"Well, I suppose, but the writers are going to have to find a way to work this out," Diva said importantly. "It's pretty difficult to sneak past my defense system."

"Oh, sure," Lazarus said. "You're absolutely right. But that's why we did the trial run this way. So they could work out the bugs in the story."

"Yeah," Sable added. "If they're going to write an AI into the script, they're going to have to figure out a good way to work that out. Maybe we should have the writers come talk to you later so you can give them some suggestions. You know, some pointers."

"Yes, that's a good idea," Diva responded excitedly. "I'd like that. All right, you can finish your test run."

"Thanks, Diva," Lazarus said, breathing a big sigh of relief. "You're a peach."

"Oh, I'll bet you say that to all the girls," Diva replied, and the figure in front of him was gone, leaving Lazarus's shadow standing by himself at the entrance to the security control center.

No, only the ones who live in a fantasy world, Lazarus thought as he proceeded to enter the system once again.

* * * * *

Still sitting in the duct, listening to Lazarus lie to the AI over her comm unit, Sable watched as the floating orb, its unblinking camera lens still facing her and the laser sight still centered on her forehead, drifted backward slowly. It disappeared around the bend in the duct, and when it was gone, Sable collapsed, burying her face in her arms and trembling. Her nerves were completely frazzled, and she wanted to cry.

"Sable, are you ready to finish?" Lazarus's voice asked quietly through the comm unit.

"No," she answered, trying to keep her voice steady. "I just spent the last five minutes hoping a little robot wouldn't blow my head off!"

"I know. I'm sorry. But you've got to move. It's going to be morning soon, and then this place will be crawling with people."

Sable sighed and straightened up again. "All right," she said, inching toward the grill once again. "I'm okay."

"Good girl. Where are you now?"

"I'm at the grate leading into the datacore room. Hang on," she said. She peered down through the grill, trying to get a good look around. "I can see the floor and the door, a bit back the way I came. It looks like there are several large cabinets in front of me, but it's hard to tell for sure."

"Those would be the databanks. It sounds like you're in the right place. You ready to go in?"

"Yeah. Let me get the grill off," she answered, beginning to examine the grating closely. "This is going to take a few minutes." She pulled out her power screwdriver and attached a special U-shaped adapter to it. It was a hollow tube that had a flexible shaft inside, allowing the motor to turn the bit, even though the bit was aimed backward from its normal direction. Sable carefully slid the adapter through a hole in the grill. Manipulating the device, she was able to hold the screwdriver pointing down so that the length of the adapter descended down through the hole and then made a U-turn out away from the center of the grill toward the edge, angled back up, and pointed directly toward the screw head, which was facing down toward the room beneath Sable. Sable seated the bit in the screw, and then pulled up on the screwdriver so it pulled the head tight against the screw. She held down the switch, and the tiny motor whined as the flanges of the screwdriver bit caught in the head of the screw and loosened it.

Sable removed all of the screws from the grill and pushed it free, holding on to it so that it wouldn't fall to the floor below. Then she turned it sideways and pulled it up beside her and set it aside. She lowered herself down through the hole and peered around upside down, getting a better look at the place.

The room was large. Dominating about two-thirds of it were several rows of cabinets, the datacore array for Diva. Along one wall was an access station, similar to the one that Lazarus had been operating from in the generator room. The only difference, Sable knew, was that this one was a direct line to the core operating system of the entire security system.

I wasn't expecting to have to monkey around with the operating system of a damned AI, Sable thought dismally. *I hope I can finish this before Diva figures out what we're doing.*

Sable took out the last of her pitons and the lone coil of rope that she had brought with her. She planted the piton against the metal ceiling of the duct, its adhesive making it stick tight, and then she tied the rope to it, dropping the rest down through the opening. She pushed across to the other side of the hole, still on her belly, so she could go feetfirst, and dropped her legs through. Slowly she began to inch her way backward, feeling her feet hanging in space.

Don't lose your grip, girl, she told herself as she continued, more and more of her body weight moving past the balance point. When she was clinging with just her arms, the edge of the duct opening at her armpits, she reached out and grabbed the rope and began to slide. Once she was clear of the opening, she easily slid the rest of the way down to the floor.

The hard part is going to be climbing back up, she thought, still feeling the soreness in her shoulder from Lazarus's grabbing her during her fall in the tunnel.

She turned and headed directly toward the access station, looking for a port to plug her Gridcaster in to. She found it right away and jacked in. Flipping a couple of switches, she immediately entered into the Grid, luxuriating for a moment in the black void. Then the connection was complete, and she was in a virtual room that looked identical to the real one, except that where the datacore cabinets would have been, normal filing cabinets existed instead. The walls were lined with an additional array of readouts and switches.

Sable's shadow rose from the virtual desk and began to scan the room, looking for the key features she needed to get to quickly, before Diva figured out their lie.

Gotta make this count, she thought, and spotted the alarm system override. There's that . . . now, where's the watchdog command panel?

She let her virtual gaze wander over the place until she found it. Then, taking a deep breath, she slapped at the alarm override, silencing it. She darted forward to the watchdog panel and shut it down just as a figure materialized in the corner near her. It was a beautiful woman, one that Sable vaguely remembered seeing on a holovideo program recently.

Ah, Sable thought grimly. Laz's new girlfriend.

"What the hell are you doing?" Diva asked, her voice filled with suspicion. "You never said anything about shutting off vital systems. What if a real break-in occurred? You lied to me, both of you. You're not part of any holovideo program. I'm calling—"

Sable didn't wait for Diva to finish her speech, activating her defense measures and then wading in to attack the Grid shadow standing before her.

In one smooth motion, her own shadow had the sword out of the sheath at her back and was going through the standard forms—the program's way of running the diagnostic code. Diva shimmered and transformed into a street punk, glistening with chrome and obviously cybered to the max. A pair of thin blades appeared in each hand. The two began to circle one another, watching for an opening to attack. Sable was careful to keep herself from straying too far from the alarm or the watchdog panels. If Diva was able to lunge over and activate either one, there would be hell to pay.

Suddenly the punk figure launched itself forward in a graceful flurry of rapid attacks at Sable, who gasped and took a step back, bringing her own defenses up in the nick of time.

Desperately parrying each stroke and thrust, Sable thought, I've never fought anything so damned *fast!* It took her complete concentration to maintain her position and not let Diva's Grid shadow get inside her own shadow's defenses. Twice the other shadow moved in, and each time Sable had to work at a feverish level to keep the blade-code away from her own shadow.

"Sable, what's happening? Give me an update." Sable jumped at the sound of Lazarus's voice, and Diva nearly got inside her defenses. But Sable was getting more used to the speed of the fight now, and she turned gracefully, moving out of the way and executing her own attack. She pushed

Diva back a few steps and then dropped back into a defensive crouch before answering.

"Can't talk right now, Laz," she said, eyeing the other shadow warily. "Got a little business to take care of."

"You're going down," the punk said, changing suddenly into a battle-armored trooper with a heavy weapon, aimed right at Sable.

Sable hissed through her teeth and leaped to the side, barely dodging the blast from the weapon. Behind her, there was a brilliant flash, and she heard a loud pop in her feed, but she didn't have time to turn around to see what Diva, in soldier form, had demolished on the command panel. Launching herself into a full roll, Sable concentrated on staying out of the line of fire of the big gun. Several times Diva fired, and each time, Sable barely ducked out of the way.

"Damn it, Sable, what's going on?"

"Shut up, Laz! I can't concentrate!" she screamed back, leaping into the air and kicking out at the barrel of the weapon. The gun went off again, aimed right at one of the datacore cabinets. There was another bright flash, and the whole virtual chamber flickered.

Stupid nutcase is wiping out her own code trying to kill me, Sable thought. Well, fine. I can use that.

Sable began to dance about, trying as often as possible to keep herself positioned between the virtual soldier and what she hoped were representations of the storage facilities for Diva's sensitive operating code, trying to anticipate when the shadow would fire the weapon and duck out of the way at the last moment. It was working. Each time Diva fired, the shot slammed into vital code storage and sent electrical surges through the crystal array and frying circuits.

Diva quickly figured out what was happening. "I know your game," she said, "Don't think you can beat me like that." In an instant, the soldier shadow was replaced by not one but three forms, all alike, all ancient samurai holding blades similar to Sable's own.

Sable dived away as the shadows closed in on her, each of them moving through martial arts forms similar to the ones her own shadow had used when she booted up. Still, Sable noticed a difference. The images seemed to flicker and jerk more than they should. The core was definitely damaged.

As two of the shadows continued to advance steadily toward her, the third one moved away, and Sable realized that it was headed toward the controls for the alarm and the watchdogs, the silver spherical probes like the one that had intercepted her in the vent duct. She feinted an attack in one direction and then lunged in another, launching herself over the cabinet that stood between her and the control panels. The third shadow reacted instantly, leaping forward, trying to get to the control panels before she got to them, but running three shadows at the same time was draining Diva's resources, and Sable was just a little faster. With one deft stroke of her digital sword, Sable cleaved the shadow in half and watched as it appeared to vaporize, a million tiny pixels of light flashing and fanning out in every conceivable direction and winking out a moment later until nothing remained.

Sable didn't waste time admiring her handiwork. She spun and crouched, barely fending off a blow from one of the two remaining shadows. The two samurai parted, sliding to each side of her, and she saw their tactic immediately. She couldn't face both of them at the same time. She waited and watched, staying in a crouch, as the pair of shadows circled her warily.

Suddenly a particularly bad electronic flicker hit the shadows, and Sable reacted. She kicked low at one of the shadows, and then quickly spun and swung behind her at the other one.

The first shadow avoided her kick, but the second one didn't react quite fast enough, and the blade caught it. The blow didn't cut it in half as it had before, but she knew she had corrupted enough of the code that the shadow wasn't long for the Grid. It staggered backward, streamers of light pouring out of a long cut across its midsection. The flickering intensified until it winked out suddenly, without fanfare. Diva had killed the program.

Sable spun to face the lone remaining shadow, but to her horror, she saw that it had reached the alarm system and was on the verge of pulling the switch.

"No!" she yelled and launched herself across the space between them, but it was too late. Somewhere outside herself, she heard the alarm begin to wail, even as her sword swiped through the shadow and split it in half.

"Shutting down secondary systems for self-preservation," Diva's voice echoed through the Grid. Sable noted absently that it was missing its former personality.

She's withdrawing, going into a pure self-preservation mode, Sable thought. Trying to keep me from wiping out her whole memory bank.

Sable considered if she should go ahead and kill the AI, thereby erasing the evidence of her invasion, but there was a part of her that actually felt some small amount of regret at the thought. Diva was really nothing more than a lonely intelligence, trapped in an isolated Grid system with no one to talk to and only old holovideo programs to entertain her. Even though one part of herself considered it silly, Sable felt that destroying the AI seemed in some way cruel.

"Sable," Lazarus's voice cut in, "I don't know what the hell you're up to right now, but I'm telling you we are out of time. The alarms are going off all over the place, and the security lights have all come up. I'm going to try to pull up the security cameras again. Whatever you're doing, do it fast and get out of there."

"Laz, I hurt Diva. Badly enough that she shouldn't be a problem for the rest of the evening. But she got to the alarms before I could stop her."

"Damn. Well, nothing we can do about that now. Just get the data and get out of there."

"Roger," Sable said. She turned to the array of data storage cabinets that filled the center of the virtual room. "Although I have no idea what I'm looking for."

"Start with HansCorp and go from there. Just hurry!"

Sable mentally ordered up a menu catalog system and input her request. The system began a search for files related to what she wanted, although the flicker was growing worse. She was worried that perhaps she had damaged enough of the system that all the data would be lost. If that was the case, the whole trip would be for nothing.

Maybe letting Diva blow herself up wasn't such a good idea after all, she thought. I wonder if the Mateo family keeps backups of its records anywhere?

At that moment, the search engine came back to her with a listing of files that were related to HansCorp Freight. She scanned through them and saw that they were all located in the same sector of storage. She called it up globally and began to download the stuff.

No time to look at it now, she told herself. Just get it all and figure it out later.

She filled the better part of two datacrystals plugged into her gauntlet with the data. When she was done, she did a quick sortable scan on key words just to see what came up. Most of it was junk, information about bank accounts and types of weapons, but one name popped up that made her catch her breath.

MicroCore Investments, a wholly owned subsidiary of

Yonce Enterprises; Minister Relitalia Yonce, primary stockholder.

Jesus, Sable thought. What the hell is a Concord Minister doing with the Mateos?

"Sable, it's time to go *now!* Move it!"

"I'm on my way. Screw the vents. I'm going through the doors. And, Laz?"

"Yeah?"

"You're never going to believe what I found. Never in a million years."

Lazarus laughed at the other end. "Fine. Surprise me later. Just get out of there."

Sable jacked out of Diva's Grid and blinked. The alarm was intense, piercing. Tucking away the cables for her gauntlet, she moved toward the door. She pulled her hood up over her face again and drew the knife from its sheath in her boot.

"Hey, Laz. Did you get back into the cameras?"

"Somewhat. I can't seem to stabilize any of the connections. There's flickering all over the place. But I can try to walk you out of there."

"Then let's go. I'm at the main door to the datacore. What's waiting for me on the other side?'

"Hang on . . . looks clear. Go, but move it, because it looks like there's a whole group of uglies making their way toward you even as we speak."

Sable didn't wait for Lazarus to finish before she was tapping the switch beside the door and slipping through it as it slid open. She hustled up to the clear door a few meters farther down the hall and tapped the switch there. Nothing happened. She hit it again. Still nothing.

"Laz. The second door's stuck shut. What can you do?" she said into the comm.

"Hang on," he sighed. "The system is really fouled up."

Sable moved nervously from foot to foot, fingering her knife and waiting for Lazarus to get the door open, fretting that security goons would turn the corner and see her there at any moment. She tried tapping the switch a couple more times, but still nothing happened.

"Come on, Laz!" she said, the panic rising. "Get me out of here!"

"I'm working on it. Just calm down."

"Look, you're not the one stuck in here. Hurry up!"

Suddenly the door slid open about halfway and stopped. Sable darted through the opening as fast as she could and took off. She ran down the hall to the intersection, cutting to her left and continuing without bothering to check for guards, headed toward the stairwell. There was a shout from behind her. She whipped her head around and saw two security guards. One was raising a pistol, aiming it at her, while the other one seemed to be speaking into a comm unit. Both of them were running directly toward her.

Sable took off, running as fast as she could, darting back and forth to make herself a more difficult target. She heard a shot and flinched as the wall next to her exploded in shards of plastic. She was about halfway to the door to the stairs now, but four more guards came into view around a corner from the other direction. Sable skidded to a stop as two of them raised pistols and took a bead on her.

"Laz, I'm cut off! Help me!"

"Damn it! The system is so screwed up, I can't get it to do anything. I've lost the cameras again."

"Don't move!" one of the guards behind her said.

Sable looked back over her shoulder and saw the pair of them closing the distance cautiously, both aiming pistols at her now. In front of her, the four new thugs were also closing the distance. She was trapped in the hallway. There was no way to get to the stairs.

"She sank down to the floor, leaning against the wall. "I can't get to you, Laz," she said, starting to lose it. "They've got me."

"No! I'm getting you out of there!"

"It's too late," Sable whispered, her voice choking as the guards arrived. Six pistols were leveled at her point-blank. She let the knife slip from her hand and went limp.

10.0:

"DON'T MOVE," ONE of the guards said, squatting near her so that his face was up in Sable's. "Who the hell are you, and how did you get in here?" he asked, pressing the barrel of his weapon against her cheek.

Sable looked at the guy squarely but remained silent. One of the men kicked the dropped knife aside as another holstered his weapon and reached down, grabbing her roughly by the shoulder and lifting her to her feet. He yanked her gauntlet and comm off her and spun her around, slamming her against the wall. She grunted as she hit, the wind knocked out of her. She felt her arms yanked behind her. Then security binders were snapped on her wrists. The guard spun her around again and shoved her forward. She stumbled and fell, unable to catch herself. She heard one of them laugh, and then she felt a hard kick in the ribs. She grunted in pain and gasped, curling up into a ball.

A second kick hit her in the kidneys, and she cried out. Then hands were grabbing her again, lifting her to her feet, cuffing her face and head. She felt several hands groping her, patting her down to look for weapons. She stayed limp. Spots swam in her vision from the blows.

A fist slammed into her stomach, and she doubled over, gagging, but she was forced up again, and they began to march her along the hall, her feet dragging. She felt as if she were going to throw up.

Suddenly her mind drifted to another time and place. She was far away, with Ana, her cruel teacher. Ana kicked her as she lay on the mat, screaming at her.

"You're weak! You're nothing, worthless!"

Sable whimpered.

Ana grabbed her hair and pulled her roughly to her feet. "Defend yourself!" she screamed at Sable, and Sable tried to assume a stance, but all she wanted to do was double over.

"P-please stop hitting me," Sable begged the woman, but in a flash, Ana spun, snapping her foot up and raking her heel across Sable's chin. The blow knocked her halfway across the mat.

Sable's vision swam, and she was back in the present, stumbling along with her six-guard escort, trying to stay on her feet as they shoved her along. She stumbled and fell again. "Please, stop," she begged breathlessly, the two visions of her life merging into one convoluted awareness. She heard several of them laugh cruelly, and she was yanked to her feet once more.

"Move it, before I decide to put a round through your head."

Once again Sable felt as if she were going to puke. Her stomach, ribs, and back ached where she had been kicked and punched. Her lip felt as if it were split, and one eye was swollen shut. She closed her other eye and thought of Gavin, saw his smiling face when they were young kids. In the park, chasing each other. She saw him dart into the bushes, trying to get away from her. Then her mother was calling them.

Suddenly the guard escort stopped. "What the hell is that?" one of them asked, and she felt him let go of her arm. She sagged downward, and the one holding her on the other side didn't seem interested in forcing her to stay on her feet.

Sable opened her good eye to see what the commotion was about and saw a spherical silver orb floating in the middle of the hallway, looking at the group of them. Floating wasn't exactly the right word, she realized. Hovering erratically was more accurate. The watchdog focused its laser sight on the chest of the lead security goon, bobbing up and down from time to time as it seemed to lose control.

"Why is it out here?" one guard asked.

"Who knows?" a second one answered. "The whole system is shot to hell tonight. She probably did it," he said, kicking her in the ribs with the side of his foot. It wasn't a hard blow, but she grunted nonetheless.

"There's another one," Sable heard as she curled up, dizzy from the pain radiating throughout her body.

"There's another one behind us. Should we shoot them?"

Sable tried to make her mind work through the haze of pain. She knew that this meant something, but she couldn't get it focused in her head. She groaned. Three watchdogs, hovering in the hallway nearby. Diva's watchdogs. Diva. It didn't make any sense. Why was the AI threatening the guards? It was her that Diva should be after. But she was already caught. She couldn't make it work out in her mind. She shook her head at the thought and groaned again when a fresh wave of pain shot through her skull.

The first shot seemed incredibly loud in her ears. At first she thought one of the guards had fired at a watchdog, but when a body collapsed on top of her, she knew one of the guards had gone down. She opened her good eye once more and witnessed a scene of total confusion. The five remaining guards were scrambling for cover, what little of it there was in the open hallway, as the watchdogs opened fire on them, popping high-pitched flechette rounds at the security goons.

Then there was a second loud shot, and this time Sable could tell it was coming from behind her, back down the hall in the direction they had come from. With some difficulty, she rolled over to see what was going on.

Lazarus! she saw, and her vision swam with spots.

He was crouched in the hallway, using a doorway for partial cover, a pistol in his hand. He aimed and squeezed off a shot, and the loud boom echoed through the hallway again. On the opposite side of the corridor from where she was sprawled out on the floor, a guard screamed and grabbed his shoulder in a splatter of blood, tumbling backward, the gun in his own hand skittering away. Lazarus was definitely not using his stutter pistol this time, Sable thought.

She had to close her eyes again, since trying to look around was making her nauseated. She remembered thinking that she ought to try to squirm down a little lower and take cover behind the dead guard lying across her feet, and then everything went black.

* * * * *

Sable's vision went from black to gray for a brief moment, but when she realized she was trying to open her eyes, she also became aware of the pounding pain behind them, and she stopped. She could tell she was moving, and after some consideration, she realized she was bouncing rather harshly in an odd position. She groaned as each bounce sent pain through her body, but she forced herself to open her eyes again to see what was happening.

She was draped across Lazarus's shoulder, being carried like a big sack. They were in the generator room, she realized. Lazarus had just passed through the door and shut it. He set Sable down gently on the floor and looked at her.

"You're awake," he commented, relief in his voice. "Hang on. I'm getting you out of here." He moved away to the computer console on the wall where he had been working before. His gauntlet was still there. Slipping it on his arm and sliding the shades into place, he tapped on the keypad for a couple of moments, and then removed the equipment and unplugged the jack from the console.

"I shut down everything. All the doors, everything. They're going to be at it for weeks, trying to get themselves out and everything running again."

Sable tried to smile, but the effort made her cheek hurt.

"Hang on, Sable. I'm taking you out of here right now." Lazarus bent down and gently picked her up, trying to get her to stand on her feet. "Can you walk at all?" he asked.

Sable groaned and shook her head.

"That's okay. I'll get Blue. He'll help me." He set her down again, and she slumped over on her side.

Somewhere in the back of her mind, Sable realized that she was no longer cuffed. She thought for a minute, making her brain work. It would be hard to raise Blue on the comm with the energy field up, unless he had actually managed to shut that down, too. She wondered how Lazarus had managed to get the remains of Diva under control enough to pull that off. Then she remembered the watchdogs. As she tried to contemplate their role in this, she blacked out again.

*   *   *   *   *

Sable briefly awoke a second time and found herself dangling in space. She groaned as she spun lazily, and then realized she was clipped by her web gear to the rope pulley, being conveyed across the shaft in the tunnel. Blue was on one side of the shaft and Lazarus on the other. She briefly wondered how Lazarus had managed to get her through the hatchway.

"Do you think they can get through the door?" Blue was asking as they moved her along.

"I don't think so, but that's not what I'm worried about. They may figure out how we got in and circle around to the club to try to cut us off. It all depends on if someone thinks to check schematics and so forth. If they can."

From that point on, Sable drifted in and out of consciousness periodically. She was aware of the passage of time, and later she could remember being in certain places from time to time, but she never really remembered much of the trip. Somehow, though, Lazarus and Blue managed to drag her through the tunnels and back into the club and beyond.

The next time Sable really came to, the three of them were in a small room that had been filled with various provisions. She was wrapped in a blanket, lying on the floor, and Lazarus was leaning over her, tending to her. He had a medical kit in his hand and was in the process of administering some drug. When he saw that she had opened her eyes—although one was still severely swollen—and she was looking at him, he smiled.

"Welcome back to the world of the living. How you doing?"

Sable merely grunted, still feeling groggy and definitely tired. "Sleepy," she finally said.

"Yeah, well, I gave you something to help you rest. It'll knock you out pretty good for a while, but it'll give my little friends, the wonder drugs here, time to work. You'll feel a lot better after some sleep."

Sable nodded and closed her eyes as Lazarus tucked the blanket around her more snugly. Then she opened them again.

"Laz," she said, fighting to stay awake.

"Yeah?"

"Thanks."

"No problem," he said, and began to gather up the discarded wrappers from the medkit.

Sable snaked one hand slowly out of her covers and reached for his. She took hold of it, stopping his work, and squeezed. "No, I mean it. Thanks for coming back for me. I didn't expect you to. If it had been the other way around . . . well, anyway, thanks."

Lazarus looked at her. "It was the only thing I could do. Besides the fact that you still had the crystals with the data on them, and besides the fact that I care deeply about you— might even say I was falling in love with you, if I was more foolish than normal—I couldn't have lived with myself if I had left you behind. So I did what I had to do. Now I want you to shut up and get some rest. We still need to get back to find out what's on those crystals."

Sable nodded again, drifting into sleep. But she smiled, feeling his hand tremble as she held it. He had said something she hadn't heard since her parents were alive. Or almost said it. But it was there, and strangely, it made her feel all the more warm and comfortable in her makeshift bed.

*   *   *   *   *

"My God," Lazarus muttered, staring at the display screen, "they've moved three times the weapons out of there that we suspected. It looks like they're outfitting an entire army!"

"Well, that should slow down for the time being, after what you two did to them last night," Director Stipelle remarked, looking over Lazarus's shoulder. "It will take them weeks to recover, and I imagine they've lost significant business records that they can't ever get back."

"Fine with me," Lazarus said dismissively. "I got what I wanted from them. But it's going to take me a little while to wade through all of this to figure out exactly how everything worked. I still can't believe that a Concord ambassador is behind this. One of the most prestigious and respected figures in all the Galactic Concord, buying weapons and supporting a terrorist group! Sable was right last night when she said I wouldn't believe it in a million years."

"Then don't."

Lazarus looked at Stipelle sharply. "What do you mean?"

"I mean, don't believe it. Don't just assume that it's the truth, just because it's in the records. Always consider other angles, other possibilities."

Lazarus nodded, troubled. He had been so eager to finally get his hands on this data that he'd neglected to do all the detective work. What Stipelle was saying made sense, certainly, but now he had to wonder just why the man was pointing all of this out right now.

"What makes you think that it isn't what it appears to be?" Lazarus asked.

"Nothing concrete, but look," Stipelle said, pointing. "This material Sable downloaded is in a handful of very carefully organized file folders. See here?" he tapped a couple of keystrokes and pointed again. "But you told me she did a massive retrieval, dumping large amounts of unsorted data onto those crystals from the datacore. You said yourself that things were crazy at the end. The alarms were going off, the system was crashing. Utter chaos. Right?"

Lazarus nodded, considering. "There's no way she would have taken the time to sort through all of that data and categorize it. But is that so strange? I mean, why wouldn't the Mateos keep meticulous records? Why wouldn't they have stored the information this way?"

"There's no reason they wouldn't, really, except that the information is supposedly produced by a wide variety of individuals. Look. In this folder, you've got shipment records under one name, while in this other folder, you've got inventory records prepared by someone else. Yet all of these, and other folders like them, are stored within this one common folder here, which was set up and maintained by yet *another* individual. Who stores their records in someone else's directories? Why would all these people be going into another person's files to save their own stuff?"

"I see what you're saying," Lazarus said, frowning. "But that could be explained easily enough by yet another person doing all of this archiving work. Perhaps the owner of the main folder gathers all of the material, sorts it by folder, and stores it like this."

Stipelle nodded. "Perhaps, but take a look at this." He made a few more keystrokes and produced a new screen of data. He pointed to a section and said, "All of those folders were created at random times throughout the last year or so. The main one was created two days ago."

"Strange . . ." Lazarus breathed.

Stipelle tapped the keypad again. "And these files are all fragmented slightly, as though they were saved, modified, and stored randomly, or over a long period of time. But these others, which all mention this holding company, MicroCore Investments, are neatly stored, with no fragmenting, and they are layered in the exact order of their dates."

"It was all manufactured and then planted where we would find it," Lazarus said, sitting back and shaking his head in amazement. "Very basic evidence of file tampering, and I didn't even bother to look for it." Lazarus felt like kicking himself. "Someone *wanted* us to get that data last night. We were meant to believe that MicroCore Investments is responsible for paying the Jamaican Syndicate to ship weapons to CFN cells throughout the Verge."

"Exactly. So I guess the question now is who—and why?"

"My first thought would be the Mateos themselves, but that just doesn't make sense," Lazarus said, thinking.

"True. If they wanted you to find all of this out, then why would they have sent a hit squad to take you out that day we brought you in? They could have let you get hold of the information without nearly so much hassle, or the loss of their agents. Not to mention the chance to avoid attracting Technospider attention."

"Or for that matter, having their facility broken into and their security system—their AI—ruined," Lazarus added.

"Right. So it wasn't the Mateos."

Lazarus considered. "It could be the true buyer. Perhaps they know they're being investigated and they're trying to throw me off the scent." He sighed. "But that seems like an awful lot of work just to preserve themselves. Why not just kill me?" He swallowed, not liking that image much at all.

"Maybe because they didn't know where to look for you."

Lazarus nodded, thinking. "Even then, if they wanted to kill me, they could have set up an ambush in GWM. No, they definitely wanted me to find this and act on it. I wish I had that crystal Germaine was going to hand over. It's really too bad he wasn't more cautious."

"What if his crystal had the same information on it?" Stipelle asked quietly.

Lazarus turned to look at him, confused. "I guess that would mean Germaine was in on it, too."

"Exactly," Stipelle said.

"But why would he be giving false data, meant for me, to someone looking to underbid the Mateos?"

"He wouldn't," Stipelle said. "But as we've already pointed out, someone wanted you to find that data. How would they even know you were planning to break in to GWM to get it unless they knew you had tried to get it once already from Germaine?"

"Hmm. Up to this point, I assumed that the only ones who knew we were trying to get the data were the Mateos themselves. But we already decided that they wouldn't have allowed themselves to suffer so much just to get it into my hands. So—"

"So," Stipelle interrupted, "it's a good bet that the crystal Germaine had did not simply contain the true names of the buyers. That's too much of a coincidence."

Lazarus nodded, not liking where this was leading. "Yes, it is."

"They wanted you to get the crystal from the start."

"They've been setting me up. Damn!" Lazarus growled, fuming. "They've been playing me for a patsy since the start. What the hell is going on?"

"You're still facing the same questions I asked earlier. Who and why?" Stipelle said, standing and stretching. "But I think you have a good idea of where to look for the answers now."

"Yes. Gillst, or whoever he really is," Lazarus said, considering. "Sable referred to him as Mr. Maxwell. But man, that's convoluted. If the whole delivery was a setup, meant to get this fake information into my hands, they would have had to expect me to go after Sable and to get her to cooperate. . . ." Lazarus trailed off, the impact of such a suggestion hitting him squarely. "Sable could be in on it. Why didn't I think of that earlier?" he said, pounding a fist into the palm of his other hand. "She's been playing me for a sucker, too. Damn!" he shouted, stalking across the room.

"Maybe," Stipelle said, "but she's pretty much a pawn in this, I think. She was in bad shape last night."

Lazarus stopped his pacing and looked at Stipelle. "I know. She's not doing it by choice. She's being coerced."

"You know this for a fact?"

"Yes," Lazarus said, nodding. "I'm absolutely certain. Don't ask me how; it's her story to tell. But trust me, I know."

"Well, there you go, then."

"Yes, but being forced to do the work doesn't change the fact that she could still be trying to hide her level of knowledge from me. She might have been told to lead me straight down this path from the start. Damn!"

Lazarus's stomach roiled. His palms were sweaty, and he couldn't stand still. He had to pace. After everything that had happened, the chaos of last night, after telling her how he felt, he found himself right back at the beginning, wondering if he should be trusting her at all.

If she's known about this all along, she's good, he told himself. She's really good. The question, though, is how much did she really know? There's only one way to find out, he decided.

"I guess there are some things I have to do now," Lazarus said to Stipelle. "I owe you a lot. All of you. But I have to get to the bottom of this."

"I understand." Stipelle crossed over and shook Lazarus's hand. "I'm sorry we can't do more to help you."

"You've done more than enough. The rest I have to do on my own."

"And the girl?"

"That depends on what she's about to tell me. If she's been playing me for the fool, it's over. I can't let her be involved any longer. If not . . ." Lazarus shrugged. "Either way, I'm taking her with me."

"Watch your back, then. The Mateos are most certainly looking for you two."

"I know. I will. Thanks. For everything."

Stipelle nodded and left the room, leaving Lazarus to his own thoughts once more. I have to talk to her, he thought. I have to know, once and for all. Damn it, Sable, why did you have to affect me like this?

Lazarus took a deep breath, which he found surprisingly difficult. He was trembling with nervousness, and his breath was shallow and rapid. He wasn't looking forward to what he was afraid he was going to hear.

* * * * *

On the *Lighthouse* Grid, a shadow arrived at the
entrance to a great hall, a data storage bank unrivaled by
any other within the Verge. The shadow passed through the
portal and moved efficiently and with purpose. The other
shadows within the place paid little notice to the conserva-
tively dressed image, their pilots busy as they were with
their own work.

The newly arrived shadow stepped up to the representation of a search interface node and began to access the menu
system. Scrolling through the choices, the shadow quickly
established a checklist of resources to consult and moved
off, heading to other address locations within the virtual hall
of records to refine its search for information.

At various selected resource collections, the shadow,
which in many ways looked like a certain Concord Investigative Bureau agent, interfaced with the hall's data
retrieval system, making requests based on the criteria it
had been given back in a small library in Port Royal on
Penates in the Lucullus System. It fed in the digitized
image of a young woman, along with her fingerprints, a
reliable scan of her bioelectrical signature, and other esti-
mated vital statistics.

The records system began combing through its vast collection of census information, weeding through countless
iterations of people whose facial structure resembled hers
by comparing the fingerprint and bioelectrical code. Eventually only a handful of choices remained, and the shadow
requested a cross-reference compilation between the quali-
fying individuals and other records on file. The shadow
specifically requested news items, genealogies, and all
available government records. Some of this last information
was, of course, restricted, but the shadow employed special

code sequences and programs that allowed it to bypass the security of the system.

At last the shadow had a concise, comprehensive data file on four individuals who matched the description of the profile the shadow had been given. It collected this information and began its return journey to the small Grid address in Port Royal.

After the shadow departed, a second shadow unfolded itself from a dormant state within the records system of the *Lighthouse* Grid. This second shadow was fairly nondescript, deliberately featureless. It had been recording detailed information about the nature of the first shadow, including a means of contacting its owner. Now it departed, bearing this digital cargo to its creator.

11.0:

SABLE HEARD THE door swish silently open, but she didn't actually open her eyes until she felt the weight on the edge of her bed. When she did open them, she saw Lazarus sitting there, and she smiled for a moment before she realized the look on his face was not happy.

"What?" she asked, worried. "What's wrong? Did you figure out who's behind the weapons sales?"

"No," Lazarus answered her, looking away. "But I did figure out a few other things, and I think that those other things will lead me to what I want to know."

"So? What did you find out?" She wanted to sit up, to move closer to him, but a medical surveillance system had her bundled up in several cables and tubes. She was also still pretty sore, although she felt much better than she had when they'd arrived. Her swollen eye was still puffy, but she could see out of it now, and her lip was healing nicely, although she thought she sounded funny when she spoke. She had not yet seen herself in a mirror, but she was afraid of what she might find if she did.

But Lazarus would not answer her. Instead, he stayed where he was, right on the edge of the bed, looking everywhere but at her.

What is it? she thought. He's scared of me. I must look like death warmed over.

"Laz, what's wrong?" Sable asked him.

For a long moment he still didn't answer, but finally, after swallowing several times, he said, "How much more of your assignment have you not told me about?"

Sable blinked, not understanding. "What are you talking about?"

"What else haven't you told me about what you were supposed to do here?"

"I—I don't understand, Laz. I explained all of that to you before. Please tell me what's wrong. You're scaring me."

Lazarus looked away from her again and studied his hands. "I'm pretty sure I know what Mr. Maxwell is up to, but I need to know from you, right now, if you've been playing along with him."

Sable was still confused, but the tone of his voice told her he was accusing her of something, of something against him, and she felt the tears spring up immediately. He still didn't trust her.

"Laz, I swear to you I don't know what you're talking about. Please tell me what you mean. I haven't lied to you anymore. Please believe me."

He turned to look at her now, leaning forward to stare directly at her face. "Are you sure? Tell me right now, to my face, that you don't know anything about Mr. Maxwell, or Gillst, or whoever the hell he really is, setting me up with false information. Tell me you aren't part of it, that you haven't been playing me for the sucker all this time."

Sable's lip trembled. Lazarus's accusations, after all they'd been through together, made her chest ache and her hands shake. A single tear ran down her cheek, but she shook her head and stared straight back at him. "I don't know what you think of me anymore, and it's killing me to hear you accusing me of such things. But I swear to you, to your face, that I did not betray you, or rat on you, or lie to you about something Mr. Maxwell is up to."

Lazarus watched her for a moment, and then finally nodded, almost imperceptibly. "Okay," he said.

"No, it's not okay," she said through her tears. Her voice, though, was strong. "You saved my life last night when you didn't have to. You came and got me and brought me back with you. I owe you my life, and those things you said to me back in the tunnels made me face up to the fact that I've been feeling the same way about you, even though I was afraid to admit it. But if you're going to go through the rest of your life, and mine, not trusting me, then let me up out of this bed right now, and I'll go my own way."

"No, it's not like that. I—"

"It *is* like that, Laz. I've spent my whole life feeling that way about everybody else. I hated it, but I had to do it. It was how I survived. You made me think differently. You made me see that not everyone is going to double-cross me the first chance they get. You actually gave me something in this stupid galaxy that I could feel good about, that I could think about without it turning my stomach. But I don't want it, not if it's tainted with the same mistrust I've felt for everybody else I've ever been around."

Lazarus reached his hand out and put it gently to her mouth, hushing her. "I'm sorry," he said. "I didn't want to ask you, but I had to know. I don't like the way I feel very much right now for doubting you, but it was a possibility, and I had to make sure. A whole lot of lives depend on it, and I couldn't have lived with myself if . . ." He looked down for a moment, and then returned his gaze to hers. "This might not make a difference after what I just did, but for what it's worth, I won't doubt you again."

Sable looked at him, struggling. She loved him. God knew how it had happened, but she did. And that was the scariest thing she had ever admitted to herself. More terrifying even than facing Maxwell.

Why did you have to come into my life, Lazarus what-ever-your-name-is? she asked herself miserably. She wanted to believe him, to know that he wouldn't question her trust-worthiness again, but it was so hard after all the times she had been betrayed before. But the ache of imagining not having him there anymore was even more painful than that, and she finally snaked an arm out of the covers, took the hand he still held to her lips, and kissed his fingers. And then she cried—the big, wet tears running down her face—but she hoped that Lazarus realized she wasn't sad.

Lazarus leaned down and took her hand in both of his and kissed it in return. "I'm sorry," he said, but he was smiling, and she knew he understood. "I hated hurting you again. I didn't want to. But I had to be sure. It'll never happen again, I swear it."

"I know," she said, laughing softly. "Somehow I do." And she laughed again, the laughter of joy, for she was feeling something amazing, and it had to bubble out of her.

Lazarus leaned in then, brought his face down to hers, and kissed her softly. "You still need to rest," he said, as if to cover for his forwardness, and rose from the bed. Sable tried to keep hold of his hand, but he gently pulled out of her grasp. "I need to go for a while. Get some sleep."

"Lazarus," Sable called after him as he turned to leave.

He turned back to her. "What?"

Sable bit her lip, trying to think of the right words. She couldn't, though, so finally she asked, "What about Gavin? What am I going to do?"

Lazarus nodded, then said, "We'll figure it out. You're not going back. I'll never let you go back to that. But right now get some rest. By tomorrow, I think, you'll be ready to travel."

"Okay," she said and grinned at him again. He turned and disappeared through the door, and she smiled ruefully when she realized that she missed him already.

You're a silly idiot, she told herself.

Maybe, she replied, but what difference does it make now? I've already gone and done it.

Done what? she wondered. What is this? Love? Is this what love feels like? But she knew very well that's exactly what she was feeling.

You *are* silly, she insisted, but this time she refused to listen.

Sable settled her head back into the pillow and closed her eyes, thinking of Lazarus in half-dreams until she finally drifted off to sleep again.

* * * * *

Lazarus scanned the street again, watching to see who might be out of place, who might be watching his apartment from some out-of-the-way spot, waiting for him to return. The Mateos were going to figure out where he had been staying sooner or later, he knew, and the quicker he got this taken care of and got away, the better. When he was certain there was no one watching the place, and no one had followed them, he and Blue crossed the street and headed up the stairs. At the landing, he studied the security panel carefully for a moment, looking for signs that it had been tampered with. Nothing. That made him more worried, rather than less.

"I almost wish there was some evidence of them. At least that way, we'd know they were onto us," he said, grimacing.

Blue merely chuckled. "If you say so. Let's just get this over with."

Lazarus punched in the code and let the system scan him.

The door slid open, and he stepped inside. "Stay here and keep an eye on things," he told Blue quietly. "I'll only be a second. If there's trouble, you come running."

"Sure," Blue replied. He slouched against the wall as if he had nothing better to do.

No reason to be stupid, Lazarus told himself, and drew his pistol as he peered around carefully.

The place looked pretty much as he would have expected. It certainly didn't look as if anyone had been here poking around. Nonetheless, he checked every room in the place carefully before holstering his weapon. He walked around again, trying to decide what to take and what to leave behind. Most of the stuff he didn't care about, but there was a certain need to eliminate evidence of what he was about. Certainly all of the computer equipment was coming with him, and some extra clothing, but beyond that, he wasn't sure.

He had brought a small satchel with him, carrying his gauntlet and some extra clips for his pistol inside, and now he began to pack more things, stuff from his bedroom, into it, sorting through his possessions with a recklessness that revealed his nervousness at being there. In addition to his clothes, he grabbed his trauma pack and supplies, his stutter pistol, the extra ammo for his sabot pistol, and a few other personal items. Back in the living room, he scooped up crystals and dumped them into the satchel, not caring too much what was on them. He could figure it all out later. When he had everything, he started gathering up Sable's gear, stuffing it into the satchel with his own stuff.

When he was finished packing, Lazarus set the bundle down near the door and pulled out his gauntlet. He went over to the desk and jacked it in, sliding the thing onto his arm. He dropped the visor over his eyes and booted the connection. He waited through the flicker and the void, and then he stepped through to the little room he called his address. One shadow was waiting for him.

"What did you find out?" Lazarus asked the shadow as he began to erase old files and other data from the place.

"There was no record of any ship registered to Quartz Pyramid Limited docking at the Port Royal spaceport within the last six months, nor was there any record in the commercial passenger manifests of a Jaren Gillst arriving or departing within the same time period."

Lazarus nodded. "Of course not. Because it doesn't exist," he said to himself.

"Pardon?" the shadow asked.

"What? Oh, sorry. Nothing. I have a new set of instructions for you." Lazarus quickly tapped out the new code on his gauntlet, uploading the commands absently as he composed the message in his head. This was going to be a little tricky.

Tap-dancing around your superior is never a good idea, he thought wryly as he worked, so if you're gonna do it, Lazarus, make it sound really good.

"This is a Priority One message for Administrator Monahan, Oslo G., at the *Lighthouse*. Clearance is Eyes Only, use fastest available traffic at all steps. The message is: 'Have managed a significant breakthrough in the case. However, believe someone on the other end is aware of efforts. Data retrieved was falsified. Have a new lead. No further contact for time being due to risk of security compromise. Believe someone on the inside is turncoat. Will report again after completion of next phase of investigation.' End message. Depart."

Lazarus sat back and considered what he had just done by sending the shadow with that message. I'd just damn well better have some interesting news for him, he told himself.

He shook his head and conjured up another shadow. With a few simple keystrokes, he had a new code programmed to his satisfaction. He spoke to the shadow as he worked.

"Stay here and detain all other shadows that return. I'll send a forwarding address when I get one," Lazarus said, typing on his gauntlet. "Two weeks ought to do it. Then wipe the place, and yourself with it." He completed the programming alterations and uploaded the code into the shadow.

"Acknowledged," the shadow said emotionlessly.

Lazarus leaned back, considering. It would be the only loose end, and if they figured out how to crack their way into his address, they could eventually find him. But he needed that other information. "Yeah," he said at last, "two weeks. Then the site goes down."

"Understood."

Lazarus nodded his head and jacked out. Back in the living room of his place, he bundled up the gauntlet and its cables, stuffed them back into the satchel, and took one more look around. It looked fine, but he still felt a strange sense that he had forgotten something. He walked through each of the rooms one more time until he was satisfied that he had taken everything important.

Lazarus stepped back to the door, scooped up the satchel, turned to look back once more, then stabbed at the door switch, and turned to leave—and found himself staring down the barrel of a flechette gun.

Time seemed to slow to a crawl as Lazarus's mind registered the fact that the barrel of the gun was protruding from the arm of the assassin who had chased Sable in the cafe. He followed the arm, clad in the immaculately pressed suit, seeing the precision of the stitching in the fabric, up to the guy's shoulder. His eyes swept up across the narrow chin, freshly shaven, to the grinning mouth. The upper lip was twisted in a vulgar smirk, and Lazarus could feel the maliciousness there, the delight at the anticipated pain to come. Then Lazarus was past the lips to the nose, small and slightly hooked, to the mirrored shades that the assassin had worn on that first day. In those shades, Lazarus could see his own face and the surprise evident on it.

Out of the corner of his eye, Lazarus could see Blue's body still slouched against the wall where he had left the kid standing. A knife protruded straight out from the young man's forehead, and a forked trail of blood cascaded down his face and was spreading through his shirt.

Son of a—! Lazarus knew he was a dead man, but that didn't stop him from trying to escape his fate.

In a single fluid motion, Lazarus dropped down, sinking to one knee, thankful that the gun was so close to him. He heard the report, felt the blast of the flechette rounds as they exploded past his shoulder, screaming from the barrel, centimeters from his ear. He flinched from the pain of the noise, and he felt shards of needle-thin metal caress his ear and shoulder, but he ignored them as he drove his fist into the assassin's gut as hard as he possibly could.

In the next instant, everything was a blur. The killer was lightning fast, flinching only slightly as Lazarus's punch thudded harmlessly into dermal armor. Then the assassin's knee was up under Lazarus's chin, snapping his head back with tremendous force, sending the CIB agent flailing backward, off balance. Lazarus reacted desperately, pushing back with his feet and throwing himself into a barrel roll, twisting and falling on his shoulder and then spinning to the side. He heard another blast from the flechette gun as it sprayed the floor where he had been a fraction of a second earlier. He rolled again and again, trying to keep himself moving to stay out of the line of sight.

By the third time Lazarus had rolled to his stomach, he was kicking himself forward into a somersault and launching himself to his feet. There was another blast from the gun, and he felt hot pain shoot through his shoulder as the spread of needles grazed him. He stumbled slightly but used his momentum to propel himself forward into a run, dashing across the room in two huge strides. He heard the report of the flechette gun again, but he launched himself into the couch, using his body weight against the upright portion of it to roll the whole thing, himself against it, backward, so that he fell in a heap to the floor behind it. The couch shuddered with the razor-thin shards of metal spraying it.

Damn, he's fast! Lazarus thought as he yanked his pistol out of the holster.

Lazarus felt the warm wetness of blood trickling down his back from his shoulder. He crouched and then flung himself to the side, gun up, and sighted. As his body skidded out from behind the couch, he targeted the approaching assassin, who was in midstep across the room, coming toward the couch. Lazarus squeezed the trigger as fast as he could, feeling some comfort finally in the heavy sound of the sabot rounds exploding into the room.

But the assassin was too fast. Even as Lazarus squeezed off the first of several shots, the killer spun out of the way and dived through the doorway into the bedroom. Lazarus's shots blew huge chunks out of the plastic, concrete, and steel wall where the guy had been standing.

Not wanting to give the assassin a chance to pin him down behind the couch, Lazarus rose to his feet and ran pell-mell across the room until he was back at the alcove by the front door. He dropped to his knees, crouching behind the wall and peering around the corner. He could see the couch, tipped backward ninety degrees.

Suddenly there were several rapid shots from the other room, and Lazarus watched, horrified, as the couch exploded in a spray of material and fabric. From his angle, he could see that a significant portion of the flechette rounds were pummeling the wall behind the couch, too. He had gotten out from behind it just in time.

Lazarus considered making a break for it; he could be out the door and down the street before the assassin recovered.

But then he realized that he had dropped the satchel in his first attempt to get away, and it was now lying in the middle of the living room floor. He had taken a big risk to come and get it, and he was damned if he was going to forget about it now.

Several more shots rang out, the high-pitched sound of the flechettes screaming through the air as the couch was pulverized. Lazarus considered whether to fire back from his new position or not.

He still thinks I'm back there, behind the couch. Don't draw attention to yourself until you have to, dummy! He frowned, considering. *Local cops will be here in a couple of minutes, if that, but I can't wait. I've got to get out of here. With the stuff.*

A new volley of shots whistled through the air, but this time they slammed into the other side of the alcove, spraying Lazarus with tiny chunks of plastic and concrete.

He flinched but remained silent. *Well, I guess he knows I'm here now.*

Lazarus waited for the next shot to pepper the wall, and then he leaned out and squeezed off a couple of shots in the direction of the doorway to the bedroom. He didn't keep his head out long enough to get it shot off, but from his quick glance, he caught sight of the assassin's reflection in the mirror on the bathroom door.

They exchanged another round of shots, and Lazarus's clip was out. He had one more in his coat pocket, he knew, but the rest were in the satchel.

I can't get to it in time, he thought. He briefly considered trying to snag the satchel with something, to lasso it with his belt, but it was too far away. Anything he did would expose him to the damned flechette gun.

He's got to run out of ammo soon, Lazarus thought. *He can't keep that thing loaded indefinitely.*

Suddenly Lazarus had an idea. He switched clips, fired off a couple of shots around the corner, and lunged up and slapped the front door switch on the side of the wall exposed to the killer. The door slid open behind him. He crammed his foot against it to keep it open and waited to see what the assassin would make of this. There was another volley of fire from the bedroom, and Lazarus returned the attack. The assassin stayed where he was.

Lazarus nodded and took a deep breath. Then he began to scoot himself backward out the door, keeping a watch on the living room as he backed his way to Blue's body. The last thing he wanted to do was turn his back on the killer. Reaching behind him, he began to pat the kid down, looking for the pistol he knew Blue carried in the small of his back. He found it there and drew it out.

Poor Blue never even got it out, Lazarus thought sadly. That bastard killed him before Blue knew he was even there. But he was in for a big surprise. Blue was packing something special.

Lazarus scrambled back inside as another shot screamed into the wall near his head. He flinched as he was peppered with more shards of wall. He fired his own pistol back into the room, watching as the shots dug huge chunks in the wall but didn't punch through.

Lazarus heard the assassin laugh. "I was afraid you had decided to leave," he called out to Lazarus. "Not as much fun to hunt you down in the middle of the street. Not very sportsmanlike."

Lazarus didn't respond. Instead, he fired his weapon three more times at the wall where the assassin was standing, watching carefully in the mirror to see how the killer reacted. There was nothing. The guy felt completely safe behind the wall. Lazarus nodded, smiling, and took Blue's pistol. He waited.

When the assassin fired another flechette round at
Lazarus, he took a breath, then leaned out, and sighted carefully down the barrel of the mass pistol. Using the reflection
in the mirror as a guide, Lazarus adjusted his aim. At that
moment, the assassin spotted the mirror and realized Lazarus
was looking at him. The killer lifted his hand in a mock
salute and raised his gun to blow the mirror away.

Too late.

Lazarus squeezed the trigger on the mass pistol three
times in rapid succession, feeling the kick of the weapon as
the rounds slammed into—and through—the wall dividing
the living room and bedroom, striking the killer squarely in
the torso. The assassin stared dumbly at Lazarus through the
mirror and took an uncertain step, wobbling on his feet.
Blood began to stain his shirt, and Lazarus watched as he
looked down, surprised and confused.

He tried to take another step, and then stumbled. Lazarus
waited, watching through the mirror. The assassin fell forward on his face, his arms sprawled out in front of him.
Lazarus still waited. The killer didn't move.

Thank God for mass pistols. Walls are kind of like armor.
There's always something to punch through them.

Lazarus crept out to retrieve his satchel. He grabbed it
and backed out the door, still watching the unmoving form
of the assassin.

Just to make sure, he told himself. I've seen cyberheads
get up before.

Out on the landing, he stopped for a moment to look at
Blue.

Sorry, Blue, he said silently.

Lazarus then turned and headed down the stairs, cutting
across the street and away from his apartment even as the
approaching sirens of the local police drew close.

*   *   *   *   *

"Blue's dead," Lazarus said as he entered Sable's room.

"You're bleeding!" she said, struggling to sit up in the bed.

"Not anymore. I got patched up before I came."

"What happened?"

"I got jumped by your friend with the gun for an arm. He's dead, too."

"Damn." Sable chewed on her lip, thinking. "I guess they're coming after us, huh?"

"Yeah. We've got to get out of here soon. I don't think they could get to us in here with the Technospiders, but I don't want to stick around and draw any more attention to them. Besides, we need to get off this rock while we can. Do you feel up to traveling?"

"I'm so sick of lying in this bed I could scream. But Stipelle and Ellesao won't let me up until you say it's okay."

"It's okay." Lazarus grinned. "I grabbed your stuff from my place. We're out of here tonight."

"Laz," Sable said, looking at him intently. "Where are we going?"

Lazarus sat down on the edge of the bed near her. "What were you supposed to do after you got the data from Germaine?"

"Catch a shuttle up to Highport Space Station, then take a flight to Aegis and meet them at Nectaris Station."

Lazarus looked thoughtful. "Then what?"

Sable looked down, frowning. "It depends."

"On what?"

Sable sighed. "On what kind of mood they're in." She hated telling him this. "Sometimes I'm just put under with a stimcrystal, and when I come out of it, we're someplace else. I don't know where."

"A ship, maybe?"

"It's possible. I don't know for sure."

"And what if they don't just put you under?" Lazarus reached out and took her hand in his.

Sable squirmed under his gaze. If they were going to get to Gavin, she knew she had to tell him everything, but it made her stomach turn somersaults even to think about it. Going back was always traumatic. "Sometimes Ana is there."

She could feel Lazarus stare at her for a long moment, but then he finally got up and began to pace.

"Your Mr. Maxwell, or whatever his real name is, is part of this. That data we stole from the syndicate was planted, just for us. Which means that I was supposed to hook up with you from the beginning, that Maxwell, or Gillst, or whoever he is, was luring me out so he could play me."

"That's why you thought I was in on it?"

"Yeah," Lazarus said quietly. "It was entirely too possible. I'm sorry."

"We already went over that. So Mr. Maxwell is in on it. Where does that leave you?"

"Pretty angry, but it makes my decision easy. I'm supposed to get this case cracked, find out who's behind the sale of arms to terrorists. But you know damned well the first thing we're doing is getting your brother. Now I can do it without having to explain to my boss why. It all ties in together."

Sable looked at Lazarus. "Okay," she said, smiling warmly.

He'd throw his career—hell, his life—away to help me, she thought. I sure hope it's worth it.

"So what's the plan?" Sable asked Lazarus.

"I don't know yet. First, we've got to get off Penates without the entire Mateo family coming down on us. We'll figure the rest of it out on the way to Aegis."

12.0:

THE NONDESCRIPT SHADOW glided through the void of the Grid once more, seeking the spot atop the tall building. As expected, the second shadow was waiting.

"We are encrypted?" the first asked, settling lightly to the surface of the roof.

"As always. The news is not good."

The first shadow nodded, as though expecting this. "Tell me. Again, no names."

The second sighed. "As we had suspected, the agent went for the source. In anticipation of that, the trail was planted, as per your instructions."

"Thus far we're on track."

"Yes, but somehow he didn't take the bait. I'm not sure how, but my ears inside tell me that he and those who crawl between the walls determined it had been fabricated."

"Your agents did not do an effective job," the first said, his annoyance evident. "You knew this man was capable and that he would have technical aid. We should have ensured that the planted evidence was flawless."

"Yes, but it didn't happen that way. There's nothing we can do about it now."

"Continue."

"The agent's most recent transmission hinted that he suspected a leak within his chain of command. He indicates that he's dropping out of sight in order to solve the case on his own."

"Damn it! He must be extracted at once! We cannot allow our work to come to light, not at this stage."

"I understand. I have my people out already, preparing to bring both him and the girl in. I intend to terminate him. There is no other way, at this stage."

The first sighed. "Yes," he said at last. "It would appear so. This makes it difficult. Elections are on the horizon. I had hoped—"

"I know. And I am sorry. But this is a last resort. I would not issue the order unless I knew it was our only way."

"What of those who crawl between the walls? How much do they know?"

"I am uncertain, although I suspect they know quite a bit. Regardless, I do not think they will act on it."

The first raised an eyebrow. "No? How can you be certain?"

"I cannot, but I suspect it. They are too wrapped up in their own affairs; they would not spare the time or the resources to pursue it. If the agent succeeds, so much the better, in their eyes, but if he does not, they have their own affairs to tend to. They will not be bothered by events taking place several systems away."

"I am not certain I want to hang my hat on such a precarious assumption. What if you're wrong?"

"It is a risk, to be sure, but we do not have much of a choice. The effort to dig them out and destroy them would be immense, and it would put the entire system into such an uproar that many other vital operations would be adversely affected. Drastically."

The first shadow was silent for a long moment, considering. Finally he said, "Very well. But keep a close watch on them. At the first sign of a problem, I want to know, and I want solutions for dealing with it already planned out."

"I understand."

"Inform me the moment you have the agent."

"I will."

The second shadow disappeared, but the first lingered awhile longer, deep in thought.

* * * * *

Sable stayed close behind Lazarus as they threaded their way through the throngs of people at the Port Royal spaceport. She eyed the crowds carefully, watching for any sign that the two of them were being followed. She kept her duffel bag close to her, one arm wrapped through the handle straps and around it, hugging it to her chest. Ahead of her, Lazarus's broad shoulders swayed slightly as he slipped through the gaps between people.

They had decided to come during the day, when the most flights would be arriving and departing. Lazarus figured that it would be safer to be out in public when the spaceport was crowded, since it would be harder for the Mateo goons to spot them, even though the same crowds would, in turn, would make it difficult for Sable and him to notice anyone following them. It was a calculated risk, Lazarus had said, but it made sense in the long run.

They had made arrangements to circumvent any security checkpoints. The Technospiders had gotten them inside the spaceport at a location beyond all checkpoints, to avoid being spotted on security cameras. Still, the Mateos would know they had the capability to do such a thing, so the watchers might be most prolific here, in the main terminals.

Stipelle had also arranged for a private charter flight for the two of them, although it had taken a significant amount of funds to pay for it. Lazarus had been forced to break into a reserve stash of working capital. Sable hoped it was worth it.

"I think it's this way," Lazarus said over his shoulder as they neared an intersection in the terminal. "All the charter flights arrive and leave from Concourse D." He turned to his right and continued, gently forcing his way through the crowd. Sable scurried to keep up with him, using him as a sort of shield.

"I just want to get there," she said to his back as she continued to watch for faces that were watching her. "The sooner we get out of this damned crowd, the better I'll feel."

Lazarus chuckled once, and then said, "Soon. We'll be safe once we're on board the ship."

I hope so, she thought. I need a little drivespace downtime to relax.

Lazarus had crossed over to one side of the concourse and was nearing a row of gates. Sable tried to remember which gate he had said they were headed toward.

Something like sixteen, she thought.

Lazarus continued to move down the large open walkway, scanning the gate numbers. Sable noticed that it had gotten a little less crowded since they had left the main terminal behind and entered the charter flight area. In a way, she was glad, although she did feel a little more exposed here.

I wonder if the Mateos will guess that we're going to charter our way out of here.

"This is it," Lazarus said, stopping at Gate Sixteen.

The gates weren't actually gates at all, but small rooms where the charter passengers could hook up with their pilots. Some of the charter companies had permanent rooms assigned to them, which they had converted into full offices, almost like their own business location. Others, such as the one they had made arrangements with, were assigned whatever gates were available at the moment, and those rooms had little more than a few chairs and a holovideo set.

Lazarus tested the door and found it to be locked. "We

must be a little early." He looked around and spotted a small food vending area with a few tables and chairs in a recessed area farther up the concourse. "We can wait over there," he said, pointing. "The pilot should be along soon."

Sable nodded and started to follow him over to an empty table, cutting through the passengers hurrying back and forth along the concourse. It was at that moment that a hand wrapped itself around her face, covering her mouth and jerking her backward, off balance. The hand was small and delicate, and the sight of it made Sable suddenly tremble with dread.

"Hello, Sable, my darling," a woman's voice said behind her, and Sable's breath caught in her throat in terror. She knew the voice. It was Ana.

Sable flailed wildly as Ana dragged her backward. The other people in the terminal either watched in suspicion or hurried on, trying not to get involved. Sable stared at Lazarus's back as he receded from her, willing him to turn around.

The barrel of a gun was planted in her ribs, and Ana whispered in Sable's ear, "Now, my darling, I think you know what I want you to do. Gavin is waiting for you. What condition we find him in when we arrive is up to you." Then she kissed Sable once, mockingly, on the cheek and took her hand away.

Shaking badly, Sable watched as Lazarus headed into the food court, obviously looking for a table. Then Ana spun her around, and she saw two more of Mr. Maxwell's thugs, Lars and Eduardo, standing there. Lars yanked her duffel bag from her grasp as Eduardo stepped to her free side, opposite Ana, and took her by the other arm. They began to lead her down the concourse.

Sable had finally had enough. Something in her snapped. Some part of her that had been held in check through fear finally bulled its way to the front, and she reacted. Jerking her arm free from Eduardo, Sable spun sideways and slammed her fist up under Ana's chin, forcing the woman back a step and causing her to let go of Sable's other arm. Spinning again, Sable planted a kick right in Eduardo's gut, hearing the audible *whoosh* of air as she drove the breath from his lungs. The thug stumbled backward, his eyes bulging in surprise and pain. Sable spun once more and tried to break away, shouting at the top of her lungs. "Lazarus!"

Sable felt something cut across her shin as she tried to run. She realized that Ana had hold of her shoulder and was trying to trip her with one leg and force her down to the floor. She struggled to catch herself, to spin away, but her cybernetically enhanced teacher was too fast. All too quickly Ana was astride Sable's back, pinning her arms to her sides.

"Grab her, you idiots!" the woman said to the two thugs, trying to keep Sable from squirming free.

Sable kicked and flailed, cursing. "Get off me! You are *not* taking me back! I'm going to kill you!" Somewhere a rational, sane part of her mind was horrified at her words, her actions. But she was in a frenzy now and would not be stopped. It was time to end the paralyzing fear. It was time to strike back, to take control, to do *something* besides cower for the rest of her days. Unfortunately, she was still only one person, and Lars, Eduardo, and Ana quickly overpowered her.

All around her, people looked away from the spectacle, hurrying to their destinations, not wanting to become involved. They rushed by, giving Sable and her escort a wide berth. Sable squeezed her eyes shut as the tears trickled down her cheek, still fighting for all she was worth but unable to free herself from Ana.

"Hey!" someone shouted from behind her, and Sable opened her eyes in time to see Lars peering back behind them. His eyes grew wide, and he went for a gun that had been tucked into his belt, hidden beneath his coat.

"Look out! He's got a gun!" someone screamed, and then Lars was aiming at something as Ana and Eduardo yanked Sable up, dragging her unwillingly away.

Sable thrashed against the two who held her, turning to look back over her shoulder as Lars fired several shots. Lazarus was running down the opposite side of the concourse, pacing them, ducking and crouching as Lars's shots sprayed the crowd. Several people screamed, and the whole concourse erupted in chaos. People were running everywhere, and she could hear gunshots from Lars as well as the deep belching rumble of Lazarus's stutter pistol.

At that moment, Eduardo said, "Put her under, for God's sake. She's fighting like a wildcat!"

"I don't know what's gotten into her, but I'll beat it back out of her later," Ana said, producing a tiny hypodermic that extended from her fingertip.

"No!" Sable screamed now, shrinking back. "Lazarus! Help me! Ana, no!" Sable jerked and thrashed, trying to kick at Ana's hand and free herself from her captors' grasps, but they were too strong.

Sable screamed again as Ana jabbed the tip of her finger into Sable's neck, injecting the needle into her skin. Sable felt a hot flash that quickly overwhelmed her. She sensed that she was getting dizzy, and then blackness swallowed her.

*   *   *   *   *

"This table okay?" Lazarus asked, turning back to Sable. She wasn't there. He jerked upright, scanning the concourse, and then suddenly heard her shout his name. He spotted her about thirty meters away. She was running toward him, pulling away from two people, a man and a woman, who seemed to be trying to grab her. A third man was carrying Sable's duffel bag and watching the two others grapple with Sable. The woman moved with lightning quickness then, grabbing Sable and throwing her to the floor in a smooth motion.

Damn it!

Lazarus jerked his stutter pistol out of his holster and darted forward, weaving through people. "Hey!" he called, rushing forward as fast as the crowd would allow. He saw the one with Sable's duffel bag turn and look at him, and then he caught sight of the flash of black metal.

Damn! Don't fire that thing in here!

"Look out!" a man close to Lazarus yelled. "He's got a gun!" and he swung a large piece of luggage toward Lazarus, trying to hit his gun arm.

Stupid tourist!

Lazarus dodged out of the way as he saw the man in front of Sable spin around and level his own pistol at Lazarus. Lazarus launched himself to one side as the thug fired, grazing the tourist in the shoulder.

Lazarus leaped up, trying to keep them in sight. The pair flanking Sable were now dragging her, struggling against them, back up the concourse. He saw Sable turn to look back, and even at this distance, Lazarus could see something wild etched on her face, a bestial quality that surprised him. He got the armed thug squarely in his sights, looking for a clean shot, but the guy was using Sable as a shield.

Lazarus ducked as another round of shots sprayed the crowd, and people were screaming and running everywhere now.

Screw it, Lazarus thought. I'm only going to wind up hitting innocents. Got to get closer.

"Lazarus! Help me!" he heard Sable scream. "Ana, no!"

Ana? Lazarus thought. Those are Maxwell's thugs!

Lazarus scrambled along the far wall from his quarry, staying low, using the crazed, panicked crowd as a screen to stay out of sight. Alarms were going off now, and Lazarus knew spaceport security was on its way. He tried to dash quickly along the concourse, hoping to get ahead of Sable and her captors. He reached a planter in the center of the concourse, slipped behind it, and then leaned out carefully to take a peek. He could see the armed thug peering around in different directions, but it was obvious that he had lost sight of Lazarus. The other two still held Sable between them, but her head lolled against her shoulder now, and they were carrying her.

Lazarus had managed to get ahead of them, but instead of coming toward him, they stopped at one of the charter flight gates and slipped inside, the armed thug hesitating before following them.

Damn!

Lazarus started to leap up from his position and dash across the way to the gate, hoping to get inside, but he spotted four spaceport security officers, weapons drawn and moving cautiously, coming that way. He froze, still concealed behind the planter. He slipped his pistol inside his holster and waited. Around him, most of the crowd had taken cover or run off completely. Lazarus ground his teeth as the seconds ticked by.

The security officers stopped, weapons drawn, scanning the area. Someone huddled behind a trash can said something to one of the officers and pointed farther down the concourse in Lazarus's direction. The officer nodded and motioned for the informant to stay down, and they continued to advance.

No, not me! Lazarus seethed. They're getting away!

The place was suddenly very quiet except for the occasional whimper or groan of a terrified or wounded civilian. Someone who was slumped over a body sobbed and begged the spaceport cops to help her husband, but the officers motioned for her to hang on.

Lazarus debated charging across the open space between his own hiding place and the gate where Ana had taken Sable.

No way I could make it, he realized.

He wasn't about to tell the spaceport cops where Sable and the others had gone, either.

They're likely to shoot her with the rest of them.

At that moment another civilian who was hiding under a bench gestured toward the gate through which Sable had been taken, and the security officers nodded and approached the open doorway. Lazarus heard one of them call in for backup.

Bloody hell! Lazarus growled.

A burst of automatic fire coming from inside the gate raked through the security officers. A couple of them managed to get off a shot or two, but the whole thing was over quickly. The four officers were down. The door slid shut.

Oh, God! Lazarus thought, reeling. That would have been me! But Sable's in there!

Realizing he had no time to waste, Lazarus leaped from his hiding place and tore across the concourse to the gate where Sable had disappeared. He kept to the wall, trying to stay out of a direct line of sight, even though the door had slid shut. When he got there, he crept close and then tried the door. It was locked, as he suspected. He checked the panel. Clenching his teeth in fury and barely controlled fear, he pulled the lock decryption card from his coat and slapped it against the panel. He waited impatiently as the readout flashed through its iterations.

One of the officers groaned and began to draw his knees up under himself, trying to stand.

"Come on!" Lazarus growled at the lock. "Open!"

Finally, with a flash of green, the sequence was displayed, and Lazarus desperately tapped the code into the lock. The door slid open and Lazarus crouched beside it, his gun in his hand. He peered around the corner into the room beyond, but it was empty.

Damn! They have a ship!

He ducked into the room and moved carefully to the door at the back, the air lock that would lead to the docking bay. He'd have to hurry if he was going to reach them before they took off. Stabbing at the switch beside this new door, he waited as the air locks on the other side sealed, and then the door slid open. Lazarus's mind raced as he proceeded through the air lock, feeling every moment stretch like an eternity.

I'm coming, Sable. Just hang on.

He ran as fast as he could down the passage to the docking bay, but before he even got to the other end, he could feel the rumble of a ship's engines powering up.

No! he cried out silently, slamming against the door.

Through a small window beside the door, he saw the ship, and beyond it, the great bay door, already open. He slumped against it, holding his head in his hands. There was no way he was getting this door open now. Beyond it was another air lock, magnetically sealed, he knew, designed to protect against exposing the entire spaceport to the deadly atmosphere of Penates. There was no way he was getting to her.

I'm sorry, Sable, he thought. Hang on. I'll find you.

*   *   *   *   *

"It was all I could do to keep from getting killed myself," Lazarus said angrily, slumped in a chair in Stipelle's office. "I just wasn't expecting anyone from that direction. Damn!" he shouted, lunging out of the chair and pacing furiously. "I'm going to kill them when I find them. I swear, if they touch her . . ." he growled, moving back and forth like a caged animal. Ellesao watched him from a chair on the far side of the room.

"Look, you did what you could," Stipelle said. "They were willing to kill innocent people to stop you. There was nothing else you could have done."

"I don't care," Lazarus said, stopping in his tracks to look Stipelle in the eye. "I wanted nothing more than to have my sabot pistol right then. I was ready to drop the three of them the first chance I had a clear shot." Lazarus sighed and dropped into the chair again. "Oh, God, why wasn't I paying attention? I could have done something if I had kept her in my sight!" He pounded his fist against the armrest.

"The question is, what are you going to do now?" Stipelle asked him.

Lazarus scowled at nothing in particular. "I don't know," he said. "She was my link to Maxwell. I was going to nail him when he tried to get her back. He's my connection to the buyer. But I have no idea who he is."

Stipelle nodded, although Lazarus was too absorbed in his thoughts to notice. "What about the holding company owned by Yonce?"

Lazarus raised an eyebrow questioningly at Stipelle. "You know that's a false trail. Why would I mess with that?"

"Well, within every lie, a certain amount of truth exists. Yonce is real. Her holding company is real, too. We know it owns HansCorp Freight. Who knows what else might be true?"

Lazarus sat up, thinking. "I've got nothing else at this

point. Maybe someone at the holding company knows something."

"I'd start with the name of the investor who shows up on all those fabricated transactions we saw. He might be real, too," Stipelle said, leaning back in his chair.

Lazarus ran his hands through his hair. "Yeah," he said absently, turning over what he knew in his head. "Yeah, that might be the way to go. I guess I'll see if I can still get that charter flight we had booked to take me off this rock." He stood up, still lost in his thoughts.

"I would like to come with you, Lazarus," Ellesao said.

Lazarus turned to look at the mechalus, surprised. "You? Why?"

Ellesao shrugged. "I also care about Sable. And"—Ellesao looked at Stipelle as she said this—"reasons/several that make it in the interest/best of the organization. Besides, I have wanted/always to see the *Lighthouse*."

Lazarus nodded and grinned briefly. "I could certainly use your help, so if you want to tag along, that's fine with me. How soon can you be ready to go?"

Ellesao smiled. "Like you, I travel lightly. I can be ready in an hour."

"Great," Lazarus replied. "I want to do one thing on the Grid first, and then I'll be ready to go." Lazarus turned to Stipelle. "If I can use one of your data nodes . . ."

Stipelle nodded and gestured toward Ellesao. "She'll get you set up. Good luck, both of you."

* * * * *

Lazarus let his view adjust to the images of the Grid as they flashed across the visor covering his eyes, and then he settled in, stroking the keys of his gauntlet with absent familiarity as he cruised through the digital city laid out before him. Typing in a data address, he watched as his shadow sped through the panorama around him. He arrived at the address, his own data node, and entered the code to gain access inside.

There were three shadows waiting for him when he arrived.

The first, of course, was the one he had left behind to look after things and to shut down the node after the time limit ran out. The second one was also his own, but the third one he did not recognize. He eyed it warily, bringing up a defensive program almost without thinking, but the shadow did not react threateningly, so he relaxed a bit. He ran a few standard scanning programs over it, making sure it was clean and wouldn't suddenly fry his hardware, and then said, "Who do you belong to, and why are you here?"

The shadow responded, "I bear a message, as follows: 'One of my shadows observed one of yours retrieving information about a certain woman named Sabine Taraen, who is presumed to be missing or dead."

Now I've got people following my *shadows!* Lazarus thought. Who the hell is Sabine Taraen? He suddenly wondered. Is he talking about Sable?

The shadow continued. " 'I am a friend of hers, although you might not believe me, as she has many enemies and often conceals her true identity. I respect your caution. I am very interested in speaking with you, but I must regretfully maintain anonymity for the time being, as it is not safe for me to reveal too much at the moment. Please, if you call yourself friend to Sabine, come to the *Lighthouse* and visit an establishment known as The Corner. Ask for Handstand Howard. We must talk. Her life depends on it.' "

When it was finished delivering the message, the shadow

stood motionless for a moment, and then suddenly vanished completely, leaving no visual remnant that it had ever been there at all.

Lazarus gaped at where the shadow had been but moments before. Programmed to erase itself once the message was delivered, he realized.

It's a trap, he thought, but for some reason it didn't feel like a trap.

Lazarus moved to the second shadow that he had created, which he quickly discovered was the one he had sent out to unearth an identity for Sable. His chest constricted in both pain and excitement at the thought of her.

Stop it. Just get her back, he told himself, and addressed the second shadow.

"Report," he said.

"I was successful in acquiring four possible matches on the subject for which you requested an identity. The selections are as follows. . . ." The shadow began delivering a detailed account of each possible subject. Lazarus listened to each description, dismissing the first two almost immediately because their whereabouts were known. The third one made Lazarus sit up.

"Subject: Sabine Taraen, date of birth, November 14, 2483. Daughter of Mitchell and Laura Taraen. One brother, Gavin, born July 13, 2488. All missing and presumed dead as of March 23, 2499, while in the Aegis system."

Sabine, he thought, fitting his mind around the name. Her name is Sabine. And she has a friend out there somewhere. He shook his head, wanting to hear more.

"What else? What about her parents?" he asked.

"I gathered very little collateral information, as it was not part of my programming."

Lazarus nodded and waved his hand dismissively. "Yes,

yes, whatever you did gather." He knew he could do more research later if he had to.

First things first, Lincoln, old boy.

"Mitchell Taraen worked for a very successful construction materials company, Malmott Supply, based in the Rigunmor Star Consortium, and he was placed in charge of a new branch distribution center in the Verge. He moved his family to Bluefall in early March of 2499 to set up operations, but the entire family vanished while on a day excursion on the surface of Bluefall before he actually got the business up and running.

"Sabine has one distinguishing mark that should make her easy to identify without additional surveillance equipment. There is a star-shaped birthmark on her left shoulder, approximately five centimeters across."

Lazarus considered this as he filed away the data on a crystal on his gauntlet. It had to be her. The left shoulder. Of course! The tattoo! She must have gotten it to hide the birthmark, Lazarus realized. More ways to mask her identity.

As a precaution, Lazarus listened to the description of the last individual, but the woman had been arrested several times for black market crimes before she had disappeared. No, Lazarus was certain Sabine was his girl.

When he was finished digesting this information, he immediately set about wiping the data node clean, eliminating all of the evidence still remaining, including the two shadows. There was no reason to leave the forwarding program in place anymore. He had all the information he needed.

When he was done, Lazarus logged off the Grid, but he sat for a long moment in the chair where he had been working, considering. No matter how he looked at the situation, only two possibilities came to mind.

The mysterious person who had contacted him was either

Maxwell or Gavin. Either way, it was a new lead. Lazarus smiled as he arose from the chair and went to find Ellesao.

Hang on, Sable. Hang in there. I'm going to find you and get you back.

13.0:

SABLE OPENED HER eyes and blinked, the sharp glare of the light stinging. Her head felt strange, as if it were stuffed with cotton, and there was a tingling sensation in her arms. She blinked several more times, trying to get her bearings. She was naked. She shivered, realizing she was cold.

She was lying on her side on a flat, hard bed, her arms pinned under her at an awkward angle. She tried to sit up and felt dizzy, almost groggy. Her arms felt leaden, as though she had slept on them and they had fallen asleep. She groaned but forced herself to sit up and look around.

She was in a small room, sparsely furnished, with the bed, a toilet, and a shower head set in one wall and a drain in the floor. There were no other discernible features, only a single door set in one wall. She brought her hand up to her face and rubbed at her eyes and temples, trying to clear her head. Then the memories flooded back to her.

She choked back a sob when she realized where she must be—on board a ship heading to Mr. Maxwell.

Oh, God, she thought. Laz!

She stood on wobbly legs and moved over to the door. She tested it, but it was locked, as she suspected. She banged on it.

"Ana! Let me out!" she shouted.

When there was no response to her noise, she turned back and stared at her prison. She wondered how long they would keep her locked in here.

They've got to feed me, she thought, but she knew they didn't have to do anything if they didn't want to. She treaded back to the bed and collapsed on it, curling into a ball, shivering from the cool air of the room.

After a while, she reached up and felt the spot on her neck where Ana had injected the drug into her. She felt a tiny welt there, but nothing else. She examined her body, by touch in places she couldn't see, to discern if anything else had been done to her while she was unconscious. It seemed that nothing had, as far as she could tell.

No implants, at least, she thought. Unless they hit me with nanotech, she added miserably.

She remembered what Ana had said when they had caught her back at the Port Royal spaceport. Gavin's condition would depend on how she acted. It made her ball up her fists in rage. She remembered snapping in the spaceport, fighting against Ana and the thugs with everything she had. She wondered briefly if she had doomed Gavin by her actions. A lump formed in her throat as she thought about such a possibility, but at the same time she knew she had reached her breaking point, and whatever happened, she was tired of cowering from them all.

I won't, she thought. Not anymore.

Sable remembered what Lazarus had said, that Mr. Maxwell had set the whole thing up. He probably knew that Lazarus was a CIB agent. It was a good bet that he was aware that she had been helping him. That wasn't going to earn her any points. She groaned as her mind went through this, the impact of her capture beating against her.

"Come and get me!" she cried out. "Let me see Gavin!"

When still no one came, she curled up again and went to sleep.

*   *   *   *   *

Sable awoke to the sound of her door opening. She blinked, confused for a moment, before she remembered where she was. Then she saw that it was Ana. Sable glared at her sullenly, waiting to see what would happen.

The woman sauntered into the room and let the door slide shut behind her. Outside, Sable caught a glimpse of Lars casually standing against the far wall of a hallway. Then the door closed. Ana moved to within a meter of the bed and stopped, looking Sable up and down appraisingly, with a slight smile on her face.

"So, you're awake at last. Good."

Sable looked at Ana, her heart racing. With Ana, she never knew if the woman was going to smother her with false compliments and sarcastic praise, or if she was simply going to beat the hell out of her and be done with it. Apparently Ana was still deciding.

"So? Do you have anything to say?" Ana asked, her voice like ice.

Sable stared back, wanting to defy the woman, but she didn't say anything.

"Cat got your tongue? Hmmm?" Ana said, smirking. "Well, maybe some exercise will help loosen it a bit."

Sable winced. Exercise to Ana meant a good beating. She had tried once or twice to fight back, to take Ana down, but she had never succeeded. No matter how hard she tried, Sable would never be as fast as Ana. The woman's cybernetic implants made her movements a blur.

"On your feet. Let's go," the other woman said coldly.

Sable knew refusing would only make it worse, but she hesitated a moment, the last vestiges of her modesty coloring her cheeks. "At least give me something to wear," she said.

"Wow. Making demands and everything. Putting on the brave face, are we?" Ana said, seemingly pleased that Sable had decided to show some backbone. "I think I'm really going to enjoy this. But, hey, if you manage to stand up to me for more than five minutes, I might let you wear something tomorrow."

Sable shook with rage as she rose from the bed, determined to surprise the hateful woman with just how much backbone she could muster. She followed Ana out of the room, trying hard to ignore the leers Lars gave her as she stepped out into the hall.

"Move it," Ana said, shoving her forward down the hall.

Sable stumbled forward, and then stalked down the passage as she had been instructed. At the end of the hall, Ana guided her into a large room with a workout mat. When they had both entered, Ana shut the door behind them and then moved to the center of the mat, bouncing on the balls of her feet and limbering up. Sable watched her for a moment, arms folded across her chest.

"Well, aren't you going to warm up?" Ana asked mockingly.

Sable shook her head once. I'm not going to give you the satisfaction, she thought. She was surprised at the amount of rage she was able to muster. "Just do what you want," Sable said finally.

Ana merely laughed. "I *want*," she emphasized, "for you to go through your lessons with me, Sable. Or were you too busy bedding the cop to remember to practice?" she finished, her voice harsh and accusing.

Sable didn't say anything, wondering if Lazarus was even alive. She didn't realize how much it could hurt to imagine him so far away and unreachable. She tried to shut it out of her mind as she watched Ana stretch.

"Defend yourself, you little brat," Ana said, dropping into a crouch.

Sable pursed her lips and took a slow, deep breath,

drawing all of her energy into herself and preparing for the onslaught she knew was coming.

In a flash, Ana lunged forward, stepping quickly through a series of kicks and punches that passed within centimeters of Sable's body. Sable moved to block each of them, but Ana was too fast, and the near-miss blows were gone before she had her defenses formed. Making a disgusted sound in her throat, Ana whirled and kicked out with her heel, raking Sable across the side of her face. Sable's head whipped around, and she stumbled sideways and fell to the mat, gasping in pain.

Ana sighed. "Looks like it's going to be a long lesson. You've got a lot of work to catch up on." Sable heard her laugh. She growled in anger as Ana strode closer, jumping to her feet and dropping into a defensive crouch again.

Fast . . . you've got to be fast, Sable chided herself. Don't anticipate her attacks. Just move like she taught you.

Ana came in again, a flurry of arms and legs, and this time Sable managed to block the first of the blows and slide out of the way, swinging her fist up into Ana's jaw before a kick landed in her gut, sending her sprawling again. She choked back the sensation of gagging and climbed to her feet again. Fury was plain on Ana's mien, and Sable noted with satisfaction that a tiny trickle of blood was running down the woman's chin. Sable had gotten to her.

Sable's pride was short-lived, though. When next her teacher moved in to attack, Sable couldn't even follow the blur of motion. Five or six solid hits rained down on her before she even hit the ground, her body wracked with pain.

"Don't ever think you can beat me," Ana said, closing in again. "You're about to find out just how much trouble you're in."

*　*　*　*　*

Lazarus was thankful that his visit to the *Lighthouse* coincided with one of its scheduled stops in the Aegis system. It was fortunate, he thought, that the trip from Lucullus had gone as fast as it had. He still had several days to poke around for information before the *Lighthouse* left to head to its next stop. He hoped he could figure out where to find Sable. If he was lucky.

They could have taken her anywhere, he told himself for the hundredth time as he and Ellesao disembarked from the charter flight they had taken from Penates. He kept finding himself resisting the urge to hold out hope that he would see her again. It hurt that way, but he didn't feel like being disappointed later.

Even after so many times, his visits to the *Lighthouse* never stopped filling him with awe. It was an amazing vessel, he had decided long ago, and something the Concord should be proud of. And it was the bustling center of most Concord activity in the Verge.

"What will we do first?" Ellesao asked as they moved through the concourse to the main terminal of the docking deck.

Lazarus led the way through the crowds, trying to reach one of the many massive elevators that ferried people up and down the length of the *Lighthouse*. "First we grab a room," he said over his shoulder as he pushed through the throngs of people. "There's a place I like to stay at when I'm here that should do nicely. Nice service, not too pricey. After that, we'll look up this MicroCore Investments and go pay them a visit."

"That sounds reasonable," Ellesao answered, following him. "What do you intend to ask/tell them?"

Lazarus shrugged as he finally reached the lifts. "I haven't thought about it yet. I've been a little preoccupied."

Ellesao stepped into the line beside him and said simply,

"Perhaps we should formulate a plan. If MicroCore is not in contact with the Mateos in any way, it would be appropriate/NEGATIVE to walk in and accuse them of it. It would be/NEGATIVE even if they *were*."

Lazarus chuckled as they moved forward in the line, waiting for the next available car. "Perhaps. But subtlety isn't really my strong suit," he quipped. As the next elevator car arrived and the pair stepped inside, Lazarus snapped his fingers. "Oh, I've got to remember to contact Monahan when we get checked into the hotel. I need to give him a call and let him know I've arrived." Lazarus chuckled again as the elevator descended rapidly. "I'm sure he's fit to be tied after that last message I sent him."

Soon enough, Lazarus and Ellesao were on Deck 198 of the *Lighthouse* and checking into the Pacific Plaza Hotel, where they quickly got settled into a comfortable suite of rooms. After inspecting the suite, Lazarus ducked back out into the streets and looked for a public vidphone booth. He dialed up Monahan's office.

The woman at the other end of the visual link, Charlotte, was polite and professional, as usual. "Administrator Monahan's office. How may I help you?"

"Charlotte, it's me, Laz. How you doing?"

"Oh, hello, Laz. Are you on board?" Charlotte smiled warmly at him.

"Actually, yes. Is the administrator in? I really need to talk to him."

"Oh, no. I'm sorry, Laz. He's away for the rest of the afternoon. Is there a number where he can reach you? I know he wants to speak with you." Charlotte leaned in conspiratorially toward the video camera at her end and whispered, "Whatever communication you sent him last time, it really got him worked up. He paced around in his office for two hours."

Lazarus chuckled at the imagery, but then he shook his head. "No, I don't want to leave a number, Charlotte. I don't know where I'm going to be. Tell him I got in. I'll track him down soon. I have some other things to take care of first anyway."

"I'll let him know. Stop in soon, though, okay? You still owe me dinner, you know."

Lazarus chuckled again. "I haven't forgotten. See you soon." He clicked off and checked his chronometer. He doubted if anyone in the office had had time to trace the call, but even if they had succeeded, they only had this street as reference. Lazarus also noted that there were still a couple of hours left in the business day.

Just enough time to swing over to MicroCore, he thought. He headed back to the Pacific Plaza to get Ellesao.

*   *   *   *   *

Sable was thankful the trip was finally over. They were home, or what passed for home, but she had no true idea where that was. Sullenly she followed Ana as they disembarked from the ship. Lars and Eduardo strolled along, one on either side of her, keeping an eye on her, but she hardly felt like running. In fact, she hardly felt like moving at all.

Ana had meted out the punishment in spades. Sable's whole body ached, and one eye was blackened and swollen. Ana refused to let her treat it, telling her that the suffering would teach her to pay attention to her lessons.

As they walked, Sable stared at the floor in front of her. She had long since stopped looking anyone in the eye. It had only earned her a backhand or kick. Her defiance wasn't gone, but she had tempered it and forced it down inside her for the time being. She could only take so much beating before her resolve to glare and talk back began to

waver. So she did exactly as she was ordered to, not daring
to cross any of the three of her captors in any way, biding
her time until she could do something productive to get out
of this predicament.

At least they let me put something on, Sable thought
fleetingly, although Ana had made her wait two days before
letting her dress again. Sable hated the way Eduardo and
Lars made a point to check up on her and her lessons whenever they could, leering at her as Ana sent her sprawling
across the mat. But there was nothing she could do about it,
so she tried to ignore them.

Her only respite was at night, or what passed for night on
the ship. At the end of each day, she was locked in her room
with a meal, and they ignored her until the morning, when
she was fed again before being hauled to the exercise room
once more.

By the end of the second day, Sable didn't care anymore.
Exhausted and aching from head to foot, she ate what they
gave her and collapsed each night on the bed, waking sleepily when Ana arrived in the morning.

The trip seemed to take forever, but in reality, only a few
days had passed in starfall. And now they were back in the
familiar surroundings that Sable had come to know as her
home, the place where Mr. Maxwell kept her. Despite herself, she trembled in dread at the thought of him. She wanted
to be able to stare him down when the time came, to make it
clear to him that he could no longer push her around, but she
knew in her heart that he still controlled her, that as long as
he had Gavin, she would do whatever he wanted in order to
protect her brother from harm. If it wasn't too late.

Sable could only guess what Mr. Maxwell would have to
say about her flagrant disregard for his instructions. She knew
she had stepped way over the line this time, and she feared for
Gavin's life, defiance or no defiance. She shuddered when

she thought of being alone with Mr. Maxwell. Unlike
Eduardo and Lars, Mr. Maxwell did more than gape at her
when he had her alone.

Sable sniffed once as she was led into her room and
looked around sadly as she heard the door being locked
behind her. It was in no way comforting to be back here. She
threw herself on the bed and buried her face in her arms, too
worn out and emotionally numb to cry.

*　*　*　*　*

Lazarus casually examined the unusual art prints on the
wall of the office where he and Ellesao waited to meet Mr.
Gordon Stillman, executive director of MicroCore Investments. MicroCore was not a large company, but Lazarus had
been impressed with the portfolio of other companies within
its folds, scattered across the four corners of the Verge. Ellesao sat beside Lazarus, staring out of the expansive windows
at the artificial sky. Lazarus decided he liked the look of the
art, graceful for its lack of electronic enhancement or
motion. It was simply abstract images displayed statically
on a flat surface, but its simplicity intrigued him.

When the door opened, Lazarus rose from his seat. A tall
man of middle years, impeccably groomed, with a touch of
gray at his temples and in the thin mustache he wore,
Gordon Stillman was obviously a man of taste and refine-
ment. He scanned Lazarus with an appraising eye as they
shook hands, and then his gaze turned to Ellesao. Lazarus
noticed one eyebrow arch slightly as Stillman took her in,
but he never hesitated to take her hand as well, and he was all
perfunctory smiles and greetings.

As he settled behind the large and stately desk in his
voluminous office, Stillman clasped his hands together in
front of him and said, "This is a most unusual visit, I must

say. I don't believe I can recall a member of the Concord's law enforcement dropping in on me before."

Lazarus smiled as he said, "Well, it's a rather unusual set of circumstances that bring us to you today, Mr. Stillman. The case I am working on is extraordinary, and—"

"Yes," Stillman interrupted, "you mentioned a case before, but I don't recall what you actually said it was you were investigating."

"I didn't," Lazarus said, drawing a slow, even breath. He didn't like this guy from the start. Gordon Stillman seemed to have an air of superiority about him just in the way he appraised everything, including his two guests. Besides, Lazarus thought sourly, I hate being interrupted. "Uh, tell me, Mr. Stillman, who within MicroCore would have decision-making power over what and where you invest Minister Yonce's assets?"

Stillman contemplated Lazarus for a moment before answering. "Well, that's quite a complicated thing, you see. There is a small team of financial advisors that plan the investing strategies for the company overall, and working beneath them, in different divisions of expertise, are a number of what we call watchdogs, individuals who constantly comb the latest financial, political, and commercial news, looking for insight into the future. They put together this information for the advisory team, who then refine the investment strategies accordingly."

"But the actual decision making about how much gets invested and where? That's the advisory team's realm?"

"Well, yes, more or less. They actually only put together recommendations, and then I sign off on the—"

"So you're actually the one who gives the yea or nay to all the spending decisions."

"Um . . . well, yes. But I obviously don't make these decisions in a—"

"So," Lazarus said, leaning forward and placing his hands on Stillman's desk, enjoying interrupting the man and watching his reaction when the shoe was on the other foot. "If I asked you if MicroCore had been secretly investing large sums of Concord dollars in a speculative venture in Port Royal that was actually a front for one of the largest crime syndicates in the Verge, you'd be able to tell me?" Lazarus tried to control his smile as Gordon Stillman's jaw dropped and his face turned a most incriminating shade of white.

"I, uh, I can assure you, *sir*," Stillman stammered, "that MicroCore Investments in no way consorts—"

"And if that money, supposedly being invested in an entertainment venture—a very speculative operation that was likely to lose money—was actually being used to purchase arms that were then being repackaged and distributed to terrorists in secret by *another* company, a freight company, *also* owned by MicroCore, you would know about it?"

Stillman only stared across his desk at Lazarus, his hands clenched tightly and his knuckles as white as his face. "Damn," he breathed at last. "There was no way—" He straightened up then, collecting himself as best as he could. "No. As I tried to explain before, MicroCore in no way deals with any businesses of that kind. Now, I have a lot to do, so I must bid you—"

"Stop lying to me, Stillman," Lazarus said. "It's written all over your face, and you've all but confessed. Now, we could do this the usual way, where I go get a warrant to examine your books, which I'm sure would be all up to snuff, but that doesn't really tell me what I want to know, does it? On the other hand," Lazarus went on, still smiling, "I could have my companion here have a sit-down with your corporate computing system, and I bet she'd dig up some pretty interesting records that looked nothing like those public books."

By this point, Stillman's hands were trembling, despite his best efforts to control them. He fumbled for something in his pocket, and then seemed to change his mind and clasped his hands together again.

"So what do you say, Gordon? You don't mind if I call you Gordon, do you?" Lazarus asked, leaning forward again. "What do you say we have a little look at your system, Gordon, take a little tour of the financials in there? Do you think I'd find out what I want to know?"

"Please," Stillman said in a whining voice, the last vestiges of his calm demeanor evaporating. "Please, you don't understand. I had no choice. They promised me—you don't know who you're dealing with here. You're in way over your head."

Lazarus noted that Stillman's words were not a threat, but in abject respect and terror were spoken. "Nonetheless, I want the names. You tell me who I'm dealing with right now."

"My G-god, I can't! They'll k-kill me! Don't you understand? This is big! We're talking the very top of the line. I can't cross them. I won't!"

"You're going to go to jail for a very long time, Mr. Stillman," Lazarus said forcefully, standing up to accentuate his point. "Nothing will change that, but if you cooperate here, tell me who is behind this, I can make sure you get off a little easier."

Gordon Stillman's lips pursed. "No," he said through clenched teeth. "You have no idea how powerful—"

The glass of the window shattered, spraying the entire room with fragments as a high-velocity mass projectile slammed through it and into Gordon Stillman. The force of the blow blasted the man, chair and all, to the opposite side of the desk, and then Gordon Stillman was off balance, a strange look on his face, as the chair tipped over and he crumpled into the corner.

Lazarus was on the floor almost instinctively when the shot was fired, reaching for his weapon. He noted somewhere, in a more lucid part of his mind, that Ellesao had dropped down immediately, too. Lazarus scrambled behind the desk and waited for another shot, but none came. He watched Stillman for a moment, but the executive director of MicroCore Investments lay unmoving on the plush carpet. Ellesao had moved against the wall, near the shattered window, staying out of sight.

When the door to the office flew open, Lazarus had his pistol up and was halfway to squeezing off a shot before he realized it was Stillman's administrative assistant. The woman had ushered them into the office when they had first arrived, but now she surveyed the room with a look of confusion.

"Get down!" Lazarus yelled, motioning with his free hand. "You'll get your head shot off!"

The assistant caught sight of Stillman's body, and her hand flew to her mouth in horror. She turned and fled, a choking sob echoing after her.

"Ellesao," Lazarus called softly. "Are you all right?"

"Yes," the mechalus woman replied.

"That was a mass rifle, I'm sure of it," Lazarus said, breathing heavily. "You realize it'll punch right through that wall you're hiding behind?"

"True, but they see me/NEGATIVE, so they would have to get a guess/lucky. *You* realize it will penetrate the desk you are hiding behind."

Lazarus's grip on his gun intensified. "I know," he said. "I don't even want to take a peek to see if the shooter's still out there."

The moments dragged on, and after what seemed like an eternity but was in reality only a minute or so, Lazarus slid along the side of the desk to place himself against the wall next to the window, on the opposite side from Ellesao. Very carefully Lazarus peered around the edge of the sill. Out on the deck, people were milling about, and he saw a squad of peace officers arriving. From this vantage, it was obvious to Lazarus that the only place the shooter could have fired the shot was from a building across a small plaza. If the window had remained intact, Laz might have been able to visually trace a line of sight back through the hole from where the shot hit Stillman and judge which floor it came from, but with the window shattered, it would be nearly impossible. At this point, Lazarus didn't care. If the shooter was still up there, he or she wouldn't be there for long.

Not with Concord Star Force running around down there, he thought.

"Ellesao," Lazarus said, "I think our shooter has cleared out. And the cavalry has just arrived. Maybe we should get out of here before they find us and ask us a lot of uncomfortable questions."

"That sounds like an idea/good," Ellseao replied.

Staying low, the two of them crossed the room and slipped out the door of Gordon Stillman's office. Beyond, in the reception area, Stillman's assistant was nowhere to be seen.

She must have cleared out and called the authorities from elsewhere, Lazarus thought. We should be doing the same, I think. Taking a back way out, Lazarus and Ellesao vanished from the premises moments before a cadre of *Lighthouse* security arrived on the scene.

14.0:

"THAT WAS CONVENIENT/UNUSUALLY," Ellesao remarked as she and Lazarus rode the lift. They had returned to the Pacific Plaza directly from their visit to MicroCore and were now heading up to their suite.

"What do you mean?" Lazarus asked absently, working over what Stillman had said before he had been killed. Who could he have been talking about? Lazarus wondered, when he referred to it going all the way to the top?

The pair reached their suite and went inside. Ellesao sat in a chair while Lazarus began to pace, thinking while he listened to the mechalus.

"I mean," Ellesao continued, "that the assassin who killed Stillman was there quickly. We were not in that office for five minutes/greater than, yet someone managed to get into position and kill him before he could tell us anything important."

Lazarus glanced over at the mechalus as he strode back and forth, absorbing this. "Hmmm," he said, considering. "It's possible they had the office bugged." He rubbed his chin, thinking. "In fact," he added, "they probably have the whole place bugged and the vidphone lines tapped, too. They reacted as soon as they knew we were there and were onto him."

"Perhaps, but it was still quick/very."

"Well, we can be sure they know we're onto them and that we're on their trail. We've got to be very careful now."

Lazarus dropped into a chair. "I've been thinking about what Stillman did tell us."

"Yes?"

"Well, he kept saying that it was big, that it went all the way to the top."

"I remember. You think you have an idea who he was talking about?"

"Maybe. But it scares the hell out of me. I keep asking myself, 'The top of what?' MicroCore? That doesn't make sense. He's the top, except for Minister Yonce, and if it was her, she wouldn't need to bribe him, and she sure as hell wouldn't be planting incriminating evidence for us to find."

"Seems rational so far," Ellesao said, stretching out on a couch.

"So it would be something external. I'm wondering if he means the top of the *Lighthouse*, or perhaps even the top of the government."

"Well, Administrator Wakefield runs the *Lighthouse*, but why would he be involved in something like this?"

"I don't have a clue. Wakefield doesn't make sense at all. Besides, when you're talking about the power around here, whether it's the *Lighthouse* or the Verge as a whole, only one person springs to mind."

"And that is . . . ?" Ellesao asked, leaning forward in anticipation.

"Undersecretary Michael Thayne."

Ellesao blinked. "Thayne? Interesting."

Lazarus mulled his own idea over in his head. Michael Thayne, undersecretary and minister of the Galactic Consulate, was probably the most powerful man in the Verge. The Galactic Consulate was the diplomatic branch of the government, composed of six ministers from each stellar nation and two from each alien nation. To the masses, the ninety-one ministers were seen as a type of modern nobility, perhaps the most prestigious positions within the Concord as a whole, and Thayne was one of them. Even more impressive was the fact that Thayne was one of six under-secretaries appointed by the first secretary, the elected leader of the consulate. Thayne also happened to be in charge of Verge affairs, responsible for protecting the Concord's interests in the frontiers of space. Of late, he had made it clear that he represented the Verge's interests as much as the Concord's.

"Think about it," Lazarus said, sitting forward and ticking points off on his fingertips. "He's a powerful force in the Verge and seems to have a lot of ambitions that no one can quite pin him down on. A lot of people say that he would like to become a true leader of an independent Verge, separate from Old Space. And—and this is reaching, I know, but hear me out—what's going to happen if CFN terrorists continue to disrupt business in the Verge, well supplied with weapons by our Jamaican friends?"

"There will eventually be pressure for some sort of action by the Galactic Concord."

"Exactly. I can't think of many reasons Yonce would want to cause such a ruckus, given her background. She has been, and always will be, interested in only one thing: the almighty dollar."

"Which she would not be making many of, were she to be supporting CFN," Ellesao said. "She would be pouring funds/ample into something she would not see a return on."

"Well, sure, except that she's not doing it. Someone conned, coerced, or bribed Stillman to do it with her money but keep it hush-hush."

"They were setting her up?"

"It seems that way. Now, if it's Thayne, as I'm starting to believe, he could have the evidence planted for me to find, which I would then take back to my superiors. A major investigation would ensue, and the Galactic Concord would clamp down hard on the Verge. You're talking about serious military presence and less individual system freedom."

"Why would Thayne want that to happen? And why pin it on Yonce?"

"Well, here's where I'm reaching. If he truly does want to rule an independent Verge, he has to convince the people to support him. What better way to do that than to make it appear that Yonce is trying for a greater Concord presence, then plan to renounce the whole thing as a scheme of the Concord's to gain tighter control?"

"Interesting. That is a stretch/considerable."

"But in its own twisted way, it makes sense. Yonce wants to make money. The Verge is a perfect place for it, provided there is a certain level of stability. So she secretly supports the Concord Free Terrorists, hoping that they will do enough damage that the Concord will come riding in and take control. At least, that's what everyone would believe, and I was going to hand them all the evidence. And then Thayne stands up and says, 'What do you take us Vergers for, a bunch of fools? We'll never let you Galactic Concord bastards come in here and strip away our freedom. We declare independence.'"

"But he is really part of the Galactic Concord, too," Ellesao said, frowning.

"Yes, that's true, but he's been very careful to position himself as a Verger rather than as an Arriver, a newcomer to the region from Old Space. He always talks as if he's been a part of things out here for a long time, that the Verge has his support, and that his loyalties lie here before the Galactic Consulate."

"I suppose your idea does make sense. But you have evidence/NEGATIVE to substantiate it."

"You're right," Lazarus admitted, standing. "But Stillman

was suitably terrified by whoever came and leaned on him. He didn't strike me as the kind of person who's going to let just anyone intimidate him. And the way he said what he did, about it going all the way to the top . . . I wouldn't have just concocted this notion if it hadn't been for those comments."

"So how do we prove your theory one way or another?"

Lazarus chuckled ruefully. "You're not going to like this much, I'm afraid."

"What?"

"I think it's time to go pay Minister Yonce a visit."

"Oh, good. Let's get her shot today, too" Ellesao quipped.

"Yeah. Two in one day might be a record. But, hey," Lazarus said, smiling at Ellesao's successful attempt at human sarcasm as the two of them headed out the door into the hallway, "if someone does try to plug her, my little theory would start to look awfully reasonable."

Ellesao rolled her eyes and said, "You are so irreverent/incredibly."

"No, just realistic."

* * * * *

"Look," Lazarus said to the man sitting behind the desk in Minister Relitalia Yonce's *Lighthouse* offices, "I understand that she doesn't accept unannounced drop-in visits, but this is a matter of extreme urgency that involves her directly. I know it's late, I know the minister is busy, but I need only a few minutes of her time. Please, just dial her up and ask."

"I'm sorry, sir, but it's just not going to happen." The fellow's tone was irritatingly polite. "You can make an appointment if you want, or I might be able to plead your case to one of her advisors who's working late, but Minister Yonce is not going to talk to you tonight."

Exasperated, Lazarus leaned forward across the front of the desk, getting his face down within inches of the other fellow's. "Now, look. I know you're doing your job and that you're following standard protocol here. But this isn't standard. You know about the minister's personal holding company here on the *Lighthouse?* MicroCore? Have you heard yet what happened there today?"

The receptionist bristled as Lazarus loomed over his desk, getting closer than was generally considered polite, but at the mention of the killing, he nodded and didn't say anything.

"Okay. I have good reason to believe that the same thing could happen to the minister unless you let me talk to her *now.*"

The receptionist blinked a couple of times and leaned back a little farther, away from Lazarus. "I see. Based on that explanation, I think you've got a pretty good idea that there's no way I'm letting you in to see her now, if there had ever been a chance before. In fact, I think perhaps it's time for me to summon security unless you leave right now."

Lazarus sighed. The last thing he wanted to do was flash his badge around. The fewer people who actually knew what he was up to, the safer they all would be, he thought, but this guy wasn't leaving him much choice. He slipped the badge from his pocket and looked around to see who else might notice, and when he was certain there was no one watching, he flashed it.

"No one knows I'm here, and I'd like to keep it that way. So you didn't see this. Do you understand?"

The guy took a look at the badge, and then blinked and did a double take. "Oh! Um, sorry, sir, I didn't—please forgive me, but I just didn't—"

"Forget it," Lazarus said, pocketing the badge as he waved his other hand in dismissal. "You were only doing your job. And I'm only doing mine. And I'm telling you, if you want to make sure the minister makes it through the night, you get me in to talk to her. Now, and in private."

The receptionist swallowed nervously at Lazarus's words, but he nodded vigorously and said, "Why don't you two have a seat over there while I get hold of her. It should take only a minute."

Lazarus nodded and turned to sit down in the waiting area. He chuckled at the receptionist's reaction.

Always the professional, even after the bomb I just dropped on him.

Lazarus shrugged his shoulders as he settled into a chair, and Ellesao dropped into one beside him. A moment later the receptionist was speaking animatedly into the vidphone and nodding his head fervently. When he finished and looked up, he motioned for Lazarus to come over. Lazarus joined him at the desk.

"Minister Yonce said to give her about five minutes, and then she would be happy to visit with you for a few moments. After that, she has a formal dinner engagement this evening."

"That's fine. It'll take me about two minutes to get my point across." Lazarus leaned in and lowered his voice. "Did you tell her I'm a cop?"

The guy nodded, not saying anything.

"Okay. We'll wait." Lazarus turned and went back to his seat.

About fifteen minutes later, the receptionist called over to Lazarus and Ellesao that the minister was ready to see them. Lazarus and the mechalus stood up and followed the guy as he led them back into the offices beyond the reception area.

Minister Relitalia Yonce's offices were spacious, tastefully decorated in a modern style that was subtle but elegant. Magnificent pieces of art of every conceivable kind from all over the galaxy were displayed, making clear to all who passed through these rooms that the minister had money and lots of it. Lazarus whistled in appreciation as they passed through a front conference room dominated by a large table surrounded by chairs. The room was filled with a collection of priceless sculpture around the perimeter.

She certainly likes to show off her money. Lazarus chuckled, wondering how much it all was worth.

Beyond the conference room was Yonce's inner sanctum, a large office with an antique desk. The minister was seated behind it, staring at a computer screen intently. She did not look up as Lazarus and Ellesao entered, but tapped occasionally on the keypad as she scanned something. The receptionist silently motioned for the two of them to seat themselves in a pair of chairs that faced the front of Yonce's desk. As Lazarus settled into the soft overstuffed chair, he studied the minister.

Yonce was a middle-aged woman with short, graying hair. She was dressed in a black formal evening dress, accentuated by a dazzlingly elegant diamond necklace. Her mouth was pursed in a deep frown as she continued to stare at the monitor in front of her. This was a woman who was used to power, who expected to be obeyed by her subordinates and cooperated with by her peers. She expected no less than the best effort from everyone around her. She was also a woman who, it seemed to Lazarus, had no patience for nonsense from anyone.

Yonce made them wait for several long minutes while she perused whatever it was she was consulting. During that time, the office seemed uncomfortably silent, and Lazarus was suddenly reminded of his days back in school when he got into mischief and was summoned to the principal's office. He tried to keep his squirming to a minimum, but he suddenly found the seat far from comfortable.

At last Yonce tapped one final key and sat back, deep in thought. Then she looked up, first at Lazarus, then at Ellesao. "Fabian tells me you have something urgent that both you and he felt needed my attention this evening, as opposed to tomorrow morning. As you can see, I am preparing to attend a speaking engagement being held this evening. Therefore, please be succinct, as I am running late."

Lazarus nodded, swallowed, and nodded again. Finally, after stealing a quick glance at Ellesao, he said, "I assume that Fabian told you who I am."

"He did."

"Then I hope you take what I am about to reveal to you as seriously as possible."

"Mr. Lazarus, I can assure you that nothing passes within my notice that I do not take seriously. Please, time is of the essence here."

"Yes, well. I have strong reason to believe that Undersecretary Michael Thayne is attempting to falsely incriminate you for political reasons."

Minister Yonce laughed, a deep, hearty chuckle that was reflected in her twinkling eyes. "Mr. Lazarus, every member of the Galactic Consulate is attempting to do the exact same thing to every other member on a daily basis. That's hardly news."

Lazarus grimaced and tried again. "I seriously believe that he has put into motion an elaborate scheme that fingers you as the mastermind behind the funding of a major terrorist operation. I believe it is his intention to expose you for these crimes and use the resulting outrage by the citizens of the Verge to set himself up to lead the Verge into gaining independence from the Galactic Concord."

Yonce looked at Lazarus, frowning deeply. She tapped her lips with the tip of one finger, and then finally said, "Mister Lazarus, that's both a very serious and a somewhat outlandish speculation on your part. I certainly hope you have some sort of evidence to back up these claims."

"I do. Well, I definitely have evidence that someone is attempting to pin these crimes on you, but as of right now, I still only suspect that Undersecretary Thayne is behind it."

"Hmm. And what evidence would that be?" Yonce asked, leaning back in her chair.

Lazarus sat forward in his own seat and began his tale, explaining everything that had happened since he had been brought into the case and stationed in Port Royal, leading up to the conversation with and the death of Gordon Stillman at MicroCore Investments. Occasionally Ellesao interjected a tidbit of information when Lazarus left something out. When Lazarus was finished, he let out a deep breath and waited for Yonce to say something.

For a very long time, the minister didn't say a word. She merely stared past Lazarus and Ellesao, seemingly lost in thought. When she finally did speak again, her question came as a surprise to Lazarus. "Although I appreciate the fact that you've come to me with this, I must ask why? Surely you have the means to open a formal investigation of Thayne within your own organization. What is it you hoped I would do with this information?"

"Well, Minister, you are correct. I am actually well past due to report in and give my superior an update. However, I don't feel that I have quite a strong enough case yet, and I suspect Thayne may have someone on the inside in the bureau. He seems to have been anticipating many of my moves. Also, I felt it important to warn you of this. One person in your employ is already dead. I fear you may be the next target."

Yonce chuckled again. "Well, your concern is appreciated, my dear Mr. Lazarus. However, a person in my position cannot simply disappear and go into hiding. There is too much government work that needs to be done, and it cannot be done invisibly. But I will take your advice to heart and watch my step. Fabian can make arrangements for additional escorts for the next several days."

Lazarus nodded, and then took a deep breath before making his last point. "Finally, I had hoped I might convince you to seek more information from sources I don't necessarily have easy access to, or in places I might not think to look. I'm still hoping to find Sable, the courier who was at the beginning of it all." He was afraid to hope too much, but he had to ask, he told himself.

"If my network had any inkling that any of this was going on, I know I would have heard about it by now. The very fact that this is news to me tells me that you are either barking up the wrong tree, or else Thayne has done a remarkable job of covering his tracks. In either case, I don't think I'm going to be of much help to you. But in the interests of helping you find this woman and to protect myself, I will get some people on it immediately. If I hear anything promising, I'll let you know instantly."

Lazarus nodded deeply in thanks. "That's all I could ask of you, Minister, and I appreciate it. And your time, which we've taken up too much of already."

"Nonsense. If I've learned anything in my years in this job, it's that you're never too well informed to be caught off guard by something. Whether Thayne is behind this or not, I'm in a much better position to react to it than before. So I thank you for bringing it to my attention. You have done anything but waste my time tonight.

"However," Yonce said, standing, "the demands of office wait for no one, and I really must say good evening. I trust you can find your own way out?"

"Certainly, Minister. Have a nice evening." Lazarus and Ellesao stood and moved to the door, leaving the minister once again keenly studying her computer terminal.

Once they were outside the offices and on their way back to the Pacific Plaza, Lazarus looked at Ellesao. "You were fairly quiet in there."

"I did not feel it was my place/truly to speak. This is your case, Lazarus. I am here to help, but I am a Concord agent/NEGATIVE. Besides, you seemed to cover the bases quite thoroughly. There was little for me to add."

"So what did you think of her reaction? Was I right to trust her? Or is she in on it?"

"I do not think she is a part of it, as we logically concluded before. It would never have made sense/any, and since you resist acting in the capacity that the enemy had hoped to manipulate you toward, your usefulness to them is gone. If she were involved in some way, I would think she would be trying to have you killed."

Lazarus shivered slightly at the thought that there was no good reason to keep him alive, and he wondered just how long that had been the case. He quickened his pace a little.

"Lazarus," Ellesao said, stopping in front of a holovideo newscast at a corner. "Look." She pointed upward at the three-dimensional display. There was an image of the CIB agent there.

He grabbed Ellesao and pulled her into the shadows of the nearest building, watching the broadcast.

". . . is being sought for questioning in connection with the brutal murder of a high-profile businessman today"—an image of Gordon Stillman replaced Lazarus's—"an investment manager for a highly successful trading company, MicroCore Investments. One of the primary stockholders is Minister Relitalia Yonce. . . ."

Lazarus sighed and shook his head. "Damn. I should have guessed they would try this. Especially when we were spotted by the secretary during the middle of it."

"What now?" Ellesao asked.

Lazarus glanced at her. "Come on. Let's get off the streets. I don't want people to start noticing me."

Leading the way, Lazarus headed back to the Pacific Plaza, entering through a side door rather than passing through the main lobby. They took the back stairs up to their room. As Lazarus approached, he got an odd feeling someone was watching him. He reached the door and let it scan him to unlock it, but he couldn't shake the feeling. As the door slid open, he glanced down the hall and saw a man standing in the elevator alcove, peeking around the corner at him. It was one of the men who had grabbed Sable at the Port Royal spaceport.

Bloody hell! The room's being watched! At the same instant, he thought, She's here! She's on the *Lighthouse*!

He wanted to lure the bastard into the stairwell and grab him there. He turned away from the door, motioning for Ellesao to head back down the hall toward the stairs, when a flash of movement caught his eye from inside the room. Instinct told him it was a figure with a gun before he even turned his head to get a good look at the motion, and he dived out of the way, crashing into Ellesao, just as the loud thump of a pistol exploded from inside. The shot whizzed past Lazarus's shoulder and embedded itself in the wall on the opposite side of the hall.

Lazarus was desperately yanking his gun out even as he dropped heavily on top of the mechalus. He rolled to one side and fired two quick shots down the hall at the man who had been near the elevators, the vibrating belch of his stutter pistol reverberating in the hallway. The figure, who had begun to run toward them, staggered and dropped in mid-stride.

Lazarus flipped himself backward as another shot erupted from inside the room, and then rolled up over his shoulders and head to land on his feet. On hands and knees, Ellesao scrambled out of the way. Lunging to one side, Lazarus fired wildly into the doorframe of the suite, feeling the burp of the gun go off and radiate into the entry hall. There was a grunt and a thump, but when Lazarus heard a shouted curse from inside, he knew he had only grazed the attacker. At the same instant, a door a few rooms down opened, and several more thugs with guns burst out into the hall. When they saw Lazarus, they began to run toward him.

"Come on!" he yelled at Ellesao, grabbing her by the arm and helping her to her feet as he rushed down the hall toward the stairwell. "We're out of here!" As they scrambled away, Lazarus turned once to fire back at the pursuing attackers. A figure stumbled out the door of their suite, holding a large pistol. Lazarus recognized him as the other creep who had nabbed Sable. The man's arm hung awkwardly at his side, and he couldn't seem to keep his balance. The shot had been direct enough. Several other shots whistled dangerously close as Ellesao hit the stairwell. Lazarus flinched as the mechalus charged through the door, and then he followed right behind her.

They were down to the main level in a matter of moments, and Lazarus motioned Ellesao out the side door they had come in through moments before. When they were outside in the streets again, Lazarus slipped his pistol back into the shoulder holster under his coat. He looked around, checking for signs that others were following them. Then he grabbed Ellesao by the arm and guided her down the street to a small cafe. He darted inside and took a booth, motioning for Ellesao to sit opposite him. He grabbed a menu and buried his face in it, watching the door for signs of pursuit.

When he was convinced that they had not been spotted, he looked at the mechalus woman. "They're turning the heat up. I think it's time to come in from the cold."

"Clarify?" Ellesao asked, confused.

"It's on old spy expression. It's time to get the cavalry on our side. It's time we brought the full weight of the Concord law and justice systems to bear on the situation. I want you to go over to the Administration Building and see my boss. Administrator Oslo Monahan. Give him this." Lazarus reached into his coat pocket and pulled out a data crystal, which he slid across the table to Ellesao. "And tell him everything. Tell him I'm on my way to report in, but I have to take care of one thing first."

"Lazarus, what are you up to?"

"Those men were the same ones who grabbed Sable. It's very possible she's on the *Lighthouse* right now. I'm going to find out."

"Do not do something rash. You cannot take them on all alone, just to get one of them to lead you back to her. That is behavior/irrational, and it does not aid Sable if you get killed."

Lazarus shook his head. "Only as a last resort. I have another idea. I'll fill you in when I see you back at Monahan's office. Now go and deliver this for me. And stay put. I'll be along shortly."

Lazarus got up from the table and headed out the door.

* * * * *

When Ana entered the room, she was carrying something that made Sable cringe. It was a diaphanous silk robe that Mr. Maxwell was particularly fond of. Ana tossed it to her, and Sable caught it and held it distastefully.

"Clean yourself up. Then put it on," the hateful woman said.

Sable hung her head, dreading this moment but knowing it was inevitable. She began to strip off the simple shift that she had been wearing for the last several days.

Ana headed out the door, saying over her shoulder as she went, "I'll be back in twenty minutes. You'd better be ready to go."

Sable slumped to the bed when the door shut, a tight lump in her throat. She hated how she was forced to rush to get ready for something she dreaded more than anything in the world. God, how she hated that woman! Only the image of Gavin made her stand and move woodenly toward the shower.

I don't even know if Gavin's still alive, she thought.

Don't! She told herself. You don't know he's not, and you're the only thing he's got. Whatever happens, you've got to save him. Just keep telling yourself that. And when the time comes, they'll pay. All of them.

She quickly finished the shower and dried off, then brushed out her hair and slipped into the hated robe. It clung to her skin and hid nothing. Still, she pulled it tightly about herself and sat down to wait.

At least, she thought with a brief flicker of satisfaction, I was ready before Ana came back.

When the door opened a second time, Sable winced at what she saw. In Ana's hands were a thick steel collar with a leash and a set of restraints. Mr. Maxwell sometimes insisted that she be presented to him in that fashion, usually when he was displeased with her.

"Turn around," Ana growled at Sable and slipped the collar around her neck.

Sable heard the click as it was locked shut. Then Ana grabbed one of her wrists and jerked it behind her, securing it in the cuffs. When her other arm was locked to the first, Ana spun her around and snapped the leash on her collar.

"Time to go," she said, smiling cruelly at Sable. With that, she headed out the door, tugging on the leash and forcing Sable to follow, the robe wafting lazily around her body with nothing to hold it closed.

As they neared Mr. Maxwell's private room, Ana said casually over her shoulder, as though they were the best of friends, "I'll bet you've missed him, seeing how long you've been away. If you're especially good tonight, I'll bet he might let you stay with him rather than send you back."

Sable refused to answer but kept an image of Gavin firmly fixed in the forefront of her mind.

For you, Gavin. To keep you alive. To keep you safe.

The door slid open, and Ana led Sable inside. Mr. Maxwell was reclining on his favorite couch, reading an actual book, one of his loves and vices, he always claimed. He was dressed in a pair of lounging pants and a loosely tied robe. The room around him had several shelves filled with other printed volumes. It was the largest collection of non-electronic information Sable had ever seen, but she cared little for it. As Ana moved with purposeful strides toward Mr. Maxwell, Sable followed grudgingly, her toes digging into the plush carpet.

"Ah, Sabine, my dear. You look lovely. Thank you, Ana. That will be fine."

Ana dropped the leash, letting it bounce against Sable's stomach, then turned and retreated from the room. Sable stared at the floor in front of her, clenching her teeth.

For you, Gavin.

"Sabine," Mr. Maxwell said quietly. She continued to look downward. "Sabine, look at me."

Slowly Sable raised her eyes and looked into the man's face. She could see the appreciation in his eyes as they roamed over her, and it made her cheeks blush hotly. She wondered if the hatred she felt for him was apparent in her face.

"Sabine, you've been a very willful and disobedient girl. Now why, do you suppose, did I have to send Ana and the others to come find you? Weren't my instructions clear?"

Sable stood rooted to the spot where Ana had left her, her gaze fixed on Mr. Maxwell's face, hearing his words but fighting to keep them outside her mind, to think only of her brother.

"I suppose Ana discussed these transgressions with you on the way back," Mr. Maxwell continued, "but I'm not sure that was sufficient to make it clear to you what I expect. Are you, Gavin, and I going to have to have a talk?"

Sable shook her head. "No, sir," she said, breathing deeply to control her loathing.

"You've learned your lesson about disobeying, have you?" Mr. Maxwell said, a mocking smile in his voice.

"Yes, sir," Sable lied, despising the words.

For Gavin, she said silently. For Gavin.

"Good. Then see that the lesson sticks with you. Now come here."

Slowly, a single escaped tear sliding down her cheek, Sable crossed the few remaining meters to the man she hated more than anyone in the galaxy.

15.0:

THE CORNER WAS a busy place, Lazarus observed as he entered through the main doors. The entire tavern and adjoining casino was one huge round room, with a second balcony level above it. The irony of the name was not lost on him. There wasn't a corner to be found in the place. A large fellow, stripped to the waist, head shaved, and body almost completely covered in tattoos, moved to block Lazarus's way.

"Readout says you're packing," the huge bouncer said, extending his hand. "I'll need to take care of that for you before I can let you through."

Lazarus sized him up for a half a second. Then he opened his coat, exposing the holstered stutter pistol. The bouncer reached in and removed the weapon, slipping it into a drawer behind a counter along the wall.

"You can get it back when you leave," he said, smiling. "Enjoy your visit."

Lazarus hesitated. Is this such a good idea? he asked himself. You're way out on a limb here, and you just gave the galaxy's biggest human art show your only weapon.

If you can think of a better way to find Sable, Lazarus, old boy, I'm all ears.

He sighed and looked at the bouncer. He leaned in a little so he wouldn't have to shout and said, "I'm looking for someone named Handstand Howard."

The bouncer pulled back and looked at Lazarus with

surprise, but then he nodded and put his fingers to his mouth and whistled shrilly. Most of the patrons in the place looked up briefly, but the bouncer caught the eye of the person he wanted and motioned whoever it was over.

A moment later another hulk of a man, almost as large as the tattooed fellow, strolled across the open floor, deftly dodging the patrons who were dancing to the lively music coming from the band on stage on the far side of the circular room. Lazarus immediately figured him for an ex-military type, probably a marine. Short burr haircut, gray camouflage fatigue pants tucked inside of combat boots, and a T-shirt that fit snugly over every bulging muscle told the tale as plainly as a standard issue uniform, to Lazarus's way of thinking.

"Yeah? What's up, Elmo?" the guy asked the tattooed bouncer, his voice raised to be heard of the din of the place.

"This guy needs to talk to Martin," Elmo said.

"No, I said I needed to talk to—" Lazarus started to correct Elmo, but the tattooed fellow cut him off.

"Shut up. Martin will understand what you want, but stop saying that name out loud here."

Lazarus bit back a retort and just nodded.

"All right, come on. I'll take you to see Martin," the ex-marine said, and he turned to lead Lazarus back through the crowd to the bar.

"Hey, Swede," Elmo called out as they moved away.

"Yeah?" the ex-marine said, looking back over his shoulder. Lazarus stopped and waited, unable to go anywhere with the huge man standing in front of him.

"I'm due for a break in a few minutes. Tell Grimy, would ya?"

In response, the ex-marine waved his hand over his head once and turned back to lead Lazarus to wherever they were going.

At the bar, the ex-marine motioned for Lazarus to have a seat on one of the barstools. "I'll get Martin. Make yourself comfortable. . . . Gr'uun!" he yelled at a huge weren who was tending bar a few meters farther down. "Can you get this gentleman something to drink? Put it on my comp card." To Lazarus, the ex-marine said, "Gr'uun'll get you a beer or something. Anything you want . . . compliments of the house."

Lazarus nodded to the ex-marine in thanks and settled onto the barstool. The weren went back to what he was doing as the ex-marine disappeared through a door that led to the interior of the place, what would be the central hub if The Corner were a giant wheel. From the sounds and the brief glimpse Lazarus caught, it had to be the kitchen. Lazarus settled on the stool at the end of the bar and looked around, wondering how someone named Handstand Howard could connect him with Sable.

Sabine. Her name is Sabine.

Lazarus was still getting used to the name, and he liked rolling it around in his head or even speaking it aloud.

"What can I get you?" the weren asked, appearing in front of Lazarus, using a rag in one massive clawed paw to wipe a mug held in the other.

"Uh, just coffee. Thanks."

"Sure. You want regular or t'sa?" the weren asked as he produced a large, heavy mug and set it in front of Lazarus.

"Just regular is fine," Lazarus said, chuckling as he imagined the buzz he would get by drinking such a huge mug of t'sa coffee.

The weren poured Lazarus a serving of black coffee, and Lazarus thanked him and began to sip at it.

A man appeared at Lazarus's elbow a moment later. "Hi. I'm Martin Skvrsky, the manager. The Swede said you were looking for someone."

Lazarus looked at the guy, who had the appearance of someone who worked hard for a living but loved what he did. "Yeah. I was told that I should talk to Handstand Howard here."

Skvrsky blinked once, and then immediately looked around to see if anyone else had heard him. "At last. Come on," he said and led Lazarus into the kitchens. Lazarus got up and followed the guy somewhat bewilderedly, wondering for the hundredth time who Handstand Howard was and hoping he was indeed a friend of Sable's.

Skvrsky led Lazarus through the kitchen to what Lazarus thought was a large broom closet. Skvrsky opened the door and stepped inside, and Lazarus followed him, one eyebrow raised in confusion. Skvrsky moved to the back of the closet and twisted a hook on the wall. A section of the plastisteel wall popped free and glided open, its seams suddenly coming into view where they had been hidden before.

Skvrsky led Lazarus through the small door and slid it shut behind them, and then the two of them were heading up a staircase that seemed to curve around, following the shape of the wall of the kitchen. The stairs wound up and up for a while, and then they were on a landing. Skvrsky stepped through an opening into a small hallway. The hallway stretched straight ahead, with several doors opening off of it. Skvrsky led Lazarus to the first door on the left and went inside. Lazarus followed and found himself in a small, sparsely decorated room, with a simple table and a couple of chairs.

Skvrsky took one of the chairs and motioned for Lazarus to have a seat in the other one. Lazarus sat across from the man, who looked at him for a several moments.

"How did you come by that name?" Skvrsky asked Lazarus point-blank.

"Why?" Lazarus asked in return, not at all comfortable with this situation.

No gun, trapped up here with someone you don't know. You're an idiot, Laz.

"Look, I can't help you unless I know I can trust you. Now, who gave you that name?"

Lazarus considered, but then he sighed and admitted, "I don't know. He wouldn't say. But I know why."

"You are certain it was a he?"

"Look, why all the questions? What is it I've asked for?"

Skvrsky drummed his fingers on the table, studying Lazarus. "Handstand Howard is a code word. It means that whoever was given it knows the whereabouts of someone very important to a friend of mine, and my friend wants very much to see this person alive and well. If my friend gave you this code name, then you know who I'm talking about. But I want to know how you came by the name."

Lazarus nodded. "I received it as part of a message delivered to me via Grid by an anonymous shadow. As a result of some research I was doing."

Skvrsky nodded. "Does she trust you?"

Lazarus snorted, realizing by the use of the word "she" that Skvrsky knew he was connected to Sable. It seemed pretty ridiculous to continue to remain aloof at this point.

Skvrsky obviously knows what the hell is going on, he thought. No backing out now.

"I think so, although I don't deserve it," Lazarus answered finally. "She trusted me to protect her, and I did a pretty lousy job of it."

Skvrksy leaned forward. "What does that mean? Is she still alive?"

Lazarus shrugged. "I don't know. I was hoping I could find out from Handstand Howard. She was grabbed a few days ago by the people who've been keeping her and Gavin against their wills."

Skvrsky frowned, but he nodded at the same time. "What's your connection with her?"

Lazarus sighed, figuring this was going to come up. "I'm CIB." Lazarus watched as Skvrsky showed the inevitable surprise. "Our paths crossed on a case I'm working on."

"Oh, my God."

"Yeah, well. I need to find her. Is Gavin the person behind Handstand Howard? How's he able to communicate with you?"

"Look, he has very little access to us. He doesn't know where his sister is either. He's trying to find *her*, not the other way around."

"I understand, but I think he can help me. I think she's here, and I think I know who's got her, got both of them. I need to confer with him."

"It's dangerous for him. I don't know if he'll let you expose him."

"Then what the hell did he plan to do once I showed up here?" Lazarus couldn't control his frustration any longer. "If he's trapped and in so much danger, why does he bother to peek out of his hole at all?"

"Don't be a jerk. He's not much more than a kid, you know. He's scared to death that they might do something to his sister if he resists them. Somehow he figured out that she leaves from time to time. He was hoping he could find out when she was out, to make contact with someone who could let him know, and then he'd try to escape himself. Or at the very least talk to her, get help."

Lazarus nodded wearily. "Yeah. That makes sense, I guess. Poor kid. So why don't you help him?"

Skvrsky shrugged. "I would if I could. But it was a complete crap shoot. None of us knew where she might be or if she was free of danger. Without that knowledge, none of us dared risk anything. He refused to allow any attempt to free him, not until he could be sure his sister was safe."

"God," Lazarus growled. "The bastard played both of them against each other. To get them to do what he wanted, he threatened each one with harm to the other."

"Oh, there's more to it than that," Skvrsky said. "Whoever he is, he uses each of them. Gavin is some kind of a Grid genius, apparently. They made him into a hell of a pilot, far and away the best I've ever seen. That's how he's managed to make contact on the sly. He writes simple programs that escape their notice, then works to get those programs to work together to make more complicated ones, and so on. Very delicate stuff. Way over my head."

Lazarus was considering this. *That's how I get to the kid*, Lazarus realized. *We have to meet on the Grid.* "Look," he said to Skvrsky, "I think I know how I can reach him. I need your help. I'm a Gridpilot, too. I can get through to him, but you have to tell me how he contacts you. How did he find you in the first place?"

Skvrsky grinned. "A chat node. It's actually a virtual version of The Corner, for folks who like the place but either can't or don't want to actually come here. He was apparently performing some service for his Mr. Maxwell and used the opportunity to drop me a note. I don't understand completely why he picked me, but he claims he was able to profile some of the people who were in there a lot and singled a few of us out as the most likely to help him."

Lazarus just sat back in his chair and marveled. "That took a hell of a lot of guts," he said.

"Yeah. Let's make it worth it to him."

Lazarus nodded and said, "Give me as many particulars as you can about him, and I'll track him down. I just need to borrow a gauntlet and jack into a node for a while."

* * * * *

It seemed humorous to Lazarus to be drifting through a digital representation of the very same bar he was already in, but the virtual version of The Corner was just as crowded as the real thing had been.

Lots of people like to socialize from the privacy of their own home, Lazarus chuckled. He followed Skvrsky's shadow, which looked pretty much exactly like the man, to the bar.

"When he has something to tell me, he always leaves a little blip somewhere for me to find. He rewrites the code somehow so that something looks a little strange."

"Like what?" Lazarus asked, finding it eerie to hear Skvrsky's voice not only through his gauntlet, but also hearing the man as he sat only a few feet away from Lazarus, piloting the Grid with him.

"I always know it when I see it. It's never the same thing twice." Skvrsky looked around carefully. "He doesn't always leave something, so we may be out of luck tonight. No, wait . . . there! See the countertop of the bar?"

Lazarus moved over to where Skvrsky was pointing with his shadow and stared. Right at the corner of the bar, somewhat out of sight of customers who might choose to hang out there, was a small three-dimensional structure, a strange sculpture of sorts, made entirely out of maraschino cherry stems.

"Wow," Lazarus said, looking at the construction. He poked at it and found that he couldn't budge it. "He rewrote your physics model code!"

"Yeah, every time it's like that. I'm the only one who can move it, too. Watch." Skvrsky nudged the little tower with his finger, causing it to topple. "That way he's assured that I spot it before someone else ruins it."

"Okay," Lazarus said. "What does the little tower mean?"

"It means," Skvrsky answered, "that he has something to ask me or tell me, or something for me to find out for him. I'm supposed to hang around so that I'll be here when he gets a chance to sneak in."

"How long does it take for him to show up?"

"Oh, not too long usually. He generally waits until he can jump back in from time to time, and that way he doesn't leave me hanging too long. The longest I ever waited was three hours. I finally had to give up on him, and I didn't hear from him again for three days. Worried me sick. Found out later that they had taken an unexpected trip somewhere. He had gotten to see his sister."

"All right," Lazarus said, summoning the HUD display for his gauntlet's chronometer briefly and then making it vanish again. "I can stay here for a little while, at least. But eventually I'm going to have to go. I'm keeping my bosses waiting."

As it turned out, Lazarus didn't have to wait long. A shadow approached the two of them, moving casually but weaving in many directions as it did so. It reminded Lazarus of someone casing a place.

"That's him," Skvrsky said quietly. "Let me talk to him first and let him know that you're a friend."

"Sure," Lazarus said, trying to contain the rapid beating of his heart. "The last thing I want to do right now is scare him away."

"Hi, Martin," the shadow said. "Can we talk? I need to ask—" At that point, it turned and stared at Lazarus. "You're the one!" the voice said, although Lazarus couldn't tell if it was a boy's voice or not because of heavy modulation. "What are you doing here?"

"Hi, Gavin," Lazarus said. "I'm Lazarus. I'm a friend of your sister."

"Sabine," Gavin's shadow breathed. "You found her. Oh, thank God."

"Gavin," Lazarus said slowly, not sure how to tell him gently, "I lost her again. She's with Mr. Maxwell now."

"What?" Gavin's voice trembled slightly, even through the modulation. "What happened?"

Lazarus sighed and explained. "Ana came and got her when I wasn't paying enough attention. I screwed up. I'm sorry."

"It's okay," Gavin said, seemingly trying to sound chipper. "Once she leaves again to run another errand, you can contact her and tell me, and then I can get out of here."

"I'm afraid it's a little more complicated than that," Lazarus said slowly. "You see, I'm a cop. And Sabine was helping me with my job. Unfortunately, Mr. Maxwell found out about it. That's why Ana grabbed her and took her back."

"Damn! She's in trouble. So am I."

"Hang in there, Gavin," Skvrsky said. "We'll figure something out. Lazarus thinks he knows where she is."

"Gavin," Lazarus asked, "what can you tell me about where you are?"

"Well," the kid answered, "I know we're on the *Lighthouse*. Martin told me that. And I've figured out that we're somewhere within a government center, because my data node originates there."

Yes! Lazarus thought exuberantly.

"Other than that, I'm not sure. I can't just go outside when I want, so I have no real bearings."

"That's all right. It's already enough. I'm pretty certain that Sable—I mean, Sabine—is here on the *Lighthouse*, too. I think I might know who Mr. Maxwell is. I think he's someone pretty important here on the *Lighthouse*."

"You do?" Gavin asked. "How do you know that?"

"Who do you think it is?" Skvrsky breathed.

"Something someone said to me earlier today gave me a hunch. But I need to figure it out for sure, so I had an idea. I never asked your sister to describe Mr. Maxwell to me. It never occurred to me that I might know him. Would you tell me what he looks like?"

"I can do better than that. I can send you an image."

Lazarus practically jerked in his seat when he heard this. What a hell of a break!

"That would be just fine," Lazarus said, his elation threatening to overwhelm him. "How come you never told anyone you had an image of him before? How come you didn't try to find out who he was yourself?"

"I'm setting up the file transfer now," Gavin said. "To answer your questions, I didn't want someone else trying to do anything for me until I knew my sister was safe; it seemed like a risk to let someone see it, so I held on to it. And as for why I didn't research it myself, that seemed too risky, too. You saw how I found out about you, by setting up a watchdog on her records. Right?"

"Yes. Very ingenious, I might add," Lazarus said, smiling. "You're one hell of a pilot, you know. Better than your sister, maybe better than me."

"Well, what's to stop Mr. Maxwell from doing the same thing? He might want to know everyone who checks him out, and if he figured out I was doing it, I'd be in big trouble."

Lazarus nodded. The logic was sound, although Gavin's expectations of other people's piloting abilities seemed a bit inflated. "All right. Well, if it turns out that Mr. Maxwell is who I think he is, we're going to have to be very careful. But I think I can get to both you and Sabine with your help."

"Here comes the file now," Gavin said.

Lazarus waited anxiously, wondering if he was going to be right. If it was Michael Thayne, having two human beings as permanent hostages was enough to take him down forever.

Unless I kill him first, Lazarus thought, seething.

When the file was finished, Lazarus switched to a different protocol so he could view the image in his gauntlet without exiting the Grid, but without anyone else seeing what he was about to superimpose on his vision. With a trembling finger, he tapped the key that opened the image.

And gasped.

It was not Michael Thayne.

It was Administrator Monahan.

16.0:

LAZARUS TRIED TO steady his breathing as he approached the offices of his immediate superior, Oslo Monahan, Concord Administrator. He wondered if he was as transparent to others as he felt right then, if his anger and betrayal showed clearly, if it would be easy to see through his facade. He wondered if he would be able to contain himself and play the part he had chosen to play.

Perhaps, he thought, I'm going to play it too well.

The image that Gavin had sent had made him reel when he first saw it. And yet, in another part of his mind, a part that had been able to separate itself from the stunned part of him on the surface, it had all made so much sense. Set up all the pieces just the way you want, make sure you have exactly the right tools for the job, and you'll get the results you want.

He used me like the fool that I am. He knew I'd do exactly what he wanted me to.

Lazarus knew now that he had been played for a fool from the very start, from that first moment that Oslo Monahan had pulled some strings to get him out of that Insight prison and gotten him assigned to CIB. That he had been part of the plan back when Monahan had him assigned to the administrator personally and told him that his talents were exactly what were needed for a special assignment, a unique case outside of the normal jurisdictions of CIB. It had been Monahan's intention from the start for Lazarus to uncover the fake trail that had been planted and expose Minister Yonce as a traitor and a criminal.

That he had fallen for it so completely did not truly bother Lazarus. It would be foolish to expect anyone to deviate from his basic nature, and he was no exception. Monahan picked him precisely because of this nature, and Lazarus had been true to himself, playing cowboy and riding in, trying to solve all the problems himself without asking for help from above. He wouldn't apologize to anyone for that, not even himself.

How can I be coldly analyzing the hell out of this, while at the same time I want to punch my fist through a wall? God, I want to strangle the bastard with my bare hands! And yet I'm debating freshman philosophy with myself.

The thing that did bother Lazarus, though, was why. He hadn't been able to figure that one out, and he had been over it probably a couple dozen times since he had seen Monahan's image. Why would a Concord Administrator want to bring about Yonce's downfall? He didn't see how they could be political rivals, since they moved in very different circles and had widely different realms of responsibility. Certainly they weren't business rivals, although Yonce had more than her share of those. There had to be something else, something under the surface, that no one knew about.

Of course, that was an obvious assumption, Lazarus realized, cerebrally smacking himself in the head. If there weren't reasons, he wouldn't be in the middle of it. You've just got to figure out what they are.

Lazarus reached the administration complex and, even though it was after hours, gained entrance to Monahan's building easily enough. After all, he worked for the guy and had access to the offices, too.

Monahan maintained a combination office and private

estate all as one facility on the *Lighthouse*, although Lazarus had only visited the personal portion of the property a couple of times. He did know, however, that Monahan had access to his own private docking bay for interstellar travel away from the *Lighthouse*.

Amazing, Lazarus thought. The guy kept his private little menagerie of slaves—for that's certainly what Sabine and Gavin have been to him—right under the noses of the entire population of the *Lighthouse*, including all its law enforcement agencies and regulating bodies.

Lazarus felt as if little explosions were going off in his mind as waves of realization hit him. To think, all that time, how physically close Sable—Sabine—and I were to each other, and yet we didn't meet until we were in another star system. Lazarus shook his head.

Get hold of yourself, Lazarus. Get over the shock and do your job.

Making his way through the public office area, Lazarus approached the administrator's private quarters. He tried to imagine what he was going to say, thinking through the words that would carry off the deception. It was an effort, resisting the urge to think of what he really wanted to say instead.

Time enough for that later, after you've beaten him senseless, Lazarus told himself. First things first. Get Sabine and Gavin out.

He arrived at the entrance and paused, taking another deep breath. He wondered just how long each of them would be able to keep up the facade. Calming himself, he tapped the door chime and waited.

The video screen to the side of the door flickered on, and Monahan peered out through it. When the administrator recognized Lazarus, he broke into a warm smile.

"Lazarus! You made it at last."

"Yeah, finally," Lazarus answered, returning the smile but mentally punching the man in the face.

"Well, come on in! Your friend arrived here hours ago. I was getting worried. We're in the study. You remember where that is? It's the second door on your left after you come inside." There was a click, and the door slid open, admitting him into a large foyer.

Monahan's apartments were beautiful. Lazarus had always admired the man's taste in decor, for the administrator had a deep love of old world things. Books, spring-and-gear driven clocks, and a variety of string and wind instruments, all but forgotten in today's digital world, were complemented by lush green plants and mood lighting. In one room the man had a huge ancient map mounted on a wall, real ink on parchment. Lazarus had stared for a long time at that map on the few occasions he had visited the administrator. But he wasn't here to admire Monahan's decorating skills tonight.

Lazarus stepped through the entryway and made his way through to the designated door. When he walked through, Monahan was seated, facing him, in a big comfortable chair, dressed in an old-fashioned smoking jacket and lounging slacks. He was pointing a gun at Lazarus. Lazarus froze in midstep.

So much for pretenses, he thought, assessing the situation.

Huddled on the floor next to Monahan's chair was Sabine, a skimpy silk gown or robe of some kind barely covering her, and a collar encircling her neck. Monahan held the other end of a leash that was attached to the collar. Sable's eyes were red and puffy, but they brightened briefly when she saw him enter and meet her gaze. Lazarus balled his hands into fists, barely able to resist the urge to leap across the distance between himself and the administrator and pummel the man into bloody oblivion.

Ellesao was crumpled to the floor off to one side, doubled up in the fetal position, a pool of blood staining the carpet beneath her. Lazarus cursed under his breath.

Lazarus figured she was dead until she groaned softly and flailed feebly with one leg. He wasn't certain, but the blood seemed to be coming from her stomach.

"You bastard," Lazarus said. I sent her right to him, he thought furiously. Every step, he's been ahead in the game. Well, no longer.

Monahan merely smiled as he brought the pistol up a little higher, aimed it a little truer at Lazarus. "Relieve him of his gun, Lars."

For the first time, Lazarus noticed that there were others in the room. The two men who had accosted Ellesao and him at the Pacific Plaza, who had grabbed Sable and dragged her away from him in the spaceport, stood in the corners that flanked the door, each holding a charge rifle.

One of the two of them moved close, rifle aimed at Lazarus, and said, "Turn around, hands on the wall, and don't even think of trying anything funny."

Lazarus did as he was instructed, and the man patted him down thoroughly, removing the pistol from its holster. It wasn't Lazarus's stutter pistol that the man removed. Lazarus had switched it for his sabot pistol before coming. When Lars was finished, he stepped back toward the corner where he had been when Lazarus first entered, resting easily but keeping the rifle aimed at Lazarus.

Lazarus turned to look at Monahan again. "So," he asked, nodding his head toward Ellesao, buying a little time to further assess the situation, "what did you do, gut-shoot her?"

Monahan chuckled. "As a matter of fact, I did. Sabine, here, got to watch, too." He smiled and reached up, stroking Sable's hair with his other hand.

Sable looked at Lazarus, her eyes smoldering, but didn't say anything.

"So why did you do it?" Lazarus said coldly but matter-of-factly. "Why set Yonce up to take the fall? Why send weapons to CFN? What's your game?"

Monahan chuckled. "Why, why, why? So many questions. Let's just say I have my reasons and leave it at that."

Lazarus shrugged. "I was thinking you might indulge me, since I was your very first patsy and all, but that's fine. I'm not sure I would trust myself to believe your answers anyway."

Monahan chuckled. "Come, come, Lazarus, my boy. You were hardly my first patsy, but you were definitely my best. At least, you would have been if Germaine had only gotten that damned crystal into your hands without the syndicate's interference. That's a darn shame. A lot of work has gone to waste because of that unfortunate incident."

"Can't say I'm too sorry about that," Lazarus said. "But I have to hand it to you. You played me well, feeding me all that crap about wanting me on the team, wanting to give me a fresh start. Tell me, did you know what you had in mind for me when you first came and plucked me out of prison back on Vision? Was that all part of your scheme? To find some idiot with the right skills who had gotten himself into trouble and groom him to become your lackey?"

Lazarus was torn. Ellesao was dying, but he needed some answers before he could act. If only he could get the bastard to talk! What were his reasons for all this? Who was he working for?

Monahan shifted in his chair. "You catch on quickly, Lazarus. But then again, that's what made you the perfect tool. Anyway, that's all water under the bridge. The thing I think we should be asking ourselves now is who else have you talked to tonight about our little secret? Who knows what's been going on?"

"Enough people that you're not going to get away with it for much longer," Lazarus said. "Regardless of what happens tonight, you're going down. I've made sure of that."

"Oh, have you, now?" Monahan said, an edge of sarcasm creeping into his voice. "Well, I don't think you know the score quite as well as you think you do. But that's irrelevant. Sable, here, is going to watch you die right alongside your mechalus, and then she and I are going to take a nice long trip somewhere so she can get her head back together. I'm sorry you won't be coming with us, Lazarus, but you know how it is."

Lazarus shrugged, deciding he had given it long enough. Ellesao wouldn't last much longer; he couldn't wait to see if Monahan would reveal any more. "Any time now, Gavin," Lazarus said loudly and clearly as he watched Monahan straighten his arm, preparing to fire the pistol.

As if on cue, the lights suddenly blinked out, leaving the room pitch-black. Lazarus, who had been expecting the sudden darkness, leaped off to one side of the doorway, tumbling and rolling across the carpet as Monahan fired his pistol where the CIB agent had been standing a heartbeat before, shattering the shocked silence. Lazarus came up into a kneeling position, activating his infrared optics and peering around the room as the others began stumbling blindly about, unable to see. The two goons with the rifles in the corners squeezed off a shot or two, peppering the door where Lazarus had been standing.

"Stop shooting!" Monahan yelled, scrambling up out of his chair. "You're going to kill each other, you bloody idiots! Get the damned lights on!"

Lazarus was already crouched and ready to spring when the second thug, Eduardo, stumbled near him, feeling around blindly with one hand in front of himself while swinging the rifle about with the other hand as though he intended to shoot blindly. Lazarus shifted his weight and swung his leg around and up in a sweeping kick, nailing the man in the solar plexus. The man crumpled over in a gasping wheeze, the wind knocked out of him. Lazarus snatched the rifle away as the goon, making a gurgling sound, fell to the floor. He quickly drew a bead on Lars and squeezed the trigger. The rifle spasmed in his hand as he fired, but he didn't waste time watching the other thug cry out and drop the floor. Instead, he slammed the butt of the rifle against the temple of the man at his feet, knocking him cold, and then stepped quickly and quietly to the side, not staying in one place too long. The others in the room could certainly home in on a muzzle flash, he knew. He moved to Ellesao's body and checked for a pulse. It was there, but it was weak and slow. She wouldn't last much longer.

Monahan fired twice in the general direction of where Lazarus had been standing a moment before. The administrator, Lazarus could see through his infrared optics, had grabbed Sable and pulled her close to him, and he now held her with his arm around her neck, using her as a shield. "I'll kill her, you bastard. You stay the hell back. If I even feel you getting close, I'll put a sabot round in her, Lazarus! Right in her pretty head!"

Lazarus froze and crouched motionless, trying not to make a sound. He waited and watched. From somewhere beyond the room, he heard yelling.

Monahan spun about slowly, keeping Sable in front of him. "So Gavin's disobeyed me and helped you, I see," he said, talking to no particular spot in the room, though his voice was considerably less steady than before. "I've got to hand it to you, Lazarus. You're quite the clever fellow."

Monahan quickly fired three shots into the darkness of the room, aiming in random directions. None of them came close to Lazarus, but he flinched and stayed low. Monahan could get lucky.

"I don't know how you managed to find him," the administrator said. "I guess I'm going to have to bring the little brat's life to an end a bit sooner than I thought. Gavin?" he called out, realizing that the boy was probably patched into the room-to-room intercom system via the Grid and could hear everything that was said. "You hear me? You're dead, you little punk!"

"No!" Sable howled, and Lazarus saw her turn and begin to pummel Monahan, beating her fists against him wildly. "You're not touching him, you bastard!" she cried out as she assaulted the man.

The sudden attack caught Monahan off guard, but before Lazarus could close in to take advantage of the surprise, the administrator swung the butt of his pistol around blindly to fend Sable off, smacking her in the temple.

"Ungh," the girl grunted weakly, staggering and dropping to her knees.

Monahan tightened his grip on the leash, grasping it directly under her chin, and raised the weapon for a second strike.

Before he could finish the blow, Lazarus raised the rifle and fired. Monahan yelped in pain as the slug entered his shoulder. He stumbled back, releasing Sable, and crawled behind his chair, cursing. Sable slumped down limply to the floor in the middle of the room.

Lazarus leveled the rifle at the wounded administrator, but he didn't fire. Monahan crouched, the pistol in his off hand, now. He swept the room with it wildly, aiming it randomly. He fired off a couple of shots, neither coming close to Lazarus.

"Don't," Lazarus said, aiming at the administrator's chest. "Don't make me shoot you again. I've got you dead in my sights."

Monahan didn't hesitate. He pointed the pistol in the direction of Lazarus's voice and squeezed the trigger.

Lazarus was already ducking, though, moving away from where he had been crouching when he spoke. Lazarus shook his head and took aim, firing once, intentionally missing the administrator's ear by centimeters. The man flinched and jerked out of the way.

"That was your final warning, Administrator. Drop the weapon. This is over." *I have to know his reasons,* Lazarus said to himself. *I have to know why he did this, why he set up this elaborate scheme.*

Lazarus saw Monahan's shoulders sag finally, and then the administrator tossed the gun to the floor, standing slowly, arms outstretched.

"Don't shoot," Monahan said, talking to where he had last heard Lazarus's voice, "I'm unarmed."

"Just tell me why," Laz asked, moving closer cautiously.

"Forget it, Laz," Monahan said. "That game won't work with me. You think you've won? Guess again, boy. This is far from over."

Sable groaned and began to stir. Lazarus moved to her side, still keeping the rifle trained on Monahan, who was standing very still. Laz dropped to one knee and reached out for her face, running his fingers softly along her temple. There was no blood. He sighed in relief.

"Sabine," he said to her softly.

For a moment she was silent, but then she finally said, "Lazarus?" Her voice was thick with emotion.

"Yes," he answered. "It's me. I'm here."

"Lazarus! Oh, God!" she sobbed, taking his hand in hers and kissing it. "I was so scared you were dead. I thought—"

Lazarus could feel her tears, wet on her cheeks. "Shh," he whispered. "It's okay. But we've got to go. Ellesao is bleeding to death."

"I can't see a thing," Sable said. "It's totally dark." She began to stand up.

"Gavin, I need the lights on," Lazarus called out. A moment later, his optics readout informed him that there was once again illumination in the room.

Sable and Monahan both flinched at the sudden glare. Lazarus switched back to normal sight, his cybernetic eyes rapidly adjusting to the level of brightness. Monahan stood there, next to his chair, one arm hanging limp, glowering at the two of them. Blood stained one shoulder of his smoking jacket.

"You bastard," Sable said, taking a step toward the man.

"Sabine, no!" Laz's voice was sharp. "Not that way. He'll get his, I promise. I need you to find my sabot pistol." He gestured to the thug lying in the far corner. "It's on him. He's just unconscious, so watch it."

Sable hesitated, hatred burning brightly in her face as she stared at Monahan, but she turned away and moved to fetch Lazarus's pistol. "What now?" she asked him, pulling her robe closed as she moved.

"Gavin has contacted Star Force. They should be getting here any minute. Then we turn the administrator here over to them and prosecute him to the fullest extent of the law. We do it the right way, Sabine. He'll go down for what he's done to you and Gavin."

At that moment the door slid open. Lazarus spun around. Framed in the doorway, crouching, a pistol aimed at the CIB agent, was Ana.

Lazarus swore and tried to bring the rifle to bear on her, but she was too fast. She fired at him and dived out of the way. His thigh was suddenly hot with pain, and he dropped the rifle as he spun about, crying out. He clenched his teeth in agony and grabbed at the wound as he dropped to the floor.

Ana sauntered into the room, her pistol aimed at Lazarus. He lay on the floor before her. He had both palms pressed into the wound in his thigh, trying to stanch the flow of blood. He stared back up at her. He saw her smile at him coldly, and then her eyes narrowed. She raised the pistol and sighted down its length, aiming straight at Lazarus's chest.

Monahan leaped to retrieve his pistol, shouting, "Look out! She's armed!"

Ana's gaze left her target for a moment as she glanced in confusion at Monahan. Then, when she saw where he was pointing, she spun around, swinging the pistol up to aim at the far corner of the room. But she wasn't fast enough.

The ear-splitting blast of Lazarus's sabot pistol was deafening as Sable fired two quick shots with it, hitting Ana twice in the chest. The woman staggered backward, her face a mask of surprise and confusion. The pistol slipped from her fingers and bounced softly to the carpeted floor as she stumbled two, three steps away from Sable, toward the door through which she had entered. She never made it, though, finally staggering sideways and bouncing against the door frame before completely losing her balance and dropping in a heap. Her mouth tried to work, and her fingers twitched as she feebly clawed at the bloody holes in her torso, and then she was still, her lifeless eyes staring at nothing.

Lazarus saw Sable move first, swinging the pistol around to take aim at Monahan, who seemed stunned by the events that had just unfolded before him. He snapped out of it quickly, leaping to the side, holding his pistol awkwardly in his off hand and firing in Sable's direction as he moved.

Sable ducked down behind a writing table as the shot slammed into the wall behind her, and then she was up again, firing the huge sabot pistol with both hands on the grip, sending Administrator Oslo G. Monahan scrambling for the exit. He darted through and was gone.

Lazarus groaned and rolled to his side, looking for the rifle he had dropped. "Gavin, on your toes. Monahan's trying to escape," he called out. "He might be headed in your direction." Using the rifle as a brace, Lazarus tried to stand, but his leg was on fire, and he couldn't.

"Sabine," he said.

Sable was standing, staring down at the lifeless body of Ana. She didn't move.

"Sabine!" Lazarus said again forcefully.

The girl blinked and looked at him. Tears were welling in her eyes. "I got her, Laz," she said. "She's dead."

"I know, baby, but Monahan is still loose. He may be going after Gavin. Help me up."

Sable's visage clouded over in rage again. "No. I won't let him. Not ever again." She turned and moved out into the hall.

"Sabine!" Lazarus called after her. "No! Wait!" Sable didn't stop. She disappeared around the corner of the door frame, sabot pistol gripped in both hands.

God! Lazarus groaned inwardly, trying to stand again. It was no use. She was going to get herself killed. Or kill Monahan. And he needed Monahan alive to answer some questions. He prayed the Star Force marines would get there soon. He turned and crawled to Ellesao, checking her pulse again.

Still alive.

* * * * *

Sable moved out into the hall and quickly glanced both ways. The entire place seemed eerily silent. She turned and headed deeper into the residence, clenching the pistol in her hands for all it was worth.

He's not going to lay a finger on Gavin. Not ever again, she repeated silently. She strode with her jaw set, determined to hunt down the man she hated, but she was nonetheless cautious. She moved carefully, ignoring the gauzy robe flapping lazily about her and the leash and collar still attached to her neck.

She darted into a large kitchen and peered around, and then headed through the doorway on the far side. When she rounded the next corner, she found herself within sight of all-too-familiar territory: the quarters where she spent the last several years of her life, subjugated to the whim of "Mr. Maxwell." Sable drew a deep, calming breath and began to traverse the length of a single straight hallway, passing her own chambers and the exercise room where she had been forced to train with Ana.

Ana is dead, she told herself. She'll never hurt you again.

The hallway she followed turned around a corner at its far end. Sable peered cautiously around the corner. Mr. Maxwell's own private rooms were in this part of the residence, as were Ana's, Lars's, and Eduardo's. She had never been able to learn where Gavin was kept.

"Sabine, Darling." It was Mr. Maxwell's voice.

She froze in midstep, looking for him.

"Sabine, Gavin is here with me. We're both watching you on the house security cameras. Say hello to your sister, Gavin."

"Sabine, just go! Don't listen to—" Gavin shouted before he was abruptly cut off. The blood ran cold in the girl's veins.

Mr. Maxwell cut in again. "I would very much like for you to join us, Sabine. In fact, I insist on it. We're down in the docking bay, getting ready to leave. Gavin and I have a proposal to discuss with you."

Wordlessly Sable continued around the corner toward the small hallway that led to Mr. Maxwell's own private docking bay and air lock. She kept the sabot pistol in front of her, moving methodically, peering through doorways to make certain she wasn't walking into a trap.

In the distance, a muffled explosion rumbled. For a second, Sable panicked, thinking Mr. Maxwell had outwitted her and doubled back behind her, but then the man's voice crackled through the intercom again.

"I would hurry if I were you, Sabine. The marines have arrived, and I don't have much time to wait."

So, Sable realized. *The troops are here. The explosion must have been set off by them, blowing open the front door. But this is my fight.* She rotated her shoulders, trying to shrug some of the tension out of them, while at the same time trying to ignore the pounding of her heart in her chest.

Sable continued on toward the docking bay, her feet padding softly on the carpeting. She turned a final corner, passed through the still-open air lock, and found herself in the large bay. It was a huge chamber, large enough to house both of Mr. Maxwell's small private ships. It smelled of grease and chemicals. The lighting was harsh and without warmth, and the floor was a neutronite-coated steel grate that felt cold on Sable's bare feet. In the background, behind the ships, was another huge air lock.

Standing near the hatchway of one of his two ships, Mr. Maxwell held Gavin before him, one arm around the boy's neck and a black baton clutched in the same hand. In his other hand, the man held his pistol against Gavin's temple, waiting. His wounded shoulder had been hurriedly bandaged. Sable came to a halt a few paces inside the chamber, Lazarus's sabot pistol leveled at Mr. Maxwell's head.

"Right on time, Sabine," Mr. Maxwell said, and he used the small remote device to close the air lock behind Sable. As the doors closed, Sable had to resist the urge to wince. They were alone now, the three of them, sealed in the docking bay. "That's not a very polite thing to do, Sabine, pointing that gun at me. Why don't you put it down?"

"Why don't you go screw yourself?" Sable replied, sweating despite her flimsy covering.

Mr. Maxwell broke into a wide grin. "Why, Sabine! I don't think I've ever seen you so defiant."

"Let Gavin go," Sable said quietly.

"Oh, come now. I thought, after all this time, you understood the arrangements. I give the instructions, and you follow them. Now put down the gun. We're leaving."

"No!" Sable replied, angry that the man was still trying to intimidate her. It almost worked. "I'm through playing that game. Let him go now, or I will shoot you."

"I think not," Mr. Maxwell replied, shifting his grip on Gavin, whose hands, Sable now saw, were cuffed behind his back. "But since we're pressed for time here, I will offer you a proposal. Surrender to me and get on the ship, and Gavin goes free. Decide quickly, though. The troops are closing in, and I don't intend to be standing here when they arrive."

Sable blinked, trying to figure out the man's intentions. He's lying, she thought. Don't buy into it.

"It's a fair deal, Sabine. Your life for your brother's. And I'll even give you a fresh start, wipe the dataslate clean. No punishments for the transgressions on your part of late. I'll take good care of you, Sabine. Of course, you'll never leave my side again, but those are the prices we pay."

Sable's stomach roiled at the thought of spending the rest of her days anywhere close to this man. But the chance to buy Gavin's freedom . . . No, she told herself firmly. I won't let the bastard walk. "No," she said quietly at last. "Never again."

Mr. Maxwell's face boiled into a rage. "Then you can just die, you worthless little—" and he raised the pistol away from Gavin, lining her up in his sight. Sable blanched and lurched to the side, averting her face from the imminent shot.

At that moment, however, Gavin lunged upward, his shoulder directly beneath Mr. Maxwell's wounded arm, shoving it skyward so that the shot the man fired flew up and wide. There was also a loud crack as the crown of Gavin's head slammed into the underside of Mr. Maxwell's chin, driving the man off his feet and snapping his head backward. A grunt of pain escaped Mr. Maxwell as he staggered backward from the blow, and in that instant, Gavin dropped to his knees on the decking of the docking bay and rolled to the side.

Mr. Maxwell caught his balance as Sable stood erect again, taking careful aim at the man. "Don't" was all she said, waiting to see if he would surrender. She knew she should give him that chance. Laz had said it should be that way. And Lazarus needed to know the reasons why they had been used, needed to know the purpose behind the scheme.

But Sable might as well have been speaking to a large rock, for Mr. Maxwell's eyes blazed with an insane fury. One hand holding his jaw, blood trickling down his chin from the blow Gavin had given him, the man turned on the boy, looming over him. "You little brat!" Mr. Maxwell growled, and raised his pistol to shoot.

Crack!

Sable fired a shot, feeling the kick of the pistol as the round screamed across the distance between herself and the man she hated. She absently saw the blossom of blood on the man's chest, perceived him quiver from the impact.

Crack!

Sable fired again, drove Mr. Maxwell back a step, his pistol slipping from his grip and beginning to fall.

Crack!

Another wound appeared on Mr. Maxwell's chest. His gun slowly, agonizingly drifted to the deck, clattering against the steel grate, as he looked around, his eyes wild with fear, seemingly unable to understand what was happening to him.

Crack!

Never again, Sable mouthed silently.

Crack!

Never . . .

Crack!

Again.

Crack!

Mr. Maxwell was going down now, pitching to one side as his leg crumpled, rolling awkwardly as he fell.

Crack! Crack! Click . . . click . . . click . . .

The clip was empty. Sable stopped depressing the trigger, but she continued to point the weapon at Mr. Maxwell's bloody, still form. She was shaking, and she couldn't seem to get any air. Her heart pounded in her chest madly. She gasped and realized she had been holding her breath. Never again, she thought. Never again will you hurt me or my brother, you bastard. "Never again!" she screamed aloud and threw the pistol at the man's corpse.

She turned to Gavin, who was crouching, hands still locked behind him, staring at her with wide eyes. She dropped to her knees next to him and hugged him, sobbing.

"Oh, Gavin. My baby brother," she cried, her voice thick with emotion. She held him, then, clung to him and let the wet tears run down her face, felt him lay his head on her shoulder.

L AZARUS SHIFTED IN the overstuffed chair, furious. He and Sabine were guests of Undersecretary Michael Thayne, discussing with the Galactic Consulate Minister some of the finer points of the case following a news conference that had been held on board the *Lighthouse* to bring to light the illicit activities of Administrator Oslo G. Monahan, a.k.a. Brandon Maxwell. Lazarus stared out the window of the man's palatial offices, barely aware of what the undersecretary was saying. Sabine was squeezing his hand reassuringly.

With the death of Monahan at Sabine's hands, Lazarus had lost his opportunity to learn the administrator's motives. He had forgiven her; her defensive reaction to the threat to herself and her brother was instinctual and understandable. Of course, emptying an entire clip into the body had taken a bit of explaining when the Star Force marines finally reached her, but it had been written up as "under extreme duress" in the reports, once they learned the whole sordid story. Sabine had been absolved of any incriminating acts very shortly after. Lazarus was disappointed that he had lost the trail with the death of Monahan, but he was far from angry with Sabine about it.

Ellesao had survived and was recovering nicely in the *Lighthouse*'s medical center. She would be released in a few days. And Gavin was found to be completely healthy, although he was going to need some counseling to help him adjust to being back in society. He had demonstrated to

Lazarus some of the methods he had used to program behind Monahan's back, and Lazarus had been stunned. The kid was a natural, a genius at manipulating code. They had begun to test him, to find out what his limits were, and so far they hadn't found many.

The best damned Gridrunner I've ever seen, Lazarus found himself thinking on more than one occasion. He'd overwhelm them even back at Insight.

No, all in all, just about everything had worked out well. But Lazarus was still furious. He had been taken off the case. Thayne had explained that it was an internal investigation now, and special agents were being dispatched to dig into the whole affair. Lazarus had been forced to file massive reports, to sit through endless hours of questioning. On the side, he had begun, with Gavin's help, to poke into Monahan's private files. Before Thayne had everything sealed as evidence, at least. Gavin was currently exploring ways to get around that, too. What the two of them found was sparse, but it definitely suggested an accomplice, or more precisely a superior, backing Monahan in his efforts. Someone was further up the chain of command, still running free, still plotting something. And Lazarus was dead certain it was Michael Thayne. Only he had no proof. Yet.

And now here I am, sitting in this bastard's office, listening to him give me the rah-rah speech. He must be feeling pretty smug, telling me what a good job I did, when he's the one behind it. Lazarus growled and nearly jerked his hand when he felt Sabine's nails dig into his palm. He looked over at her and saw her pointed expression, realized that Thayne had stopped talking and was staring at him.

"Is everything all right, Agent Lazarus?" Thayne asked, a mild expression of annoyance mixed with confusion on his mien.

"Yeah, I'm sorry, Undersecretary. It's been a very long few days. I apologize."

"Not at all," their host replied. "On the contrary, I've been very insensitive and kept you here overly long already, listening to me prattle on. Forgive me."

Lazarus motioned dismissively with his hand. "No, it was rude of me to drift off there. It's a privilege to us for you to welcome us up here to your offices, Undersecretary."

"Yes, quite," Sabine added, smiling warmly to the man across the desk from them. "I can't tell you how much I appreciate all you've done, for both me and my brother."

"Oh, think nothing of it. By the way, I hear he's getting on quite nicely, in good health and all that."

"Yes, he's fine," Sabine said, her face flush with happiness. "It's going to take a while for us to find some sense of normalcy, but I think we're going to make it."

"Good, good," Thayne said. "And your mechalus friend? I understand she's faring better?"

"Yes, sir," Lazarus said, trying not to clench his teeth in disgust. "They should be releasing her from Galinda Medical Center in just a few days."

"Wonderful," Thayne gushed. "Well, then, let me thank you again for coming by. I can't tell you how thankful the entire Galactic Concord, the Verge, and everyone on board this station is for what you've managed to do, Agent Lazarus. It's quite the proverbial feather in your cap."

Lazarus smiled weakly in response, and then the undersecretary was rising and showing them to the door, begging their forgiveness and apologizing for his busy schedule.

Once they were out in the streets and beyond the holonews reporters, Lazarus swore softly.

"What the hell is wrong with you?" Sabine asked, still holding his hand and spinning him around by it to face her. "You've been acting like a grouch for three days now."

Lazarus sighed. "I'm sorry. I just know that damned man has something to do with all this. I just know it! And it chaps my hide to have to sit there and listen to him spout pleasantries at us."

"Hey," Sabine said, putting her hands to either side of Lazarus's face and forcing him to look at her. "You saved my life. And my brother's. Ellesao made it. It could have turned out a lot worse."

"Yeah. Yeah, I know," Lazarus said sheepishly. "I'm sorry."

"And I know you and Gavin will figure out what's going on. You just have to give it some time. If it's him, you're going to nail him. If it's someone else, you'll be glad you didn't get on the undersecretary's bad side for no good reason."

Lazarus chuckled and leaned in to kiss Sabine. "Okay," he said. "I'll shape up."

"You damn well better, mister," she said, kissing him back. "By the way," she said as they turned and continued their stroll through the streets of the *Lighthouse*. "You never told me how you found out how to meet Gavin."

"Oh, that," Lazarus said, smiling. "I was spying on you, actually."

"What? You bastard!" Sabine said, her warm smile belying her words. "I guess I'm never going to be able to trust you."

"Yep. That's how I found out your real name and everything." Sabine groaned and rolled her eyes as they walked. They were on their way to visit Ellesao. "You know," Lazarus continued, teasing, "Lazarus isn't my real name."

Sabine stopped in mid stride. "I've been wondering when you'd finally get around to this. So what is it?"

"Hah!" Lazarus said, pulling her along by the hand.

"Are you going to tell me?" Sabine asked.

"Maybe," he replied, not looking at her.

"Tell me!" she said, laughing.

And he did.

GLOSSARY

Aegis - A G2 yellow star. The metropolitan center of the Verge.

AI - Artificial Intelligence. Sentient computer programming whose sophistication varies from model to model.

Aleerin - see mechalus.

AU - Astronomical Unit. 150 million km.

Bluefall - Capital planet of the Aegis system. The world is almost completely covered by water.

cerametal - An extremely strong alloy made from laminated ceramics and lightweight metals.

CFN - see Concord Free Now.

charge weapon - A firearm in which an electric firing pin ignites a chemical explosive into a white-hot plasma propellant, thus expelling a cerametallic slug at extremely high velocity.

CIB - see Concord Investigative Bureau.

CM armor - Cerametal armor.

Concord - see Galactic Concord.

Concord Administrator - A high-ranking law enforcement official of the Galactic Concord. Administrators have the power of judge, jury, and executioner in their assigned jurisdiction.

Concord Free Now (CFN) - A terrorist organization dedicated to maintaining the independence of the Verge from the stellar nations.

Concord Investigative Bureau (CIB) - The intelligence-gathering arm of the Galactic Concord. Often named "the Silent Bureau," it is famed for its secret covert operatives throughout known space.

Concord Survey Service (CSS) - A division of Star Force dedicated to scouting, surveying, and first contacts.

CSS - see Concord Survey Service.

cytronic - A biomechanical device that bridges the gap between biological nerve endings and bionic implants.

drivecore - The central engine core of a stardrive.

drivesat - A communications satellite that drops into drivespace in order to transmit and receive messages.

driveship - Any spaceship that is equipped with a stardrive.

drivespace - The dimension into which starships enter through use of the stardrive. In this dimension, gravity works on a quantum level, thus enabling movement of a ship from one point in space to another in only 121 hours.

durasteel - Steel that has been strengthened at the molecular level.

ecodome - Any enclosed facility whose primary purpose is to maintain a habitable environment on uninhabitable worlds.

e-suit - An environment suit intended to keep the wearer safe from vacuum, extreme temperatures, and radiation.

flechette gun - Any firearm that utilizes bundles of tiny, razor-sharp aerofoils as projectiles.

fraal - A non-Terran sentient species. Fraal are very slender, large-eyed humanoids.

Galactic Concord - The thirteenth stellar nation. Formed by the Treaty of Concord, Concord law and administration rule in the Verge.

Galactic Standard - The lingua franca of known space.

Gibson-Williams Multimedia (GWM) - A producer and multisystem distributor specializing in a wide variety of entertainment packages, ranging from interactive holo and Gridware to live stage productions and sporting events. Some speculate that GWM may actually be the

main front for the Mateo crime family's various
business interests.

gravity induction - A process whereby a cyclotron accelerates
particles to near-light speeds, thereby creating gravitons
between the particle and the surrounding mass. This
process can be adjusted and redirected, thus allowing
the force of gravity to be overcome. Most starships use
a gravity induction engine for in-system travel.

Grid - An interstellar computer network.

Gridcaster - A computer, most often in the form of a gauntlet,
that enables the user to connect to the Grid.

Gridpilot - A term used to describe a person using the Grid,
especially as a profession.

Gridrunner - A colloquial term used to describe someone who
is an expert in navigating the Grid.

Grid shadow - A virtual reality representation of a user in the
Grid that can be customized to the user's needs and
desires.

holocomm - Holographic communication.

holodisplay - The display of a holocomm that can be viewed in
either one, two, or three dimensions.

Inseer - A citizen of Insight.

Insight - A subsidiary of VoidCorp that broke away to form a
separate stellar nation. Citizenry is dominated by
freethinking Gridpilots who believe that humanity can
reach its destiny only in Gridspace.

Ianth cell - The standard lanthanide battery used to power
most small electronic equipment and firearms.

Lighthouse - A huge space station, capable of 50 light-year
starfalls, that roams the Verge.

Long Silence, the - That period of time when the Stellar
Nations lost contact with the Verge because of the
Second Galactic War.

Lucullus - A trinary star system consisting of two blue-white stars and a distant red dwarf. A former penal colony, it is now a haven for organized crime and hedonistic entertainment.

mass reactor - The primary power source of a stardrive. The reactor collects, stores, and processes dark matter, thus producing massive amounts of energy.

mass weapon - A weapon that fires a ripple of intense gravity waves, striking its target like a massive physical blow.

mechalus - The most common term used for an Aleerin, a sentient humanoid symbiote species that has achieved a union between biological life and cybernetic enhancements.

mindwalker - Any being proficient with psionic powers.

neurocircuitry - Cybernetic implants intended to fuse electronic or mechanical systems with a living biological entity.

NIJack (neural interface jack) - A plug located in the neck or head that allows data cables to be connected to a user's cytronic circuitry system.

plasma weapon - A weapon that converts an electrochemical mixture into white-hot plasma and then utilizes a magnetic accelerator to throw a blast of the plasma at the target. The super-heated plasma explodes upon striking its target.

sabot weapon - A firearm that uses electromagnetic pulses to accelerate a discarding-rocket slug at hypersonic speeds.

sesheyan - A bipedal sentient species possessing a long, bulbous head, large ears, and eight light-sensitive eyes. Most sesheyans are about 1.7 meters tall and have two leathery wings that span between 2.5 and 4 meters. Sheya, the sesheyan homeworld, has been subjugated by VoidCorp. However, a substantial population of "free sesheyans" live on Grith.

Silence, the - see the Long Silence.

spaceport - A planetary landing zone for driveships.

Standard - see Galactic Standard.

stardrive - The standard starship engine that combines a gravity induction coil and a mass reactor to open a temporary singularity in space and thus allow a ship to enter drive-space. All jumps take 121 hours, no matter the distance.

starfall - The term used to describe a ship entering drivespace.

Star Force - The naval branch of the Concord military.

starport - A zero-g, orbital docking zone for driveships.

starrise - The term used to describe a ship leaving drivespace.

stellar nations - The thirteeen sovereign nations governing the Stellar Ring, the center of which is Sol (Earth).

Stellar Ring - The systems that make up the thirteen stellar nations, the center of which is Sol.

stimcrystal - A microchip whose primary purpose is to stimulate the brain's pleasure centers.

stutter pistol - A nonlethal weapon that uses blasts of sonic energy to render targets unconscious without causing serious harm.

system drive - Any form of non-stardrive propulsion used for inner system traffic.

Technospiders - A political faction—ostensibly dedicated to freedom and the rule of law—of Lucullus that maintains heavy control of Penates' environmental control systems.

Thuldan Empire - A militaristic, fiercely patriotic stellar nation that considers the unity of humanity under the Thuldan banner to be its manifest destiny. The largest of the stellar nations.

t'sa - A sentient species native to the T'sa Cluster in the Stellar Ring. Most t'sa stand about 1.4 meters tall and are covered in thick, interlocking scales. Combined with a tail and a bony head-ridge, the t'sa resemble large bipedal Solar reptiles.

Verge, the - A frontier region of space originally colonized by the stellar nations that was cut off during the Second Galactic War.

Vision - Capital world of Insight.

VoidCorp - A corporate stellar nation. Citizens are referred to as Employees and all have an assigned number.

weren - A sentient species native to the planet Kurg in the Stellar Ring. Most weren stand well over two meters tall, are covered in thick fur, and have sharp claws. Male weren have large tusks protruding from the bottom jaw.

chapter
1NE

"**W**orking late tonight, Dr. Doyle?"

Dr. Shani Doyle smiled at the orderly in the corridor and eased the door to room 923 of the Presbyterian-St. Luke's Medical Center intensive care unit closed behind herself. "My shift's almost over, Jenny. Just looking in on Mrs. Tavish before I go."

"Anything new?"

"No change, I'm afraid." Shani shook her head and brought up her clipboard to make a few notes.

"Anything . . . unusual?"

Shani's pen froze on the paper, but she glanced up with clinical detachment. "Such as?" she asked lightly.

Jenny flushed a guilty red. "Body temperature?" she stammered. "Heart rate? Just anything the night shift should keep an eye on over night. You know."

"I know." Shani turned her attention back to the

clipboard. "Don't worry, Jenny. If anything comes up, I'll pass it on, okay?"

"Uh . . . sure." Jenny shuffled nervously. Shani kept her eyes on the clipboard. Finally, the orderly added. "I'm going around and turning the lights in the halls down for the night. You want me to leave this one on for you?"

"Don't worry about it. I'll be only a minute." Eyes on the clipboard. Voice distant and dismissive.

"Oh. Okay. Good night, Dr. Doyle."

"Good night, Jenny."

Shani waited until the orderly's soft footsteps had receded down the corridor before closing her eyes for a moment, drawing a deep breath, and allowing herself to relax. When had one of the friendliest doctors in the hospital started getting so nervous around the staff? Bad question. She knew the answer to that. She opened her eyes to stare at the top sheet on her clipboard. All of the standard notes on vital signs and physician observations. This information would go into Laurel Tavish's official charts, opened two weeks ago when the woman in room 923 had been rushed in from Midlothian, already deep in a coma. Shani put her initials at the bottom of the page and flipped to the last sheet on the clipboard. That paper would go no further than a private file in her office.

"Anything unusual, Jenny?" she muttered to herself. "Hopefully not tonight."

Not long after Laurel's arrival at Presbyterian-St. Luke's, things had started happening in the intensive care unit. As far as Shani had been able to determine, the first to experience anything unusual was one of the nurses on duty the night after Laurel was brought in. She had been walking down the hall outside Laurel's room when she looked up and found herself surrounded by a drifting mist. Others had seen the same mist since then, always somewhere around Laurel's room, mostly at night, but sometimes during the day. It showed up, lingered for a short time, and then vanished. There had been reports of a weird odor of wet dirt and dry leaves sometimes as well. And a couple of people on the night shift had seen a blue glow coming from under the door of Laurel's room, like a light was moving around in the room. Jenny had been one of those people.

On her clipboard, Shani made a few quick notes. No mist tonight. No odor. No glow. No . . . Shani held her breath for a moment and listened. All she heard were the night sounds of the hospital. No, she wrote on the clipboard, children.

Four nights ago, the patient in the room next to Laurel's had awakened to the sound of children playing and laughing. He had blamed the noises on his medication, but two nurses on duty that night had also heard them. Last night, Shani had heard the sounds herself, the only reported phenomenon that she had experienced personally. The mist, the odor, the lights—somehow she suspected that if she did eventually experience them, they couldn't possibly be more eerie than the disembodied sound of happy children.

And yet eerie or not, she wanted to know more. She wanted to see the mist. She wanted to smell dirt and leaves and glimpse blue lights under the door of room 923. More importantly, she wanted to *understand* them, to figure it all out. The intellectual challenge made her heart race and her brain burn. The file in her office was slowly filling with notes documenting every incident that she could ferret out. Soon she would . . .

Intellectual challenge or not, the sudden dimming of the corridor lights still made her jump and it took her a minute to realize it was just Jenny turning down the lights. Just the lights—some investigator she was. How silly was that? She shook her head as she made a few last notes. How silly was this whole thing? What had she been thinking? It would all probably turn out to be nothing, just a series of coincidences strung together by imagination. Or maybe not. Either way, she wanted to know. She flipped the papers on the clipboard back down and headed for the elevators.

Her first step revealed that something was wrong. The air around her ankles and shins was cold, as if she had stepped into a draft. She glanced down.

Drifting mist surrounded her. As high as her knee, cool and clammy, it shrouded the corridor for a good fifteen feet on either side of her. There was no motion to it at all. When she took a step, the passage of her leg should have sent the mist swirling. It didn't. The mist—everything in fact—was very, very still. A shallow, tentative breath carried the taste of wet earth and dry leaves. Shani swallowed. She had wanted to experience the other phenomena that had been reported to her. Here they were.

She turned slowly back toward the door of room 923, a hollow feeling growing in her stomach. There was movement by the door, a lazy swirling as mist spilled out from under the door to fill the spreading cloud in the corridor. What must it be like inside the room? Shani stepped forward and reached for the doorknob—reached and gasped.

There was something in the mist, something as cold as the vapor, but dry and firm. It stroked across her calves and wrapped around her shins, tangling around her legs like a cat in the dark. Feet trapped, Shani swayed for a moment and almost fell. Clenching her teeth, she recovered her balance and thrust herself forward. She was going to open that door. Her hand closed around the cool, condensation-slick metal of the doorknob.

And the touch in the mist was more than firm. For a moment, it was solid. Horribly solid. It wasn't just tangling her legs, it was tearing at them, pulling them out from under her while reaching up to shove back on her torso. The force was irresistible. It tumbled her like a ball of fluff and slammed her hard into the floor. Air fled her lungs in one great, frightened gasp, and for a moment she couldn't breathe. Dark blobs of shadow swam across her vision, and she couldn't see, but she could hear footsteps come racing along the corridor, and Jenny was there. She helped her up, Shani blinking and wheezing.

"Are you all right?"

Shani glanced around. The mist was gone. Vanished. Under the door of room 923, a blue glow winked once and faded away. Had Jenny seen it this time? Shani looked up at her, but the orderly's eyes were on her. "Fine," she said. She managed a smile. "I tripped on my own feet. Long day, I guess."

"You're sure you're okay?"

"Absolutely."

The shock of the impact with the floor lingered. Shani felt nothing but a kind of stunned numbness as she went down to her office, revised her notes on the night, and slipped the sheet of paper into her secret file. The shock stayed with her on the drive home. It stayed with her as she climbed into bed. It stayed with her through restless sleep that saw her awake at dawn, watching the sun rise. Her brain wasn't burning now. Her heart was racing, yes, but not from any intellectual challenge. What had she been thinking? She was no investigator. Fortunately, she knew people who were.

At precisely nine o'clock, she picked up the telephone, dialed a number that she had been given a long time ago but had never called before, and then waited nervously, fingers twisting the phone cord, until a voice on the other end of the line said, "Hoffmann Institute."

Michael McCain drew a deep breath and brought the basketball up to his chest. He held it there for a moment. Forty-seven feet away, the basket waited for his approach, mocking him under the cold, grey mid-November sky.

McCain snapped into action, dropping the ball down into a dribble and moving it up the court. At the twenty-two foot line, he broke into a crossover dribble and zigzagged in toward the basket. He imagined a defense spread out in front of him. Crossover left. Crossover right. For a moment he paused, confronted by another imaginary guard. A fast reverse dribble and he was past, going for the basket. He took two quick steps, planted his foot, and pushed off. His arm came up, pushing the ball toward the basket. Up. Up.

Too high. Too close. The ball ricocheted off the backboard and went spinning across the court. McCain bent over for a minute, hands on his knees, blowing hard, his breath making clouds in the cool air. The basket, towering overheard, continued its morning of silent mockery. McCain watched the ball roll on across the asphalt—until a foot came down on top of it.

"Yours?" A woman in her late-thirties with long, straight, red-brown hair scooped the ball into the air with a flick of her toe and caught it. She passed it back to him, bouncing it off the pavement in a smooth motion. McCain scrambled to catch it.

"Jeane," he panted, "aren't you supposed to be at the Institute today, doing something like . . . oh, I don't know—working?"

"I am working. I've been looking for you." Jeane Meara walked onto the court so they could talk without shouting. McCain watched her approach. Only a few weeks ago, he had been a fresh young agent of the Hoffmann Institute in Washington, D.C. Jeane had been an even fresher recruit though she was almost ten years older than he and a veteran of the Bureau of Alcohol, Tobacco, and Firearms. The Institute had a way of making even the most hardened veterans feel like rookies, at least for a little while.

That D.C. investigation had left Jeane with a disgraced dismissal from the ATF and him with more than a few uncomfortable revelations about his past. It had also, however, made them a team, and its resolution had earned them a transfer to Chicago. Them and the third member of their team. McCain grimaced. "Ngan?"

Jeane stopped. "He sent me to collect you. He tried calling you, but there was no answer, either on your home line or your cell phone."

McCain sighed and began dribbling the ball. "I had a feeling you were going to say that. It is supposed to be my day off, you know."

"You shouldn't have stuck so close to home then. Nice place, by the way." She gestured around them. The basketball court was located atop one of the warehouse-loft conversions that cluttered Chicago's River North district. McCain had taken to the area immediately on his arrival in Chicago. It had required some work with his connections to get his hands on the loft, but it had been worth the effort. "The security guy at the door told me you were up here."

"How nice of him," muttered McCain. He turned around and aimed at the basket.

Jeane cleared her throat. "Ngan does seem kind of eager," she pointed out. "Something's up. He's meeting us at a hospital—Presbyterian-St. Luke's."

"I'm not finished with my workout." McCain jumped and shot. The ball bounced off the rim of the basket with a dull ring.

"Graceful," Jeane commented as he went after it. "How long are you going to be?"

McCain caught up to the ball and brought it back into a tightly controlled dribble. "I'm out here until I get twenty-one good shots." One of Jeane's eyebrows rose slightly and suddenly McCain was very conscious of the sweat that soaked his workout clothes. "I'm not just shooting baskets," he said defensively.

"I saw. How many shots have you got to go?"

"Six," McCain lied smoothly. He could almost feel the basket smirking at him.

"All right." Jeane pulled off the fleece jacket she wore. "Just to get us out of here, I'll play you for them."

"What?" McCain's hand faltered on the ball, and it bounced over in Jeane's direction. She captured it easily.

"Based on those last two shots, if I have to wait for you to sink six more it's going to be an hour before you're even off the court. And this gives you a chance to practice against a real opponent." She paused, ball held at chest level. "Worried?"

McCain's eyes narrowed. Jeane was thirty-nine. He was barely thirty-one. She was wearing office shoes. He had sneakers. She was coming in cold. He had the advantage of being warmed up and talking to her had given him a chance to catch his breath. "No," he said and moved forward to block her. Her feet betrayed a step to the left. He moved to intercept.

Jeane crossed one leg over the other and swiftly broke right, driving past him and into a perfect lay-up. The ball barely even touched the hoop as it sank through. Jeane caught it underneath and tossed it to him. "One," she said as he walked back out to the three-point line.

"Lucky." He walked around the outside of the circle, dribbling slowly. "All right, Agent Meara, the gloves are off."

She beat him with five more baskets in a row. After the last basket, she threw the ball to him and asked, "Ready to go?" She'd barely even broken a sweat.

McCain sucked in a deep breath, trying to get his wind back. "Give me fifteen minutes to wash the egg off my face. This way." He led her back to the stairwell that went down into the building. She glanced at him as they descended.

"You know, Fitz, you really suck at basketball."

The words echoed in the stairwell. He smiled. "Ah, now there's the Jeane Meara I've come to know. Always sweet, always tactful."

"I mean it." She looked him over. "I bet you'd be better at football."

"High school quarterback," he admitted. They reached his floor. He held the door open for her. His loft was just a little ways down the hall. "And my team won Yale intramural five years running."

Jeane spread her hands. "So why play basketball now?"

"Because he didn't."

"Who?"

"Never mind." McCain unlocked his apartment door and swung it wide. To some eyes, his loft might look sparsely furnished, stark and minimalist. He liked it that way. A sofa with clean straight lines, a few bookshelves, an entertainment stand with a miniature stereo system and a flat screen TV. Simple black and white photographs complimented the room and the glass-panel warehouse windows.

Jeane pointed at one prominently displayed photograph in particular, a striking cityscape that had been his most recent purchase. "Dallas. Have you ever been there?"

"Not as such," McCain said dryly. He headed for his bedroom and a hot shower. "Kitchen's through there. There's water in the fridge and glasses above the sink. Knock yourself out."

Presbyterian-St. Luke's Medical Center was a tall and sprawling white building just off the Eisenhower expressway at the Ashland/Paulina exit, barely fifteen minutes away from River North and McCain's loft. Fifteen minutes, that is, once Jeane finally had McCain ready to go. It took him longer to dress and get ready than it ever took her. Then again, she favored simple, practical fashions. McCain had a predilection toward sharp, stylish suits, expensive ties, and careful grooming. It must have been the lawyer in him. At least he carried it off well.

She looked at him out of the corner of her eye and asked, "New haircut?"

"Yeah."

"Good." She stepped on the gas and moved smoothly into the exit lane, accelerating past a big moving van. "It makes you look less like a damn JFK clone." McCain coughed suddenly, almost choking. "You okay?"

He nodded, clearing his throat. "It's just your driving. What's the speed limit on this expressway again?"

Jeane smiled tightly. "Not high enough, junior." She sailed around the Ashland/Paulina ramp without slowing down.

Ngan was waiting for them in the hospital's crowded lobby. In spite of the busy masses of people Jeane didn't have any trouble spotting him. Ngan Song Kun'dren was a small man, Tibetan by birth. He had to be close to seventy, though only his eyes showed it. His face was leathery and creased, the roundness of it emphasized by a smoothly shaved scalp. In sharp contrast to McCain's stylish suits, Ngan habitually wore very simple, plain suits of navy or grey. He always seemed so calm and composed that it was almost eerie. Jeane had never known him even to raise his voice. He was so unassuming that it seemed he should just vanish into a crowd. In fact, just the opposite was true. People seemed to subconsciously avoid him, leaving little pockets of space around him. It was those pockets more than anything else that made him easy to find. If he wanted you to find him.

He saw them coming from across the lobby and gestured for them to meet him by the elevators. Easy for him, thought Jeane. The crowd was, naturally, thickest near the elevators and while she and McCain were closer to them initially, Ngan still got there first. The crowd just melted away before him. He held the door of an elevator open so that McCain and Jeane could squeeze into the car after him. "Hello again, Jeane. Good morning, Michael."

"It was until you pulled me in." McCain turned to face the front of the elevator, putting his broad back to her and Ngan. "There was a matter of a day off. I watched you sign the paper yourself."

Ngan sighed. "I have a lot of papers to sign now, Michael."

"Yes, well, I guess the promotion wasn't all just authority and hobnobbing, was it?" McCain looked back over his shoulder at them. "There's some real work involved."

Ouch. Jeane held her breath, waiting for a reaction. The comment even earned darting glances from the strangers in the elevator with them. A pair of nurses exchanged knowing looks. They might not have known the whole story behind McCain's comment, but they didn't have to. Someone was bucking under a new boss. Jeane on the other hand did know the whole story. With the team's transfer to Chicago, the higher-ups in the Hoffmann Institute had decided they needed a liaison and Ngan had found himself saddled with the title of agent-in-charge. As far as she could see, the old man was the only logical choice. It wasn't like McCain or she were even potential candidates. They were inexperienced in Institute operations. Ngan had been around for years. No contest.

Yet McCain never missed an opportunity to needle Ngan hard about his new responsibilities. Ngan never said anything, just rolled along in calm serenity. True to form, he didn't say anything now. Jeane let her breath out in a puff and raised her eyes to the flickering numbers over the door. Moving from the ATF to the Hoffmann Institute hadn't been easy—quite aside from the weirdness of aliens and ancient spaceships buried under D.C. It was strange to be working for a civilian agency. In the ATF, McCain's attitude would have gotten him slapped down long ago.

She knew. That's what had happened to her.

The elevator car stopped on a floor of offices. Ngan led them down a long hall lined with honey-colored wood doors. There was a quiet hum in the background, the universal office noise of fluorescent lights, distant air circulation systems, and radios turned low behind closed doors. Very normal, very professional. Strangely soothing. Jeane knew that could be deceptive. She wondered why Ngan had brought them here. She had asked when he had dispatched her collect McCain. His answer had been as distant as he was. "Your first investigation in Chicago." Very helpful. It was a relief when he finally knocked on one of the doors. The simple plastic name plate read Dr. S. Doyle—Neurology.

"Come in."

The doctor was already rising and coming around her desk by the time Ngan had the door open. She was a tall, attractive women with coffee-cream skin and long, luxurious black hair. Even in a lab coat, she had a sophisticated elegance about her. "Mr. Kun'dren?" She had her hand out.

"Ngan, please, Dr. Doyle." He shook her hand. "My apologies. We were delayed." Jeane noticed he didn't even hesitate in his explanation. No fuss, no blame. That was part of what made dealing with him both a pleasure and a frustration. "My colleagues, Jeane Meara and Michael McCain."

Jeane offered her hand to the doctor, but McCain beat her to the punch, slipping in between them with the speed and grace of a snake in an apple tree. "My friends call me Fitz."

The doctor gave McCain's hand the briefest of squeezes. "My friends call me Shani, but I'll let you know when you can." She reached past him. "Ms. Meara."

"Jeane." She liked this woman already. As the doctor retreated behind her desk and gestured for them to take seats in the chairs arranged before it, Jeane flashed McCain a thumbs up. "Stud," she whispered, brushing past him.

He growled at her. "My last prostate exam was warmer."

Ngan gave them both a look that made Jeane feel like a schoolgirl caught passing a note. Dr. Doyle didn't seem to have noticed anything. She sat down at her desk, hands resting lightly on top. It struck Jeane that they were too still, as though Dr. Doyle was trying very hard to keep herself from fidgeting. She looked to Ngan. "Where should I start? How much have you told them?"

"From the beginning, please. Michael and Jeane know nothing at all."

"Thanks." Jeane pulled out a notebook and pen. "I guess that means I have a lot of writing to do." Ngan had taken the chair closest to the doctor's desk. He had to turn around to look at her and McCain. At least he had the decency to look a little embarrassed this time.

"A poor choice of words. What I meant, of course, was that I've told you nothing about this case. I wanted you to start with an open mind." He nodded to the doctor. "Perhaps the first thing you should know, however, is that Dr. Doyle is a trusted ally of the Institute and has been for several years. She called the Institute this morning on a matter of urgency—thus my rush to recall you, Michael." McCain didn't look impressed, but Ngan didn't wait for his approval. He turned back to Dr. Doyle. "Tell them exactly what you told me."

Dr. Doyle took a deep breath, and her hands left the desktop to knot around each other. "First," she said, "I want you to know that I'm not the kind of person who's given to imagining things. I'm a doctor and a scientist. I read biographies and mysteries—I don't even like science fiction."

The first word Jeane wrote down on her notebook was "denial." She underlined it. The motion must have drawn Dr. Doyle's attention to her, though, because when she looked up again, the doctor was looking at her. Her eyes, Jeane noted, were hollow and afraid. "About two weeks ago," Dr. Doyle continued, "I took on a new patient who had just arrived in our intensive care unit from the ER. Her name is Laurel Tavish. Her husband says she tripped and hit her head."

"Oh?" asked McCain. He was sitting back in his chair, legs crossed and a skeptical expression on his face. "What does she have to say about it?"

Dr. Doyle turned to him. "Nothing. Laurel is in a coma."

"That must have been some whack to the head."

"It was."

Jeane tapped her pen against her teeth. Against the wall behind Dr. Doyle was a fully loaded bookcase that included several books on head trauma. "It was definitely an accident?"

"Definitely." Dr. Doyle sat back in her chair. Her hands unwound and came to rest on the arms of the chair. Jeane could hear confidence in her voice now. She knew what she was talking about. "I can see where you're going with this. The wound was consistent with a very hard fall—as were other bruises and scrapes on Laurel's body. The police investigated. It *was* an accident. Not exactly routine, but mundane. I wouldn't have contacted the Institute if that's all there was."

"Then why did you call the Institute?" Jeane asked.

The doctor brought her hands up again, steepling her fingers and resting them against her chin. She took another deep breath and looked up at the ceiling, and then began to speak. Jeane recognized the clinical detachment in her voice. She had used the same cadence herself many times in presenting evidence. She liked to think, however, that the evidence she had presented was a little more substantial than the events Dr. Doyle described. Strange mists? Lights? A funny smell? As the doctor's recitation continued, Jeane glanced over at Ngan. He looked back at her with absolute neutrality. No help there. She kept writing, waiting for all of the insubstantial evidence to present itself.

When Dr. Doyle finally finished, an uncomfortable silence fell in the room. The background hum of the office reasserted itself in Jeane's ears. McCain was frowning. Ngan was watching both him and her, clearly waiting for some kind of response. Jeane looked down at her notebook and the list of occurrences that she had jotted down. There was a familiar pattern to the events.

"Dr. Doyle," she asked bluntly. "Has the hospital been doing any work on the ventilation system in the last two weeks?"

The doctor gave a short laugh tinged with irony. "That's certainly what I've been trying to convince people of." She spread her arms wide. "It's all a coincidence. Just a fluke of the temporary ductwork. Except for the lights, of course—they're just reflections from lights outside the hospital. A helicopter. Lights bouncing off the building from traffic on 290. Spotlights from the United Center—the room faces that direction."

Jeane looked at her carefully. "But you don't believe that yourself."

"Maybe I did once." Dr. Doyle drew her arms in again, folding them across her body. "But not after the attack last night."

"Then what do you think is creating these events?"

Dr. Doyle didn't answer, but an embarrassed flush crept across her face.

McCain leaned forward and looked at the doctor sharply. "It's a ghost."

STAR★DRIVE®

Adventure beyond the stars with Diane Duane

The Harbinger Trilogy

Starrise at Corrivale
Volume One

Gabriel Connor is up against it. Expelled from the Concord
Marines and exiled in disgrace, he's offered one last chance by
the Concord to redeem himself. All it involves is gambling
his life in a vicious game of death.

Storm at Eldala
Volume Two

Gabriel and his fraal companion are scratching out a
living among the dangerous stars of the Verge when they
stumble onto new, unknown forces. Only their deaths seem
likely to avert disaster. But an astonishing revelation from the
depths of time makes the prospect of survival even
more terrible than a clean death.

Nightfall at Algemron
Volume Three

Gabriel Connor's quest to save the Verge and clear his
name leads him to a system ravaged by war and to the ruins of
a long-dead alien civilization. Along the way, he discovers that
to save himself and all he holds dear, his one salvation may
also be his ultimate destruction.

Available April 2000

☉TAR☉DRIVE®

*To the edge of the galaxy
and back!*

Two of Minds
Williams H. Keith, Jr.

In the urban underground hell of Tribon
on the planet Oberon, life in a street gang
doesn't offer many possibilities. That is,
until one day Kai St. Kyr robs the wrong
man and finds himself in the middle
of a power struggle that stretches
beyond the stars.

Available July 2000

Gridrunner
Thomas M. Reid

When a black market courier journeys to the Verge, she must
enter the virtual world of the mysterious Grid. Together with an
undercover agent, she finds herself embroiled in a desperate
conflict between a crime syndicate, terrorists, and her
own boss. The solution lies in the Grid.

Available September 2000

Zero Point
Richard Baker

Peter Sokolov is a bounty hunter and killer for hire. Geille Monashi,
a brilliant data engineer, is his quarry. After Sokolov and Monashi
encounter an alien derelict in the farthest reaches of space, they
have only one chance to survive. They've got to trust each other.

On the Verge
Roland J. Green

War erupts on Arist, a frozen world on the borders of known space.
The Concord Marines charge in to prevent the conflict from escalat-
ing, but soon discover that an even darker threat awaits them.

Legend of the Five Rings ®

The Clan War

A legend of the Emerald Throne of the emperors. Of a struggle among the clans for power. And of a war that would devastate all Rokugan.

The Scorpion
Stephen Sullivan
Available July 2000

The Unicorn
Allison Lassieur
Available September 2000

The Crane
Ree Soesbee
Available November 2000

Live the legend!